You're The Best Part

CHENELL PARKER

Text ChenellParker
to 22828 to be
added to my emailing list

Join my reader's group Chenell's Chatty Corner on FaceBook

WHEN IT COMES BACK AROUND

Gianni stood outside of the church, trying hard to get her emotions together. She wasn't ready to say goodbye to the only woman who genuinely loved her, aside from her mother. It was only three years ago that she stood outside of the same church, preparing to say goodbye to her mother, Janessa. Now, her maternal grandmother, Agnes, had left her and she felt lost already.

She still had her auntie, Karen, but that wasn't much. Karen loved her men too much to even pretend to care about anyone else. Karen's daughter, Kori, had moved out of her mother's house a long time ago because she got tired of Karen putting the men in her life first. Her relationships never lasted long, but that didn't stop her from finding another man whenever one of them left her. Kori lived with yet another one of her boyfriends and she barely visited her mother. She and Gianni were close, so they always stayed in touch. They argued like two old women but the mutual love was there.

"Gianni, I'm so sorry for your loss," one of her grandmother's church members and best friend said when she walked up and hugged her.

"Thanks Mrs. Flo," Gianni replied with a faint smile.

"You let me know if you need anything. Agnes would want me to make sure that her baby girl was okay."

Florence and Agnes had been good friends for years, up until the other woman died. They had been members of the same church for most of those years until their pastor took sick and died. They had three other pastors that were under him, so service went on as usual.

Unfortunately, everyone didn't agree with all of the changes that they were making. Things seemed to be getting out of hand once their pastor became too ill to preach. Since then, most of the younger parishioners moved on to different congregations. Unlike before, their church had become too judgmental, especially towards the youth. They frowned down upon everything, including the way they dressed. The church was supposed to be a welcoming sanctuary, but they dropped the ball on that theory. Gianni was one of the few youngsters who stayed and that was only because of her grandmother.

Flo admired the young woman for staying around to take care of her grandmother. When Agnes had a stroke, Gianni put her own needs to the side to care for the needs of someone else. She did the same thing for her own mother and that was commendable. She was going to be blessed and

Flo prayed for it to happen every time she talked to God. Agnes' own daughter was too selfish to take care of anybody but herself and her men.

"I appreciate that, Mrs. Flo. I'm just trying to get through today and I'll be okay."

"We're all praying for you, sweetheart. I know that this has to be hard. I can't even imagine how you feel. First your mama and now your grandmother."

The older woman walked away shaking her head sadly and Gianni was happy. She was depressed enough and she didn't need anyone to make her feel worse.

"They act like you were grandma's only living relative. She did have another daughter and granddaughter," Kori said as she walked over and stood next to her cousin. Agnes had a grandson too, but he wasn't shit. Truthfully, Kori's mother wasn't shit either but she was the only living child since Janessa died.

"It's not like that cousin. They just know me from living with her after my mama died and coming to church with her all the time."

"We both used to come to church with her when we were younger. I just stopped when I got older."

"I'm just ready for everything to be over with. I hate funerals. I need something to smoke."

"So do I. Have you thought about what you're gonna do about your living arrangements?" Kori asked her.

"I haven't had time to think of too much lately, but I'll figure it out. I definitely want to get back in school though."

"School can wait. You got more important shit to worry about. You know Biggie's fat ass might want you to come stay with him," Kori said, speaking of Gianni's boyfriend, Nolan.

"Girl, bye. You already know that ain't happening," Gianni replied with a roll of her eyes. Biggie was always begging her to stay the night at his house but she never did. She had a good reason why she couldn't but that didn't stop him from getting upset every time she said no. She couldn't leave her grandmother home alone and she didn't give a fuck how he felt about it.

"You better grow the fuck up Gianni. You really don't have many options right now. Me and my man are already sleeping on top of each other in our small ass apartment. We don't have room for nobody else. And I hope you're not depending on my mama to help you out. I'm her only daughter and she never gave a fuck about me. Grandma is gone, so you can't depend on her or use her for an excuse anymore."

"Bitch please. Depending on anybody will get you fucked over every time. That's something that I've never made a habit of doing. I'll go without before I look for a handout. I'm all that I got and I know that for sure now. Besides my mama, grandma was the only one who showed love without looking for something in return."

Kori had her fucked up talking like she had all the answers. She was a younger version of her mama and she needed a nigga on her arm to feel validated too. She was only twenty-four years old and was living with her third boyfriend. All of them were pedophiles in Gianni's opinion because they were all over forty. She moved in with the first one when she was only sixteen, but Karen didn't care. In her eyes, Kori was well taken care of and out of her hair.

"You already know that grandma was gonna make sure that you were straight. You were her favorite. She was willing to get put out to make sure that you had somewhere

10

to stay. She didn't even bother extending that invitation to me when I needed somewhere to go."

"Why, so you could turn her home into a hoe house?"

She was tired of Kori always bringing up the same old shit. Agnes lived in a senior facility and Gianni wasn't even supposed to be living with her. When her mother died, her grandmother purchased a sofa bed and wasted no time moving her in. Kori was salty about it and she made it a point to always bring it up. The circumstances were completely different but she wasn't trying to hear that. There was no way in hell she would have taken care of their grandmother the way Gianni did, so everything happened for a reason.

Gianni was supposed to go to college as soon as she finished high school but she postponed when her mother got sick. Even after Janessa died, she was so grief stricken and depressed, furthering her education was nowhere on her mind. After a while, her grandmother convinced her to do the right thing. She always told her that her mother was smiling down her and she needed to make her proud. Gianni agreed and she was happy that she was finally doing what she'd always wanted to do.

She had just finished her freshman year of college when she came home one day and found her grandmother laid out on the living room floor. Agnes had a stroke and the entire left side of her body was paralyzed as a result. Although she had a nurse that visited daily, the bulk of the responsibility fell on Gianni's shoulders. She had to drop out of school to take care of her, but she didn't mind. They had a small family but she still couldn't depend on anyone else to do it. She didn't really have a life outside of caring for her grandmother and she was surprised that she was even able to keep a man. She hated that her education was put aside once again, but it was for a good cause.

11

Gianni and Biggie met about a year ago at the movies and had been dating for about six months. She tried to push him away for a while but he wasn't having it. Her grandmother's nurse felt bad that she was always inside, so she agreed to stay with Agnes while she went out and had some free time. Kori suggested going to the movies and Gianni was happy that she went. Living with Biggie wasn't what she wanted, but Kori was right. She didn't have very many options at the moment.

Gianni had an older brother, Greg, but she would have died before she went to live anywhere near him. It was sad but she hated everything about him. To her, he was partially to blame for their mother's death. He was locked up anyway and she was hoping that his grimy ass never got out.

Greg was ten years her senior at thirty three years old but he acted nothing like a big brother should have. Janessa always said that Gianni was her miracle baby because she didn't think that she could ever conceive again. Janessa was a horrible mother to her firstborn, but she catered to Gianni. Greg resented his baby sister because of it and they never had the best relationship. Janessa had her son at fifteen years old and they were more like friends than anything else. She didn't know who their fathers were and there was a good reason for that.

Janessa was a well-paid hoe and Greg made sure that she never changed professions. He was the one who went out and recruited customers for her and their home served as her work space. Gianni's room was all the way down the hall but she was no fool. She knew what her mother did for a living. Janessa made good money with the world's oldest profession, as her grandmother used to call it.

Even still, Janessa was the best mother that Gianni could have ever asked for. It didn't matter how late her mother stayed up the night before, Gianni always had a hot breakfast waiting for her every morning. Janessa walked her to school in the morning and was there waiting for her every afternoon. She helped her with homework and they had a girls' night every Saturday or Sunday. Gianni's room was filled with everything that she wanted, including a closet full of clothes and shoes. She never lacked anything, especially love and attention.

She never remembered Janessa having a steady boyfriend, but she always told her about the one man who had managed to capture her heart. Gianni loved to see the look in her mother's eyes and the smile on her face whenever she talked about the one who got away. She never said his name but Gianni knew that her mother was in love with him. She didn't know what happened for them to break up but she wished that he was still around. Maybe then, her mother would have settled down and not have had so many men in and out of her life and body. Janessa would have probably been married and still alive and happy.

As much as she loved her mother, not everyone felt the same way. Gianni basically fought her way through high school and she became good at it. A few of the girls that she went to school with learned that their fathers were customers of her mother and that didn't sit too well with them. Gianni got jumped more times than she could count but she always fought back. They soon figured out that they couldn't handle her one on one, so they stopped trying. It was crazy that some grown ass women tried to fight her or they sent their daughters at her if they couldn't.

It got so bad that Janessa gave her a small blade to carry. When Gianni got caught with it at school, her mother was the first one there to act a fool and tell them why she had it. She didn't play behind her baby girl and Greg hated the pedestal that their mother put his sister on. He was always throwing it in her face how she showed favoritism, and Janessa never denied it. He used to looked at Gianni like she disgusted him and he sometimes told her so.

13

When she got a little older, Greg used to always tell her how pretty she was. He swore that she could make even more money than their mother, but Gianni wasn't the one. He was actually asking to pimp her out until she told Janessa about it. Their mother went off and Greg never came at her sideways again.

Gianni was happy for a while until her mother hit her with a bomb only three months after her eighteenth birthday. Janessa had full blown AIDS and Gianni felt like her entire life was over. She'd been diagnosed with HIV years before but she didn't take care of herself like she was supposed to. That was obvious seeing as how she was still sleeping with men for money. Two years later, she was gone and she took a part of Gianni with her. She didn't know about the HIV diagnosis and everything seemed to happen so suddenly.

For a while, she was angry with her mother for not taking better care of herself. She was upset that Janessa didn't love her enough to want to do better. It took her grandmother to point out a few things to her and Gianni got over her feelings eventually. Now, she had to prepare to say goodbye to her second mother and she just wasn't ready.

Gianni was thankful that her grandmother had insurance, but it was barely enough to bury her. The funeral home took pity and didn't stress them about the difference in cost. Karen was pissed that there would be no money left, but Gianni was just happy that they didn't have to raise funds to lay her grandmother to rest. Janessa was the same way and her insurance policy was just enough to bury her with a few dollars left over. Gianni used the remaining money to buy herself a used car that broke down every other week.

"Girl, I can't believe that they let Greg out to come to the funeral," Kori said, pulling Gianni away from her thoughts.

She looked up, shocked to see her brother being escorted off the prison van by two deputies. Greg had been locked up for about a year but he looked like the same slimy snake that she remembered. She hated the signature smirk that always seemed to grace his face. It made him look even sneakier than he was if that was even possible.

"Look at my beautiful baby sister. Come give your big brother a hug." Greg smiled while looking at Gianni. She didn't know why he wasn't handcuffed, but she backed away when he tried to embrace her.

"Don't touch me!" Gianni snapped.

"Come on now sis. It's been years and you're still in your feelings. Mama was a grown ass woman. I couldn't make her do nothing that she wasn't willing to do. Besides, she wouldn't want her favorite child to be acting like that. What do you think she would say?"

He touched the chain on her neck and it made her skin crawl. The deputies didn't seem to care one way or another. She could have slipped him a weapon or anything since they weren't paying attention. They weren't even supposed to let him get that close to anyone.

"I'm really starting to feel threatened. Maybe I need to voice my concerns to one of these deputies, so they can bring you back to your cell."

Greg's expression turned serious when she said that because he knew that she would do it. Gianni hated him since she felt that he was responsible for their mother's death. Truthfully, she seemed to hate him even before that and the feelings were mutual.

Janessa didn't give a fuck about him when he was younger and he was thankful for his grandmother. Agnes was more of a mother to him since his own mama was too busy chasing niggas to care. He could have probably overlooked a lot of things that she did if she were a junkie or an alcoholic. None of that was the case for Janessa though. She was just a hoe.

Janessa was giving her body away for free and Greg didn't understand the logic behind that. He went at her about a way to make both of them some money and she quickly jumped at the chance. His mother was beautiful with her butterscotch complexion, slanted hazel eyes, and naturally curly hair. She had a banging ass body and men, young and old, wanted a piece of her. Gianna was a younger version of her and Greg knew that she would make twice as much. She had a fit when he went at her on some hoeing shit and Janessa almost died when Gianni told her about it. His mother cursed him out and threatened to disown him. She loved his baby sister more than life itself and that hurt him more than anything.

All the things that he fantasized about his mother doing with him, she did with his sister. Gianni had the best of everything and he resented her for that. He never even knew that Janessa knew how to be a mother until her second child came along. Greg was a grown man before he went on his first vacation, but Janessa took his sister to Disney World every year when she was younger. He confronted her about it a few times but he was a grown man by then. And that's exactly what she always told him whenever he complained. She told him to get over it and stop being envious of a child. It pained him that she never even tried to acknowledge his feelings or even talk to him about it.

At first, Greg thought that Janessa was that way with him because she didn't know who his father was. That wasn't the case though because she didn't know who Gianni's father was either. At least that's what he assumed. She never mentioned anything about their fathers and none of them ever came around. He wasn't even sad about his mother's passing. If anything, he was pissed that he was gonna be losing out on money. The death of his grandmother hit him harder because she was the only one who'd ever shown him unconditional love.

"Don't be like that baby sis. I'm rolling out in another month or two. Maybe we can work something out so you can make some money. With both grandma and mama being gone, it's gonna be kind of rough. You know you're used to somebody taking care of you. I got you if you stop being so stubborn."

Gianna was about to reply until the deputies escorted her brother away. He wasn't allowed to walk in with the family and she was grateful for that much.

"What the hell was that all about? I never understood why you and Greg never got along. That's your only brother. What did he ever do to you?" Kori asked.

"I think it's time for us to walk in," Gianni replied as she saw one of the pastors walk out of the church and start looking around.

To her knowledge, none of her family members knew about the arrangement between her brother and mother, and she wanted it to stay that way. It was bad enough that people looked at her sideways because of the way that her mother died. Having them find out who inadvertently contributed to her death was just too embarrassing. Granted, her mother was grown and capable of making her own decisions. It was just sad that the person who she brought into the world had a hand in taking her out of it.

"Gianni!" the pastor yelled as he waved her over. "We're ready to get started sweetheart."

"Excuse me, but that's my mother. You should be talking to me," Karen said while rudely interrupting.

17

"Excuse my ignorance, but who are you?" the reverend asked.

Gianni wanted to laugh at her auntie's astonished expression. Karen always wanted to feel important, but she didn't do a damn thing for nobody but the men in her life. It was sad that Gianni had to postpone her education to take care of her grandmother, when her only living child didn't even work. Gianni begged Karen to sit with her mother three days a week while she went to class, but she refused. She was selfish but always the first one to cry and pass out when something happened.

"That's my auntie, Karen," Gianni spoke up.

"My apologies but I don't think we've ever met. However, we're ready to get started, so I need the family to line up behind me and we'll walk in shortly," the pastor instructed.

Karen hurried to stand behind him so that she could be the first one to enter. She was always doing too much but it wasn't that serious. Their family wasn't even that big for her to be so extra about it. Since Greg was already inside, it was only three of them that had to be led in. Their family was small and her grandmother was the last one left among her siblings. They had other family out there somewhere but they hadn't seen or heard from them in years.

Gianni snapped out of her thoughts when the pastor started reciting a prayer. She stood shoulder to shoulder with Kori as they were led into the church and escorted up to the front row. Biggie gave her a faint smile as she passed by the pew that he was sitting on. His mother and sister had come along with him to give Gianni some support. They were good to her and she appreciated them.

Once the hour-long service was over with, they went to the graveyard before heading back to the church hall where the repast was being held. Gianni was grateful for her

18

grandmother's church members for stepping up to the plate and making things happen. Karen did more for her man when his mother died a year ago but she barely lifted a finger for her own.

"You good baby?" Biggie asked when he walked over and snaked his arm around Gianni's waist. She was standing outside alone, deep in thought. Her appetite was gone so she didn't bother trying to eat anything.

"Yeah, I'm straight," she replied with a forced smile.

She played with her mother's chain that she decided to wear that day. The pendant that dangled from it was the initial of her mother's first name covered in diamonds. Janessa loved that chain and Gianni treasured it just as she had. She didn't wear it all the time but she felt the need to have it on that day. In her eyes, that day was equivalent to a holiday. Nothing was more special than seeing her grandmother for the last time.

"You know I got you, baby. My mama said that you can stay with us for as long as you want to. We can even get a place of our own if that'll make you feel better."

"We'll talk about that later Biggie. I still gotta clear out the apartment and pack up all my shit," Gianni sighed.

"Didn't I just say that I got you? Me and my boys can have that shit done in a day or two. Don't stress baby. Let your man take care of you."

Biggie hated that Gianna lost her grandmother but he was looking forward to them spending some time together. Sitting on the sofa watching movies while her sickly grandmother was in the other room wasn't his idea of romance. Even when Gianni managed to get away and come to his house, she was always on edge. She wondered if her grandmother was okay and she called the nurse every five minutes. Since Ms. Agnes was gone, he was hoping that Gianni would finally loosen up and get a life of her own. Most of all, he was hoping that she stopped being stingy and finally gave up the pussy.

Thanks to Kori's big mouth ass, he knew that Gianni's mother died of AIDS. He also knew that she was afraid of being intimate with anyone because of that. It all made sense to him once it was revealed though. Gianni always got nervous whenever he mentioned sex. He just assumed that she wasn't ready. But having a twenty-three year old virgin for a girlfriend was almost unheard of. He was excited to be her first and he was hoping to be her last.

"What are you over here lying to my cousin about now?" Kori asked when she walked up and bumped into Biggie.

"Move your thot ass around somewhere and mind your business." Biggie frowned.

He and Kori were cool in the beginning, but she was a hater. She smiled in Gianni's face but was always throwing shade when she wasn't around. Gianni didn't club and hang out as much as her cousin did. Every time somebody asked Biggie about his girl, Kori made it a point to say how lame and inexperienced her cousin was. Biggie was happy that his girl wasn't out there bad like her cousin and some of the others. Kori had made her way through his entire crew and still didn't get chosen. She did right to stick with older men because none of the younger ones wanted her hoe ass.

"We're hitting up the club tonight cousin. You don't have no more excuses not to come," Kori said while ignoring her cousin's man.

"Are you serious right now?" Gianni asked in shock.

"What?" Kori shrugged.

"Bitch, grandma ain't even warm yet and you're talking about going out. Fuck a club!"

"Sad as fuck man," Biggie mumbled.

"Fuck you, Biggie!" Kori spat angrily.

"Nah, I already got a girl. Besides, my niggas already told me that it was trash."

"Will y'all please stop? I'm not in the mood for this bullshit right now!" Gianni yelled.

"My fault baby. I'm going back inside," Biggie said before he kissed her cheek and walked away.

"That fat muthafucker makes me sick. That nigga ain't slick though. He's working hard as fuck to get some pussy. I hope you don't be stupid enough to give it to him!" Kori yelled.

"Nah, stupid is giving it away for free. You muthafucking right a nigga gone work hard to get this."

"Don't even flatter yourself boo. Knowing him, he's probably getting it from somewhere else anyway."

"Good, then I can keep my untouched sweet virgin pussy all to myself. Not too many girls my age can say that," Gianni smirked as she watched her cousin angrily walk away.

She was making light of the situation, but the thought of sex terrified her. She was no fool and she knew that Biggie was out there doing him. He was a street nigga and there was no way he was sitting around waiting for her to give it up. Oral sex was all that ever went down but that was getting old now. Intimacy was a beautiful thing, but the thought of it all terrified her. She was well educated about HIV and AIDS but that didn't stop her from being afraid. The risk of her contracting the disease through oral was almost nonexistent, so she played it safe. She knew that she could get other STD's that way too, but none of them were as deadly. She never expressed her feelings to Biggie and he never asked.

Besides the hints that Kori always threw, she had never heard anything about him and other females. Honestly, Gianni really didn't care. She had feelings for him but they weren't that deep. If ever he got tired of waiting, he could move on and she would do the same. She had already lost the two most important people in her life, so she knew that she would be okay. Nobody was gonna rush her to make one of the most important decisions of her life. If she had to die a virgin, she was prepared to meet her maker pure and untouched.

"Come on Ma. I hate when you start up with all that crying," Nix said as he pulled his grandmother into a comforting hug.

"Leave her alone and let her cry. You're the first college graduate in the family. You made us proud and I know that Jake would be proud of you too," his grandfather, JB, replied.

Nix looked away, hoping to hide the tears that suddenly formed in his eyes. The subject of his uncle, Jake, was always a touchy one. He and Jake were raised more like brothers and they were only three years apart. Nix's mother had him when she was only thirteen years old but she was confined to a juvenile facility when she did. She and his father, Quick, who was only fourteen at the time of his birth, had been wanted for a string of robberies but she got caught and arrested before he did. They had sex only a few hours after they met and Nix was conceived. They were both toxic as fuck and that's what bonded them.

According to his grandparents, they showed up to the hospital with Quick and a lawyer when his mother went into labor with him. His father wanted his first son to have his last name, so he refused to turn himself in until he witnessed his birth and made that happen. Soon after, he was taken into custody and Jacobi Latrell Nixon Jr., better known as Nix, was signed over to his paternal grandparents. Jake was only three years old and their youngest child at the time. He and Nix were close and grew up like siblings instead of uncle and nephew.

Jake was killed in a carjacking a few years ago and life for them was never the same. Nix was with him at the time and he was blessed to still be alive. Jake was shot three times, with two of them being in his head. Nix was shot four times and spent almost an entire month in the hospital. Whoever did it took the car and anything else of value before leaving them for dead in the middle of the street like wounded animals. Nix was in a medically induced coma for over a week and they had already buried his uncle by the time he came out of it. That hurt even more because he wasn't able to say a proper goodbye. Jake was the first person that he asked for when he got up and his family had a hard time breaking the news to him.

Nix was distraught and so were his grandparents. They had three other sons and two daughters, but Jake was their last born and baby of the bunch. That was before Nix came along and stole their hearts once again.

Thanks to having a good lawyer, Nix's parents were released from prison when he was two years old. They were still heavy in the streets and going to jail did nothing to change that. They were still babies and his grandparents refused to let them ruin his life, much like they'd done their own. They were in and out of jail for most of their childhood and they didn't want their grandson to be caught up in that life. They kept Nix with them and they were the only parents that he really knew. His mother was just plain ole Nichelle and his father was Quick, a nickname that was given to him when he was younger. Nix's grandparents were his mother and father and that's how he addressed them. He got along great with his parents but it was more of a friendship than anything else. They finally calmed down and got married some years later but they never had any more kids. His father was rumored to have another son that was around his age, but he didn't claim nor acknowledge him. Nichelle always threatened to leave him if he even tried.

"Okay, enough tears. This is supposed to be a celebration. Turn the music up and let's muthafucking celebrate!" Nichelle yelled as she raised her glass high in the air.

Their family on both sides were there and Nix appreciated the love. Nichelle rented a hall and Quick had more liquor than they could drink. Nix knew that he didn't purchase any of it. His father always had some kind of hookup and they always came through. He got all the food catered too and there was more than enough to go around.

"I'm so happy for you, baby," Dior, Nix's longtime girlfriend, said while hugging him from behind.

Since she had been taking college courses in high school, Dior graduated the year before him with a degree in early childhood education. She had three older sisters, her father, and aunts, but she still considered Nix's family as more of her own. She never knew her mother since she died while giving birth to her. Dior's father blamed her for taking his wife away and they never had a good relationship. He raised her, but she felt like she didn't even know him. He didn't look at her the same way he looked at her sisters and that hurt more than she cared to admit. She was being blamed for something that was out of her control and that wasn't fair.

Dior had been with Nix since she was fifteen and he was sixteen. They were now twenty-four and twenty-five years old and still going strong. They had a few bumps in the road that caused them to separate temporarily, but they always found their way back to each other. She wanted them to have that everlasting love, something like his parents had, minus the jail time and cheating.

Quick and Nichelle were hood as fuck but they loved each other unconditionally. They were the epitome of ride or die and they had each other's backs. Although they didn't raise Nix, they loved him more than life. They loved her too since she had been around them for so long.

"It's only up from here baby," Nix said as he turned around and embraced her.

Dior was a plus sized beauty with dark chocolate skin and full pouty lips. She was always so insecure about her size, but Nix always made her feel beautiful. He always told her that she was perfect just the way she was and that always gave her the boost of confidence that she needed.

She was way shorter than him, so she melted into his tall, athletic frame and inhaled his scent. Nix was perfect to her with his velvety chocolate skin that was littered with tattoos. His hair was cut low and his beard was always neatly trimmed. His lips were full and he had the sexiest bedroom eyes that she'd ever seen. He was rough around the edges but he was always gentle with her. His outspoken personality was both a blessing and a curse, depending on who you asked. Nix loved hard and he believed in monogamy more than any man his age that she'd ever encountered. He wanted a wife and kids, but bearing his

26

kids seemed to be the one thing that Dior wasn't sure that she could ever do.

Some of the women in her family had fertility issues and, sadly, she was one of them. Her oldest sister was too and she was never able to conceive. She and her husband ended up using a surrogate to give them their two kids, but Dior didn't want to go that route unless she absolutely had no other choice. She looked forward to walking around with a swollen belly for Nix to rub. One of her sisters had three kids with no problems while the other used in vitro to have her set of twins. She was one of the lucky ones and got pregnant on her very first try. Since Nix now had his business degree, Dior was hoping that they could do the same thing to start their family. The process was expensive but well worth the price. They were still young but she wanted them to start a family before they turned thirty. Nix was fine either way. He wanted kids too but he never tried to pressure her or make her feel bad about it. He always said that even if they never had any, he would still love her just the same. Dior had always dreamed of being a mother and, being that she was a school teacher, that only made her want them more.

Thanks to his grandfather, Nix already had a solid income. He and his best friend, Aldrin, already owned a franchise restaurant in the airport and a gas station. Al had graduated with Nix and they were already discussing what business ventures they wanted to explore next. They really wanted to invest in medical marijuana but it was expensive to start. Since it was a billion dollar industry, the return on their investment would be well worth it.

"We're a muthafucking power couple for real now baby." Dior smiled as she snapped out of her thoughts.

"Yep, now all y'all need to do now is buy a big ass house and fill it up with some babies. I run the streets too much to babysit but a bitch still want some grandkids one day," Nichelle chimed in as she walked over with a bottle of champagne.

The smile on Dior's face faded and Nix could have killed his mother. No one knew about Dior's fertility issues, but she needed to chill on the grandkids talk. She didn't even raise him, so she was worried about the wrong thing.

"I'll be back. I'm going get a drink," Dior said as she walked away and joined a few of his cousins at the bar.

"I wish you chill out with all that baby shit. Nigga just graduated yesterday. I'm not trying to have no damn kids right now," Nix argued while looking at his mother.

"Boy bye. It ain't like you can't afford it. You got money coming in from your businesses and JB is paying you a grip to do nothing at that construction site," Nichelle replied before she walked away.

Nix's grandfather had owned a construction site since before he was born. He started out as an independent contractor and single handedly grew his company into a multimillion dollar success. His sons ran the place for him and it was mostly family who worked there. Nix had been working there for a little over three years and he was in charge of securing the contracts. He got paid good for what he did and some of his uncles and cousins didn't like that. They always accused JB of showing favoritism, but he didn't care. To JB, Nix did everything right. He graduated high school and college, something that he'd always wanted his own kids to do. In his mind, it was only right that he rewarded his accomplishments. It was crazy that Nix was raised with his father's side of the family but was closer to his mother's side. He wasn't with all that hating shit and that's what some of the Nixon's did best.

They were really gonna be pissed if JB was on board with what he wanted. Nix was hoping that his grandfather let him manage his night club once the renovations were complete. Club Nixon was a hot spot before it closed down four months ago to be upgraded. JB was expanding so that they would have sections of the club to be rented out for parties and special occasions. He was also adding a top level for VIP and a stage for live performances. It was set to be complete in another two months and he already had a lot of great ideas. JB still managed the club himself but he was getting tired and ready to retire. Nix's uncles seemed content with running the construction company, so he made his request known more than once. He was hoping that JB agreed because he was ready to work.

By society's standards, Nix was already a statistic. He was born to unwed teenage parents who had no education and a lengthy criminal record. He was already labeled as a failure in his mother's womb but he proved a lot of people wrong. He heard the whispering around him and that was all the more reason why he decided to educate himself in the streets as well as the books.

Nix could cook dope, break it down and sell it too. He could also stand in a room full of college educated individuals and hold an intelligent conversation with ease. He knew how to hold his own in any situation and that was intimidating to a lot of people. His pants hung low and he was full of tattoos, labeling him as a thug to mostly anyone who didn't know him. He was slow to speak but he listened to everything around him.

"What are you over here daydreaming about nigga?" Al asked when he walked over to his best friend.

"Man, I'm hoping that JB will let me manage the club once it opens up again. I told him that I was interested, but he ain't say shit. With the right people running it, that bitch is a for sure moneymaker."

"Damn, Nix, bruh. We just graduated yesterday and you're trying to work already. Relax and enjoy life a minute nigga."

"I'll enjoy life when I get a few millions in my account. Money don't sleep nigga. I'm trying to get it. And you should be trying to get it too. My niece gon' hit them pockets hard as fuck when she gets a little older," Nix laughed, referring to Aldrin's three year old daughter, Alexa.

"Shit, she's already hitting my shit hard now. Her and her begging ass mama."

"I don't know why you still be playing with that broad. Life is too short for all the bullshit. Fuck what people say."

"Come on Nix, bruh. You know me better than anybody. Shit ain't that easy for me," Al sighed.

He and Nix had been best friends since they were babies. They grew up right next door to each other and their grandparents were good friends. They went to school together all the way through college, where they both got business degrees on the same day. They trusted each other more than they trusted anybody else. Nix found his soulmate in Dior, but Al hadn't been so lucky.

Unlike Nix, Aldrin grew up in an overly religious household. His mother was a pastor and she frowned down on anything that she thought was ungodly. When he had a baby out of wedlock, she preached to him and the mother of his child for months. She tried to pressure them to get married but Al wasn't having it. Kinsley, his daughter's mother, was down for it but he didn't love her the same way that she loved him. Truthfully, aside from her being the mother of his only child, he didn't love her at all.

"It's as easy as you make it. You gotta stop living for other people bruh," Nix said, pulling him away from his thoughts.

"Yeah, I know. But man, listen, we need to get our money up for real. That medical marijuana is where it's at. That's a billion dollar industry and we need to get in on it."

"I know man. If JB lets me manage the club like I want to, I can have that shit in no time. You already know I want you on board if he do. We'll have that bitch lit every night of the week. I already got a few ideas."

"Damn man. What did he say when you asked him?"

"He ain't say shit. You know how JB is, bruh. He just nodded and kept smoking his cigar. That nigga move on his own time. Working at the construction site was cool as long as I was still in school, but I'm trying to make some real money now. I'll still help out if they need me but I'm not trying to be there full time no more."

"The weed money is good too nigga. Don't sleep on our hustle," Al pointed out.

"That's straight too but think about how much better it'll be if we were pushing that shit from inside the club. We can triple what we sell now and make even more to invest."

"Yeah, another legal business would definitely help."

"Yeah, and managing the club is where it's at," Nix said, right as Nichelle's loud mouth could be heard on the mic.

"I want to thank everybody for coming out to celebrate my baby's big day. Nix! Come over here baby."

"The fuck is she doing now," Nix mumbled as he and Al got up and walked over to where his mother was.

"Is it that time?" Al asked.

31

"Fuck no and she don't even know about it. She's too damn extra for me to tell her anything," Nix said as he looked around the crowded hall for Dior. He didn't see her and that was unusual.

"Come here Nix! Why are you standing all the way over there?" his mother yelled.

"What's good Nichelle?" Nix asked when he walked closer to where she was. His father came and stood beside them, smiling like he had a secret that no one else knew.

"Many people might not know this, but Quick and I were only thirteen and fourteen when Nix was born. We were just babies ourselves and it was hard trying to figure shit out. I'm so thankful to my in-laws, who stepped in and gave him the life that we couldn't. Quick and I never had to worry about him because we knew that he was okay. But, still, we're so proud of you, baby, and we wanted to do something to show you just how much," Nichelle said as she grabbed her son's hand and led him outside.

Everybody followed to see exactly what was going on. A few seconds later, a black Bentley Bentayga pulled up with a huge white bow on top. The grill was silver and sparkled like diamonds.

"Surprise!" Dior yelled when she jumped out of the truck and handed him the keys.

"From us to you. Congrats bruh. I'm proud of you," Quick said as he pulled his son in for a hug.

"Damn," Nix replied as he looked on in shock.

Besides clothes and shoes, he couldn't really remember his parents doing much of anything for him. It's not that they didn't want to. They were never home enough to take care of him like they should have. He already had a Suburban, but they got him a grown man ride and he was feeling it. He looked inside and smiled when he saw his name engraved in the head rest. The inside was chrome plated and nice as fuck.

"Do you like it baby?" Nichelle asked.

"Hell yeah. This bitch is nice. Aye, this shit is legal, right?" Nix asked lowly while looking at Quick.

He was grateful but he had to be sure. Quick and Nichelle used to get into all kinds of shit back in the day. They robbed delivery trucks and anything in between that guaranteed them a payout. Nix had never been to jail and he wasn't trying to go.

"Yeah nigga. I'm good on all that other shit. This is legit and we got the papers to prove it." The money that he used to buy it wasn't legal, but Nix didn't need to know all the details.

"Damn man, I appreciate y'all," Nix said as he gave his parents a hug.

He took a few more minutes to admire his new machinery before they all went back inside. When Al nudged him, Nix nodded his head to let him know that he was ready.

"Come here Dior," Al said, calling his best friend's girlfriend over to him.

Dior looked around in confusion when he pulled out a chair for her to sit in. Al gave the DJ the thumbs up and the music switched almost instantly. When *Why I Love You* by Major started to play, Dior smiled. She loved the bounce version more but the original would do. That was one of her favorite songs and she closed her eyes and started singing. When she opened them, she smiled when she saw Nix standing in front of her. She was about to get up and sing to her man, but he got down on one knee before she could. Dior gasped when he pulled out a ring box and showed her what was inside. Tears fell from her eyes as everybody whistled and cheered. She could barely make out what Nix was saying over all the loud commotion but she clearly heard when he asked her to be his wife.

"Yes baby! Yes, I'll marry you!" she yelled as she stood up and hugged him.

Her hand trembled when he slipped the ring on her finger and she couldn't stop crying. His big day turned into a big day for both of them. She and Nix had talked about marriage lots of times, but she wasn't expecting a proposal so soon after he graduated.

"Yes bitch, that ring is everything," Nichelle said when she grabbed Dior's hand to inspect it.

"Get ready Nichelle. We're going dress shopping soon," Dior replied excitedly.

"Just let me know when girl. I'm always ready. I can't believe that my baby is getting married. You already know I'm showing the fuck out!"

"Go chill with Nichelle and my cousins for a minute baby. I'm going rap with JB for a minute," Nix said as he walked away with Quick.

His grandfather, uncles and a few of his male cousins were all sitting in a corner of the hall and he requested their presence. JB was almost seventy years old but he was still full of life. He was big on family and all about making his legal money make even more money. He never got involved in the dope game and he didn't agree with his kids and grandkids doing it either. He didn't know that Nix sold weed and he wanted to keep it that way. Nix didn't know why he asked to speak with all of them, but he was curious. He noticed that all of them who worked at the construction company were present.

"The man of the hour. Come sit down and have a drink with your pops," JB said while smiling at Nix.

He pointed to a chair that was right next to him, telling him to sit down. Nix's uncles hated when their father referred to him as his son. He was a grandson and they didn't care that JB raised him like his own.

"What's up?" Nix asked as he grabbed a beer from the cooler that was on the table.

"I wanted to let y'all know about a few changes that I'm making to the company," JB started.

"Aww shit," his oldest son, Jessie Jr., groaned. He managed the construction site and had been in charge for ten years. He didn't know what kind of changes his father was trying to make but he was hoping that it didn't involve him.

"Relax, Junior, you still got your job," JB assured him.

"What's good Pops?" Nix asked.

"As y'all all know, I'm getting up in age. My wife is ready for me to spend more time at home with her and I'm ready to relax. I've been working since I was fifteen years old and I'm tired."

"What are you saying grandpa? You're not gonna be managing the club no more?" Nix's cousin, Ryan, asked excitedly. He was a regular at the club before it closed for renovations but he didn't mind working there if given the opportunity. He was Jessie's middle son and he also worked at the family's construction company. That was the first job for most of the men in the Nixon family.

"Nah, I'm done working altogether. I've made enough money for me and my wife to live comfortably and travel the world ten times if we wanted to."

"What does that mean for us then? I hope you're not planning to sell," Jessie said.

"I told you a long time ago that these were family businesses. I'm keeping everything in the family," JB said as he pulled two sets of keys out of his pocket and handed them over to Nix.

"The fuck is that Pops? I've been managing the construction site for ten years," Jessie complained.

"And you still do. Nix is not the manager. He's the new owner," JB said as he smiled proudly.

"Is this some kind of joke?" Jessie yelled out angrily.

"Do you see me smiling nigga?" JB countered just as upset.

"I can't believe this shit. We busted our asses for months renovating that club, only for you to go hand the shit over to somebody else. You got all these kids and grandkids and you hand everything over to Nix like we don't mean shit," Jessie fumed.

Everyone else was just as upset but he was vocal about how he felt. He had two sons and a daughter of his own, and JB didn't even try to acknowledge them. He understood that he was proud of Nix for graduating college because that was something that no one else in the family did. But, to overlook everyone else and give everything to him was fucked up on a whole other level.

"First off, you better watch how the hell you talk to me. You didn't do a damn thing for that club for free. You and everybody else got paid to do your jobs. Nobody even gave a damn about the club before now. Nix was the only one whose ever shown interest in it."

"That may be true but the same can't be said about the construction site. I've worked there longer than anybody else."

"That's true but work is all you can do. I can't deny that you're good with your hands, but running a business takes more than that. You don't know how to negotiate contracts or nothing else. Besides me, Nix is the only one who knows everything on the back end."

"I'm trying to see what the problem is. I think you made the right choice," Quick said as he mean mugged his brothers and nephews.

"Yeah, I bet you do." Jessie frowned as he grabbed his drink and walked away. After a few minutes, everyone else walked away too, leaving Nix and Quick there alone with JB.

"Man, I would hate to fuck somebody up behind my son, but I will. Hating ass muthafuckers," Quick fussed as he grabbed a beer and walked away.

"Man, I appreciate this Pops but you know it's about to be some shit," Nix said as he looked over at his grandfather.

"As if I give a fuck. I don't need nobody's approval for nothing that I do. This has been in the works for months now. And, honestly, it was your grandmother's idea. I was only giving you the club, but she made a lot of sense when she said that you should run the construction site too. Nobody else knows the ins and outs like you do and I don't have the patience to train them."

"What's your price? I know you're not just handing everything over to me without getting some kind of profit from it."

"You know me too well. Let's talk numbers," JB said, as Nix gave him his undivided attention.

They sat and talked for over an hour before they finalized their plans. JB was confident that Nix was the man for the job and he knew that he'd made the right decision. His other kids and grandkids were in their feelings, but they would just have to get over it. Most of them dropped out of high school, so college wasn't happening. The others either had an extensive criminal record or struggled with drug addiction at one point in their lives. If it weren't for him having a family business, some of them wouldn't even have a job.

"What's good bruh? You and JB were over there running it for a minute," Al said when Nix walked back over to him.

"It's on nigga," Nix replied excitedly.

"He agreed to let you manage it?"

"Nah nigga, he let me have that shit."

"What do you mean he let you have it?"

"It's mine nigga. Ain't no managing. I'm the muthafucking owner!" Nix replied excitedly.

"Real shit?"

"I gotta give him ten grand a month. Five for each business."

"Wait, I'm confused."

"He gave me the construction site and the club. He's transferring ownership to me bright and early Monday morning."

"Damn bruh, that's what's up. But do you think you can swing ten grand a month? That seems kind of steep," Al noted.

"Man, that ain't shit. The construction site can make that in one day. I negotiate the contracts, so I know. Man, this shit is about to be on and poppin' but you might not like what I'm about to say."

"Aww shit. I should have known that there was a catch," Al sighed.

"It ain't no catch, but I really wanna get Danny on board. I know shit ain't been sweet with y'all in a minute but we can really use him at the club."

Danny was one of their middle school best friends who they clicked with almost instantly. He and Al had a falling out in high school, but Nix remained in contact with him. Thanks to his popularity, Danny was one of the hottest promoters in New Orleans. He didn't work for anyone, so every dollar that he made was his to keep. He was always invited to the hottest parties and he had connections to a few rappers and managers. He could be an asset to Club Nixon and Nix wanted him on board. He wouldn't do it at the expense of making his best friend uncomfortable though.

"Man, we're grown ass men. We don't have to be best friends to work together. I'm about my money and nothing is gonna stop that. Bring that nigga on board if you think it'll help."

"That's what the fuck I'm talking about. If all goes well, we'll be ready to invest in less than a year," Nix said, as Al nodded in agreement.

Nix was hoping to be a married homeowner within another year. His bank account was nice but he was ready to add a few more zeroes to it and he was gonna grind until he did. .

Chapter 7

"Shit!" Gianni hissed when she got up and saw the long line of people waiting to use the bathroom.

She set the alarm on her phone but she slept right through it. Between work, school and just life itself, Gianni felt like there were never enough hours in the day. She was drained most of the time, but it would all be worth it. She was in her senior year of college and she would have her degree in finance soon.

"Last call for breakfast ladies!" one of the counselors walked into the room and yelled.

A few ladies got out of the line to go eat, but it was still too long for Gianni. She didn't want to be late, so she would just have to improvise.

"Fuck it," she mumbled while getting out of the line and rushing over to her cot. Once she had it made, she grabbed her duffel bag and headed out of the women and children's shelter that she had called home for the past four months.

It had been a little over a year since Gianni's grandmother passed and everything in her life changed. She ended up getting an apartment with Biggie, but that didn't last very long. After only five months of moving in, Gianni was looking for somewhere else to stay.

Biggie started out being understanding but he started to show his true colors after about two months. He was getting impatient with Gianni holding out on him and he always complained about being sexually frustrated. He was getting tired of them sleeping in the same bed and not having sex. He was out there fucking other women, so Gianni didn't know why he was so pressed. Kori made sure to let her know everything that he did but she never confronted him about it. She even stopped going down on him because his name was ringing bells in the streets. She really didn't care about any of that until he got one of his side bitches pregnant.

Kori told her all about the rumors that were going around, but Gianni never entertained it. She believed her man when he told her that it was all a lie, but he turned out to be the liar. When a woman showed up to their house to confront her, Gianni was done. Biggie thought that he had the upper hand on her because she didn't have anywhere else to go. He soon found out how wrong he was when he came home one day and she was gone. He tried reaching out to her a few times until she got her number changed. She hadn't seen him in a while and she wanted it to stay that

42

way. It was crazy because she was ready to take that next step with him, but it obviously wasn't meant to be.

Kori always made it known that she didn't have enough room for her to stay there, so she never even bothered to ask. She ended up sleeping on the sofa by one of her classmates but that was only a temporary fix. When her man came home from jail, Gianni already knew what was up.

Surprisingly, her auntie, Karen, opened her door and let her stay with her for a while. She had just broken up with her man and was living alone. Gianni had a part time job, so she was able to help her out with bills. As soon as Karen found another man to lay up under, she gave her niece the boot.

One of the academic advisors at the school told Gianni about the shelter and she had been living there ever since. She regretted not signing up to live on campus but she didn't think she would ever have a reason to.

After leaving the shelter, Gianna hopped into her Nissan Rogue and headed to a nearby gas station. The SUV was only four months old and the only thing of value that she owned. Gianni traded her old car in and got some reliable transportation. Between her car note and three different insurances, she couldn't afford a place to stay even if she wanted to. She rented hotel rooms a lot if the price was right but, sometimes, her truck served as her home for the night.

The shelter had strict rules and they didn't allow residents to come in after certain hours. They had to pay two dollars a day if they had a job and she always paid for the entire month. That basically guaranteed that her cot wouldn't be given away to any newcomers. They didn't allow them to have cars either, so Gianni always parked around the corner and walked. She also had a small storage unit where she kept her clothes and other personal items.

Her living arrangements weren't the best but she never complained. Gianna had been bent by life but she refused to be broken.

"Hey. Can I have the key to the bathroom?" she asked the gas station cashier who stood behind the counter.

Once he gave it to her, Gianni went into the bathroom and completed her morning hygiene. She used the wipes that she had in her duffle bag and cleaned herself up. She got dressed in record speed and moussed her naturally curly hair. After putting on her eyeliner and gloss, she looked at her reflection in the mirror. She smiled, satisfied with the way she quickly got herself together. She was happy that she took her shower the night before but she was ready to take another one.

Over time, Gianni had mastered the art of being cute on a budget. YouTube tutorials taught her how to do her brows and natural hair. She purchased all of her clothes on clearance but she had a gift with putting it all together. After spraying herself with some body mist, she exited the bathroom and got ready to start her day.

It took about fifteen minutes to get to her destination but she made it five minutes before time. It wouldn't have been a problem if she was late, but that wasn't professional. She took the gun that she always carried out of her purse and put it under her seat. She was a single woman living in a shelter, so she had to be careful. Gianni walked into the library and waved at the employees who knew her very well. She sat at her favorite table and got ready to work.

A few minutes later, the door opened and a man who resembled a black sumo wrestler entered the building. To most, he looked mean and intimidating. In the beginning, he intimidated Gianni too. Now that she knew him, he was the sweetest man that she'd ever had the pleasure of meeting. Before he had a chance to say anything, a little girl ran from behind him with a piece of paper in her hand.

44

You're The Best Part

"I made a B on my test! Can you believe it? I've never made that kind of grade in her class before," Tiana said as she wrapped her arms around Gianni's neck.

"Aww, I'm so proud of you, boo. You're gonna make an A next time. Hey Heavy." Gianni smiled while speaking to Tiana's father.

"What's up Gianni? I'm happy that she can finally tell you her good news. I'm so tired of hearing about this damn B," Heavy laughed.

"Don't do her like that. She worked hard for that grade."

"I sure did and I made the highest grade in the class. That test was hard."

"It's gonna be even higher next time. I made a few notes for you to study. We'll go over everything and I'll explain it all to you."

"Okay. I'm going run to the bathroom before we get started," Tiana said as she hurriedly walked away.

Gianni always went to the library to study whenever time permitted. About two months ago, she spotted a very frustrated seventh grader who seemed to be having a mental meltdown. Gianni didn't like to pry but she hated to see the little girl crying. When she learned that she was having a hard time in her math class, Gianni stepped in and offered her assistance. She was a finance major, so math was like second nature to her. After a while, she had taught Tiana a few tricks to solve the problems that she had trouble with and that seemed to work. When her father came to pick her up, he asked Gianni about being his daughter's tutor. Since she could use the money, she jumped at the chance. She was only gonna charge them forty dollars for each session, but he offered her sixty.

Gianni was doing so well with Tiana that a few of her friends' parents asked her to tutor them too. She had a total of five clients and that was the money that she used to pay for her car. Heavy and his wife, Nadia, took an instant liking to Gianni. They were the only ones who knew about her living arrangements other than her cousin, Kori. They offered her a room in their home, but she graciously declined. They were nice, but Gianni didn't want to impose on anyone. Nadia's niece worked at the hotel that she frequented on the weekends and she always gave Gianni her discount if the hotel didn't have an event and allowed her to.

"I need to make a few runs for my brother but I'll be back in an hour. Oh, and let me give you this before I forget," Heavy said as he handed Gianni her room key and an envelope with cash inside. Nadia's niece knew to rent her a room every Friday and she already had Gianni's debit card on file.

"Thanks for the room key but keep the money. I told you that it's no charge. You and Nadia are too good to me. This is the least that I can do to show my appreciation." She tried to give him the money back, but he raised his hands and backed away.

"Stop insulting us girl. Seeing my baby smile is worth way more than what you're charging us. That math shit was starting to fuck with her self-esteem. Trust me, we appreciate you just as much. I'm gone but I'll see you tonight," Heavy said before he walked away.

Besides the hookup that Nadia got her for the room, Heavy got her a part time job on the weekends. He was a bouncer at a club and he was tight with the manager. It was crazy because Kori worked there too. She used to always brag to Gianni about all the men who wanted her and how much she made in tips. She claimed that the owner was after her too but she didn't know how true that was. Gianni used to beg her to get her on but she always had an excuse as to why she couldn't. It was cool though because Heavy came through for her. It had only been a month but Gianni was able to save a little more money. She was now up to five thousand in her savings and she was hoping to be at ten in the next few months. She wanted to make sure that when she finally got her own place, she would be able to afford to keep it.

"Okay, I'm ready." Tiana smiled when she came back and sat down.

"Let's do it," Gianni replied while pulling out her notepad and pencil.

"Bitch, hurry up! I'm trying to get out there before them other vultures get here. I wanna make sure I'm working in the section where Nix is sitting," Kori said, as Gianni touched up her brows.

One of Nix's cousins was having his thirtieth birthday party in his club and he had the entire top half reserved just for him. All of the other private sections were rented out as well, but Kori wanted to work the party.

"I would have been finished a long time ago if you keep still," Gianni fussed.

"I'm happy that I came up in here early before the rest of them hoes."

"I don't know why. Y'all be doing too much just to get next to one man. This ain't The Players Club and that nigga ain't Dollar Bill."

"Bitch, you must be blind. Stop acting like you don't see how fine that nigga is."

"He is, but it's not that deep."

"It's very deep for me. I be seeing the nigga checking me out, but he hasn't made a move yet. I'm tired of waiting so I plan to get the ball rolling tonight."

"You had me thinking that y'all were already fucking."

"Who says we're not?"

"Girl bye. You just said that he hasn't made a move yet. As much as you talk, I know y'all ain't doing shit." Gianni rolled her eyes, not believing a word that she was saying.

If that were true, Gianni wondered why Kori could never get her on when she used to beg her to. It was fucked up because she had hooked her up with a job a few months before, even though it didn't work out. One of Gianni's classmates told her about the strip club that she worked in and she was intrigued. With that kind of money, she knew that she would have her own place in no time. Gianni told Kori about it and they both showed up to the club, ready to work. Things quickly went left when Gianni got there and saw her brother, Greg. He and a few of his friends were seated right by the stage and that put a damper on her plans. She didn't even know that he was home from one of his frequent trips to jail but she damn sure wasn't about to dance in front of him.

You're The Best Part

When Greg saw her, he looked at her like she was a snack instead of his little sister. He was asking her what time she was going on, but she left without even replying. Kori stayed and ended up working there for almost a month. When she got into a fight with the owner's sister, that was the end of that. She started working at Club Nixon soon after but she never tried to look out for Gianni like she had done for her. Greg went back to jail soon after and that was the best news that Gianni had heard in a while. She never did try to go back to work at the strip club. She had lost her nerve to do it by then.

"Bitch, I don't tell you everything. But, no, we haven't had sex yet," Kori said, interrupting Gianni's thoughts.

She was embellishing but Gianni didn't need to know that. Nix never even looked her way, but she was trying to change that.

"I just wanna get my tips and get the fuck up out of here. I'm tired already and my shift hasn't even started."

"Did you get a room this weekend?" Kori asked her.

"I sure did."

"Good. I might need to use it for a few hours if I can get close enough to Nix."

"I don't see how that's gonna be possible when his fiancée is always around."

"I heard that they're not together anymore. I don't know why she still be hanging around here all the time. That nigga ain't checking for her fat ass no more. He don't even acknowledge her."

"How do you know that?" Gianni asked.

"His cousin is one of the bartenders. She said they broke up, but Dior still be saying that they're together."

"Oh, well, you're all done," Gianni said while handing her a mirror to see the finished product.

"Thanks cousin. Wish me luck. If all goes well, I'm getting me some new dick tonight," Kori replied while looking at her reflection in the floor length mirror.

The bottle girls all wore the same uniform but they didn't all look the same in them. The black leather bodysuit, fishnets and combat boots made her feel sexy. Kori knew that she was the shit with her caramel complexion, slim waist, and large breasts. She wished she had more ass but she was hoping to rectify that problem soon. She was saving her money to get it done and she almost had enough. The tips that she got from Club Nixon was making it happen sooner than she thought. She was used to being the center of attention, but now she had to share the spotlight.

She hated that Gianni worked there now and she tried her best to avoid that from happening. Kori always had an excuse whenever her cousin asked her to get her on. She didn't count on Gianni meeting and forming a friendship with Heavy. He was one of the head bouncers and he and Al were tight. Gianni got hired on the spot, no questions asked.

When Kori first saw her there, she wanted to die. Her cousin was shapely with a beautiful face and Kori didn't want her to steal her shine. Gianni turned a few heads but she wasn't as friendly as her cousin. She didn't do small talk and she barely smiled. She did her job and went home, nothing in between. Kori had a man, but she didn't mind flirting a little if it meant getting a bigger tip. Sometimes, she did more than flirt but that's what made her the most popular bottle girl in the club.

Once she made sure that her appearance was on point, Kori sashayed out of the employee break room, ready to get her day started. She looked up at the top level of the club, but Nix wasn't holding down his usual spot yet. He was probably in his office, but she knew that he would be coming out soon. The crowd usually came in around ten and it was a little after nine.

"What's up Al? Can I work the upper level tonight?" Kori asked, beating the other bottle girls to the punch.

"Yeah, you got that," Al replied, exciting her.

"Thanks boss man."

"I'm putting your cousin up there with you."

"For what? She don't even like working up there."

"Do you have a problem with the way I run shit around here Kori?"

"I'm just saying. We're not joined at the hip. Gianni don't have to go everywhere I go."

"Maybe I'll send her up there by herself and you can work the bottom level."

"No, sorry about that, Al. I'm cool with however you want to do it," Kori hurriedly apologized before he walked away.

Al was Nix's righthand man and manager of the club. Nix called all the shots, but Al was his mouthpiece. Al was cool but he didn't like it when anyone questioned his authority. He was fair and that's what Kori liked about him the most. He didn't play favorites and the only reason why he agreed to let her work the top level was because she asked him first.

Unlike Nix, Al knew all that there was to know about every one of the employees. He knew who was fucking who and everything else. He was never one to talk anyone's business, so Kori had mad respect for him. She had run through a few niggas in the club and he knew all about it. As long as she did the job that she was being paid to do, he turned the blind eye to her whorish ways.

"What you sippin' on?" Alicia, one of the bartenders, asked.

"Nothing, I'm good," Kori replied as she walked over to Nix's cousin, Rachelle.

Alicia was married, but it was no secret that she was crushing on Nix too. He was the boss so that was to be expected. She watched him just as much as Kori did, but he didn't pay them any mind. Truthfully, there wasn't a woman there that he gave a second glance. That made Kori feel good because she knew that he wasn't just ignoring her.

"What do you need boo?" Rachelle asked her.

"Give me a strawberry Hennessey cousin," Dior interrupted when she walked up with her friends, Crystal, and River.

"Stop being so rude Dior. Did you want something Kori?" Rachelle asked.

"Nah, I'm straight," Kori replied as she discreetly looked at Dior.

She was a big girl but she was bad as fuck. Dior's makeup stayed flawless and she dressed better than any BBW that had ever graced a magazine. She had confidence and she walked like she owned the place. Kori could see why Nix was with her, but she was happy that it was over. She wanted a chance with him and she would gladly leave her man if he gave her one.

"Twelve dollars," Rachelle said once she was done fixing Dior's drink.

"Really?" Dior questioned as she looked at her sideways. Alicia was helping her friends and she was sorry that she didn't ask her to help her too. Rachelle was the only one who charged Dior for anything but the others never even dared.

"Yes, really," Rachelle snapped. Dior pulled a twenty from her purse and threw it on the bar.

"The change is not yours to keep. I'll be back for round two."

"I'll be here," Rachelle assured her before she walked off.

"When did she start paying for drinks?" Kori asked once they were alone again.

"Since her and my cousin broke up. He said no more freebies. I need my job, so I do what he says."

"What happened between the two of them?"

"I don't even know. Nix ain't the type to put everybody in his business like that. Nobody even knew that they broke up until Nichelle told us that the wedding was off. Her stupid ass be walking around here barking out orders like she's still the boss' fiancée," Rachelle replied before she walked away to go help another customer.

Kori grabbed two ice buckets and prepared to head upstairs. When Gianni walked out front, she grabbed her ice buckets and prepared to do the same.

"I hate working the top level," she complained.

"Why didn't you tell that to Al?" Kori questioned as they headed upstairs.

"Nah, I'm good. I just got here and I'm not trying to start complaining. I'm grateful just to have a job. I definitely need the money."

"You should be about ready to get you an apartment by now. I don't know why you left from by Biggie."

"Because the nigga had his hoes coming there like it was cool. Not to mention the baby that he made. Ain't no telling what else he did that I don't know about."

"I wouldn't have cared what he did. He took care of you and had a roof over your head. Besides, you ain't giving up the pussy. What did you expect him to do?"

Gianni kept her composure, but that comment hurt her feelings. Kori knew better than anyone how she felt about having sex. She was ready to be intimate with Biggie but his impatience was what stopped her. He had no compassion for her feelings and that's what turned her off. She wanted to experience the feelings that she kept hearing so much about but only when she was ready. The way her mother died scared her and she had to get over those feelings. She was well educated on sex and the risks that came along with it. Still, she wasn't about to knowingly put herself in a fucked up situation.

"I'm happy that I didn't give it up. I don't give a fuck what he did for me. I'm not about to let a nigga do me dirty just because he's taking care of me. I'll sleep under a bridge first."

"You're close to it," Kori replied sarcastically.

"Girl, fuck you, Kori. You seem to be more worried about my life than I am. There go your new dick, go hop on it," Gianni snapped when she saw Nix walk into the upper VIP section.

Kori instantly perked up when she saw him. She felt bad about what she'd said to Gianni but she would

54

apologize later. It wasn't their first argument and she was sure that it wouldn't be their last.

"What are y'all drinking tonight?" Kori asked as she walked up to Nix's table. He was playing on his phone while Al and Danny sat next to him. They were the three who ran the place so that wasn't unusual. The other two men appeared to be arguing but they got quiet as soon as she made her presence known.

"Just bring us a few bottles of Hennessey and Tito's," Al said with an annoyed frown. Nix seemed preoccupied by whatever was on his phone. Kori wanted him to look up at her, but he never did.

She went back to the bar and grabbed a few bottles. After a while, the birthday boy showed up and the entire club was jumping. Unlike the rest of the men in his section, Nix was chillin', just like always. He behaved like a boss and that shit turned Kori on more than anything. She made sure to stay close to him, hoping that he noticed her. When the birthday boy started talking, she tuned in when she thought they were discussing her.

"Aye cuz!" Nix's cousin, Ryan, yelled while slapping his leg.

"What's up?" Nix asked while looking up at him.

Ryan had just started coming back to the club. A few of his family members were still salty about him owning the place and he was one of them. Ryan was a regular there for years before the place closed for renovations. He went at Nix about being a manager, but that idea was quickly struck down. All Ryan cared about was fucking different hoes and that was his only reason for wanting to work there. He had a girl but that never did mean anything to him. The nigga had three kids but none of them were with his girlfriend, even though they were together when all three of the kids were conceived. His next words proved that Nix had made the right decision in not giving him a job.

"What's good with your bottle girl? She fine as fuck."

"Which one?"

"Baby over there with the curly hair," Ryan replied while nodding his head towards Gianni.

"Shit, I don't know. Ask Al," Nix said as he looked around.

He did a double take when he glanced over at Gianni. It was the hazel eyes that did it for him. They were beautiful and so was she. His gaze lingered a little too long for Kori's liking. She had never seen him do that before and she wasn't feeling it. She would die if Nix wanted her cousin and not her. Gianni was busy fulfilling orders and she wasn't paying attention. Kori was over Nix and his staring, so she decided to interrupt.

"Don't waste your time love. She don't like men," Kori smirked.

"Damn man. She's gay?" Ryan asked.

"Nah, she's just scared of men for her own personal reasons and she got a lot going on right now." Gianni was prepared to die with her virginity intact, so he was wasting his time inquiring about her.

"Like what?"

"For one, she's a fulltime student. She's also homeless and living in a women's shelter. Trust me, dating is the last thing on her mind."

"Fuck that, I'll pass. She's fine and all, but baby girl sounds like a liability. I got enough bills and she sounds like she'll only be another one."

"Believe me, she will be."

"How do you know so much about her?"

"Because she's my first cousin."

"Is that why you feel so comfortable telling all her business?" Nix asked angrily.

He heard the entire exchange and it was fucked up how she was doing her own cousin. The look that he was giving Kori made her skin crawl. She wanted him to notice her but not that way. He looked pissed, but that wasn't her intentions. His scratchy voice sent chills down her spine but not in a good way.

"Grab us a few more bottles Kori," Al requested, making her happy for the temporary distraction. Kori rushed down the stairs to the bar at the same time as Gianni.

"Tips are good as hell tonight," Gianni said.

"Yeah, they are. Look, I'm sorry about what I said earlier. I was out of line," Kori apologized.

"It's cool. No love lost. How did it go with the boss man? Do you still need to use the room?"

"It went good but we're getting our own room," Kori replied with a sneaky smirk.

She was lying her ass off, but Gianni didn't need to know that. She knew her cousin very well. As long as she thought that Kori was fucking with Nix, she would stay away from him. That was exactly what Kori wanted her to do.

Chapter 2

"Shit," Nix hissed, as Alicia's head bobbed up and down.

She slobbered all over his dick as she took him to the back of her throat. She was humming and the vibration combined with what she was doing had him ready to blow. He pulled her hair tight and it only took another five minutes before a few of his babies were sliding down her throat. Alicia stood to her feet, but the wall assisted with helping Nix keep standing.

"Come get this pussy," Alicia purred as she bent over the sofa and placed her hands on the back of it.

She made her ass clap, and Nix was ready to beat it out the frame. He rolled a condom over his erection and walked over to her. He stood behind her and grabbed a handful of her hair. Alicia moaned his name and closed her eyes when he entered her. Nix had the best stroke game out of every man that she'd ever been with, including her husband.

Alicia's husband was a fireman who also worked as an online college professor. She loved him more than life, but he just wasn't the same man that she'd married eight years ago. They barely had sex because he was either at the firehouse or busy with his students. He hadn't touched her in four months and he didn't see anything wrong with that. They were only thirty years old and it felt like their marriage was already over. She was very sexually satisfied with him whenever they did have sex. He knew her body inside and out but he needed to do better.

Alicia was a freak, but her husband was too reserved sometimes. He didn't even like her to swallow when she gave him oral, but that turned her on. She loved to use toys but he wasn't with that either. She was tired of begging him for something that he should have given willingly, so she stopped. It was wrong, but she sought companionship outside of her marriage.

"Stop running," Nix growled while wrapping her hair around his huge hand and pulling her back into him.

"Damn Nix," Alicia moaned while enjoying the feel of his thick, long dick sliding in and out of her.

She was begging him not to stop as he gave her long, deep strokes. When he picked up one of her legs and placed it on the cheap sofa, Alicia braced herself for what she knew was coming. He fucked her with no mercy while she tried her best not to fall. She looked back at him and got even wetter when she looked into his handsome face. His bottom lip was stuck in between his teeth and his reddened eyes were low. Alicia's legs started to quiver when he wrapped his hand around her neck. She screamed as she came and she knew that he wasn't too far behind. When his breathing became short and labored, she already knew what was up.

"I'm almost there," Nix huffed while pulling out of her.

Alicia hurriedly dropped down to her knees and pulled off the condom. She quickly took him into her mouth again, anticipating the reward that she was about to receive. Nix held the sides of her head and fucked her face like she was begging him to. She felt his dick pulsating in her mouth right before he erupted like a volcano. Just like before, she drank his juices like water and wiped her mouth when she was done.

"Shit, I need a blunt after that," Nix panted while dropping down on the sofa.

"When don't you need a blunt?" Alicia laughed.

He smoked more than any man she'd ever known and red seemed to be the permanent color of his eyes. She got up from her place on the floor and grabbed his blunt. After lighting it for him, she took a pull before handing it over.

"Preciate it," Nix said while taking the blunt from her.

"I'm going take a shower. I'll leave the water on for you."

Nix nodded as he continued to smoke. Alicia always rented a room when she wanted to see him and they had been there since leaving his club the night before. She used to beg him to come to her house but she had him fucked up. It was bad enough that he was fucking with another man's wife. He wasn't about to do the shit in their house.

Since his split with Dior eight months ago, Nix had a few females that he chilled with. All of them were either married or had a man at home. He didn't want them to get attached, so he preferred not to deal with single women at the moment. Nix still wanted a wife and kids one day but he was having fun in the meantime. Everybody seemed to only want sex and that was all that he gave them. He'd only run across one other woman who he thought about settling down with since calling off his engagement. When she told him that she wanted to travel and didn't want kids, he ended things and kept it moving.

When Alicia approached him, she was straight up about it. Her husband wasn't handling business at home and she had needs. She didn't bother Nix or try to make their arrangement more than what it was. She got some dick and went on her way. She was a bartender at his club and she kept it classy there too. She stole glances at him from time to time but she stayed in her lane. Besides Al and Danny, no one else knew what was up.

Once she was out of the shower, Nix hopped in and freshened up. Alicia had the room for a few more hours, but he got dressed and got ready to leave. She laid in the bed, preparing to take a quick nap when Nix headed for the door.

"I'm out!" Nix yelled right before walking out the door.

He checked his messages on his phone as he walked to his car. As soon as he got in, Nix did a double take when he saw Gianni coming from a room on the bottom level. She was already pretty, but the blunt that she had dangling from her glossy lips made her fucking beautiful. She was a woman after his heart and he was intrigued. Her golden tinted eyes sparkled in the sunlight right before she put on a pair of shades to hide them. Just then, the things that her cousin said replayed in his head like a record. She said that her cousin was homeless but she wasn't in a homeless shelter like she said. Nix was curious and he made a mental note to ask Al more about her. He watched as Gianni got into her truck and pulled off before he did the same. He was up for most of the night with Alicia and he needed a nap before he had to be back at the club later that night.

"Fuck," Nix sighed in disgust when he pulled up to his house.

He wanted to drive off and go somewhere else when he spotted Dior's silver Benz parked in his driveway. It would have been perfect if he could have parked in his enclosed garage before she came. That way, she wouldn't have known if he was there or not. Knowing her disgusting ass, she probably would have waited anyway just to see. Both his cars usually stayed out of sight and that's how he preferred it.

Nix loved his home but he was sorry that it wasn't in a gated community. As much as he adored Dior before, he couldn't stand the sight of her now. She got out of her car when she saw him get out of his. Nix wasn't in the mood to keep having the same conversation with her. She broke his heart in a way that he never imagined. It took a while, but he was finally over it.

"Hey," Dior said when he got closer to her.

"I'm tired Dior. I need a nap before I have to be back at the club tonight," Nix replied as he kept walking.

"I guess you are tired since you didn't sleep home last night. Where were you?"

She had passed by his house twice the night before and once earlier that morning. He hadn't been home either time. He usually kept all the lights off when he was home. If ever his porch light was on, she knew that he was gone. When she went back again, she decided to wait until he showed up.

"I'm a grown ass single man. I don't have to answer to you and nobody else."

"Can we at least talk without arguing Nix?"

"We don't have shit else to talk about. The fuck, man. It's been eight months now Dior. Whatever we had is over and there's no coming back."

"I'm sorry, okay? How many times do I need to apologize to show you how sincere I am? I gave you the money back. What more do you want from me?" she cried.

"The fact that you felt that you had to take anything from me in the first place is what I have a problem with. I gave you the fucking world and you still weren't satisfied. You think I gave a fuck about buying this big ass house. I got this shit because of you. We were supposed to grow old and raise our kids in this bitch."

"We still can Nix. Please baby, I'll do anything for you to forgive me."

"I already forgave you. I just can't fuck with you no more. I'll never be with somebody that I can't trust and I'll never trust you again." Dior broke down and cried but that was nothing new. He didn't feel an ounce of sympathy for her and he never would.

A little over a year had passed since he proposed to her and they were supposed to be married by now. He'd spent thousands of dollars on a wedding that never happened. He would have lost out on all of his money if his grandparents didn't have a special occasion coming up around that time. Instead of using the hall, photographer, and caterers for his wedding reception, he used it to throw them a surprise anniversary party instead. He'd spent even more on the fertility doctor that she went to and he was happy that the treatments didn't work the first time around.

Nix still wanted kids. He just no longer wanted Dior to be their mother.

A year ago, Nix was negotiating a few contracts for his construction company. One of the contractors was in the process of building his house from the ground up and the foundation was already there. He and his wife decided to scrap those plans and buy something bigger when she got pregnant with twins, giving them a total of seven kids. Nix told him that he was interested in purchasing the property since Dior loved the area so much. She fell in love with the blueprint design and didn't want to change a thing. It was too big to Nix but he wanted her to be happy. The contractor not only sold him the house, he and his crew completed the work too. He failed to tell Nix about the cameras that he had installed in the common areas of the home until a few weeks later. Every area of the house was equipped with surveillance equipment except the bedrooms and bathrooms. Since they had small kids, he and his wife felt that it was necessary to have an extra set of eyes on them at all times.

Being curious, Nix decided to tap into the system once he learned how it worked. Dior was there with his mother, trying to figure out how they were going to decorate. Nix didn't know where Nichelle was, but Dior was in the kitchen talking on the phone to her friends. It broke his heart to hear her discuss how she'd been stealing money from him for months. Dior did the books for both his companies and he had no reason not to trust her. She was going to be his wife and he gave her whatever her heart desired. She didn't have to take anything that was freely given to her.

Nix didn't want to believe it but he hired an independent auditor just to be sure. Two weeks later, his worst fears had been confirmed. Dior had stolen over fifty thousand dollars from his companies and was stashing it in a private account. She tried to deny it, but he had too much evidence for her to even go there. She tried to make excuses for why she did it but there was nothing that she could say. That shit broke him and it took a minute for him to bounce back. He entertained the idea of getting back with her but he just couldn't do it. He didn't trust easily and she had broken their bond. Now, he just had no strings attached sex and he was good with that.

"I told you why I did it. I was scared Nix," Dior said, pulling him away from his thoughts of the past.

Dior sounded like a damn fool and he was tired of hearing her voice. She claimed that she only did what she did just in case things didn't work out between them. She swore that she was scared of him leaving her broke and alone. She had access to any and everything that he had, so he wasn't buying it. Aside from that, she had a degree and was making her own money being an elementary school teacher. She was just being greedy and got caught.

"That excuse was bullshit when you first said it and nothing has changed. Stealing Dior? That's some shit that you never had to do. I would have given you every dime in my account. I didn't love my money more than I loved you. And stop poppin' up at my house. The shit is mad annoying and I'm losing my patience."

Nix was done, so he left her standing there just like he often did. He and Dior had been together for years but time meant nothing to him. She couldn't get over the fact that they were done but she had no choice. Nix felt like he would never recover from her betrayal but, in time, he did. He hadn't shed tears since his uncle Jake got killed but he wept like a baby when it was all over with. He got pissy drunk the night they broke up and one of her friends helped to alleviate some of his pain. The same shady bitch who she felt comfortable telling her business to was the same one swallowing his babies that night. Nix felt like fucking her girl was payback for what she'd done, but the pain lingered long after the deed was done.

Once he was inside, Nix went straight upstairs to his bedroom, stripping out of his clothes as he went along. His house was a mess but that was nothing new. His hygiene was always on point but he was horrible at housekeeping. He had his grandmother to thank for that because he never lifted a finger when he lived with her. It was the same when he got with Dior because she did it all. Nix was tired. He put his phone on do not disturb and drifted off into a deep sleep soon after.

Nix woke up hours later to loud talking and he already knew who it was. Nichelle was there and she was on the phone and she had her call on speaker. As if she wasn't loud enough, she was talking to her sister and her voice was just as deafening.

"This is a damn shame girl. This house is too nice for him to keep it so dirty," Nichelle fussed.

"What happened with him and Dior?" Nicole, his auntie, asked.

"Bitch, I don't even know. All I know is we were planning a wedding one day and it was cancelled the next. She never even finished helping me decorate the house because she didn't move in."

Listening to his mother talk was the reason why Nix never told anyone his business. Nichelle talked too damn much. Besides Al and Danny, nobody knew what happened between him and Dior. They speculated but nothing was ever confirmed.

"Chill out with all that noise, Nichelle," Nix fussed when he got up from his bed and headed for the bathroom. He was clad in nothing but his boxers, but she didn't care.

His voice was deep and raspy, making him automatically seem mean to some people. It hadn't always been that way but he'd damaged his vocal cords years ago when he was in the hospital recovering from being shot. Nix kept removing the uncomfortable tube that was in his throat and they had to keep putting it back in.

"You need to do better Nix. This house is too nice for you to keep it like this. It's bad enough that I have to clean up behind your daddy. I shouldn't have to do it for you too."

Nichelle fussed about the same thing all the time and he always ignored her. She was going off on him as she made his bed and swept his floors. Nix took a shower and found him something to wear for later. He had a few hours left before he had to be at the club and he wanted to relax.

"What's that?" he asked when he walked into the kitchen and saw his mother turning off a few pots that were on the stove.

"Pot roast, potatoes and vegetables. I'm about to fix my man a plate and go home. What do you want to eat tomorrow?"

It was crazy how she did more for him as an adult than she ever did when he was a child. She was still a child herself, so she really didn't know how.

"It don't matter," Nix replied as he went to fix himself something to eat.

Unless it was in a restaurant, Nix never ate out. He didn't do fast food at all and he would starve before he did. If he ate a hamburger and fries, it was made with real ground meat and peeled potatoes. That was something else that his grandmother could be blamed for. She was old school and she was responsible for him being the way he was. He didn't start eating candy and other junk foods until he moved out of her house.

"I'm leaving. I'm cooking at home tomorrow but I'll drop something off to you," Nichelle said as she walked to the door. As soon as she opened it, Al was standing there getting ready to ring the doorbell.

"What's up Nichelle?" he asked when he saw her.

"Ain't shit. You know I gotta make sure my baby's house is clean. Go fix yourself something to eat. I just cooked," she replied while walking away to her car.

"The fuck is wrong with you," Nix said when he saw his best friend.

To most people, Al looked normal but Nix knew better. Something was bothering him and he saw it the minute he walked through the door.

"Same shit different day. Maybe I just need to stay single. My love life is all fucked up." Al fixed himself something to eat before joining his best friend on the sofa.

"Nigga, look at who you're talking to. I'm supposed to be happily married and trying to make some babies right now."

It was crazy how they had money coming in by the thousands but they still weren't happy. They finally invested in the medical marijuana business like they'd always wanted to. Add the income from the club and the construction company to that and Nix was set for life. All he was missing was the right woman to share it with. He was slowly giving up hope of that ever happening.

"I'm good on the babies and probably the marriage too."

"That's all on you though, bruh. You give a fuck about what people say too much. What happened this time?"

"We got into it just like always. You know I don't like having nobody around my baby like that."

"Cut the bullshit Al. This ain't about Alexa. You be worried about what her mama gon' say. Kinsley is good people, but whatever y'all had is over. It really shouldn't have started in the first place. You got a right to move on and be happy without her getting in her feelings about the shit. Alexa is gonna have to meet whoever you decide to be with eventually. You can't hide that shit forever."

"Come on now bruh. You know it's way more complicated than you're trying to make it seem. No matter what I decide to do, I can't make everybody happy."

"Besides Alexa, you don't owe nobody a muthafucking thing. Worry about making yourself happy."

"Yeah, you're right. I'm not having shit be a repeat of what it was before."

"Please don't. I'm not trying to be in here listening to you crying all day and night," Nix joked.

"Nigga, fuck you. You gon' listen to me cry for as long as I want you to. The same way I did for you when shit went left with you and Dior."

"Her stupid ass was parked out front earlier when I came home. Doing all that crying and shit like I'm supposed to feel sorry for her ass." Nix frowned.

"I had to go in on her ass last night. She be talking to the bottle girls like she's the boss. She got mad because one of the girls ran a tab and gave her a bill before she left. I told her ass that ain't shit free. Not a spot in VIP nor the drinks. She gotta pay just like everybody else. We might have to call a staff meeting just to let everybody know what's up."

"Man, fuck all that. What's good with the new bottle girl?"

"Who?" Al asked.

"The fine one who Ryan was asking about last night."

"Oh, Gianni. I really don't know too much about her. I hired her as a favor for Heavy."

"Heavy? He's never asked you to hire nobody before. She must be fucking with that nigga or something."

"I don't know. Why do you even care?"

"I'm interested," Nix admitted.

"Since when. She's been working there for an entire month and you barely looked her way."

"True but, now that I saw her, I'm interested. Do you think the shit that her cousin said is true? If so, it's fucked up if Heavy is dealing with her and not making sure she's straight."

"That nigga got a wife and kids, so he probably don't even care. Her cousin was wrong as fuck for putting her business out there like that though."

"What's up with her shady ass anyway?" Nix asked, referring to Kori.

"She's a typical hoe. Bitch be looking at you like you're her favorite meal. She must be trying to fuck her way to the top. She already ran through a few bouncers and the DJ."

"She's wasting her time. She left with Ryan after the club closed. She didn't have a chance with me even if she didn't. She's easy on the eyes, but I don't respect the shit that she did last night. I can't stand a hating ass bitch." Nix frowned.

Her hoe ass had the nerve to tell Ryan not to tell anybody but that's what he was known for. Ryan told all his business and everybody else's too. He told Nix about their plans before they even left the club. If his girl, Krista, found out, she would be dragging Kori's slutty ass out of there by her weave. Ryan was a dog and his girl fought everybody but him.

"Yeah, that was foul. Baby girl don't say much, so I don't know if it's true or not. She do her job and get the fuck on."

"I'm thinking that what her cousin said might be true though. I chilled with Alicia last night and I saw her coming out of one of the hotel rooms this morning. I wonder what her story is. She's young as fuck. Shit like that don't just happen. I wonder if she got any other family. We need to do some investigating."

"Who the fuck is we? I got my own shit to deal with. I'm not trying to add nothing else to my already full plate," Al replied.

"Make sure she works the top level all week. Mostly in my personal section."

"She only works the weekends."

"Why?" Nix questioned.

"That's the only shift that I needed somebody to work at the time."

"Damn man. I need to know what's up with her. I hate feeling like I'm in the dark about shit."

"Since when are you so interested in one of your employees?"

"I'm usually not but her cousin put it on my mind."

He and Al sat there and talked for a while until it was time for them to go to the club. Nix was determined to find out what was up with Gianni and he planned to start that night. He went straight to his office when he got to the club but he didn't stay in there long. Unlike the night before, he wasn't preoccupied with Ryan and his party. He had lots of time to observe his surroundings. Nix had his own private section on the top level and he made sure that Al had her working it.

About an hour later, Gianni and her cousin made it up to the top level and got right to work taking orders. Danny and Al were busy, so he was chillin' by himself.

"Hey Nix. What can I get for you?" Kori asked with a flirtatious smile.

"I'm straight," he replied, never looking up at her.

"Are you sure?"

"I'm good," he snapped, finally giving her an annoyed glare.

"Okay. Just let me know if you change your mind," she replied before walking away. It took a few more minutes, but Gianni finally made her way over to where he was.

"Can I get anything for you?" she asked while looking at Nix.

He was stuck for a minute. Gianni was even more beautiful up close and personal. Her eyes were alluring and he was mesmerized. He must have stared too long because she cleared her throat, waiting for him to speak.

73

"What's your name?" Nix finally asked. Al had told him more than once, but he couldn't remember.

"Gianni. Do you need anything?" She seemed impatient and not in the mood for small talk. She definitely didn't look at him like the rest of the bottle girls did.

"Yeah. Let me get some Hennessey."

"A glass or a full bottle?"

"A bottle," he replied right before she nodded and walked away.

His eyes stayed on her the entire time until she went down the stairs. Kori watched the entire exchange and she followed right behind her.

"What did he want?" Kori asked when she walked up behind her cousin. She had just tried to assist him, but he declined her offer.

"Hennessey," Gianni replied.

"Bitch, you know I left with him last night."

"What happened?"

"Bitch! What do you think happened? We fucked all over the hotel room," Kori lied.

She did get fucked all over the hotel room but not by Nix. She was with his cousin instead. She swore Ryan to secrecy because she didn't want it to get back to the man who she really wanted. Nix would never give her a chance if he knew that she'd slept with his cousin.

"Girl, Larry is gonna kill you," Gianna laughed, referring to Kori's boyfriend.

"If all goes well, Larry is about to be replaced."

"I'm not mad at you, boo. These hoes are really about to hate on you now."

"I already know," Kori boasted.

The hoes definitely were hating, but Gianni didn't know that Kori was one of them. Nix seemed to be interested but it wasn't her who he was interested in. Kori was happy that her cousin only worked on the weekends. That meant that she had to work extra hard to get closer to Nix on the days that she wasn't there.

Chapter 3

Dior looked at her watch, wishing that she could be anywhere else but where she was at the moment. It was her father's seventy-fifth birthday and she and her sisters had taken him out to dinner. They were now back at his house with the grandkids, waiting for him to open his gifts. Holidays and birthdays were the only times that Dior stepped foot in the house that she was raised in and she hated whenever she had to. She wanted to decline but her sisters always made her feel bad whenever she did. She wasn't welcomed there like they were, but they didn't seem to understand that. Her childhood was hell until she met Nix and his family. Nichelle was like a breath of fresh air and she loved spending time at her house.

"Yay!" Everyone clapped and cheered when her father, Walter, blew out the candles on his cake.

"Okay daddy, open your gifts," Grace, her oldest sister, said.

It was long ago discovered that Grace was the favorite child. Not only was she named after their mother, she looked exactly like her. Dior had never met her but she slightly favored her as well from what she'd seen on the pictures. Grace looked like a younger version of her and their father adored her.

"Aww, thanks baby. I really appreciate this. You know I love my linen." Walter smiled as he admired the three linen pantsuits that Grace had purchased for him.

Elise and Daria, her other two sisters, gave him their gifts and snapped pictures of him opening them. When it was time for Dior to give him what she had, the climate in the room changed. Walter was no longer smiling, but she didn't expect him to. Her father loved to fish, so she got him an expensive new fishing rod with a few other accessories to match.

"This is beautiful. Do you like it daddy?" Grace asked as she snapped a few more pictures of him with the gift.

"I got enough fishing equipment as it is. I don't like these new rods that they're making nowadays."

"Can you stop complaining and just say thank you?" Grace scolded.

"It's okay. I can return it and exchange it for something else," Dior said, trying hard to hold in her tears.

She refused to let him see her cry. It seemed to give him pleasure whenever she was in pain. He tossed her gift to the side like it was nothing, and that hurt. Nothing that she ever did was good enough and she was tired of trying.

Their mother was a nurse and all of her sisters went into the medical profession except her. That was something else that he hated about her. Dior always felt like her sisters could have done more about the toxic situation that she was in. They were all in their forties, so they were adults by the time she was born. She always wondered why none of them ever took on the task of raising her, instead of leaving her in such a toxic environment. They would let her spend some nights with them but they always returned her to her mental tormentor.

Dior was happy to see her sister start to cut the cake because she knew that it was almost time to go. When her ten year old niece, Ava, walked over to sit on her lap, she smiled and gave her a tight hug.

"Am I still gonna be in your wedding auntie?" Ava asked sweetly.

"Ain't gonna be no wedding. Just like there ain't gonna be no babies. Her coming into this world took my wife out of it. God won't allow her to be a mother when she's the one who killed her own," Walter hatefully replied.

"Daddy! I can't believe that you just said that!" Grace yelled.

"Well, it's true." Walter didn't have an ounce of remorse as he watched his youngest daughter get up and storm out of his house. Her sisters ran after her, but Dior didn't want to hear shit that they had to say. In her mind, they were a part of the problem.

"Dior, stop! You know how daddy is. He didn't mean it," Grace said as she grabbed her arm to stop her. Her other two sisters stood on the porch looking at her in pity.

"He meant every word he said and he doesn't feel bad about saying it. I'm done Grace. I have feelings too and I'm tired of him disregarding them. This is my last time stepping foot in this house. Don't tell me shit about holidays, birthdays and nothing else."

"You already know how he is, Dior. Daddy is old and stuck in his ways, but he's still your father."

"So, that gives him the right to treat me the way that he does? I'm tired of y'all acting like y'all don't see the shit that he does or hear the shit that he says. He made it clear that he didn't give a fuck about me the day that he was forced to bring me home from the hospital."

"He was hurt Dior. He had just lost his wife and he had displaced anger."

"I get it but that wasn't my fault. How do you think I felt? At least y'all got a chance to meet her. I never knew how it felt to even have a mother. None of what happened was my fault and I'm tired of taking the blame for it. I'm tired of feeling tolerated and not loved. Fuck that! I'm done and nothing that y'all say will change my mind," Dior cried as she got into her car and sped away.

She had so much more to say but her emotions got the best of her. She was tired of pretending that she was okay when she was hurting inside. Her sisters didn't know how she felt because they never had to experience it. The closest she'd ever come to having a real family was when she was with Nix. Nichelle and Quick weren't the ideal parents, but they were better than what she had. She and Nichelle were still tight, even though she and Nix were no longer together.

You're The Best Part

Dior kicked herself every day for how things with them ended. It was because of her sisters and friends that she even started to doubt her man. They kept telling her how important it was for her to have her own and not depend on a man for everything. Dior had a small savings account but they convinced her that she needed more. It was then that she opened another account and started dipping into Nix's business accounts. He trusted her so much that he never even tried to double check his records. It was obviously meant for her to get caught because it was weird how it all happened. Nix always gave her whatever she wanted and she was a fool for ruining what they had. Now, she was all alone while her sisters lived happily with their husbands and kids.

Dior was down and she needed someone to talk to. Not many people knew about her family drama and she wasn't about to put them in her business. Nichelle was always there when she needed her, so she decided to give her a call.

"Hey boo," Nichelle said when she answered the phone.

"What's up? What are you getting into today?"

"Me and my husband are about to head out for a while. Why? What's up?"

"Nothing much. I just had a fucked up day and needed to talk," Dior sighed.

"Quick is still in the shower, so I have a few minutes. What happened?"

"Today was my daddy's birthday," Dior replied as she ran the entire story down to her. She tried to keep it together but it was too hard.

"Girl, I know that's your daddy and all, but fuck him. It's unfortunate but lots of women die in childbirth. I was blessed that I made it out alive. I was a baby when I had Nix and my body was barely developed. It's fucked up that he blames you for that though."

"Nix told me to stay away a long time ago, but my stupid ass didn't listen. I'm hurting myself more by continuing to go around."

"I agree. You should stay away. And if your sisters don't understand that, then fuck them too. His old ass is wrong for that shit. I wish we could go out somewhere and have drinks. One of Quick's friends is having a party though."

"That's cool. I might pass by your son's club and have a few drinks."

Since it was Sunday, she couldn't do too much. Trying to teach small kids with a hangover was not fun. She'd done it once before and she swore that she was never doing it again.

"You and Nix need to stop playing and get back together. The fuck did y'all break up for anyway?" Nichelle pried.

"It's a long story. I want us to get back together too, but your son be on that bullshit."

Dior was happy as hell that Nix never told his parents and grandparents about their breakup. That one act let her know that he was still in love with her. He would have been all too happy to tarnish her name if he weren't.

Nichelle loved her but she loved her son even more. There was no doubt in Dior's mind that she would stop fucking with her if she knew the truth. Nix wasn't the petty type. He never even stopped her from coming to his club like she thought he would. He did stop her from drinking for free, but she still managed to finesse a few of his bottle girls. Some of them thought that she was still the boss' fiancée, so it was easy. Al was in his feelings about it but she didn't care.

"Oh well. He's probably out there fucking with some lil hood rats but he never brings anybody to the house."

Dior already knew that because she popped up over there all the time. Even when he wasn't home, she passed in front of his house just to be sure. She never knew if he was home or not because he parked his cars in his garage. She got lucky a few times and caught him as he drove up. Occasionally, she would see Nichelle, Quick or Al's cars in the driveway, but that was about it. She was happy to know that Nix hadn't moved on and she hoped that he never did.

"Well, I'm not gonna hold you, Nichelle. I'm going get me a drink and bring my ass home," Dior replied before she hung up.

She contemplated grabbing a bottle of wine from the store and going home. The thought of possibly seeing Nix had her driving in the direction of his club instead. It was early, so she wasn't sure if he was there or not. Al and Danny were always there but his hours varied.

It was dark when she pulled up to the club but Nix was just getting out of his truck. Dior had to park a few spots over but she wanted to catch up to him before he got too far. When Alicia walked out, she paused when she saw her smile at him. Nix wasn't the friendliest nigga in the world, so that was strange. Dior killed her headlights and watched them talk briefly.

"The fuck!" She frowned when she saw her grab his dick through his jeans.

She expected Nix to slap her hand or at least frown at her. Instead, he smirked and watched as she walked away to her car. Of all the bitches that she suspected him of dealing with, Alicia was never one of them. She was married and she and Dior were cool. Alicia always looked out for her with the drinks and they were always talking. She must have worked the early shift because she appeared to be leaving for the day. Instead of going inside like she originally planned to, Dior stayed in her car and followed right behind her.

"Bitch, I told you that Nix and Dior weren't together anymore. We had a staff meeting Wednesday and I heard it from his own mouth," Kori said excitedly to Gianni when she walked into the breakroom.

They were all shocked when they walked into the breakroom and found Nix sitting in there with Al and Danny. Kori had never seen him in there before and they all assumed that it had to be something serious that he wanted to discuss with them. Nix basically told them that nobody, including Dior, was to drink for free. He made it clear that they were to only take orders from him and Al. Danny was only the promoter, so he wasn't considered a supervisor. He didn't come right out and say that they weren't together anymore but they all read in between the lines.

"Oh okay," Gianni said unenthusiastically.

"What's wrong with you?"

"Nothing, just kind of tired."

She didn't want to disclose too much to her cousin but she was annoyed. Her living arrangements were beginning to get the best of her but she was trying. They had a festival in the city that weekend, so Nadia's niece couldn't get the hotel room for her. Gianni tried to book a room somewhere else, but the rates were ridiculous. They usually were whenever they had tourists in the city. She wasn't opposed to sleeping in her car. She just had to park somewhere safe when she did. She also had to find somewhere to take a shower but she could probably do that by Kori or her auntie.

"I know the feeling cousin. I haven't had an off day in two weeks. That overtime has been kicking my ass," Kori said, interrupting Gianni's thoughts.

"What else did I miss at the staff meeting?"

Since Gianni only worked on weekends, she usually missed the weekday meetings. Heavy or Kori usually filled her in, but it was never really too much.

"Nothing much. It's gonna be lit in here tomorrow though. Danny got Kevin Gates coming through. Those tips are about to be good as fuck."

"That's what's up. I damn sure can use them."

"I hope Al lets me work up top tonight."

"Aren't you fucking the boss? Why didn't you tell him to put you up there?" Gianni questioned.

"Girl, Nix don't be worrying about shit like that. He leaves all that kind of stuff up to Al."

"Well, I hope they don't put me up there. I like the lower level better," Gianni noted, right as Al walked into the room.

"What's good Al?" Kori asked.

"Gianni, you're up top tonight," Al said, calling out all the areas that the bottle girls were going to be working. Kori was pissed that she had to work the bottom level. Gianni had been up there a lot lately and she didn't like that.

"Can I switch with somebody? I'm not really feeling the top level like that," Gianni said, shocking Al.

She would usually go with the flow and he didn't expect her to speak up. He would have probably granted her request if Nix hadn't personally told him that he wanted her up top. His boy was intrigued but he was trying to feel her out first.

"I'll go up there," Kori hurriedly volunteered.

"Not my decision sweetheart. Talk to the boss man if y'all have a problem with your work assignments," Al replied before he walked away.

"Since when does Nix care about the schedule? You just said that he don't be worrying about stuff like that," Gianni said while looking at her cousin.

"Al is lying. He might be crushing on you and want you to work close to him."

"I seriously doubt that. His ass don't stay still long enough to even care. He be all over the place."

Gianni was right, but Kori would never admit it. Al and Danny were usually in the mix of everything while Nix stayed put. She didn't know how but she was gonna find a way to get up to that top level. She needed to see what was up.

86

Kori and Gianni got their ice buckets and went their separate ways. Nix perked up when he saw Gianni headed his way and he waved her over.

"What's up G?" he asked while smiling at her. Gianni had never seen him smile before, so she was kind of shocked. He was even more handsome when he didn't look so mean.

"Hey. What can I get for you?"

"Nothing, I'm good for right now."

Gianni nodded as she walked away and went to assist someone else. The first table that she serviced gave her a hundred dollar tip and that was just the beginning. The men flirted like crazy, but it was nothing that she couldn't handle. After a few hours, Kori made her way up the stairs and over to her.

"How's it going cousin?" Kori asked. Before Gianni had a chance to answer, Nix was calling out to her.

"Aye G! Let me get a bottle of Hennessey," he yelled.

"I got you," Gianni replied as she walked down the stairs with Kori hot on her heels.

"G? You and boss man got cool real quick, huh?" Kori asked.

"Girl, bye. His illiterate ass probably just don't remember my name."

"Has he been flirting with you?"

"Why would he when y'all are fucking?"

"Yeah, that's true. I was going up there and check his ass if he was."

Chenell Parker

"You don't have nothing to worry about boo. I don't play those kinds of games. We're family."

"I know you ain't shady like some of these other hoes around here. Let me get back to my section before Al's disgusting ass have a fit," Kori replied as she walked away.

Gianni went back upstairs and continued to do what she was being paid to do. After a while, Nix grabbed his bottle and left. The club was about to be closing soon and she was happy for that. When the crowd started getting thin, the bartenders yelled for last call. That was the best sound that Gianni had heard all night.

Once the club closed, Gianni met Kori outside by her car. She needed to make sure that it was cool for her to take a shower at her house. She already had her clothes in the car and she was happy that her cousin was okay with it. Gianni followed Kori to her house, not knowing that she was being followed too.

"Are you serious right now, bruh?" Al asked Nix over the phone.

"Hell yeah I am. I want to know what's going on," Nix replied as he continued to follow Gianni.

"This nigga is obsessed," Al laughed.

"Nah, more like concerned," Nix corrected.

He parked on the corner when Gianni and her hoe ass cousin pulled up to a fourplex apartment. They both got out of their cars and walked inside a short time later. Nix talked to Al for about thirty minutes until he saw Gianni come back out. When she pulled off, he drove off right behind her. It was after three in the morning, but Gianni still stopped at a gas station. She came out a few minutes later with a bag and started driving again. It took about ten minutes before she pulled up into the parking lot of the police station. She didn't get too close to the door but she parked in between a few police cruisers.

"The fuck is she doing?" Nix asked himself out loud.

He watched and waited for Gianni to get out of the car. Almost thirty minutes had passed, and she never drove off or got out. His heart broke once he realized what Gianni was doing. Her cousin was right about her being homeless and she was spending the night in her car. She obviously felt safe in the police station parking lot, but it was still dangerous. Nix pulled out his phone and made a call to Al. He was hoping that they were still at the club because he was curious about a few things.

"What's good bro?" Al asked when he answered the phone. Nix knew just by the noise in the background that his best friend was still at work. The club was closed, but Al and the security team were always the last ones to leave.

"Aye, is Heavy still there?"

"Yeah, we're about to lock up in a few minutes."

"Nah, I'm on my way back over that way. Tell that nigga to hold up a few minutes."

"You good bruh. Is everything alright?" Al asked in concern.

"I'm straight. Just tell him to hang around for about ten more minutes."

"We'll be here," Al assured him before he hung up.

Nix sped all that way back to his club and parked out front. Heavy, Al and Danny were sitting at the bar having drinks when he walked in. They all looked at him strangely but no one said anything. Nix grabbed a beer and sat down with them.

"What's good boss man?" Heavy asked after they sat in silence for a while.

"Tell me what you know about Gianni."

"Not much but she's good people."

"Are y'all fucking?" Nix asked, making Heavy choke on his beer.

"I'm a happily married man," Heavy replied, causing Nix to look at him sideways.

"You already know that don't mean shit these days."

"Nah man. I wouldn't even disrespect her or my wife like that. She and Nadia are cool and they talk all the time."

"How do y'all know her though?"

"She tutors my daughter and some of her friends in math."

Heavy ran the entire story down to them about how Gianni and his daughter met. Nix wasn't expecting to hear that but he was impressed.

"Is she really homeless?"

"Man, that's really not my story to tell. It's not my place to put nobody in her business like that."

"I respect that." Nix nodded.

He appreciated the way that Heavy handled the situation. Nix was sure that he knew more than he was saying but he respected him for not saying it. He was more solid than her shady ass cousin. Nix didn't really need Heavy for anything else, so he left once thy finished talking. Danny left right after, leaving him and Al alone.

"What's good bruh? I can already see that something is on your mind," Al observed.

"She's really homeless," Nix replied sadly.

He didn't know why but his heart went out to the young beauty who didn't talk or smile very much. Thanks to his grandparents, he had a great childhood and he couldn't imagine what Gianni must have had to endure. He didn't know why but he wanted to save her. He was attracted to her too but that wasn't the reason why.

"Damn man. So, her cousin was right. She really does live in a homeless shelter."

"Nah, she didn't go to no homeless shelter. She's sleeping in her car."

"Aww man, no. Seriously?"

"Yeah man, but I don't understand. Her cousin got a house. I followed her over there and watched her go inside. She came right back out, only to post up in a fucking car for the night. What kind of shit is that?" Nix was fuming and he hated Kori even more now than he did before.

"That's fuck up. Come on bruh, we make enough money to put her up in a room for a while. At least until she gets on her feet."

"Nah, I got something even better than that," Nix replied.

"Well, whatever it is, you can count me in. Maybe I can offer her fulltime hours to put more money in her pockets. We can use the extra help," Al said as he got up and stretched.

He and Nix set the alarm and locked up the club. They got into their cars and went their separate ways soon after. Al prepared to go home while Nix drove in the direction of the police station where he planned to post up for the rest of the night. Gianni didn't know it but she had her own personal one man security team now.

Chapter 4

"This ain't even like you, bruh. I ain't never known you to be on no creep shit," Al said as he talked to Nix on the phone.

"I ain't on no creep shit now. I was trying to talk to her mean ass, but she be giving a nigga them one word answers. I know everything that I need to know now though," Nix replied as he continued to follow Gianni. That had been his routine for the past two weeks and he pretty much had her figured out.

"Everything like what?"

"Well, she does live in the women's shelter but she stays in the hotel sometimes on the weekends. She must have her clothes and shit up in storage because she goes there a few times a week and then she goes straight to the laundromat afterwards. Besides school, the library and work, she don't really go nowhere else. She did go to the graveyard once, but I don't know what that was about. I still haven't figured out why she slept in her car that weekend though."

"Probably the same reason why you slept in yours," Al laughed.

"I was just looking out for her. Like I said, that shit is dangerous. It don't matter that she was in the parking lot of the police station. Some of them muthafuckers are crooks too."

"Yeah, you're right about that. Where your stalking ass at now?"

"She just left the nail salon and pulled up to the shelter. It's Friday, so I know she's not sleeping here tonight."

"Man, I can't believe this shit. You got the girl schedule figured out and everything. And I thought my life was fucked up. You got me beat."

"Her stubborn ass gon' say something to me tonight. Nigga trying to help her out and she be acting like she don't wanna talk and shit."

"I told you that she's not like the rest of the bottle girls. She do her job and go home."

"Did you ever talk to her about working fulltime?"

"Yeah, she said she'll let me know but she hasn't said anything yet."

"Alright bruh, I'll get at you later," Nix said before he hung up.

He watched as Gianni parked and got out of her car. He made sure to park a few cars down so that he wouldn't be seen. She looked around the parking lot for a minute before she disappeared into the building. He was deep in thought, thinking about how he wanted to approach the subject of Gianni being homeless. He didn't want to offend her but he did want to help. Some people had pride and that was probably the reason why she was in a shelter and not living with a family member. He wanted to know her story and he was curious as to how she ended up that way. Nix didn't see when someone approached his car and it was too late for him to react. When the barrel of a gun was placed to his head, he froze as memories from his past resurfaced.

"Why the fuck have you been following me all day?" Gianni asked angrily.

She didn't care that Nix was her boss. She would probably lose her job but she didn't give a fuck about that either. She thought she was trippin' at first when she noticed him following her from the library earlier that day. When she saw him at the nail salon, gas station and now, the shelter, she knew that it wasn't a coincidence.

"I've actually been following you for two weeks if we're keeping it real," Nix confessed.

"Why? What do you want with me?"

"Either shoot me or move that gun out of my face."

"Start talking or shoot is exactly what I'm about to do," she threatened.

"Have a seat," Nix requested as he popped the locks on his truck.

"No, I'm fine right here. I work for you but I don't know you like that."

"My name is Jacobi Nixon and I'll be twenty-seven years old soon. I'm an only child who was raised by my grandparents since my mother gave birth to me while she was in jail. Besides the club, I also own a construction company that my grandfather started before I was even born. I've never been married and I don't have any kids. What else do you want to know?"

Gianni wasn't expecting that but it kind of put her at ease. She lowered her gun and slipped it back into her purse. When Nix leaned over and opened the door, she walked around to the passenger side and got in.

"What are you following me for?"

"Just curious, I guess." He shrugged.

"Curious about what?"

"You don't say much and I wanted to know a few things about you."

He didn't want to come right out and tell her what her cousin had said. That would have put them at odds with each other and that wasn't his goal.

"Why couldn't you just ask me?"

"Would you have told me if I did?"

"Yes. I don't have anything to hide. I'm not ashamed of who I am or what I'm going through. This is a temporary situation that I'm making the best of."

"Okay, I can respect that. I'm not gonna even insult you by asking if you have a man."

"What would you say if I did?"

"I would tell you to leave that fuck boy alone. You shouldn't want or need nothing if you got a real nigga on your team. How old are you?"

"Almost twenty-five."

"You don't look that old. How did you end up here?" Nix asked while pointing to the shelter.

Gianni sighed, "My mom died when I was younger and I went to live with my grandmother afterwards. Once she died, I lived with my boyfriend for a while but that didn't work out. I slept on a few sofas here and there but I never had a permanent spot. My family is small, so I didn't have many options. Someone told me about this place a few months ago and I've been here ever since."

"What about your cousin? Doesn't she have her own house?"

"Yeah but she doesn't have enough room. It's only a small one bedroom apartment and she lives there with her boyfriend. There's nowhere for me to sleep."

"Does she have a sofa?"

"Yes."

"What about a floor?"

"That's a stupid question. Of course she has a floor." Gianni frowned.

"Exactly, so there's always somewhere for you to sleep. You're family."

"I know but I'm okay. I'm not trying to force my way into anyone's home."

"Are you an only child?"

97

"No but I might as well be. I have an older brother who ain't shit. If it was up to him, I would be selling pussy to the highest bidder. But that's a different story for a different day."

Nix wanted to reach over and hug her, but she probably would have shot him if he did. She was so young to have gone through so much but she appeared to be so strong. Her circumstances didn't break her and that was commendable.

"How would you feel about working at the club full time?"

"Al already asked but I can't. I could really use the extra money, but we're not allowed to come into the shelter after eight."

"I can help you with that too."

"How? And why do you want to help me at all? We don't even really know each other."

"True, but I'm trying to change all that," Nix flirted.

"I'll pass. I would never play my cousin like that."

"What does your cousin have to do with anything?"

"Thank you for offering but I can't work fulltime," Gianni said as she attempted to get out of the car.

"Wait a second. I have a spare bedroom that I'm willing to offer you," Nix said as he lightly grabbed her arm to stop her from leaving. He actually had a few spare bedrooms but that wasn't relevant at the moment.

"A room? In your house?"

"Yes, it has a connecting bathroom and it's yours if you want it. I live alone and you'll have all the privacy you need."

"What's the catch?" Gianni questioned skeptically. The thought of the arrangement that her mother and brother had made her skin crawl.

"I just need a little help around the house every now and then. You know, cooking, cleaning, laundry, shit like that."

"So, you basically want a live-in maid. Thanks, but I'll pass."

"Don't get it twisted love. My mama can and will do whatever needs to be done. I'm only trying to figure out a way for us to help each other. You need a place to stay and I need my house to always look like a home. The way I see it, we're doing each other a favor."

"Look, I apologize for sounding ungrateful. I really do appreciate everything that you're trying to do for me, but I'm gonna have to decline. I try my best not to depend on anybody if I don't have to."

"So, you'd rather sleep in your car in the parking lot of the police station before you put your pride aside and accept my offer."

"Fuck you and kiss my ass!" Gianni snapped as she grabbed the handle of the door.

"I would love to." Nix licked his full lips while looking at her lustfully.

"Please stop following me. And if I'm fired, let me know now before I waste my time showing up to work."

"Nah love, your job is good."

"Thanks," Gianni replied as she got out of the car and walked away.

"I love that feisty shit with your sexy ass. Alright beautiful, let the games begin." Nix smiled as he drove away and headed home.

"Are you serious right now bro?" Al asked as he looked over at Nix.

"Stop judging me," Nix replied, making his friend laugh.

"Boy, you know I'm never letting you forget this shit. This nigga is taking stalking to a whole new level."

"Stop worrying about what's going on with me. You got some problems of your own," Nix said while looking at the monitor that sat on his desk. Kinsley, Al's baby mama, had just walked in with one of her friends.

"Damn man! Shit is already fucked up for me at home. I don't need her coming in here making shit worse."

"Don't trip bro. I'm coming out there with you."

"Please do. I need her to stay as far away from me as possible. I don't need to be dealing with no more drama"

"I hope you made sure that my wifey is working the top level tonight."

"Every day just like you requested. I hope this girl hurry up and start noticing your ass. You getting on my damn nerves with this shit now," Al laughed as they walked out of the office.

He had never seen Nix work so hard to get a female before. Truthfully, he never had to. He had been with Dior since they were kids, so approaching another woman was something that he never had to do. Even after they broke up, females came to him. Nix believed in love and happily ever after. Al believed in it too but he was skeptical about ever obtaining it.

"What's up baby daddy?" Kinsley smiled as soon as she saw Al. She stood up and tried to walk closer to him, but Nix intervened before she could.

"First bottle of the night is on me. What are you ladies drinking?" Nix put his arm around Kinsley's neck and led her back to her seat.

"You know I'm a light weight. We'll pass on the bottle but a Long Island with pineapple juice will do." Kinsley sat down and Nix was happy to be of assistance.

Al let out a breath of relief as he locked eyes with Danny. He was coming up the stairs with Gianni and Kori following behind him. When Nix saw Gianni, she immediately had his undivided attention. His eyes were on her and Kori's were on him.

"Hey Nix. What can I get for you?" Kori asked.

"I already got it," Gianni spoke up as she handed him a bottle of Hennessey and a glass of ice.

She had been working the top level for a few weeks now and Nix always wanted the same thing every time. Crazy thing was, he always declined when one of the other bottle girls offered to assist him. He waited until Gianni came around for her to get whatever he needed.

"Let me find out," Nix smirked while looking at her.

He bit his bottom lip as he studied her from head to toe. Gianni was bad as fuck but she seemed oblivious to that fact. She obviously didn't know her worth, but he was about to teach her how to count. Gianni wasn't a dime. She was a whole damn dollar.

"Can you grab two Long Islands with pineapple juice?" Al asked while looking at Kori. Gianni took a few orders and met her cousin at the bar.

"Girl, niggas ain't shit," Kori said while looking at her phone.

"Why? What happened?"

"That was Nix texting me. He was trying to flirt with you but asking to get a room with me tonight," Kori lied.

Nix didn't even have her number. She was in her feelings about him crushing on her cousin. She was no fool and it wasn't hard to see. He didn't even try to hide it. The way he looked at Gianni said it all. Not to mention, she had been working the top level every day. She knew that it wasn't a coincidence. That was all Nix's doing and that much she was sure of.

"Fuck him. He's wasting him time flirting with me. I would never fuck with a nigga that one of my family members or friends had first."

Gianni didn't know why but she was kind of salty about what her cousin had just said. Nix was just asking her to occupy one of the spare bedrooms at his house. She was heated to know that he was fucking her cousin and was probably trying to fuck her too. Truthfully, she enjoyed it when he flirted with her but she knew that it wouldn't go any further than that. Nix was fine as fuck and it just felt good to be noticed sometimes.

"I know that's right cousin. I couldn't see myself doing that either." She smiled triumphantly, knowing that her mission was accomplished.

Gianni followed her back upstairs and passed out everyone's drinks. Kori watched from the corner of her eyes as Nix talked to her cousin. She was too far away to hear what they were saying but the smirk on Gianni's face let her know that he was probably flirting again. Kori was in her feelings but she had to smile and play it off. She didn't care that she had a man at home. She wanted Nix and she would do anything to get him.

"Girl, Danny is working on getting Jeezy to do a concert in here. We're getting new uniforms for that night if he do," Gianni said when she and Kori met up at the bar again.

"How do you know that?"

"Nix just told me. He already got Rod Wave and Big Freedia secured. We're getting something new to wear for those days too. That nigga, Danny, know everybody."

"Yeah, Nix already told me about them. He'll probably tell me about Jeezy when we hook up tonight."

Once again, Kori was lying because she was in her feelings. Besides Danny and Al, Nix never talked to anyone. If he did, it was never about anything pertaining to the club. She didn't understand why he felt so comfortable talking to her cousin about anything. Gianni wasn't really a people person and she was nowhere near friendly. She barely smiled and she talked only when it was necessary.

"What do you tell Larry when you stay out all night?"

103

"I don't have to tell him shit. When he starts helping out with some of the bills again, then he can ask questions."

"That's fucked up Kori. The man got laid off. You act like he's just a bum ass nigga who's laying up on you. He paid all the bills before he lost his job."

"He's my man and that's his job. It's all good though. Once Nix and I make things official, I won't even have to work at all."

"That will never be my life. I don't give a damn if I marry a millionaire, I'm always gonna work and have my own. Life has taught me to never depend on anyone else," Gianni said as they walked off and headed back upstairs.

"Who is she?" Kori asked while discreetly nodding at Kinsley. She was all over Al and he looked aggravated.

"That's Al's baby mama."

"Al has kids?" Kori asked in shock. Besides him managing the club, she didn't know anything about him either.

"A daughter," Gianni replied, repeating something else that Nix had told her.

"She is too thirsty." Kori frowned when they walked by them and heard some of what Kinsley was saying. She was basically begging Al to fuck her while grabbing his dick through his jeans. She was trying to undo his belt until Nix walked over and stopped her.

"Chill out girl. This ain't that kind of club. Sit your ass down and catch the beat," Nix said while leading her over to her seat. He told Kori to get her and her girl another round of drinks right before he and Al walked off towards his office.

"Good looking bro," Al said once they were behind closed doors.

"Yeah nigga, you just better make sure you handle that business for me."

"I got you, fam," Al replied, right as Danny came bursting through the closed door.

"Chill out nigga. That man wasn't even doing shit."

"Yeah, well that's not what it looked like to me. If you wouldn't have stepped in, his dick would have probably been in her mouth by now," Danny fumed.

"I'm gone. I don't need to hear nothing else," Nix said as he headed for the door.

"Hold up bro!" Al called out, stopping him before he left.

"What does he need to hold up for? What, you don't want your baby mama to see us walking out together? You're the one hiding who you are from that bitch because I don't give a fuck!" Danny yelled angrily as he and Al argued back and forth.

It had been that way since they were in high school and nothing much had changed. While Danny was an openly gay man, Al was discreet with his sexual preferences. Neither of them looked or dressed feminine, so it was hard to tell.

Danny didn't come right out and tell anyone but he didn't care if they found out. Most people knew and he wasn't ashamed of who he was. Sometimes, the way he talked gave him away immediately, but he never tried to switch it up. He came from an affluent family and he was willing to risk it all just to be himself. Danny's parents ran a family law firm and they represented some of the richest people from all over the world. He worked only because he wanted to. He was spoiled and they had no problem taking care of him.

Al came from an overly religious family, so it was a little more complicated for him. His mother was a pastor and he knew that she wouldn't approve of his lifestyle. She still fussed at him for having a baby out of wedlock and that was years ago. He hated to go around her because he felt condemned whenever he did.

They were only thirteen years old when Al confided in him about his feelings. Nix had always been attracted to women, so he didn't quite understand. Still, Al was his best friend and he never looked at him differently because of the choices that he made. He was upset with him about hiding it though. Al was a good dude with a good heart and Nix felt like that should have been enough. If people didn't accept him for who he was, they could move the fuck on.

He and Danny started crushing on each other when they were in middle school but they didn't start dating until they got to high school. They did it discreetly until Danny decided to start living in his truth. He didn't mind that Al wasn't ready to disclose his sexual preference to anyone. It wasn't a problem until Al started trying to prove a point to other people. Although Nix knew what was up, some of their other friends didn't. They knew that Nix was with Dior but they used to clown Al for not getting at all the women who wanted him. After a while, he started fucking with females, just to throw them off.

That was it for Danny and he left Al alone. He wasn't about to keep being his secret while he tried to discover himself. Al had a few flings with other men behind closed doors but he kept a woman on his arm for appearances. That was how he ended up with his daughter. He didn't regret Alexa but he knew that she wouldn't have even existed if he was being true to himself. Now, Kinsley was in love with him and he wasn't even attracted to her.

Their daughter was all that there was between them, but she wanted more. Nix always told him that he was playing a dangerous game by sleeping with women, knowing that he really wanted men.

Even now, he was too afraid to be himself. He and Danny always stayed the night at each other's houses but he always made sure that his daughter never saw anything. He would have Danny up at the crack of dawn to make sure that she didn't. They always argued about it and they broke up every few weeks. Since Nix was friends with both of them, he often had to play mediator. They both called him with their problems and he always gave them honest advice. As much as he loved Al, he agreed with Danny more.

"Fuck it. I'm done with this shit," Danny snapped angrily, shaking Nix from his thoughts of the past.

"You doing all that trippin' for nothing," Al replied as he tried to stop him from leaving.

"If you think I feel like this for nothing, then I'm clearly wasting my time."

"Fuck!" Al hissed when Danny stormed out of the office and slammed the door behind him.

"That's all on you though, bruh," Nix said.

"I don't know what the fuck he wants me to do."

"Yes, you do."

"Shit ain't that easy for me though and y'all know that."

"Man, I'm not about to keep having this same conversation with you. We've been doing this shit for years and nothing has changed."

"I don't know why you're in such a hurry for me to come out of the closet. As much as we be together, everybody might think you're gay too," Al laughed.

"Do you honestly think I give a fuck about what people say or believe? I'm very secure in my manhood. Who you stick dick to or get it from don't have shit to do with our friendship or my masculinity. Muthafuckers be looking at me sideways for leaving Dior alone. Bitch was robbing me blind but because I didn't put nobody in my business, I'm the bad guy. Truthfully, I was looking out for her ass up until the end. Nichelle and nobody else would even fuck with her no more if they knew the truth. I wasn't trying to do her dirty like that though. But, seriously, you need to do some self-evaluation. You say that Danny is who you really want."

"He is who I want."

"Well, you need to act like it then. Shit, I'm going harder for Gianni and she ain't even mine yet."

"Yeah, you're going too damn hard. I hope this shit pays off."

"It will. You know I'm always up for a good challenge. I love a woman who makes a man work hard to get her. That'll make me appreciate her more."

"Well, look out for a few minutes while I go handle that business for you," Al said as he stood up and prepared to leave with Nix following right behind him. He locked eyes with Danny and motioned with his eyes for him to follow him out back.

Nix continued to watch Gianni all night until it was time for the club to close. Usually, he would be gone, leaving Al, Danny and Heavy to handle everything. Since he had something to do, he hung around and waited until all the bottle girls left and walked out to the back employee parking lot. Nix always parked in the first spot but he didn't immediately pull off when he got into his truck. He watched as Gianni and Kori walked to their cars and waited.

"The fuck!" Gianni yelled.

"What's wrong?" Kori asked.

"Two of my tires are flat. I can see one but two of them. That shit seems suspicious as hell."

"Damn cousin. Who did you piss off?"

"I don't even fuck with nobody to piss them off."

"What are you gonna do? You already know that I got plans tonight."

"I know. You can go ahead. I'll figure it out," Gianni sighed in disgust. She already didn't have a room. Now, she wouldn't even be able to sleep in her car since she couldn't move it. She grabbed her duffle bag from her trunk as she tried to come up with a plan. She hated to bother Heavy and his wife but she couldn't really think of anyone else to call.

"What's good? Everything alright?" Nix asked when he rolled up on them.

"You need to roll back the cameras or some shit. I got two flat tires and I know that ain't no coincidence. One of these hoes are about to catch these hands if they fucked with my car," Gianni snapped, making Kori look at her like she was crazy.

She had never heard anyone talk to Nix like that before and she knew that her cousin had gone too far. As much as she hated Gianni working there, she didn't want her to get fired. She needed the money and she needed to act like it.

"It's okay Nix. She's just upset. I'm gonna give her a ride home," Kori replied.

Nix looked at her in disgust. She knew that Gianni didn't have a home to go to but she never even tried to offer hers. The mere sight of Kori was starting to annoy him, but he had to put on his game face.

"Nah, you can burn out. I'll take care of everything," Nix replied.

Kori was skeptical about leaving the two of them alone but she really didn't have a choice. She wanted to protest but Gianni wasn't the only one who needed her job. Since her man had been laid off, she had to pay most of the bills. He got unemployment but it didn't compare to the salary that he used to make.

"Okay, I'll see you tomorrow cousin."

"Come on," Nix said to Gianni once her cousin was gone.

"What do you mean come on? I need my car."

"Do you have a room?"

"No," Gianni said as she looked away in embarrassment.

Nix already knew that she didn't because Heavy told him. It was like pulling teeth to get information out of him, but Nix was persistent. He found out that Heavy's niece by marriage was getting the rooms for her, but it wasn't always possible. They had some type of political event in the hotel's ballroom and the employees weren't allowed to use their discount rates that weekend.

"Come on G. It's late as fuck sweetheart. You don't have a room and you can't drive your car. I'm not trying to see you out here fucked up like that. I can get somebody to take care of your car but nothing is open at this hour."

"Well, where are you trying to take me?"

"Home," Nix replied.

"I don't have a home."

"To my house," he countered.

"Nah, I'll pass. I don't have to drive my car. I'll just stay here until your people come through."

"Are you serious Gianni? It's lit up right now because Al and a few other people are still inside. It be dark as fuck out here when they shut everything off. Ain't no way in hell am I leaving you out here. Nigga ain't trying to do shit to you. I just want to make sure you're straight. Trust me, you won't even have to see me once you get there. My house is big enough to make sure we both have our own space."

Gianni had trust issues and that wasn't hard to see. She had been let down by a lot of people, so she kept her guard up to keep it from happening again. Besides being physically attracted to her, Nix really wanted to get to know her. He wanted to be there for her but he had to get her to trust him first. That's why he had Al to make sure that she couldn't leave the club when it closed.

"Okay, but just one night. I'm not trying to be your live-in slave. And I'll pay for my own tires," Gianni said as she got into his truck and buckled up.

"Nah, I'll take care of it. I feel responsible since it happened on my property. It's the least I can do." Technically, he was responsible but she didn't need to know that.

"Thank you." Gianni smiled.

111

Nix nodded his head before he drove off and headed to his house. He had already made plans with Alicia but he wanted to get Gianni settled in first. His goal was to make her see how good it would be to take him up on his offer and utilize one of his spare bedrooms. He didn't want to overwhelm her by trying to get with her too soon. If all went according to plan, that would happen eventually.

When he pulled up to his house, Gianni's face didn't show any emotion. He expected her to be in awe of the size, but she looked indifferent. She simply got out of the car and followed him to the front door. Nix grabbed her duffel bag before they went inside.

"Let me give you a little tour," Nix said as he walked Gianni around the house. He showed her where everything was before showing her to the room that she would be sleeping in.

"Your house is beautiful," Gianni complimented.

"Thanks. Make yourself comfortable. There's soap and clean towels in the bathroom. The remote is on the nightstand and help yourself to whatever is in the kitchen."

Gianni didn't know why but she got a little annoyed when he kept looking at his phone and replying to messages. A part of her knew that it was probably Kori, trying to see what time they were gonna hook up. Nix was obviously a pro at playing games. He pretended that he wasn't even interested in her cousin in the presence of others.

"Any idea on how long it'll be before my car gets straight?"

"Nah but I'll hit up my boy when his shop opens to take care of it."

"Thanks, I appreciate it."

"No problem. I need to make a run right quick but I'll be right back," Nix said as he turned and walked away.

"Yeah, making a run to go fuck my cousin," Gianni replied as she rolled her eyes.

She was pissed with herself for even caring about what he was doing. Gianni could deny it all she wanted to but she was attracted to him. Even still, she would never give him the satisfaction of being with her and her cousin. Even though she wasn't sexually active, she knew that she wouldn't stay a virgin forever. If she were being honest, she was tired of holding on to it. That didn't mean that she was willing to give it up to just anybody though.

When she heard the front door open and close, Gianni grabbed her duffel bag and headed for the bathroom. Once she took a long hot shower, she ventured into the kitchen to see what she could snack on. An hour had passed since Nix left and she had a feeling that he wasn't coming back anytime soon. Gianni laid in the bed and relaxed her mind and body for the first time in a while. She planned to get a few hours of sleep and be gone by the time Nix returned, if he ever did.

Chapter 5

"**S**hit baby! I'm about to cum again!" Alicia yelled right before she collapsed on top of Nix.

She had given him the ride of his life and she was drained. It was almost nine in the morning and they hadn't gone to sleep since they got to the hotel around four. Alicia's husband knew that she worked late at the bar, so she wasn't worried about him calling. Besides that, he wasn't due to be home from the firehouse for another few hours. Aside from work, she probably wasn't gonna see Nix for a few days since she wouldn't be able to get away. Her husband promised her some intimate time and she was hoping that he delivered. Her sex drive was too high for him to be so nonchalant about it.

"I gotta get the fuck up outta here," Nix said as he got up and headed for the bathroom.

He didn't plan to fuck with her so long, especially since Gianni was at his house. He was hoping to be home before she woke up. He didn't know how to cook but he wanted to take her out somewhere decent for breakfast. He wanted to know more about her in hopes of her getting comfortable being around him.

"Yeah, I gotta get home too. I feel like I'm wasting money renting these rooms for a few hours when I have a big ass empty house that we can use." Alicia followed him to the bathroom and turned on the water.

"You must be smoking dope." Nix frowned as they stepped into the shower together.

"What do you mean?" Alicia questioned in confusion.

"It's bad enough that I'm fucking another man's wife. I'm not trying to do it in his house."

"I don't know why. He's never there anyway. He basically lives at the firehouse."

"Man, y'all hoes are scandalous."

"Excuse me. I'm not a hoe."

"What do you call it then? Inviting another nigga into that man's personal space is foul as fuck."

"You fucking me is foul too but that never stopped you before."

"It's just pussy for me, sweetheart. It's not that deep. I'm not the one who took vows with somebody else. I didn't stand before God and promise nobody a muthafucking thing. I'm the wrong nigga for you to risk your marriage for love. You're the only one here with something to lose."

"I guess the old saying is true. Hurt people really do hurt people," Alicia said as she laughed sarcastically.

Her feelings were kind of hurt and she was sure that her expression gave it away. She liked Nix but she wasn't dumb enough to think that what they had would go further than the bedroom. Besides, she loved her husband. She just wanted him to get his shit together. Still, Nix's words were harsh, mainly because they were true. She did have a lot to lose but it was all fun and games to him.

"Meaning what?" Nix asked, pulling her away from her thoughts.

"I don't know what happened between you and Dior, but she obviously cut you deep. Now, every woman you encounter is going to pay a debt that she owes."

"The way that I feel has nothing to do with Dior. Shit didn't work out with us but that's life. I'll never give up on finding love. But I'll never look for it in another man's wife."

He could tell that Alicia was in her feelings but he didn't give a fuck. She approached him about sex and he did what any other man in his position would do. Alicia paid for the rooms and fucked him like he put a ring on her finger.

Once they showered and got dressed, Alicia used the phone in the room to check out. She hadn't said anything to Nix for over half an hour but she had a lot on her mind.

"You were right about everything that you said. I'm really the only one who's taking all the risks here. I'll be losing my husband and you'll be on to the next fuck buddy as soon as this is over with. Maybe we need to cool off for a while," Alicia said while grabbing her purse and preparing to leave.

"That's cool love. I get it," Nix said as he nodded in understanding.

"Well, I guess I'll see you at the club later."

"No doubt." Nix followed her to the door, preparing to leave.

As soon as she opened it, she was forcefully shoved back inside. Alicia stumbled into Nix, but he caught her before she fell to the floor.

"Lying ass bitch! Always talking about you're with your girls when I call you. I'm out here busting my ass trying to make a living for us and this is what you do. Taking my hard earned money to buy dick!" Alicia's husband, Mikell, said.

He told his superiors that he had a family emergency and they allowed him to leave the firehouse a little earlier. Truthfully, it was a family emergency since he felt like he was losing his wife. Granted, Mikell knew that he wasn't there like he should have been but he was out there working hard to make sure that his wife didn't have to. Her bartending job was just extra money, but she didn't need it.

"It's not even like that," Alicia replied as tears fell from her eyes.

"How is it then Alicia? I found the statements to your little secret bank account that you've been using to rent these rooms. You've been paying for dick for months when you can get it for free at home."

"When Mikell? You haven't fucked me in months. You barely even look at me. I have needs and I'm too young to go without them being fulfilled."

"Y'all need to have this conversation without me," Nix said as he headed for the door.

"You grimy muthafucker!" Mikell raged as he rushed Nix and tried to hit him in the face.

Since he was much shorter, he punched him in the chest instead. Nix wasn't trying to fight him, so he pushed him away. He understood him being angry. He would have felt the exact same way if the roles were reversed. Still, he wasn't about to let another nigga get away with putting his hands on him just because he was in his feelings.

Mikell was enraged, so he went at him again and swung. He managed to land one of his licks to Nix's chin and it was over from there. Nix swung twice and had Mikell on the floor in seconds. He was going at him again until Alicia stopped him.

"Nix, no, please," she begged while placing her petite hands on his chest to push him back.

"Make a decision Alicia. Right here, right now. It's either me or him," Mikell said as he slowly stood to his feet.

"The fuck. Nigga, it's you. No need to even make me an option. I don't want your wife like that," Nix assured him.

"I don't want you working at that bar no more either."

"No worries fam, her last check will be in the mail today."

Nix was pissed as he walked out of the room and slammed the door behind him. Dior watched from her parking spot behind the dumpster with an amused smirk on her face. Her plan worked perfectly if she had to say so herself. She had followed Nix and Alicia on more than one occasion to the same hotel room. She knew that Alicia's

119

husband was a fireman, so he wasn't hard to find. Dior went to his job and put a bug in his ear almost two weeks ago. She didn't know why he took so long to confront them but she was happy that he finally did. She was the one who called and told him what room they were in. Mikell swore that he wasn't gonna tell anyone about her involvement in everything and she hoped that he was a man of his word.

Alicia had the entire game fucked up if she thought she was gonna have Nix all to herself. If Dior had anything to do with it, Nix was gonna remain single unless he decided to get back with her.

When Nix pulled off from the hotel, Dior waited a few minutes before she pulled off and followed him. She was content when she saw him going in the direction of his house. She didn't want to run the risk of being seen, so she dropped down off the bridge and went her own way.

Nix was fuming when he pulled up to his house. His knuckles were throbbing and so was his head. He couldn't believe that Alicia's husband showed up to their room. She had obviously gotten sloppy with how she moved because he had never suspected anything before.

"Yeah!" Nix yelled when he answered the phone for Quick.

"What do you want me to do with this car bruh? I got my boy to tow it to his body shop, but he said ain't shit wrong with it except the two flat tires," Quick noted.

"Tell him to hold it there for a few days. I'll pay him for storage."

"You ain't gotta pay that nigga shit. It's because of me that he got that shop. He'll hold it for as long as I tell him to."

"Cool but I might need a favor tonight if you're free."

"I'm free. What's up?"

"I might need you to help Rachelle out at the bar until I can find a replacement."

"I can do that. I'll be there tonight," Quick replied before he hung up.

Nix hopped out of his car, preparing to go see what Gianni was up to. He felt bad for being gone so long but he was sure that she was okay. His house was comfortable and safe.

"G! What's good love? You trying to go grab something to eat with a nigga or what?" Nix yelled when he walked into the house.

He walked down the hall to the bedroom that Gianni occupied, but she wasn't in there. The bathroom door was open, so he knew that she wasn't in there either. The bed was made and it was as if she had never even been there. Nix pulled his phone from his front pocket and checked his camera app. He watched as Gianni walked out of the bedroom with her duffel bag and left his house. That was almost two hours ago and he was curious as to where she went. At least she had the decency to lock his front door, but he was pissed that he forgot to set his alarm. If or when she came back, he swore that he would never forget to do it again. When he looked at the camera that was outside, he got pissed when he saw an Uber picking her up. It wasn't even noon yet and his day was already fucked up. He was just about to call Al but his best friend must have known that he needed him. Al called him first and his timing was perfect.

"What's good boy. How did everything go?" Al asked.

"Fucked up is how it went?"

"Why? What happened?"

"Her lil stubborn ass left. Send her ass straight to my office when she comes in to work tonight."

"How did she leave without a car? I know you ain't let that girl walk nowhere."

"Hell no, stupid. I'll tell you about that in a minute. We got other shit that needs to be handled right now."

"Like what?" Al asked, dreading Nix's answer.

"We need to hire a new bartender. I got Quick coming to help Rachelle out tonight."

"Quick! Fuck no. Come on Nix. Quick gon' get us shut the fuck down. You remember what happened when we let him help the bouncers out that last time. That nigga pistol-whipped somebody for trying to skip the line. He's too unstable."

Al loved and respected his friend's father, but Quick needed Jesus. Nix was always getting him to help out if they were anticipating a large crowd. Granted, Quick knew how to run every area of the club but he had a short fuse. If anyone went to the bar, they had to know exactly what they wanted. He didn't like nobody to hold up his line. "Get the fuck on and let somebody else come through" was how he dismissed anybody who was thinking or undecided.

"I know bruh, but he knows how to run the bar. We're in a bind right now. I'll talk to that nigga to make sure he got his head on straight. Shit, I might need Nichelle to come help out for a little while too. The crowd has been getting thick as fuck lately."

Nix was right. They had been having a larger crowd than normal but they weren't complaining. Money was good and the club had made a name for itself. Plus, with Danny doing concerts and promoting, things were going way better than they imagined. He was already in the process of hiring three more bottle girls. Now, he had to add bartenders to that list.

"Damn man. We were already short a bartender. We're supposed to have three."

"Well, hire two. Man, I really don't give a fuck right now. I had the morning from hell."

"Damn bruh. What happened?" Al inquired.

He tuned in and laughed his ass off as Nix filled him in on everything that happened. It was still early, but Nix was right. He really did have the morning from hell.

"Where is your car?" Kori asked when she picked Gianni up for work that night.

Gianni had never asked her for a ride before and she was shocked when she did. She was at one of her classmate's house and she didn't live too far from Kori's apartment.

"I don't know but I'm gonna find out as soon as we get to work," Gianni replied in disgust.

When she left from Nix's house, she planned to go back to the shelter. They weren't allowed to hang around all day but a few of the counselors were cool. Gianni was happy when her classmate called and asked her if she wanted to study for a while. She ended up taking a nap and a shower at her house before Kori picked her up. Gianni needed her car, especially since it was the only place that she had to sleep for the night.

She was very comfortable at Nix's house but she barely got any sleep. The thought of her being under his roof while he was laid up somewhere with her cousin pissed her off. She kept getting up to see if he had come back home, but he never even bothered. Gianni was in her feelings, so she called an Uber and left.

"What do you mean you're gonna find out. I thought Nix was taking care of it."

"Fuck Nix!" Gianni snapped.

"Not too much on my man now, bitch. But, seriously though cousin, what happened?"

"I really don't know. He told me that his boy was gonna tow my car and fix it but I haven't heard anything since then."

"Where did he drop you off at last night?"

"My hotel room," Gianni lied.

She didn't want to seem shady and she was sure that she would if she told Kori the truth. Nothing happened between her and Nix, but she was sure that her cousin wouldn't buy it. It was her who he was laid up with, so she shouldn't have felt no kind of way about it.

"Baby, that nigga had a bitch climbing the walls in that room," Kori boasted.

124

She smirked when she looked out of the corner of her eye and saw Gianni frown. Kori actually went home, showered, and went straight to bed when they left the club. She would never let her cousin know that though, especially since she seemed to be feeling some kind of way about her and Nix.

"I might be getting fired tonight."

"Why?" Kori asked in shock.

"Because I'm not working the top level. I don't give a fuck what Nix has to say. All I want is my car and I'm good on everything else."

"What do you mean everything else?" Kori asked as she pulled up to the club and parked.

Gianni got out of the car without even bothering to answer. They both went into the employee breakroom but nobody was in there. Gianni took a few minutes to fill in her brows and put on some lashes. After a while, the other bottle girls started coming in getting ready for the crowd. It was about fifteen minutes before they were scheduled to start their shift when Al walked in holding his clipboard.

"Hey Al. Can I work the bottom level tonight?" Gianni asked.

"That's not my call sweetheart. Besides, the boss man wants to see you in his office ASAP."

"For what?"

"I guess you'll have to go up there and see," he replied before he started barking out orders. Once everyone was told what to do, Al left them alone.

"What the hell is that all about? Why does Nix wanna see you?" Kori asked her cousin.

125

"I don't know and I don't give a fuck. I'm not going to his office," Gianni replied as she walked away.

She and Kori grabbed their ice buckets from behind the counter and headed to their separate work areas. Kori was pissed that she wasn't working the top level but she planned to make her way up there as often as she could.

"Al, I'm sorry but I can't work up top tonight. One of my exes is up there and we'll be fighting before the night is out if I do," one of the bottle girls fussed as she walked downstairs. Kori didn't even know that Al was behind her since she was standing there daydreaming. She was happy that she didn't move when she was supposed to. That was her chance and she was taking it.

"I'll do it," Kori hurriedly offered.

"Switch places with Kori," Al ordered before he walked away. He was too busy to be stressing over minor bullshit that wasn't really a big deal.

"I'll be happy to. It's all yours boo," the other bottle girl said before she walked away.

"Yes!" Kori cheered as she hurriedly made her way upstairs and rushed over to her cousin.

"Girl, the damn shift just started and they were about to have a fight already. Al better send another bottle girl up here before shit gets real," Gianni said.

"That's why I'm here."

"Thank God. I wasn't trying to spend my entire shift playing referee."

The two of them got busy taking and fulfilling drink orders. Before long, two hours had passed and every section of the club was filled. Well, almost every section. Nix wasn't in his usual spot and no one else was there either.

126

Kori had been looking high and low but she hadn't seen him yet.

"I wonder where my future baby daddy is," Kori said as she and Gianni stood up against the wall. Gianni had just done another setup at a VIP table and received a big tip that she was discreetly counting.

"Don't know and don't care," Gianni replied, right as Al walked over to them.

"Didn't I tell you that Nix wanted to see you in his office?"

His gaze was fixated on Gianni and Kori's was too. Al was always nice but he was a no-nonsense supervisor. He hated to repeat himself, but it was different with Gianni. His boy wanted her and it was his job to help him get her. Nix had been watching Gianni all night from the camera in his office and he was tired of waiting for her. He called Al again and he wanted to make sure that she did what she was told this time.

"Yeah but it was too busy," Gianni said after a while.

"It's okay now. I'll help Kori out if I need to. Go handle that business."

Gianni sighed in disgust while handing Al her ice bucket. It felt like she was walking the green mile and she wasn't in a hurry to get to her destination. Her heart was thumping in her chest as she raised her hand to knock on his office door.

"Come in!" Nix yelled before she even had a chance to knock.

Gianni walked into his office and paused in the doorway. Black and silver must have been his colors because his office and some parts of his house were

127

decorated exactly the same. Nix sat behind a huge black and silver desk in a high-back black leather chair. There were four different monitors on the desk, so she knew that he saw everything that happened inside and out of the club.

"You asked to see me," Gianni said as she folded her arms across her chest.

"When I said come in, that meant to come all the way in. Close the door."

She rolled her eyes but she did what he asked her to do. Once the door was closed, she walked closer to his desk.

"Where is my car?" Gianni asked.

"Being repaired but that's not why I wanted to see you. What's good G? Why did you leave?"

"I don't know what kind of games you're playing but I don't have time. Why would you want me to stay in your house, so you can leave to go get a room with my cousin?"

"That's the second time that you said something to me about your cousin. Now, I won't lie and say that I wasn't with a female when I left but it damn sure wasn't your hoe ass cousin."

"My cousin ain't no hoe!" Gianni snapped.

"Your opinion but I disagree."

"She can't be too much of a hoe if you're fucking her."

"I wouldn't fuck your cousin with my daddy's dick. I don't do too well with subliminals love. Speak up and say what you have to say."

"Well, she said that y'all are fucking."

128

"And I said that we're not and never have. I've never even seen your cousin outside of this club and I have no desire to."

"Why would she lie?"

"Because she's a liar." Nix shrugged.

"Look, I just need my car. It doesn't need to be repaired. I only had two flat tires."

"And I'm taking care of it. You can catch a ride home with me when the club closes."

"No! I'm not going back to your house."

"Do you have anywhere else to go Gianni? You have no room and no car. I don't even know why this is up for debate. It looks like they can use your help out there. I'll be ready whenever you are," Nix said as he dismissed her and focused on the monitors that were on his desk.

"Bastard!" Gianni huffed as she walked out of his office.

Admittedly, Nix was right, but she would never give him the satisfaction of admitting it. He was cocky enough and didn't need any more help from her.

"What happened?" Kori rushed over to her and asked. Nix's office was kind of ducked off, so it was hard to see who went in and out of it.

"Nothing," Gianni replied dismissively.

"Bitch, you were in there for a long ass time to say it was nothing."

"He just wanted to know if I wanted to work fulltime."

"What did you tell him?"

"I said that I'd think about it. I can use the money but I don't know."

Gianni was telling a partial truth but she didn't want to put Kori in her business with Nix. He had Gianni looking at her cousin sideways about some of the things he said. Nix was so convincing about never having been with Kori and she was torn on who or what to believe. She had never known her cousin to lie but maybe she felt that it was necessary.

"There go my boo," Kori said as she spotted Nix walking out of his office.

He made eye contact with her and she almost creamed in her thong when he smiled. He sat in his personal area and she put an extra switch in her hips when she walked away. Nix watched his surroundings for hours until it was closing time. He hung around with Al and waited for Gianni to be done.

"Do you need a ride to your room cousin?" Kori asked Gianni once they were done putting everything in its place behind the bar.

"Uh, no, Heavy is taking me."

"That's even better. More time for me to spend with my boo."

"What boo?"

"Nix," Kori said as she stuck her tongue out and twerked.

"Have fun."

"We always do." Gianni saw her cousin off and went back to the top level.

"Ready?" Nix asked when he saw her.

You're The Best Part

"Yeah," Gianni replied, finally coming to terms that she was going home with her boss. She really didn't have much of a choice since she didn't have anywhere else to go. She had no room and no car, so a park bench or under a bridge were her only other options. None of those sounded appealing, so it was Nix or nothing.

Chapter 6

“Tell me a little something about yourself,” Nix requested as he and Gianni drove to his house.

“What do you wanna know?”

“Everything. You told me the short version a few weeks ago. Now, I want all the details.”

He listened as Gianni told him a little bit more about herself. Surprisingly, she had a wonderful childhood. She smiled in adoration whenever she spoke of her mother and grandmother. That look was replaced with one of disdain when she mentioned her only brother. Her family was small, so he understood why she didn't have many people to turn to for help. To him, that was even more of a reason why Kori and her mother should have stepped up to the plate.

Gianni wasn't a slacker and he could tell that just by talking to her. She was always saying how she helped out with bills wherever she stayed so that was commendable. She didn't elaborate on her mother's death the same way she spoke about her grandmother's. Nix wondered if she was probably killed and it was hard for her to talk about.

"What about you? Aside from you being born to teenaged parents, what else should I know about you?"

She gave him her undivided attention as he told her a little about himself. Looks were deceiving because she would have never known that Nix had a degree. He had a huge family and he wanted a big family of his own. Gianni wanted to ask him about his breakup with Dior but she didn't want to pry. Nix was an open book, but she didn't want to take it too far.

"Are you hungry?" Nix asked when they walked into the house. He wasn't leaving out again, so he set his alarm. He didn't want Gianni trying to sneak off and leave before he woke up in the morning.

"Yeah. What do you have to eat?"

"My mama made some spaghetti and garlic bread for me earlier."

"Seriously Nix? Your mama still cooks for you." Gianni smirked as she watched him get the containers of food from the fridge.

"Shit, I don't know how to cook. Somebody gotta feed a nigga since you refused my offer."

"I appreciate the offer. I just don't think it's a good idea."

"Why? Because you think I'm sticking dick to your lying ass cousin."

"I really don't know what to believe. She told me that she was hooking up with you again tonight."

"Call her right now and I'll prove it to you. Hell, I'm here with you so you already know what it is."

"It's not even that deep."

"It is that deep when she got you not wanting to fuck with a nigga. The fuck is she lying on my dick for? That bitch can't come to our house. We don't need that kind of negative energy."

"Don't call my cousin a bitch. And this is your house, not ours," Gianni corrected.

"Just one week G. That's all I'm asking. This can work out if you stop being so stubborn and just try. See how easy it was tonight when you didn't fight me."

"What other choice did I have? I have no car and no room. I'm drained and trying to find a place to lay my head every night is exhausting."

"You don't even have to do all that love. Real shit. You don't ever have to cook or clean and the room is yours for as long as you need it. I can't lie; I'm feeling the fuck out of you, but it ain't no pressure with that either. Just ease my mind and accept the offer."

"Okay. I'll accept under one condition."

"What's that?" he asked.

"I have to pay rent. I paid half the rent when I lived with my boyfriend. I've always paid my way, even in the shelter. Honestly, I would love to have a permanent place to call home but I don't want it for free."

"Okay, I can respect that. I have a condition too."

"I'm listening," Gianni replied.

"Let me take you out. Just one date. If you ain't feeling us doing it again, it'll be no hard feelings."

"I don't know Nix. I haven't dated in over a year. Dating my boss might feel too weird."

"Technically, Al is your boss," he pointed out.

"That's even worse. I'll be going on a date with my boss' boss."

"I'm a cool ass nigga if you give me a chance."

"I don't know Nix. I already feel weird just being here," Gianni sighed.

"That's because your lying ass cousin got you thinking some shit that ain't true. I'm telling you, G; she know a nigga is feeling you. That's why she told you that shit. But I swear on my uncle's grave, I never touched that girl."

"This is good," Gianni said while shoving a forkful of spaghetti into her mouth.

"How you just up and change the subject like that?"

"Can I just think about it Nix?"

"Most definitely. I'm just happy that you didn't flat out say no."

He and Gianni continued to make small talk while they ate. Afterwards, she cleaned up the kitchen while Nix put the leftover food away. He carried her duffle bag down the hall to the bedroom that was officially hers.

"This closet is huge," Gianni said as she marveled at the space.

"Yeah and these drawers are empty too. You can store all your personal items in the bathroom cabinet and there's extra towels in the closet down the hall. We can get the rest of your stuff from your storage whenever you're ready."

"Damn nigga. You really were following me."

"Stop making it sound like I was on some creep shit."

"But, you were," Gianni laughed.

"Nah, I was just concerned about you."

"How did you even know about my situation? That's not something that I go around telling everybody."

"I got my ways," Nix replied as he winked at her.

"I'm sure it was Heavy."

"No, it wasn't. I did ask him but he didn't offer up any info. Heavy is a solid dude."

"Yeah, he is. But, what's up with my car? I only had two flat tires. That should have been fixed by now."

"It's being fixed. Don't trip baby, I got you. I'll take you wherever you need to go and you can ride to work with me."

"Hell no! People will really start talking if they see us riding to work together every day."

"There's one thing that you're gonna learn about me, G. I don't, never did and never will give a fuck about what nobody say or how they feel. The odds were stacked against me at birth and I proved a lot of muthafuckers wrong."

"I need to take a shower," Gianni said.

"Yeah, me too. Come back to the front room when you're done. Maybe we can watch a movie. I'll take my date any way I can get it," Nix replied before walking out of the room.

Gianni smiled as she gathered her items for her shower. She felt better than she did in a long time and she was hoping that she wasn't making a mistake. She didn't really know Nix, but he seemed genuine. Her grandmother always told her that the eyes never lied and she saw sincerity in his.

"Okay, my guardian angels, I need y'all to watch over me. Send me a sign if I'm making a mistake. God knows I've made enough of those to last me a lifetime," Gianni said as she looked at the picture of her mother and grandmother that was the screensaver on her phone. It was the last picture that they took together and it was in both their funeral programs.

When she stepped under the hot stream of water, Gianni's body instantly relaxed. She looked forward to having all of her belongings with her under one roof. She knew that she couldn't live with Nix forever and she wasn't trying to. She was in her last year of college and she planned to make enough money to be able to get a permanent place of her own.

"What made you change your mind? You were so against it at first," Kori said while looking at Gianni.

Gianni had started working at the club fulltime two weeks ago and Kori was shocked. She always said that she wanted to but she was too afraid of losing her bed at the shelter. She was blessed that she didn't have to get on the waiting list to get in.

"I told you, bitch; I need the money. I have car, health, and life insurance, plus my car note. My tutoring fees help but it's still not enough. I'm trying to save," Gianni replied.

"Girl, you could have gotten Medicaid or gone to the free clinic."

"I don't have nothing against that but I prefer to have a primary doctor who can see me when I need to be seen. I hate having to see a different doctor every time I go to the free clinic."

Having life insurance was more important than anything. Gianni didn't want anyone trying to raise money to bury her. If she was blessed enough to ever have kids, she wanted to leave them something behind. She didn't want them to have it as hard as she did. Besides her aunt and cousin, she didn't even have anyone else to name as the beneficiary. That part of the document could be changed at any time, so she wasn't worried. God forbid if anything happened to her, the shelter would benefit more than anyone else.

"I thought the shelter didn't allow y'all to come in after certain hours."

"They don't."

"Where have you been staying?"

"What's up with all the questions?"

"I just wanna make sure you're good," Kori said, making Gianni look at her sideways. It was funny how she was so concerned about her now but she never once offered her a place to sleep. Not even for one night.

"Thanks but I'm straight," Gianni assured her with a smile.

For the first time in a while, she was good. She had been living with Nix for almost three weeks now and he made her feel right at home. Their chemistry was great and they had mutual respect for each other. Although he told her that she didn't have to, Gianni assumed the responsibility of cooking and cleaning. She'd learned a few things about Nix in just a short period of time. He was clean as hell with his body but he was horrible with housekeeping. He was careless with his money and that was proven by how many times she found hundred dollar bills lying around all over the house. He hated fast food but he loved to shop. He smoked so much weed that he had a room with a built-in ventilation system. It was decorated in reggae colors with jars of every flavor of weed imaginable.

A few times Gianni came home from school and food would already be cooked. Nix's mother would come through sometimes, but they had never met. She saw his parents at the club several times before but they had never been formerly introduced.

She still hadn't gone on a date with Nix, even though he'd asked her several times. She just couldn't get over him possibly sleeping with her cousin. He swore that it wasn't true, but she didn't know what to believe. Kori was still swearing that it happened several times and was still happening.

"I can't believe that you still don't have your car. How have you been getting around?" Kori asked, shaking Gianni from her thoughts.

"I got my ways," Gianni replied with a wink.

Kori would be pissed if she knew that Nix had become her personal chauffeur. They were discreet with it and never entered the building together. Gianni asked about her car all the time during her first week living with him and he always had the same answer. He kept saying that it was being fixed, but it shouldn't have taken almost a month to fix two flat tires. Nix claimed that his friend was backed up at his automotive shop and he didn't trust taking it anywhere else. Gianni stopped asking after a while because she enjoyed being driven around. Biggie used to do it all the time and she kind of missed the feeling.

"Alright with your secretive ass," Kori said as they walked away and headed for the bar.

They both grabbed the items they needed and went their separate ways. There was no need for Gianni to even ask where she was working every night. She no longer rotated like the other bottle girls and the top level was her permanent spot. Al had hired some more bottle girls and even they worked up top more than Kori did. She wanted to ask him about making the top level her permanent spot, but Al didn't like to be told what to do.

"What's good beautiful?" someone asked, making Kori spin around to see who it was.

She smiled when she saw Nix's cousin, Ryan, standing there. Kori blushed when she thought back to the night that she'd spent with him. She hadn't heard from him since then but she really wasn't expecting to. He had a girl and Kori heard about how possessive she was.

"Hey handsome. What can I get for you?" she flirted.

"You on all fours later on tonight. But, for now, give me a bottle of Tito's."

"I got you boo, on everything," she replied before she sashayed over to the bar.

Kori busied herself fulfilling drink orders and making sure that everyone in her section was straight. She wanted to sneak off to see what was happening upstairs but it was too busy for her to disappear. She had about another thirty minutes before her break and she planned to make her way up there then.

"Aye Kori," Al said when he walked up to her.

"What's up Al?" she countered, hoping he wasn't about to start up with his usual reprimands about them being too overly friendly with the customers.

"Boss man wants you in his office. When you finish with that customer, go up there and see him."

Kori was too excited for words and she couldn't contain it even if she wanted to. She knew that she wasn't trippin'. For the past few weeks, Nix had been staring at her a lot. He never looked away when she saw him. He would only nod or wink at her. She didn't know what he wanted but she hurriedly went to the bathroom to check her appearance before she went to go see.

Kori's nerves were on edge as she walked up the stairs and looked around for Gianni. She didn't see her anywhere but she was trying to prove a point. She needed her cousin to see her going into Nix's office so that her claims of them being together would seem even more legit. Kori checked the bathroom and bar area but her cousin was nowhere to be found. Heavy hadn't seen her, and she didn't want to ask Al or Danny. She wasn't trying to get her cousin in trouble. After a while, Kori gave up and headed to her destination. Her hand shook a little when she raised it and knocked on Nix's door.

"Come in!" he yelled right before she entered.

Kori looked around in awe. She had never seen the inside of Nix's office before but it was just as nice as the rest of the club. He sat behind the huge desk like the boss he was and looked up from his computer monitor.

"Hey. You wanted to see me." Kori smiled timidly.

"I did. Have a seat." He motioned at one of the leather chairs that sat in front of his desk. Kori said down and crossed her legs seductively.

"What's up?" she questioned.

"That's what I'm trying to see." Nix steepled his hands while sitting up in his seat to look directly into her eyes.

"I'm confused. What are you trying to see?"

"Have I ever gotten out of the way with you at any time since you've been working here Kori?"

"Uh, you... um... no, you haven't," she stuttered.

"Did I ever say or do anything to make you feel uncomfortable in any way?"

"No, never." Kori's heart was racing in her chest at his line of questioning. She didn't know where he was going with it but she was curious. She was just about to ask, but he answered the questions that were swirling around in her head before she could.

"I'm just confused as to why some people think that you and I have or have had an intimate relationship."

"I don't know. I've never told anybody that we did."

"Are you sure about that?"

The skeptical look that he was giving her made her hands start to sweat. She'd obviously misinterpreted the looks that he had been giving her because he was saying something totally different now.

"Yes, I am. We've never had sex and I've never told anyone that we did. I don't know what kind of games people are playing, but that's not funny. You're my boss and I would never jeopardize my job that way."

She was pissed to think that one of them jealous ass hoes that she worked with was telling her business. They'd obviously overheard her talking to Gianni about him and went back and repeated what she said. More than likely, one of them probably wanted him too.

"That makes two of us. I take my business seriously and being involved in rumors like that is not a good look."

"I understand, but I swear to you that somebody is lying on me. I've never even seen you outside of the club."

"Exactly but it's all good. I'm happy that we were able to clear up any misunderstandings. You can get back to it," Nix replied, dismissing her.

You're The Best Part

Kori almost tripped over her own feet trying to rush out of the office. She was ashamed and embarrassed and she was happy that nobody was around to witness it.

"Wow," Gianni said as she walked out of the bathroom in Nix's office.

She heard the entire exchange and was shocked by her cousin's admittance. Kori had been lying to her since before she started working there and she stupidly believed her. She didn't think her cousin would lie to her about something so mediocre because she had no reason to. Nix got tired of her shooting him down, so he decided to take matters into his own hands. He wanted Gianni to hear it directly from Kori's mouth and his mission was accomplished.

"I tried to tell you but you had to hear it for yourself." Nix shrugged.

"I'm just so confused. Why would she lie about something like that?"

"I told you why, love. She know that a nigga is feeling you. She's a hater. You need to believe your man next time."

"I don't have a man but I apologize. She's my cousin, so taking her side came naturally."

"Nah, I don't accept that. I want a proper apology over dinner tomorrow night. I want the date that I've been begging you for. You're off and I'm taking off."

Nix got up and walked closer to her. Gianni got nervous when he used his body to pin her up against his office door. He smelled good and looked even better. When he brushed his lips against hers, she closed her eyes and savored the feeling.

"See you tomorrow night," Gianni mumbled.

"Stop acting like we don't live under the same roof. You'll see me after the club closes."

"Okay. I gotta get back to work."

He licked his lips lustfully and watched as Gianni left out of his office. After grabbing his phone from his desk, Nix left out soon after. He sighed in disgust when he saw Dior and her girls coming up the steps. Dior walked right over to Nix and stood in front of him while her girls waited nearby.

"What's up with you?" Dior asked him.

"Work Dior. Always work. What's good Crystal?" Nix asked with a smile.

"Hey Nix," Crystal replied as she looked away guiltily.

She was a shady bitch to even still be in Dior's face after fucking him. Crystal and River were the friends who Dior was on the phone bragging to about how much money she'd been taking from him. Nix always told her that her girls were jealous of her, but she couldn't see it. When he saw Crystal the night they broke up, she talked about Dior like a dog before renting a room for her and Nix to go to. She elaborated on some of the things Dior did that he didn't know about and made his decision to leave final. He made it a point to speak to her whenever they saw each other. The look on her face was always priceless. Nix walked off and laughed, leaving Dior and her girls behind.

"What's the deal Crystal? Is there something that I need to know?" Dior asked her friend.

"No. What are you even talking about?" Crystal asked.

"I'm trying to see why Nix makes it a point to always go out of his way to speak to you."

"Yeah because he never speaks to me. Hell, Dior is his ex-fiancée and he doesn't speak to her either," River pointed out.

"Maybe y'all need to ask him that," Crystal said, right as Gianni walked over to them.

She was happy as hell for the temporary distraction. Nix was petty as hell for always speaking to her in Dior's presence. He was trying to make her uncomfortable and he succeeded.

"Hey. What's your name?" Dior asked.

"Gianni."

"That's pretty."

"Thanks. What can I get for you?"

"Let us get a strawberry Hennessey set up," Dior requested.

Gianni nodded and walked away. She met up with Kori at the bar and had to resist the urge to call her out on her bullshit. She didn't want to cause a scene, so she decided to let it go. Besides, she wanted to see just how far Kori was willing to take her lies.

"Girl, Nix told Al to call me into his office." Kori smiled.

"For what?" Gianni asked.

"What do you think?"

"Wow," Gianni laughed.

"What's funny?"

"This entire conversation is hilarious."

Gianni walked away without a second glance. She was over Kori and her imaginary relationship with Nix. Admittedly, she had her fooled for a while but her eyes were wide open now. She was denying her attraction to him because of Kori, but that was a done deal. Gianni decided to let things fall into place naturally. If she and Nix were meant to be, she was no longer going to fight it.

Chapter 7

Nix smiled as he looked at Gianni dancing around the kitchen as she cooked. It was inventory day at the club, so he had to go in early to give Al and Danny a hand. She was off that day, so she planned to do a few things around the house and study. He was just about to call to ask her what she was doing. He went into his office and looked at his home cameras to see for himself instead. Gianni was sexy as hell in her Nike sports bra and tights. Her hair was hidden underneath a bonnet and her feet were covered in a pair of thick socks. She was comfortable but she still looked cute to him.

Thanks to his persistence, he and Gianni had gone on three dates so far. She was letting her guard down and talking to him more. The subject of her family was always touchy, so he tried not to bring it up too much. Gianni hadn't asked about her car in a while, but he was ready to stop hiding it from her. He was confident that she wouldn't disappear or try to leave again and that was the only reason why he kept it so long.

"Man, you can bring your ass home. I don't even know why you came. You've been on the phone or glued to that computer since you got here," Al fussed when he and Danny walked into the office.

"He's trying to make sure that the stranger he invited to live with him won't run off with all of his belongings," Danny joked.

"She's not a stranger," Nix defended.

"What do you really know about her, Nix? Hell, her cousin is a compulsive lying hoe. Ain't no telling what's wrong with her."

"How long have you been knowing me, Danny?"

"Shit, since we were about twelve or thirteen."

"And in all that time, have you ever known me to make a move without thinking about it first?"

"No, I can't say that I have."

"Gianni is cool. She's just kind of closed off," Al noted.

"She's only like that with people that she don't know. Trust me, she's an entirely different person behind closed doors," Nix revealed.

"Meaning what? She's a freak," Danny assumed.

"No, nigga. And I wouldn't know that anyway."

"Wait a minute. I know damn well Jacobi Nixon ain't checking for a female this hard and he ain't even hit it yet," Danny smirked.

He was only joking because he knew that his friend was nothing like that. Nix wore his heart on his sleeve and he wasn't ashamed to admit it. Unlike some men, he was open to love and finding the right woman to spend the rest of his life with. He was old fashioned in that sense because that's what he grew up around. His grandparents were the epitome of black love and he wanted what they had.

"I love pussy just as much as the next nigga. Well, as much as most niggas," Nix said as he looked at them and laughed.

"You digressed." Danny rolled his eyes at his lame attempt at a joke.

"I can get sex from anywhere but I'm not even on that right now. I really like her."

"Trust me, baby, he's downplaying the hell out of his feelings. This nigga did some shit that I'm too embarrassed to repeat. Hell, she's living with him and he's still stalking her," Al laughed while motioning at the computer monitor.

"No way! Are you seriously spying on her?" Danny yelled as he got up to see for himself.

"The nigga be leaving money on the floor and shit trying to see if she's gonna keep it," Al said.

"Oh okay, you're trying to see if she's another Dior. That's different though Nix. Dior deliberately stole your money. You're trying to tempt Gianni into stealing from you. Did she ever take the bait?" Danny questioned.

"Nah. Every time I come home; the money be on my dresser. It's not that I'm trying to tempt her. I just feel like if she can't be trusted with a few hundred, then she damn sure can't be trusted with a few thousand."

"Well, I wish y'all all the best. Hopefully, somebody can have a happy ending," Danny said while cutting his eyes at Al.

"Here we go with this bullshit again. Come on man. Let's finish doing this inventory. I need a nap before I have to come back here tonight," Al replied before he and Danny walked away.

Nix continued to watch Gianni on the cameras. She had just walked back into the kitchen with a basket full of towels. He picked up the phone and called her right as she started to fold them.

"Hey," Gianni said when she answered the phone. She was smiling when she did and that made him smile too. She was feeling him just as much but she was too scared to admit it.

"What's good?" Nix asked.

"Nothing. Just folding some towels."

"What are you cooking?"

She paused when he said that, and he wanted to kick his own ass. She didn't say anything about cooking and he was giving himself away.

"How do you know that I'm cooking?"

"I don't. Are you?"

"Yeah. I'm making a baked potato casserole with steaks and gravy."

"Damn. Let me finish, so I can hurry up and get some of that."

You're The Best Part

Gianni was a great cook. She learned from her grandmother, so she did everything from scratch. That was a plus for him because he was raised on home cooked meals that were made the exact same way.

"It's almost done," she noted.

"Have you thought more about what we discussed last night?"

Nix asked her about being in a relationship, but she wasn't so sure. She was still holding back for some reason, but he wasn't sure why. They cleared up the bullshit with her cousin so that was no longer an issue.

"Yes," she blushed.

"Yes, you want to give us a try or, yes, you've been thinking about it?"

"I've been thinking about it."

"And?" He wasn't trying to press her for an answer but he needed to know what was on her mind.

"I'm still thinking."

"What can I do to make the decision a little easier for you?"

"You're doing everything right Nix. There's just a few things about me that you don't know. I have a lot of hang ups about relationships that I've never gotten over," she confessed.

"Don't do that G. Don't put me in the category with them other niggas."

"No, it's nothing like that. We'll talk about it later."

"Alright love. I'll let you get back to what you were doing. I should be there in about another hour or so."

"Okay. See you later," Gianni replied before hanging up.

Gianni sighed, disappointed with herself. She was trying her best to go with the flow but she was scared. She never told Nix that she was a virgin. He didn't know that the thought of intimacy frightened her and why. She didn't want to agree to be in a relationship with him, only for him to cheat like Biggie did. He was a grown ass man and waiting around until she got over her fears was probably something that he wasn't willing to do. Being honest with him about her feelings was the only thing that she could do. The ball would be in his court after that. If he still wanted them to be together, she wasn't opposed to giving it a try.

Once she was done folding the towels, Gianni headed down the hall to put them away. As soon as she did, she heard the alarm in the front room, followed by a woman's loud voice.

"Bitch, I told you! They got pots on the stove right now and this house is spotless. Nix don't know how to cook and I know damn well he ain't been cleaning up like that," Nichelle said as she looked around her son's house.

She was on the phone with her sister, Nicole, telling her about her suspicions. Nichelle barely cooked for Nix over the past few weeks and she never had to clean. She was no fool and she knew that another woman was in the picture. The placed even smelled feminine with the plug-ins that were strategically placed in every outlet in the room.

"Is anybody in there?" Nicole asked. Nichelle was just about to say that she didn't see anybody until Gianni emerged from the hallway closet.

"Bitch, yes. Who the hell are you?" Nichelle asked the younger woman who looked slightly familiar. She ended the call with her sister as she looked Gianni up and down.

154

"Hi, I'm Gianni." She smiled at Nix's mother as she politely extended her hand.

"What are you doing in my son's house?" Nichelle looked at her outstretched hand and frowned.

"I live here, temporarily."

"Since when did he start letting his hoes live in his house?"

"I'm nobody's hoe and that includes your son," Gianni snapped angrily. She didn't give a fuck about Nichelle being Nix's mother. She wasn't about to stand there and let her talk crazy to her. She would pack her shit up and be back at the shelter before she let that happen.

"Don't get shit twisted just because you're fucking my son."

Nichelle's phone started ringing but she didn't bother answering it. Nix was probably watching his cameras and calling to tell her to chill. He already knew how she was, so he shouldn't have been surprised.

"I don't want you to get shit twisted just because you're his mother. And who I'm fucking is not your concern."

"And then you got the nerve to be disrespectful."

"I match energy. I show people the same respect they show me. I don't know what you thought but you're not exempt."

The two women stared each other down, both refusing to look away or back down. Gianni was ready for whatever, even if it meant that she would be homeless again. She was on edge until Nichelle cracked a smile that made her visibly relax.

"Alright then bitch, get me all the way together. That's what I'm talking about. Don't let nobody play in your face. Fix me a plate and tell me how you ended up living here with my son. You work at the club, don't you?" Nichelle asked as she took a seat on a bar stool in the kitchen.

"Yeah, I'm a bottle girl."

Gianni fixed Nichelle a plate and sat down next to her. She gave her the short, filtered version of why she was living with Nix. She didn't know her like that to put her in her business. She seemed nice enough but she wasn't taking any chances. They talked for over an hour and she enjoyed her company.

"Well, it was nice talking to you, boo, but I need to get going. Shit, I'm happy that you're here. I don't have to be over here cooking and cleaning for his ass no more. That food was good too. Not better than mine but good."

"Thanks, I guess." Gianni smiled as she walked her to the door. Nix was pulling up right as Nichelle got into her car and pulled off. She waved at her son as she sped out of his driveway.

"I see you met my sister," Nix laughed when he walked inside and followed Gianni to the kitchen.

He heard the entire exchange between her and Nichelle and he was trying to call his mama before shit got real. When he saw the way that Gianni handled herself, he knew that he didn't have anything to worry about. He was happy that she didn't back down to Nichelle. She would have fucked with her every time she saw her if she did. After a while, they started talking and he went and helped Al finish doing inventory.

"Yeah because she damn sure don't act like nobody's mama. Are you ready to eat?"

"Hell yeah, my stomach is growling loud as fuck." Nix kicked off his shoes and left them right in the middle of the floor. He took off his shirt and threw it on the counter right next to his keys.

"Really Nix?" Gianni asked as she looked at him like he was crazy.

"Oh, shit, my fault."

He grabbed everything and went to put it where it belonged. He hadn't lived with a woman in almost a year, but Gianni wasn't like Dior. She didn't just pick up after him like his ex-girlfriend did. She held him accountable and made him do things for himself. It would take some getting used to but he wasn't complaining. When he got back to the kitchen, Gianni had his food waiting for him.

"What do you want to drink?"

"Look at you acting like the woman of the house and shit. You need to stop playing and just make this shit official."

"Sweet tea or water?" Gianni asked, making him laugh.

She was a pro at changing the subject, but he wasn't letting her off the hook that easily. Gianni was in the fridge when he walked up and stood behind her. She jumped and almost dropped the bottle of water that she was holding. Nix took it from her and sat it on the counter behind them. He pinned her body against the fridge with his own and used his muscular tattooed arms to cage her in.

"You can't run from this conversation forever. I'm good with whatever you decide, but I want you to look me in the eyes when you say it."

He was too close for her to even answer. Gianni wanted to say something but words escaped her. His warm minty breath tickled her nostrils, as well as the scent of his intoxicating cologne. Gianni opened her mouth to speak but the feel of his lips against hers ceased all conversation. She wrapped her arms around his neck, right as he slipped his tongue in her mouth. She was nervous because she didn't know how far things between them would go. She was inexperienced with sex but she had become a pro at oral. Maybe if she gave him some bomb ass head, he would be satisfied and leave it at that.

Nix was shocked when Gianni broke their kiss and dropped down to her knees. She wasn't really shy, but he wasn't expecting that. He was dressed comfortably since he was doing inventory, so she pulled down his Nike sweats and boxers in one swift move. She licked her full, plump lips before taking him into her mouth.

He more than doubled Biggie in size, so Gianni gagged a little at first. She opened her mouth a little wider and relaxed her cheeks. Nix groaned at the feel of her warm mouth enveloping his dick. He yanked her bonnet off and started pulling at her freshly flat ironed hair. Gianni's head bobbed up and down his dick as she pumped the base of his shaft. Saliva trickled down her chin as she glided it along her lips and tongue before taking him all the way to the back of her throat.

"Fuck!" Nix yelled as he fucked her face.

His eyes were closed tight as his grip on her hair got tighter. Gianni didn't look like the type to suck a dick like that but she had him fooled. Nix was no longer giving her a choice. She was his and he wasn't taking no for an answer. She had him feeling lightheaded as she used her mouth like a suction cup. When one of her small hands reached up to massage his balls, he almost lost it. Nix couldn't hold on any longer. He didn't know how Gianni felt about swallowing, so he tried to pull himself out of her mouth. Instead of moving, she gripped his thighs tighter. Nix looked down at her in shock but he got his answer. A few seconds later, he spilled his seeds into her mouth and she swallowed it all like it was nothing.

"Damn girl," he panted when Gianni stood to her feet. She tried to walk away, but he pulled her back before she could.

"What are you doing?" Gianni gasped when he picked her up and sat her on the counter. She thought that he would be good after some bomb ass head, but he seemed to want more.

"I'm returning the favor," Nix smirked as he quickly undressed her.

Gianni was sexy with and without clothes, and that was a plus. Besides Dior, he had never gone down on another woman. Since Gianni had blessed him with her superb oral skills, he was ready to do the same for her.

"Oh shit!" Gianni hissed when she felt the first flick of his tongue.

She held on to the counter as Nix lifted her legs up into the air and snaked his tongue up and down her lower lips. He flicked his tongue over her clit rapidly and Gianni almost lost it. It had been over a year since she'd had any kind of physical action and her body was trembling in a matter of minutes.

"You taste good as fuck," Nix mumbled in between sucking and licking. She smelled even better and that was yet something else that he liked about her. Good hygiene was a must and she had that part covered.

"Don't stop." She was begging him to keep going and he didn't disappoint. She almost lost it when he licked his middle finger and stuck it inside of her. Gianni's body arched upwards, but he didn't let her fall.

"Damn. You tight as fuck." Her walls gripped his finger and sucked it in deeper. Her insides felt warm and he couldn't wait to be inside of her.

"I'm gonna cum," Gianni moaned while rotating her hips.

She squealed when Nix picked her up and carried her over to the sofa. He never broke their connection as he sat her down and kneeled in front of her. His head was moving from side to side rapidly as her body quivered. She grabbed a pillow and held it close as her stomach muscles tightened. She came hard and Nix was right there, lapping up her juices like a famished kitten. Once he was done, he stood up and undressed himself.

Gianni's heart pounded in her chest as she looked at his perfectly sculpted body. She wanted to keep going but her anxiety was already getting the best of her. The room was cold but she started sweating like crazy. Her entire body started shaking and she felt like she was about to start hyperventilating when Nix lowered his body onto hers. When she felt the tip of his dick at her opening, Gianni felt like she was about to pass out.

"No! Stop!" she yelled as tears poured from her eyes. She felt like she was suffocating as she pushed Nix away and ran down the hall to her bedroom.

"The fuck!" Nix was confused as to what had just happened. He and Gianni were on the same page, or so he thought. He would have never forced himself on her and she needed to know that. He threw his sweats back on and went down the hall to find her.

Gianni was standing at the bathroom sink splashing cold water on her face when he walked in. Nix grabbed a big towel and wrapped it around her naked body. She jumped when he touched her and he didn't know what was wrong with her. He was hoping that she hadn't been raped before or something like that. Sometimes, certain things acted as triggers and reminded people of their past. Nix still got anxiety at red lights sometimes because he and his uncle were shot up when they stopped at one.

"I'm sorry," Gianni apologized as she wiped her teary eyes.

"Don't apologize love. I just want to make sure that you're okay."

"Yeah, I'm okay now." Gianni took a few deep breaths until her heart rate returned to normal. She was embarrassed, but Nix didn't seem to mind. He looked more concerned than anything. Once she seemed to feel better, he led her over to the bed where they both sat down.

"Listen, I want you to know that I would never force you to do anything that you don't want to do. I apologize if I took things too far."

"No, you didn't do anything wrong Nix. I have my own hang-ups that I need to get over. It has nothing to do with you. That's why I told you earlier that we needed to talk."

"I'm listening," he said while grabbing her hand. He gave it a reassuring kiss that made her smile.

"My mother died of AIDS," Gianni confessed.

"Damn baby. I'm sorry to hear that."

Nix listened in awe as Gianni told him all about her mother's death and her brother's role in it. She didn't blame him for what happened but she wholeheartedly felt that he was a contributing factor to her demise. Nix completely understood her reservations and he didn't mind using a condom when or if they were ever intimate.

"There's something else."

"What's up?"

"I'm a virgin."

"A virgin!" he yelled in shock. That was almost unheard of these days, especially with females her age.

"Why do you sound so astonished?" Gianni was laughing, but his reaction wasn't a surprise. Biggie felt the same way when they first met. She was in college and a lot of girls already had kids by then.

"Shit, I've never met a female virgin that was over eighteen years old. Dior was a virgin when we met but we were teenagers at the time."

"Can I ask you a question?"

"You can ask me anything."

"Why did you and Dior break up? When I first started at the club, people were saying that she was your fiancée. Then, Kori told me that y'all weren't together anymore."

"Kori seems to know more about me than I know about my damn self. But, Dior and I haven't been together for almost a year now. I don't like to put nobody in my business, so no one knew when we broke up. She still comes around so everybody just assumed that we were still together."

"Why did y'all break up?"

"She stole from me," Nix sighed. He didn't tell that to too many people but he wanted to be straight up with Gianni about everything.

"Oh okay. I get it now."

"You get what?"

162

"You can stop leaving your money lying around. I don't steal," Gianni said, making him laugh.

"My fault sweetheart. I can't lie and say that I don't have trust issues with that, but you proved me wrong. I have a few questions for you too."

"Okay. What do you want to know?"

"I thought you said that you lived with your nigga once before."

"Yeah, I did."

"And you never had sex with him. I find that hard to believe."

"Just oral."

"Yeah, I can see that." Nix nodded. Gianni had skills and he knew damn well that wasn't her first time sucking dick.

"It's not that I didn't want to. He was a hoe. Nigga was pressuring me to have sex with him when he was already fucking a bunch of other hoes. Kori used to put me down on a lot of the shit that he did."

"That bitch is like ants at a picnic. The fuck she be so worried about you for. Her hating ass was probably lying on that man too." Nix frowned.

"Nah, she was telling the truth that time. His baby mama showed up to our house and confirmed it. I packed my shit and left the same day. Not only was he having sex with other women, he wasn't using protection while doing it. I asked him to get tested and he went off. I got on birth control pills and he thought that was all the protection we needed. Never having sex with him was one of the best decisions that I've ever made. That's why I'm leery about us being together. Intimacy is a big part of relationships and that's usually a deal breaker for most men."

"That's bullshit G. Intimacy is more than just sex. We're being intimate right now," he pointed out.

"How?" she questioned in confusion.

"It's called emotional intimacy. That's when people feel comfortable sharing their feelings with each other, even the bad, embarrassing shit. There's different levels to intimacy and they don't all involve fucking. Sex is a big part of a relationship, but it's a problem if it's the biggest part. I don't want your lack of sexual experience to stop you from giving us a chance. I'm not pressed over sex and there's no rush. Only you will know when you're ready. If me getting tested will ease your fears, then consider it done. Still, I don't want you to feel obligated to do anything."

Gianni was speechless but in a good way. She hadn't even known Nix that long and he seemed more concerned about her than some of her own family did. Kori made her feel like it was her fault that Biggie cheated. She always told her that she was being childish for holding on to her virginity. Gianni always prayed and asked God for signs and He hadn't let her down yet. The day after she prayed that prayer, Biggie's baby mama showed up to their house ready to fight. She blamed Gianni for him not claiming a baby that she didn't even know about. Gianni gave her a pass since she was pregnant but that was the end of her relationship with him.

"Yes," Gianni said after they were quiet for a while.

"What are you saying yes to?" Nix asked.

"I'm saying yes to us. I want us to be official."

"After that bomb ass blow job, we already are."

"Oh God."

Nix laughed when she covered her face in embarrassment but she had nothing to be ashamed of.

"I got a confession to make."

"Aww damn. This is about to be the shortest relationship in history."

"Nah, it ain't nothing like that. I don't want you to think I'm on no stalking shit but I got cameras in here."

"I know you better be fucking lying! You see me when I shower and shit!"

She jumped up from the bed, ready to swing on him if she had to. She had just agreed to be with him and she was ready to break up with his ass already.

"No, it's nothing like that. Sit down girl."

Nix pulled her back down on the bed and explained everything to her. He even showed her the cameras on his phone so that she could see what areas were under surveillance. She visibly relaxed once she saw that her intimate moments weren't being captured.

"So, what we just did in the kitchen and living room was being recorded"

"Yeah but I'm gonna delete it," he assured her.

"No, let me see it first."

"Are you serious?" He was shocked that she asked but he thought she was playing.

"Yeah, let me see it."

Nix was all smiles as he pressed a few buttons on his phone to rewind the camera footage. He and Gianni watched themselves in action while bragging on their oral skills. After talking for a little longer, they both went back to the kitchen and ate. Since Mondays were usually slow at the club, Nix took off and spent the rest of the day with Gianni. They watched movies and pigged out on junk food. When it was time to go to sleep, he led her upstairs where they slept together in his bed for the first time. Since they were a couple now, he was sure that it would be the first time of many.

Chapter 8

"**N**ix stoooop," Gianni whined, as he planted kisses all over her face and neck.

"What took you so long to come see what I wanted?" he asked, biting her bottom lip.

"You can't keep calling me to come in here every five minutes. People are gonna start getting suspicious."

"As if I give a fuck."

"You're gonna get me in trouble with Al. You know he's gonna fuss at me for being gone so long."

"That nigga better not fuss at my baby."

"Move Jacobi. I'm still mad with you anyway."

"Don't be mad with me, baby. At least I came clean and told you the truth."

Nix finally gave Gianni her car back. When she questioned him about where it had been, he told her the truth, including the reason behind her having the two flat tires. She couldn't believe that Al was in on it with him but she shouldn't have been surprised. They were best friends that were more like brothers.

"I gotta get going before Al starts looking for me." As soon as the words left her mouth, the office door flew open and Al walked in.

"Don't let Nix get you fired Gianni," Al smirked.

"I just told him that I had to go." Gianni tried to wiggle out of Nix's hold but that only made him hold her tighter.

"Don't worry about him, baby. He can't fire the wife of the boss," Nix said.

"I just became the girlfriend two weeks ago. I got upgraded quick."

Their relationship was new but Gianni was happier than she'd been in a while. Besides oral, she and Nix still hadn't had sex. He was true to his word and went and got tested a few days after they became official. It was a small gesture that meant so much to her. She was with Biggie for over a year and he got offended whenever she even mentioned it. He would always say that he was clean, but she wasn't buying it.

You're The Best Part

"It'll really be official once you meet my mama and daddy this weekend," Nix said, referring to his grandparents.

They were excited when he told them that he wanted them to meet his new girlfriend. They knew that it had to be somebody that he really liked. Besides Dior, they had never been introduced to anyone else. They hated when they broke up but they knew that Nix didn't do anything without a good reason.

"Okay but I gotta go." Gianni gave him another quick peck on the lips before he finally released her.

"It looks like everything is going good with y'all," Al observed.

"Yeah, we're straight. The real test is gonna be this weekend. You know how my mama is. She puts everybody under a microscope."

Nix's grandmother swore that she had a sixth sense. She called it a spirit of discernment and she could look at a person and tell if they had a genuine heart. He never told her, but she missed the mark on Dior. She gave her the stamp of approval and she turned out to be a villain in disguise.

"Shit, ain't nobody worse than my people. At least she won't condemn her to hell like my mama would." Al was laughing but he was dead ass serious. He knew that if his family ever found about his secrets, he would be disowned in the name of the Lord.

"I mean, I value my mama's opinion but it's my decision at the end of the day."

"Yeah, that's true," Al sighed.

"What's good bro? I can tell that something is bothering you."

"This behind the scenes shit is starting to stress me out. Danny is pissed and I can't even blame him."

"What happened this time?"

"Same shit as always. He stayed the night at my house but Kinsley had to drop Alexa off early this morning."

"And you woke him up and put him out," Nix said, knowing exactly what happened.

"Don't say it like that. I didn't put him out but I did ask him to leave. He started up with all that bullshit and we broke up again. I can't fucking win for losing."

"Nah nigga, you don't wanna win. Fuck that. Life is too short to be unhappy. You gon' fuck around and end up alone, all because you're afraid of what the next muthafucker got to say. Look at Danny. His family didn't fuck with him for an entire year when he finally came out. When they saw that he didn't give a fuck, they came around and accepted him for who he was. If you have to lose a few people just to find yourself, so be it. If they can't love you for who you are, maybe they shouldn't be in your life to begin with."

"Yeah but Danny is talking about us buying a house and all that other shit."

"What's the problem?"

"Marriage though, bruh?"

"That's what most people do when they're in love and want to spend the rest of their lives together."

"I just need some time man."

"I get it but don't expect that man to sit around and wait until you figure it out," Nix replied as he walked out of the office.

Al sat there, deep in thought. He knew that his friend was right but he was having an inner battle with himself. He couldn't help who he loved and he wasn't trying to. He loved his family but he loved Danny just as much. He didn't want to compromise his happiness for the sake of others, but that's exactly what he was doing.

After trying to find the right words, Al left out of the office in search of Danny. When he saw him, he motioned with his head for him to follow him out back. Al made sure that the coast was clear before Danny came out there. Usually, Nix was the only one who went back there when he wanted to smoke. It was near the dumpsters, so it wasn't the ideal place to be.

"What!" Danny snapped as soon as he stepped outside.

"I'm sorry," Al said sadly.

"What's new? You can save the pitiful voice because I'm not buying it."

"I don't want you to pity me. I was wrong and I apologize."

"The best apology is changed behavior Aldrin. This is a never ending cycle with us and I'm tired. My love for you is the only reason why I'm still here but I'm getting fed up. I get it, Alexa is young and she might not understand. But it's not just her who we're hiding from. I don't want to be with someone who's ashamed of me."

"I'm not ashamed of you. I love you more than anything but this is hard for me."

"Well, let me make it easier. I'm done. I'd rather hurt a little now than to hurt a lot later. I've spent too many years hiding from other people. It felt good when I finally took off the mask. I really hope you can experience that one day," Danny said as he tried to walk away.

Al grabbed him before he got too far and pulled him back. He pressed his forehead to Danny's and sighed deeply.

"I need you. You and my daughter are the only things that make me happy. I know what I have to do and I swear that I will. It won't happen overnight but, please, don't leave me."

Danny wanted to walk away but he just couldn't do it. He'd loved Al since they were teenagers and their time apart did nothing to change that. Al was his first and he wanted him to be his last. They were soulmates and that much he was sure of.

"You should have been out of chances with me a long time ago. Don't make me regret this Aldrin."

"You won't, I promise," Al swore. He gave Danny a peck on the lips before he left to go back inside. Al pulled his half smoked blunt from his back pocket and was about to spark it up.

"Well, I guess my drinks will be on the house again," Dior smirked as she walked over to him.

"What?" Al asked with an annoyed frown.

"Now I see why you don't want Kinsley anymore. You're too busy fucking one of your best friends. Hell, maybe that's why Nix broke up with me. He might be a down low nigga too."

She was trying to find a parking spot up front but she didn't have any luck. She drove around back to turn

172

around when she saw Al and Danny standing back there talking. Dior didn't hear their conversation but she didn't have to. She saw all that she needed to see and more. Al and Danny were lovers and she never suspected a thing. She'd been around them more times than she could count and it went right over her head. As far as she knew, they had a falling out in high school and hated each other. Nix remained friends with them both, but the three of them rarely hung out at the same time. Dior thought that he told her everything when they were together but he failed to mention that his two best friends were gay. Al kept a woman on his arm so that was news to her.

"Nah, your sticky fingers is why he don't fuck with you no more. Mind your business Dior. What I do has nothing to do with you."

"I wonder how Kinsley would feel if she knew what was going on. I'm sure she wouldn't even let Alexa come around you and her uncle Danny anymore if she did," Dior smirked menacingly.

Al's heart dropped when she said that. His daughter was his world and he would never do anything to jeopardize his relationship with her. There would be no doubt in his mind about what Kinsley would do. She used to try to keep his daughter away when she suspected him of dealing with other women. He probably would never see his daughter again if she found out that he was with Danny. Not to mention the backlash that he would receive from his family.

"What do you want Dior?"

"Who, me?" She smirked while pointing to herself.

"I don't have time to play these lil childish ass games with you."

"We're friends Al. Why would you think I'd want anything from you? Maybe you can be a sweetheart and reserve me and my girls a spot in VIP sometimes. You know, just to be nice. You can also keep our glasses filled when we're here. You know, since we're friends and all."

"Yeah, I hear you." Al frowned.

"Thanks bestie. I'll see you inside." Dior got back into her car and drove back up front, leaving Al standing there alone.

"Fuck!" Al yelled as he punched the dumpster.

He was pissed with himself for being so careless with Danny. If he were keeping it real, he hated himself for not being honest about who he really was. One thing he knew for sure and that was something had to give. There was no way in hell he could be Dior's puppet since she knew his secret. Unfortunately, he knew that that was exactly what was about to happen.

"Are you nervous?" Nix asked as he held Gianni's hand.

"No. Are you?" she countered.

"Nah, I'm straight. I mean, I want my people to like you but that won't change my mind about being with you if they don't."

"Same here. It'll make it easier if we do get along though."

Nix nodded his head in agreement because he felt the exact same way. Quick and Nichelle's opinion didn't matter to him, but he wanted his grandparents to like her. Gianni didn't seem like she was scared and that made him feel better. Her opinion mattered too but not more than theirs.

"We're here," Nix said when they pulled up into the driveway of a beautifully landscaped ranch style home.

The front porch wrapped all the way around to the back with lots of rocking chairs on it. Gianni hadn't even gotten out of the car and she loved the cozy feel of the home already. She could just see herself sitting on the shaded porch doing homework or reading one of her books. It looked even better up close and personal.

"I love this," Gianni said, motioning to the porch and chairs.

"Yeah, this is my mama's favorite spot. She'll be out here all day sometimes."

"I can see why."

Nix grabbed her hand and walked up to the door. He used his key to enter the home and the aroma of whatever was cooking hit them as soon as they walked in.

"Ma!" Nix yelled as he and Gianni stood in the living room.

He didn't want to venture too far into the house until they were invited. His grandmother was old school and she did things a certain way. Nix heard her footsteps getting closer until she walked into the living room. She had a big smile on her face until she looked over at them.

"Lord, have mercy! Gianni! Oh baby! Come here and give me a hug!" Mrs. Flo yelled. She didn't wait for Gianni to come to her. She walked over and pulled her into a bone crushing hug.

"Hey Mrs. Flo." Gianni smiled while hugging her back.

"Where have you been girl? I tried calling to check on you one day and the number was changed."

"Yeah, I lost my phone and all of my contacts a while ago."

"What am I missing here? How do you know my grandmother?" Nix asked.

"This is Agnes' granddaughter. JB! Come in here!" Mrs. Flo yelled, calling her husband.

"Damn, this is a small world. Your grandmother used to come over here all the time," Nix said while looking at Gianni.

Ms. Agnes and his grandmother had been friends for years. They were also good friends with Al's grandparents, who used to oversee the church that they went to. Al grew up right next door to Nix, which was how they became good friends. His grandmother still lived there but his grandfather died. That was how his mother, Amelia, became the pastor of the church. She was also the reason why so many members left, according to Flo.

"Girl, look at you. How have you been?" JB smiled when he walked into the living room and saw Gianni.

You're The Best Part

"Hey Mr. Jessie. I'm good. How about you?" Gianni replied as she hugged him.

"You just know the whole family, huh?" Nix smirked.

He was actually happy that Gianni was already familiar with his family. He used to go to church with them sometimes when he was younger but they never forced him to. He never saw Gianni there though or maybe he was too young to remember her. She didn't really become an active member until she went to live with her grandmother. Before, she just used to visit. By then, Nix hadn't gone in years. Al went more than he did but he didn't really have a choice in the matter. He had probably stopped going by the time Gianni became a member.

"I can't believe that you're the girlfriend that my baby has been telling us about." Flo smiled.

"I guess that means that you approve." Nix smiled.

"Yes, I do. Come on in the kitchen Gianni. We can play catch up while I put the finishing touches on this food."

Gianni followed his grandmother to the kitchen while Nix sat in the living room and talked to his grandfather. JB explained to him how Gianni unselfishly put her life on hold, not once but twice, to look after her mother and grandmother. He told him about her sad ass brother too, but Gianni had already filled him in about that. Nix had a newfound respect for Gianni and he was happy that she decided to give him a chance.

"Damn man. How can you pimp your own mama?" Nix said while shaking his head.

"Janessa wasn't a child. She knew what she was doing and she made a choice to do it. She took good care of her daughter though."

Nix knew that to be true just by the many conversations that he and Gianni had. Despite her situation when she got older, Gianni had a pretty good childhood. She was loved and well taken care of. The photo album that she showed him reflected that. She and her mother were close. They vacationed often and spent a lot of time together.

JB also filled him in on Kori's mother, Karen. Apparently, she was a piece of work and he understood why Kori behaved the way that she did. It was learned behavior. It was fucked up that Gianni considered Kori to be one of her best friends. He didn't know her cousin very well but he knew that the feelings weren't mutual. Gianni told him that she lived with her aunt for a while but she put her out once she got another man. Nix didn't even know Karen but he didn't like her already.

"The food is done! Y'all come wash up so we can eat," Flo yelled into the living room.

The four of them talked for hours as they ate. It was after eight that night when Nix and Gianni finally left and they had been there since around one. His grandmother made them promise to come back the following week and they happily agreed.

"I can't believe that Pastor Amelia is Al's mother. She's a mess," Gianni said as Nix drove them home.

She remembered a lot of the younger members stopped going to the church because of the new pastor. She used the pulpit to condemn the way they dressed, among other things. She frowned down on everything and a lot of the older members didn't agree with all the changes that she'd made. They weren't used to having ATM's in the lobby or deacons walking around with credit card swipers on their phones. She sometimes gave a shout out to the highest tithers and they hated that more than anything.

"Man, you have no idea. I be feeling bad for my boy sometimes. She don't give Al a break," Nix said while shaking his head.

"I can only imagine," Gianni said when they pulled up to the house. Gianni's car, as well as Nix's other truck, was parked in the garage. She didn't know who the silver Benz belonged to that was parked in the driveway, but he didn't seem too happy about it.

"Man fuck!" Nix was heated as he used his remote to open his garage.

"Who is that?" Gianni could see that it was a woman just by the hair but she couldn't make out who it was.

"Nobody important. Go inside baby. Let me get rid of her annoying ass."

Gianni was about to snap on him but she decided to let it go. She would just wait until she got inside to look at the cameras to see exactly who it was that had him so annoyed. They walked into the house together, but Nix went back outside through the front door. Gianni looked at the camera right as Dior walked over to him.

"Who was that Nix? Huh? You bringing these hoes to your house now?" Dior fumed.

"Nah, my girl lives here but that ain't none of your fucking business. I've asked you more than once not to come to my house. I'm trying to be grown about this shit but it's getting old."

"Your girl! Since when do you have a girlfriend, Jacobi?"

"Leave Dior. Don't make me be petty and get some paperwork on your ass."

"I can't believe that you're doing this to me. I fucked up but I made it right. You're willing to throw away all our years and history over one stupid mistake. The only mistake that I've ever made since we've been together. That's not fair Nix and you know it."

Dior was crying from somewhere deep within. True, months had passed since she and Nix broke up but, to her knowledge, he'd never had another woman. If he did, he never claimed her or was seen out in public with her. Dior was just about to leave until she saw him pulling up. She saw that he had a female passenger but his windows were too dark for her to make out who she was. Nichelle's fortieth birthday was coming up in two months and she wanted to talk to him about giving his mother a surprise party at his club. His birthday was coming up too, but she was sure that he wasn't going to include her in whatever plans he made. She tried calling him but he never answered his phone for her.

Gianni had seen and heard enough. Nix looked like he was aggravated but he was still out there entertaining his ex. Maybe he felt sorry for her but she wasn't about to sit around while he consoled her. She went upstairs to Nix's bedroom and grabbed some clothes and other items. She went back to the bedroom that she once occupied and started the shower.

Once he got rid of Dior, Nix went inside in search of Gianni. When he didn't see her upstairs in his bedroom, he went back down to the room that she once occupied. He heard the shower water running, so he sat on the bed and waited until she was done.

Gianni jumped when she walked out of the bathroom and saw Nix sitting on the bed. She dropped the towel that was wrapped around her waist and slipped on one of his oversized t-shirts. She lotioned her body and put on her bonnet, never even acknowledging him.

"You just gon' ignore me like you don't see me sitting here," Nix said while looking at her.

"Would you rather I dismissed you like you just did me a little while ago?"

"I apologize but I didn't dismiss you. I just wanted Dior to go on about her business without all the added drama."

"Or maybe you didn't want your old bitch to run into your new one."

"I don't have a problem with people knowing that we're together. You were the one who wanted to be discreet with it. I know you only said that to spare your hoe ass cousin's feelings. I don't know why because she damn sure wouldn't have done the same for you. Hell, she was the reason why it took us so long to get together."

"This ain't about Kori, so don't change the subject and bring her into it. It's real strange to me how your ex-fiancée feels so comfortable just popping up over here."

"You act like I invited the bitch over here."

"Did you?" Gianni asked.

"Are you serious right now Gianni? I was done with Dior for months before I even knew you. If I wanted to be with her, I could have done that shit a long time ago."

"I'm going to bed Nix. Good night."

She pulled the covers back on the bed and laid down. She turned her back to him, signaling the end of their conversation.

"You ain't sleeping in here. We're not even about to start that shit."

"Turn the light off on your way out," Gianni replied before she pulled the covers up to her neck.

"Man, I don't even have time for this bullshit," Nix fumed as he walked away. He turned the light off and slammed the door before he headed upstairs to take a shower and go to bed.

Chapter 9

Gianna was awakened from a deep sleep by the best feeling ever. She instinctively rotated her hips and grabbed the back of Nix's head that was positioned between her legs. He parted his full lips and sucked her clit up into his mouth. They were both moaning as he twisted his head from side to side. He alternated from sucking to rapidly flicking his tongue over her sensitive flesh.

"Shit, don't stop baby," Gianni begged as she humped his face.

"I couldn't sleep. Don't be mad at me," Nix said as he looked up at her.

The lamp in the room gave off just enough light for them to be able to see each other. He was kissing the insides of her thighs in between talking to her. He tossed and turned for over an hour before he got up to go make up with Gianni. He didn't want her to think that he was on no dumb shit with Dior because that would never happen.

"I'm not mad with you."

She was at first but she had time to think about it before she went to sleep. Nix couldn't control Dior's actions and it wasn't fair for her to take that out on him. She planned to talk to him about it first thing in the morning, but he beat her to it.

"I'm falling baby. I'm falling hard and fast."

He wasn't afraid to express himself vocally. In the short time that he'd known her, Gianni had already secured a place in his heart. Their bond wasn't as strong as the one he had with Dior but that took years to build. He was confident that with time, he and Gianni could have something even stronger. They started out with honesty and that was what he loved the most.

"Me too," Gianni admitted. She didn't know if she was making a mistake by moving so fast with Nix but only time would tell.

"Do you remember the night you slept in your car outside of the police station?"

"Yeah? What about it?" Gianni was writhing underneath him. He was teasing her with his warm breath and the tip of his tongue. He was in the mood to talk, but she wanted him to use his mouth for something else.

"I was out there with you. I wanted to make sure you were okay, so I slept in my truck and watched you all night," Nix confessed right before he started flicking his tongue up and down her lower lips again.

You're The Best Part

Gianni stiffened at his admittance as a lone tear rolled down her cheek. It was crazy how a man who hardly knew her cared about her so much. He was her silent protector and she would be forever grateful for him. Nix was the one. Almost twenty-five years of saving herself just for him. She grabbed him by his shoulders and pulled him up on top of her. She captured his lips in a passionate kiss, tasting her salty sweetness on his tongue.

"Put it in," Gianni said as she reached in between them and grabbed his erection. Nix looked at her skeptically as if he was contemplating her request.

"Are you sure that you're ready? There's no rush love, I promise."

"I know. I'm ready. Just go slow."

Nix was hesitating, so Gianni got the ball rolling. She opened her legs wider and grabbed his dick. She didn't know what she was doing and she was happy when he decided to take over.

"I don't have any condoms," Nix said.

"We don't need them. I know you're good."

Gianni was nervous but she trusted him. He was clean and she had the paperwork to prove it. She'd come to the realization that it wasn't just sex that she really feared. It was the thought of dying from it that frightened her. She was no fool and she knew that her mother's illegal profession and numerous sex partners was the cause of her diagnosis. She was only trying to make money. It wasn't like she screened any of the men that she slept with. Unlike Biggie, Nix showed her different levels of intimacy. He also eased her fears when he got a clean bill of health and she was ready to take their new relationship to the next level.

"Are you really sure about this baby? I don't want you to wake up in the morning with regrets."

"I'm sure and I'm ready."

"We might need some lubricant.

"I'm wet enough. Maybe it's you who's not ready."

"I'm always ready but this is a big decision. It's not like you can change your mind tomorrow. Once you lose it, you can't get it back."

"Thanks for the speech, now put it in."

"Just promise that you'll let me know if the pain is too much for you."

"I promise," Gianni replied nervously.

She said that she was wet enough, but Nix wanted to be sure. He captured her lips in a passionate kiss as he inserted his middle finger inside of her. Gianni grinded on his hand while arching her back. She moaned into his mouth right as he inserted another finger. Gianni almost jumped out of the bed, but his grip on her was too tight. She was soaking wet when Nix pulled his fingers out of her.

"Relax baby," Nix coaxed as he lined his erection up at her opening.

Gianni nodded as she prepared for the pain that she'd heard so much about. Nix kissed her as he pushed his way into her virgin walls.

"Ummm," Gianni groaned into his mouth.

It hurt but it wasn't unbearable like Kori and so many others told her it would be. It was more uncomfortable than anything but the hard part was over with.

"You good?" Nix asked while looking down at her.

"Yeah, I'm okay. Am I bleeding?"

"No, you're good," Nix replied as he looked down in between them to check.

Once he was sure that she was alright, Nix started moving slowly inside of her. Gianni frowned because it still hurt a little. After a while, the pain slowly started to subside. She wrapped her arms around Nix's neck as he continued to stroke her. The more he opened her up, the better it started to feel. He was moaning in her ear, telling her how good she felt and she was starting to feel the same way. She was inexperienced, so she really didn't know what to do. Kori always told her that men hated a boring sex partner and she knew that's exactly what she was. Just that fast, Gianni started to feel self-conscience. It was almost as if Nix had read her mind when he spoke up.

"Don't worry about nothing baby. I'm gonna teach you everything that you need to know. Just follow my lead. If you don't like something, let me know."

"Okay." Gianni nodded, as Nix continued to stroke her into ecstasy and give her pointers in the bedroom. After a few more minutes, he pulled out of her again and sat up.

"Turn over and lay on your stomach," he instructed.

Gianni wasted no time doing what he told her to do. She laid on her stomach and waited for him to give her further instruction. Nix pulled her up to her knees and pushed her head down into the mattress. Once she had the perfect arch in her back, he entered her again and grabbed her hips. Gianni gasped when he started moving faster. She felt his balls slapping against her clit and that was the best feeling in the world.

"This feels good baby. Don't stop," Gianni moaned, enjoying the new position that he'd put her in. She felt every inch of him and she knew that sex with Nix was about to be her new favorite thing to do.

"I got you, love," Nix replied as he slapped her ass and continued to please her.

He had to learn Gianni's body but he was up for the challenge. He was happy that she wasn't shy and she told him exactly what she liked. Nix had fun teaching her a few new things. He was sure that it was only the first time of many.

"Are you sure that it'll be okay for me to be off for an entire week?" Gianni asked as she and Nix took a shower.

A little over two weeks had passed since he took her virginity and she was hooked. It was crazy how Gianni went from never having sex before to wanting it multiple times a day. Nix was just as bad and he wanted it just as much. He taught Gianni how to please him and he learned how to satisfy her too. She was still a beginner but she caught on quick. Gianni wasted no time getting back on her birth control because she had a reason to take them now. It turned Nix on to know that he was the first and only man to receive all that she had to offer. Besides Dior, she was the first virgin that he'd ever been with. Nichelle really liked her, but Quick thought he was moving too fast. Nix didn't give a damn what either of them thought. His grandparents gave their stamp of approval and their opinions were the only ones that mattered.

"Stop acting like it's not my club. You can take off however long you want to," Nix replied after a while.

"Nix, no. I told you that I don't want any special treatment."

"You're already getting special treatment. Not every bottle girl can fuck the boss in his office on her lunch break." Nix laughed at the expression on Gianni's face.

"Don't get one of them hoes cut."

"I'm just fucking with you, baby. But seriously, you're good love."

"I just don't wanna leave Al in a bind. I haven't even been working fulltime that long."

"Al is good. We already discussed it. He said the three new girls that he just hired can handle it."

Nichelle had planned a couple's vacation to Jamaica for her fortieth birthday and she invited them to come along. Neither of them had ever been before, so they were looking forward to it. Nix thought it was funny but cute that Gianni paid for the entire trip. He called to give Nichelle his credit card info, but she had beat him to it. She had a heart of gold to say that she didn't have very much. She paid for all the groceries and other household necessities on top of giving him money for rent. She was selfless with the little that she had and that only made him want to give her more. She never asked him for anything and he never heard her complain.

"Okay. I've already emailed my professors. I only have two in-person classes. The rest are online. I'll be done with my assignments before we go."

"Do you ever talk to your auntie?" Nix asked, referring to Kori's mother.

That was a question that he'd always wanted to ask since Gianni never really talked about her. Karen was her only auntie and he found that odd. He didn't talk to his aunts and uncles every day but he did see them sometimes.

"Only when she's calling to beg."

"You can't be serious. You better not give her a muthafucking thing!"

Nix was heated and he couldn't hide his feelings even if he tried. Karen was a selfish bitch and he knew that just by some of the things that he heard Gianni say about her. Kori was definitely her mother's child and that wasn't hard to see.

"It's okay. She never really ask for much."

"No, it's not okay. I'm sorry baby but fuck her and her daughter. Ain't no way in hell you should have been living in no shelter and they both have a roof over their heads. It might not bother you but it disturbs the fuck out of me."

"I know Nix and I get it. I used to question it a lot too, but I'm over it now. My grandma used to always say that you can't expect you from other people. It took me a long time to get it but I finally understand what she meant."

"Nah, I don't agree with that. I'm your man and I want you to expect the world from me. And you should leave me the fuck alone if I don't provide it for you. You were surrounded by a bunch of self-serving muthafuckers but it's all good. I dare anybody to ask you for anything now. You ain't got it and I'll be happy to tell them if you don't want to."

"I sure don't," Gianni agreed with a nod of her head.

Once they took their showers, Nix got dressed and left about an hour before she did. Al was interviewing another bartender and he needed Nix to sit in to get his input. It was another word of mouth thing, so he didn't go through the whole process of making her fill out an application. It was someone who Vic, one of the bouncers, knew and Al was doing him a favor.

After she was dressed, Gianni took some meat out of the freezer and put it in the sink to thaw out. Nix had been begging her to cook another pot roast and she promised him that she would. When she got dressed, she set the alarm and locked up the house. As soon as she pulled up to the club, Kori pulled up right beside her. They got out of their cars at the same time and walked up to the employee's entrance.

"What's going on with you stranger? We work together and I feel like I barely see you anymore," Kori said while looking at her cousin.

"Nothing much girl. Same shit as always. Work and school." Gianni shrugged.

"Bitch! When did you get a tattoo?"

Kori was full of ink, but Gianni didn't have any. She now had a set of praying hands with a bible and cross. Her mother and their grandmother's name, along with the dates they died, were underneath. It was beautiful but Kori was shocked that she had it.

"Oh, I got that a few days ago when you were off." Nix went to get another tattoo and Gianni decided to get one too. It hurt like hell but it was well worth it. She loved her tribute to two of the most important women in her life.

191

"You've been acting some funny lately. We barely talk anymore if we're not at work. I was off for a few days and you didn't answer for me once."

"I did call to check on you. How do you feel?"

Kori had been sick for the past few days and she hadn't been at work. At least that was the story that she told everyone. In actuality, she took a flight to get rid of the unwanted pregnancy that threatened to disrupt her life. She wasn't ready for kids, especially since she didn't really know who the father was. Besides her man, Kori had been fucking with Nix's cousin, Ryan, as well as Vic. She never did tell her boyfriend about it but she had Ryan and Vic both thinking that the baby was theirs. Ryan had a girl and Vic had a wife. They both wasted no time giving her the money to get rid of it. Vic went as far as paying for her flight and hotel stay too. His niece, Amya, accompanied her there since she and Kori were cool. Hopefully, she would be bartending there if Al decided to hire her like Vic had asked him to.

"I'm okay girl. I gotta work extra hard to get my money back up. You know how much I hate missing out on my tips," Kori said when they walked into the breakroom.

They were both shocked to see a huge bouquet of beautiful flowers sitting on the counter. Gianni's name was written big on the card that Kori snatched out of them. She was about to open it until Gianni took it from her.

"Excuse you. When did you change your name to Gianni?"

She rolled her eyes as she walked away and opened the card. She was smiling too hard as she read what it said. Nix was always full of surprises and she loved it. That was his third time buying her flowers, but he had the first two bouquets delivered to the house. He was always thinking of her and that was the best feeling ever.

192

"No need to ask who they're from. I better be the only nigga sending you flowers," Kori said, reading the card out loud.

"You are so nosy."

Gianni put her flowers away when the other employees started filing into the room. She didn't know them like that and she was hoping that Kori left it alone. That was too much like right. Her cousin followed her around the breakroom, still asking her a bunch of questions.

"Why are you being so secretive? I tell you everything. Let me find out that you ain't a virgin no more. Spill the tea bitch."

"There's nothing to spill. It ain't like it's the first time I got flowers."

"Yeah but it's been a minute. And don't think I missed the way you ignored my statement about you still being a virgin. Who's the new man?" Kori asked, right as Al walked into the room.

"G, you already know where your spot is. Everybody else, listen up for your work assignments!" he yelled. As soon as he was done, everyone left to go do their own thing.

"How did you get a permanent spot upstairs?" Kori asked as they walked up to the bar.

"I don't know. Ask Al." Gianni shrugged. She smiled when she saw Nichelle walking over to her. She stopped and spoke to a few people before she got over there.

"Hey boo. I hope you're ready. We got three more weeks and it's on!" Nichelle yelled over the music. She gave Gianni a hug and spoke to Kori.

"Yeah, I'm ready. What are you drinking? You can go upstairs and I'll bring it to you." Gianni was trying to get rid of her before she said too much.

"Thanks boo. Bring me a strawberry Hennessey when you get a minute." Nichelle barely walked away before Kori started being nosy again.

"Girl nah. When did you get cool with her?" Kori asked, referring to Nix's mother.

"Bitch, you sure got a lot of questions tonight. She's always in VIP and we talk a lot. Anything else you wanna know?"

"No need to get snappy boo. I was just asking. I don't care about being cool with the mama. I'm fucking the son, not her," Kori replied as she did a little dance.

She hadn't said anything about Nix in a while and Gianni thought she had given up. Obviously, she hadn't since she was still on that dumb shit. Things were different now though. Nix was no longer just a nigga who was crushing on Gianni. He was her man now. The same man who took her virginity. The same one who she shared space with and was slowly falling in love with. Kori needed to know that her lies had caught up with her.

"How long are you gonna keep up with that lie?" Gianni asked.

"Why would I have to lie about something like that?"

"That's what I've been trying to figure out. You ain't fucking Nix and you never were. You've never even seen him outside of the club and I heard that from your own mouth."

Gianni laughed as she shook her head and walked away. Kori was pissed as she watched her cousin go to the upper level. She was confused as to how Gianni knew that since she and Nix were the only two in the room at the time when she said it. She was embarrassed to think that Nix confided in her cousin about their conversation. Since Gianni worked upstairs so much, they seemed to have gotten awfully close. They talked all the time and she always saw him watching her cousin. She stared as Gianni went over to Nichelle and took a seat. They started talking and laughing like old friends and she wished she could have heard what they were saying.

"Are you here to work or daydream?" Al asked when he walked up on her.

"Sorry Al." Kori grabbed her ice bucket and got to work.

Hours had passed and she was still in her feelings about what Gianni had said. She wanted to go upstairs and finish their conversation, but Nix was up there. She didn't want to have an argument with her cousin in his presence. She did want to tell Gianni off though. She also knew that her cousin wasn't a pushover and wasn't gonna let her have the last word. She had Kori fucked up though and she couldn't wait to tell her that. They had about another hour until closing time and she was happy that they were parked right next to each other.

Kori was supposed to be hooking up with Ryan but she was too aggravated to think about it. It pissed her off to see Gianni prancing around the club like she owned the place. She had confidence that wasn't there before and Kori wondered why. It was like she was a part of Nix's inner circle and she hated that the most. She was so busy watching her cousin, she didn't even see when someone walked over to her. Kori dropped the ice bucket that was in her hand when she was hit from the side. The lick dazed her but not for long. Kori was livid when she saw Ryan's girlfriend,

195

Krista, standing there. The other woman tried to rush her, but she was ready for her.

Kori hit her with a vicious right hook that made her stumble. When Krista got right, she started swinging again. People moved out of the way as she and Kori went into a vicious mix. They were both holding their own until Krista's sister decided to jump in. They were tagging Kori from the front and the back but she was still going strong. She was getting tired and feeling like she was about to fall. Just went she'd given up hope, there was a little light at the end of the tunnel.

"Y'all got life fucked up!" Gianni yelled as she pulled Krista's sister off of her cousin and starting swinging on her.

Kori was so thankful for her cousin. Krista started getting the best of her, but she had a better chance in a one on one fight. The club was in an uproar as the bouncers made their way through the crowd. Nix was heated as he raced down the stairs to get Gianni. He had just walked into his office right before the fight started. He was gonna let the bouncers handle it until he looked on the camera and saw that it was Gianni's slutty ass cousin. He knew how she was and he knew that it was only a matter of time before she went to go help her. He was right because she was already swinging by the time he got up from his desk. He didn't want the bouncers to manhandle his girl. They would be looking for another job if they did.

"Aye, get these hoes the fuck up out of my club!" Nix yelled as he picked Gianni up.

Heavy and Vic sprang right into action and did their jobs. He didn't give a fuck about Krista being his cousin's girl. She had him fucked up. Coming to his club to fight wasn't a good look and she should have known better.

"Nasty ass bitch! This ain't over hoe! You fucked the wrong nigga!" Krista yelled as she was being led out of the club.

"Are you serious right now Gianni?" Nix asked as he looked at her and frowned.

"What did you want me to do? They were jumping my cousin."

"Go sit in my office and don't come out until the club is closed!" Nix yelled as he looked at her.

Kori looked at her cousin in shock, waiting for her to go off on him. Gianni was flip as hell and she popped off for less. When she saw her cousin turn to walk away, she was more confused than ever.

"Thanks for having my back cousin! I'll call you later!" Kori yelled to her departing back.

"You can clock out and go home."

Nix looked at Kori with disgust as she hurriedly walked away. She wasn't trippin' because the club was about to close anyway. She had made more than enough tips so she was straight. Something was up with Gianni though and she wasn't gonna rest until she found out what it was.

Chapter 10

Gianni walked into the bathroom to brush her teeth. Nix was standing at the double sink washing his face but he didn't bother saying anything to her. Three days had passed since she helped her cousin fight at the club and he was still pissed about it. They argued about it and ended up going to bed mad at each other. That didn't stop him from waking her up for sex all times of the night though. Since Gianni always wanted it too, she never turned him down.

"How long are we gonna do this Nix?" Gianni asked.

"I'm good baby. We talked about it and I'm done

with it."

"Obviously not since you're still clearly upset about it."

"I'm not upset, I'm aggravated. I get that your family is small baby, but fuck that. You be doing shit for people that they wouldn't even attempt to do for you. Do you honestly think that Kori would have broken her neck to help you fight if the roles were reversed?"

"Yes, I do," Gianni answered confidently.

"See, and that pisses me off too. You give that hoe too much credit."

"Can you please stop being disrespectful?" Gianni asked while brushing her teeth.

"Man, fuck her. We can't even be out in the open with our relationship because you're trying to spare her feelings. It's like what I say don't even matter."

"Everything that you say matters Nix. You never make a big deal out of anything, so I just assumed that you be okay with it."

"Nah, it's a lot of shit that I'm not okay with. I let a lot of shit ride because of my feelings for you."

"Okay. Tell me what you don't like and we can fix it. We're too grown to be walking around not speaking to each other. You know how to talk when you want some pussy though."

"I'll never be too mad for that," Nix assured her.

"But, seriously baby, my feelings aren't the only ones that matter. I want to know how you feel about everything so we can be on the same page."

"Well, for one, I don't want our relationship to be a secret. I don't give a fuck what nobody has to say or what they think."

"Okay, I can respect that. I'll let Kori know that we're together."

"I'm not asking you to do that. I just don't want you to deny it when she finds out. Don't try to spare her feelings because she wouldn't try to spare yours."

"Anything else?"

"Give me a kiss," Nix demanded as he pulled her close.

He missed their daily talks, but Gianni pissed him off. She was out there fighting for Kori when she didn't even know what was going on. Her cousin was a hoe and she was gonna stay in fights when she fucked with other women's men. He just didn't want his girl to get caught up in all their bullshit.

"I gotta go baby. I'm meeting a few of my classmates at the campus library to get some last minute studying done for this test. I'll see you later." Gianni gave him one last peck on the lips before she got dressed and left.

Nix got dressed and left soon after she did. He needed to check on things at the construction company and he had a few contracts to negotiate. Things were always tense when he went there because his uncle Jessie was still in his feelings about Nix owning the place. He didn't like answering to his nephew but he really didn't have a choice. Jessie was even mad that Nix didn't let him have the office. There was no need for him to even be in there since he didn't know how to do anything dealing with paperwork.

"What's up nephew?" Jessie asked when Nix walked into the building. He was sitting behind the receptionist desk with his feet propped up. It was too early for him to be on break, but he was the manager and Nix wasn't trying to be petty.

"Ain't shit. Just coming through to do some work. Where is she?" Nix asked, pointing to the desk that belonged to the receptionist.

"Bitch called off again. All she do is party and drink. She might be hungover somewhere. I think it's time for her to be replaced."

"You're the manager. Replace her." Nix was walking to his office but his uncle's next words stopped him.

"Yeah, my daughter-in-law is looking for a job. I might hire her."

"What daughter-in-law?"

"Krista. Her job just relocated to Mississippi and she got laid off."

"Nah, she ain't coming to work here."

"Why not? Like you just said, I'm the manager." Jessie put his feet on the floor before he stood up.

"Man look, this ain't no pissing contest. You can hire whoever you want just as long as it's not Krista. You already know that's not a good look for business. Her and Ryan working together is a recipe for disaster. They can barely live together without trying to kill each other."

"I'll make sure that she behaves herself."

"I know she will because she's not coming to work here. Don't get her hopes up high only to get her fired. Ain't no compromising on that one."

"Man, JB better do something about this shit," Jessie argued.

He was always threatening to get JB involved as if Nix was supposed to be scared. His grandfather didn't care how he ran his businesses, just as long as he got the cut that they agreed upon every month. When JB retired, he didn't look back. He didn't even discuss the businesses because they were no longer his to worry about. Everybody adjusted to the changes eventually but his uncle was still salty about the shit.

Jessie was mumbling under his breath as he walked away, but Nix didn't give a fuck. The nigga was over fifty years old and childish as fuck. He was like a spoiled kid when he didn't get his way. After battling with drug addiction for most of his life, he should have been happy for second chances. Jessie was good with his hands and that was the only thing that worked in his favor. JB was ready to wash his hands with him until he went to rehab.

After about three hours of work, Nix locked up his office and decided to go see Quick. His father was outside washing Nichelle's car when he pulled up. She was sitting in the living room but she went out and sat on the porch when she saw him. Nix sparked up a blunt and passed it back and forth with his mother while talking to his father.

"Man, your brother gon' make me fuck him up," Nix said as he handed the blunt back to Nichelle.

"Which one?" Quick stopped to look up at his son, letting him know that he had his undivided attention.

"Who else? Jessie ole complaining ass. Nigga was talking about getting rid of the receptionist and hiring Krista. He got me fucked up with that one."

"Why would he even think about doing something so stupid? He know how much Ryan and that girl fight. I'm sorry that they're coming on my birthday trip. I know Gianni beat her sister up and she might be in her feelings about it."

"Fuck her. As long as she don't tell my girl nothing, it's all good. Her and Ryan can get dealt with in New Orleans or Jamaica."

"I know that's right. I like Gianni, so I'm already on her side."

"I might need to go pay that nigga Jessie a visit. I be trying to stay out of the shit but he already know that I'm not the one for him to fuck with."

"You don't need to tell that nigga nothing on my behalf. I can handle me. It was all love with us before JB gave me the businesses. That nigga Ryan used to be in his feelings too but he got over it eventually."

"His daddy better get over it too. I'm going to war over mine and I'm sure they don't want these troubles," Quick said, right as a car was pulling up in front of their house. When Nix saw who it was, he knew that it was time for him to go.

"I'll see y'all later. I'm gone."

He got up and walked to his car, right as Dior was getting out of hers. Quick was done with his wife's car, so he went inside when his son's ex-girlfriend sat on the porch with his wife.

"What's up with you, girl?" Nichelle asked Dior.

"Nothing much. I had a doctor's appointment, so I was off today. Did you ever figure out what you wanted to do for your birthday? I was trying to get with your son to make something happen but shit went left."

"Girl, I'm going to Jamaica. My sisters and a few other people are coming too and I can't wait."

"Why didn't you tell me? I got some vacation time at work. I could have put in to have some days off. When are y'all leaving?"

"Nix is coming and I don't want it to be no drama."

"Really Nichelle? Nix and I aren't together anymore but I would never try to ruin your birthday."

"His girlfriend is coming too," Nichelle said, making Dior's heart drop.

"What girlfriend? Who is she?"

"That's not my place to tell you all that."

"Wow. So, you've met her."

"That's my only son Dior. Of course I met her."

"You must like her if she's going on vacation with y'all and shit."

She knew Nichelle very well. She didn't like to share her personal space with just anybody. She could be mean at times and Dior knew that better than anyone. She had been around for years and that was the only reason why they were so close. To know that she was gonna be bonding with Nix's new girlfriend made her feel some kind of way. She prided herself on being the only woman who had ever met his parents. Now, she wasn't only being pushed away by Nix, Nichelle was inadvertently pushing her away too.

"I do like her. Look Dior, you and I will always be cool but I have to respect my son's decision to move on. I wanted y'all to get back together but that's obviously not what he wants. Don't sit around and let years pass you by waiting for Nix to take you back. He's going on with his life and you need to do the same."

Dior nodded, deciding not to reply. She knew that her voice would crack and the tears that she was trying to hold back would spill over her eyelids. She walked to her car feeling more alone than ever. She already felt rejected by her own family. Now, the only other family that she considered her own were welcoming another woman into their circle. She didn't know who the other woman was but she wasn't gonna rest until she found out. She planned to make her life a living hell whenever she did.

"Hey Heavy," Gianni said when she walked into the VIP section on the upper level.

She was surprised to see Heavy dressed in anything outside of his all black bouncer's uniform. Truthfully, she was shocked to see him anywhere else in the club besides the front door. He looked nice in his jeans, vest, and dress shirt. The term big and tall fit him perfectly but he was a gentle giant.

"What's up Gianni? Are you working this section tonight?" Heavy asked.

"Yeah. What can I get for you?"

"I don't even know what that nigga likes to drink."

"Who?" Gianni questioned.

"My brother."

"Aww, your brother is home. I'm so happy to hear that."

Heavy's only brother had been in jail for over twenty years. He was always sending him money or going to see him. Nadia told Gianni that he was a big time drug dealer who got caught up with a snitch. He was locked up on two manslaughter charges, as well as drug possession. He supposedly left all of his money with Heavy and he refused to touch any of it. Besides paying for a lawyer, Heavy didn't spend a dime of his brother's money, even though his wife wanted him to. She thought her brother-in-law was gonna die in jail but his lawyers made sure that didn't happen. He was given a life sentence but it was reduced to thirty years.

"Yeah, I'm happy as hell too. Boss man gave me the night off and let us have one of the VIP sections."

"Cool and all your drinks are on me. Don't even try to fight me because I'm not taking no for an answer."

"I appreciate you, G, but don't be mad if your tab be a few hundred dollars. Besides my brother, a few of our cousins are coming through. Nadia and her sisters will be here too and they don't know how to sip slow."

"That's okay. I can probably work something out with the boss," she smirked.

"I'm sure you can," Heavy laughed.

Besides Al and Danny, Heavy was the only employee who knew that they were together. He thought they were a good fit and he was happy for them.

Gianni walked downstairs to the bar. Kori was standing there talking to the new bartender, Amya, who she appeared to already know. Nix told her that the newest hire was Vic's niece so that was no surprise, seeing as how Kori was fucking him too. Nix told her about her cousin fucking Ryan and that was one of the reasons why he was pissed at her for helping Kori fight. He felt like she put herself in those situations and she deserved what she was getting.

Kori seemed to be in her feelings since the fight with Krista. She got mad because Gianni didn't put her in her business like she wanted her to. She was doing too much and they ended up arguing a few days ago. Kori went to the shelter looking for her and learned that she was no longer a resident. She questioned Gianni about her living arrangements like she was entitled to some answers. Gianni was so mad that Nix was talking about firing her cousin. She had to talk him out of it and assure him that it wasn't that deep. Kori needed her money and she wasn't trying to see her get done dirty like that.

"What's up y'all. Let me get a few bottles," Gianni requested as she told Amya what she wanted.

"Damn cousin. What's going on up there for somebody to need all that?" Kori asked once Amya walked away.

"Heavy's brother just came home from jail and he's doing something for him." Gianni was void of any emotion and the tension was thick. Kori felt bad about their last argument because she knew that it was her fault.

"Look, I'm sorry about how I came at you the other day. I overstepped and I can admit that. I'm just not used to us keeping secrets from each other."

"It's not that I'm keeping secrets. Shit is just a little more complicated for me to explain." Gianni was no fool and she knew that her cousin wanted Nix. She wasn't trying

208

to seem like she was on no snake shit and she wasn't trying to rub their relationship in Kori's face. They couldn't hide it forever and she wasn't trying to.

"I understand cousin. I hope there are no hard feelings."

"Never that. We're good and we always will be." Kori walked over and bumped hips with her before giving Gianni a one-armed hug.

"Maybe we can hook up this weekend and do something before work. Let's do lunch and shopping."

"I can't. My entire week is booked but I'll be free the week after."

They were leaving for Jamaica over the weekend and Gianni couldn't wait. She hadn't had a vacation in a while and she was looking forward to it. She hadn't turned up in a minute and Nix was about to see the other side of her soon. Kori was about to reply until Amya walked back over with Gianni's liquor.

"I got you, G. I'll take the rest," Al offered when he walked over. Gianni grabbed a few bottles and walked away while he grabbed the others and followed her. Al cringed when he saw Dior heading in his direction.

"What's good Al? I need a spot in VIP. I know you got me, right," Dior smirked. Al wanted to grab her by the sleek ponytail that she was wearing and sling her down the stairs.

"Yeah, I got you. What are you sippin' on tonight?"

"Nothing yet. I'm waiting on my girls to get here. We'll put in our orders then." Dior walked over to the section that Al told her was hers. She was right across from Nix's personal spot, so she would be able to watch him all night.

"Why did you sit her there? You know Nix is gonna have a fit," Gianni whispered as she looked back at Al.

"That nigga ain't worried about her stupid ass. Besides, that was the only spot available."

Gianni set Heavy's section up for him while Al went on his way. About an hour later, Nadia and her crew showed up with Heavy's brother and cousins. She had never seen Heavy smile so much since she met him, but he seemed genuinely happy. She could tell that he and his brother were close and they almost looked like twins.

"What's your name sweetheart?" Heavy's brother, Gio, yelled over the music and asked her.

"Gianni. Can I get something for you?"

"What's your last name?"

"Porter."

"Who are you related to Gianni?"

"What do you mean?" she asked in confusion.

"Your family. Who is your parents, siblings, shit like that?"

"Um, my mom's name was Janessa, but she died. My aunt's name is Karen and her daughter's name is Kori. My family is small but I doubt if you know any of them."

"What about you? Are you married or have any kids?"

"Chill out bro," Heavy said while placing a hand on his brother's chest.

"I'm not even doing shit. I'm just trying to make conversation," Gio replied innocently.

Gianni had walked off by then, but Heavy saw Nix motioning for him to come over. Nix walked towards his office and Heavy got up and followed behind him.

"What's good boss man?"

"I know it's your brother's first day out and shit but I need fam to chill. He's been watching my girl all night and I'm not feeling that shit. He can have whoever he wants but Gianni is off limits."

Nix had been watching the cameras all night and peeped what was going on. He wasn't in a hurry to go to his section since Dior and her crew would be sitting right next to him. Heavy's brother couldn't seem to keep his eyes off of Gianni. She wasn't paying attention but he watched her every move.

"I apologize bruh, but I'll get that nigga in check. Nigga bout to get fucked up on his first day home," Heavy laughed.

"Nah, I ain't even on it like that. He don't know what's up. I just don't want it to be no beef over something that can be avoided."

"I understand boss man and I'm on it," Heavy assured him before leaving his office.

Nix continued to watch the cameras as Heavy made his way over to his people. He sat down next to his brother and started a conversation with him. The other man nodded as Heavy whispered in his ear. He stole another quick glance at Gianni before he picked up his drink and start sippin'. Things seemed to be calm for a while and they had about another hour until the club closed. Nix stayed in his office most of the time because he wasn't trying to look in Dior's face. He monitored the cameras all night, so he didn't miss anything. He was just about to send Gianni a text when he saw her on the bottom level arguing with someone.

211

Besides Kori, there were about eight other men in the section. Nix jumped over his desk and took the stairs two at a time, trying to get to her as fast as he could.

"Don't put your muthafucking hands on me!" Gianni yelled.

"Relax cousin. You got people looking over here like something is wrong," Kori said.

"I don't give a fuck. Why would you even call me over here for him?"

"Damn, I didn't know it was that serious."

"What's wrong G?" Nix asked once he made it to her.

"Nothing, I'm good."

Nix did a double take when he saw a familiar face sitting amongst the crowd of men. Jaron, or Ronnie as he was known, was the second child who Quick was said to have fathered. When he was on the run from the police all those years ago, Quick stayed with Ronnie's grandmother. He supposedly started fucking Ronnie's mother and got her pregnant while Nichelle was already pregnant and in jail. He denied it from day one and Nichelle threatened to leave him if she found out that it was true. Truthfully, Ronnie favored the Nixon's but they never had a relationship with him. He and Nix saw each other around sometimes but that was his first time seeing him in his club.

Gianni walked away, as Nix and the other men stared each other down. He went to go see about his girl, not knowing that he was still being watched like a hawk. Gianni didn't even feel like working anymore. She went upstairs and Nix was right behind her. He nodded his head for her to follow him to his office.

"What happened baby? Who was that nigga that you were arguing with?" Nix asked once they were alone. Gianni was pissed and her body language showed it. She didn't relax until Nix pulled her into him for a hug.

"That was my pathetic, no good ass brother."

"Which one?" Nix pulled back to look in her face. He was praying that she wasn't referring to Ronnie. That would have been too eerie if she was. He and Gianni walked over to the camera so that she could point him out.

"The sneaky looking one with the black and white shirt on." He was happy to see that she pointed to another man and not his supposed brother.

"That nigga with the red shirt on is the one who's supposed to be Quick's son. That's who I thought you were talking about."

"Nah, I don't even know him. I just can't believe that Kori's stupid ass called me over there for him. She had to tell him that I work here. I haven't seen him in years."

"That bitch really been testing my gangsta lately."

"She don't really know why I don't fuck with him but she know that I can't stand his ass. Perverted bastard tried to hug me and I lost it."

"Just chill in here until it's time to go. We're going home and smoke something," Nix said, right before he walked out of the office.

Dior didn't smoke, but Gianni got just as twisted as he did. Nix helped Al and Danny close up and made sure that everything was back in place. Afterwards, he and Gianni went home and smoked until they passed out.

Chapter 11

"Aye, big ole freak. Big booty, big ole treat," Gianni sang as she backed it up on Nix.

It was their third day in Jamaica and Nichelle's fortieth birthday. Quick had rented a waterfront cabana that came with unlimited drinks and food. Gianni had more than enough to drink and she was feeling herself. Nix was seeing an entirely different side of her, not that he was complaining. She became a straight up freak when she got a little liquor in her system. Either that or she was doing something daring.

The day before, they crashed an island wedding. Nix

didn't want to do it but she insisted. Gianni had the bride thinking that she was a guest of the groom. Then, when the groom asked who she was there for, she claimed to be a friend of the bride. They ended up eating and drinking good and no one knew or cared who they were. They were in a bunch of pictures with people who they had never seen before and would probably never see again. Admittedly, he had a good time and they had a funny ass story to tell everybody.

"Yeah Gianni! You better show us why you got all that ass!" Nichelle yelled, encouraging her to cut up. She had been hyping her up all night and that only made her go harder.

Nix had a blunt dangling from his lips, as Gianni twerked her ass all in his face. A few of his aunts, uncles and cousins were there enjoying themselves as well. Ryan was there but Krista was upstairs in their room. She was in her feelings when Ryan apologized to Nix about her behavior at his club. She didn't feel like she'd done anything wrong but her man disagreed. Ryan was still fucking with Kori's thot ass, so Krista did all that for nothing.

"Nah, don't give her nothing else to drink," Nix said when Nichelle tried to hand Gianni another cup of liquor.

"Come on Nix. It's my birthday. Let her have fun." Nichelle frowned.

"She's had enough fun. She's good on drinks for the night."

"Whhhhy? Let's go get in the pool. I wanna suck your dick under water," Gianni whispered as she straddled him. Nix's eyes grew in size as she licked his neck and started grinding on him. If he didn't know better, he wouldn't have thought that Gianni was still a virgin up until a few months ago.

"Shit baby, you gotta chill out. They got too many people out here."

"Fuck them." Gianni reached her hand into the front of his MCM swimming trunks, but he grabbed it to stop her.

"Aye Nichelle, get her some water."

"Scary ass nigga." Gianni got up and walked over to his mother. She wasn't drunk but she was definitely tipsy. Dior was a little more reserved, but Gianni liked to turn up.

"Damn cousin. How did you manage to pull that one? I didn't think you were interested when I inquired about her at the club," Ryan said when he got up and took a seat next to Nix.

"Shit happens." Nix shrugged.

"I'm saying though, are you sharing or what?"

"The fuck you just say nigga?" Nix looked at him sideways like he'd heard him wrong. He would have hated to ruin Nichelle's birthday, but Ryan was about to get knocked the fuck out.

"I was just asking if you're being selfish or sharing."

"You seriously got me fucked up right now. When have I ever shared a female with you?"

"Shit, not too long ago. You didn't mind me fucking with the other bottle girl that works for you." Nix knew that he was speaking of Kori and he got tired of hearing that slut's name.

"I never fucked with that bitch and I never will. That's my girl's first cousin."

"That bitch told me that y'all were fucking around. That's why she told me not to tell you what went down between us."

217

"It obviously didn't matter if I fucked with her or not. That didn't stop you from going there with her, did it?"

"Man, she came at me. You already know me, fam. I don't ever turn down pussy or money."

"I don't give a fuck what you do with that bitch. You ever go at Gianni sideways and I'm breaking your jaw. Ain't no muthafucking sharing when it comes to mine," Nix warned.

"Point taken," Ryan smirked as he continued to sip his drink.

He had on shades but he kept his eyes on Gianni the entire night. Nix knew that he was interested in her first, but it was all good. He had too many hoes on his team to complain about the one that he couldn't have. That didn't stop him from lusting over her though. Gianni had on a two-piece MCM halter bathing suit with the boy cut bottoms that matched her man's trunks. She was sexy as hell but looking was all that Ryan would ever do. They didn't always get along, but Nix was still family and his boss.

"What's wrong?" Gianni asked when she took a seat next to Nix. He was frowning but he smiled when he saw her.

"Nothing baby, I'm good. Just ready to go back to the room." He winked.

"Nichelle is about to cut her cake, so it shouldn't be too much longer."

Gianni was right. About an hour later, they sang happy birthday and Nichelle cut her cake. Quick paid one of the staff members to clean up while they all headed back to their rooms. Nix carried Gianni on his back because she claimed to be too tired to walk.

"You can chill out with all that yawning. You been fucking with a nigga all night. You ain't going to sleep no time soon," Nix said when they got on the elevator.

As soon as they walked into the room, he pulled off Gianni's bathing suit before stepping out of his swimming trunks. She had been teasing him all night and he was hard as a brick. He picked her up and carried her to the bed as they engaged in a sloppy kiss. Nix kissed down her body while she rubbed his head. He wrapped his arms around her thighs when he settled in between her legs. He placed soft kisses on her clit before gently sucking it up into his mouth. Gianni's body shivered when he inserted a finger inside of her.

"Shit, baby, don't stop," she begged while gyrating her hips. When he inserted a second finger into her, she rocked her hips, encouraging him to go faster.

"Damn G. You wet as fuck," Nix mumbled with a mouthful of her goodies.

Gianni was wild, but he loved that side of her. She had her lip pinched in between her teeth as she looked down at him.

"Do it baby." Gianni was panting and her moans sounded sexy as fuck. Nix knew what she wanted but he liked when she begged.

"You taste so good love."

He had Gianni's bottom half lifted off the bed and she was going crazy. He was finger fucking her while flicking his tongue faster than the speed of light. As good as it felt, Gianni was still begging him for more. Nix smiled as she pleaded with him to bring her over the edge. He had created a monster and he was the only one who knew how to tame the beast inside of her. Nix licked his thumb and Gianni got excited. When he stuck it in her asshole, she almost bucked off the bed but his hold on her was too strong.

"Oh God! Fuck!" she screamed while cumming at the same time.

It felt funny when Nix first did that to her, but she craved it now. Gianni was spent when he flipped her over onto her stomach and entered her. He paused once he was fully inside because it felt too good. After a while, he gripped her hips and started to give her slow strokes. He pulled Gianni into him by her hair and turned her head for a kiss. She moaned when he grabbed her neck and pushed her head back down into the mattress. Nix pulled back and she thought that he was about to pull out. Instead, he slammed into her and had the bed knocking up against the wall. The sounds of their skin slapping filled the quiet room. Their moans and labored breaths were like an offbeat song that only they knew the words too. Nix was fucking her like it was his last time, but she wasn't complaining. He slapped her ass repeatedly while swearing that he would die before he let another nigga have her. Nix was always vocal during sex and however he was feeling always came out. When he came, Gianni was happy because she needed some sleep. Since he had the stamina of three men, she knew that he wasn't done with her.

"Wake that ass up!" Nix yelled while kissing her neck and back. Gianni had collapsed on her stomach, but he was wide awake.

"I need a nap."

"I already told you what it was. You can sleep later." Nix picked her up and carried her outside on the private balcony. He sat in the oversized wicker chair and pulled Gianni onto his lap.

"Are you serious right now Jacobi? Somebody might see us."

"That's what makes it so exciting," he replied while lighting his blunt.

He took a pull and gave Gianni a shotgun. He tapped her thigh and she lifted up, allowing him to enter her. She wrapped her arms around his neck and rode him until the sun came up.

Kori pulled up to the club and parked right next to Gianni's car. She hadn't seen or talked to her cousin in over a week. Gianni told her that she was booked for the week but she just assumed she meant school. She didn't know that she was gonna drop off the face of the earth.

She tried calling and texting to apologize about the situation with Greg. Gianni never answered and she hadn't been to work. That was strange in itself, but it wasn't the only thing that she peeped out. Nix hadn't been there either and that couldn't have been a coincidence. Kori's chest tightened at the thought of her cousin messing with the only man that she wanted and couldn't have.

It all made sense to her though. Gianni had gotten close with Al and Danny over the past few months. Not to mention the bond that she seemed to have formed with his mother. Kori didn't have any solid proof but she was determined to find some.

When she walked into the club, a few of the other bottle girls were sitting around talking and eating. They were all excited because they were getting another new uniform for the Big Freedia concert that was coming up. That was the second one and it sold out faster than the first. Danny used his head and doubled the price on the tickets. He almost tripled the price of the sections and nobody complained about paying it.

"You gotta see Al to get your fit for tomorrow. They're doing the sports bar theme and that shit it hot," one of the bottle girls said as she looked at Kori.

She nodded her head and walked out of the breakroom. Rachelle was busy behind the bar, so she waved at her and kept going. Kori walked up the stairs and paused when she saw Gianni, Nix and Al in one of the VIP sections. Nix was whispering in her cousin's ear while she giggled and blushed. Al was on his phone and didn't seem to be paying attention to them.

"Hey Al. They told me to come get my outfit from you for tomorrow," Kori said when she walked up. Nix frowned at her, but Gianni stood to her feet.

"I'll get it for her," her cousin said while grabbing the keys from Nix's hands.

Kori followed her to his office and waited while she opened the door. She didn't miss the passion marks that littered Gianni's neck but she didn't want to speak on it. Her cousin was already pissed with her and she didn't want to give her another reason to stop fucking with her.

"Gianni, listen, I'm sorry for what happened with Greg. I didn't know that you didn't want to see him. I know y'all don't always get along but I know you haven't seen him in a while."

"I get it Kori but there's a lot that you don't know. Greg and I didn't have the best relationship when our mother was living and nothing has changed. I don't care if I ever see or talk to him again."

"I understand cousin and it won't happen again. I just feel like we're drifting apart. I thought us working together would have made us closer. I tried calling you all week but you didn't answer."

"I know. I was busy."

"Busy doing what? Or should I say who? Don't think I missed those passion marks on your neck. Somebody is keeping secrets." Kori laughed, trying to make light of the situation and not offend her.

"It's not a secret but me and-"

"It don't take that damn long to get a uniform," Nix interrupted when he walked into the office. Gianni was just about to tell her cousin about them being together before they were disrupted.

"Your nosy ass. Here you go cousin," Gianni said as she handed Kori the bag with her clothes inside.

Kori left, expecting her cousin to be right behind her. When the door closed, she looked back and didn't see either of them come out of the office. They were confirming her suspicions more and more and she was more determined than ever to get some answers.

"Shady ass bitch." Nix frowned once he and Gianni were alone.

"Stop being disrespectful."

"Fuck that hoe." Nix pulled her onto his lap and started kissing her neck.

"I was about to tell her about us until you walked in."

"Yeah?" Nix questioned while looking at her skeptically.

"She said something about all these marks that you put on my neck. I just feel like I'm lying and that's not me."

"First off, you ain't no liar. And you don't owe her and nobody else no explanations. It's not like we're hiding the shit no more. If they know they know."

"Yeah, I guess but I gotta get to work," Gianni sighed as she stood up.

"You gotta stop caring about other people's feelings so much baby. Trust me, you'll be much happier when you do."

As soon as Nix finished talking, someone knocked on his office door. He looked on the camera and was shocked to see Heavy standing there. He never really came to Nix's office. He either talked to Al or they all used the walkie talkies to communicate with each other. Gianni was about to leave, so she opened the door to let him in.

"Hey Heavy." She smiled while granting him access. He smiled and spoke back before she left and closed the door behind her.

"What's up Heavy? Everything alright?"

"Yeah, I mean, I guess so." He exhaled while running his hand down his face. Nix could tell that he had something to say. Judging by the look on his face, he knew that it couldn't have been good.

"Talk to me, bruh. What's good?"

"My brother wanted to come rap with you but I didn't think it was a good idea. Y'all don't really know each other and I didn't want the shit to go left."

"What did he want to talk to me about?"

"Well, he really wanted to talk to Gianni."

"Man," Nix drawled as he sat up in his chair.

"Nah, it ain't nothing like that. He knows that Gianni is your girl. He ain't on no disrespectful shit."

"He don't know her either. What could he possibly have to discuss with Gianni?"

"A blood test," Heavy replied.

"What!" Nix jumped up and looked at him like he was crazy.

"I know man. The shit sounds crazy but he thinks that Gianni is his daughter."

"How is that even possible?"

"He said that he used to fuck with her mama for an entire year before he got locked up. They lost contact after that and he didn't know that she was pregnant. That's why he was watching her all night when he came here. He said she looks just like her mama."

"Damn man," Nix replied as he sat back down. He was at a loss for words and that didn't happen too often. The shit sounded unbelievable to him, so he could only imagine how Gianni would feel.

"I already know bruh. I wanted to tell you and maybe you can talk to her about it. I don't even feel right going at her about that shit."

"I get that he was fucking with her mama before he went to jail, but what makes him think that Gianni is his?"

"I don't know but she did name her after him."

"What's your brother's name?"

"Giovanni but we call him Gio."

"Damn man. Her mama is a touchy subject for her. I would hate to open up old wounds for nothing. But it's not my place to keep it from her either."

"What do you want me to tell him? He's adamant about them doing a blood test but that's up to Gianni."

"I don't want to discuss it at work. I'll talk to her about it when we get home. I'll call you and let you know what's up."

"I appreciate that bruh. This shit is crazy as hell. I can't believe that I could have possibly been around my own niece all this time and didn't even know it."

"Maybe y'all crossed paths for a reason." Nix shrugged as they walked out of the office together.

Heavy went back downstairs while Nix went to his section and took a seat. He watched everything that was happening around him, but his mind was all over the place. When Gianni walked up, she smiled and winked at him. He smiled back but he wasn't in the best mood. He was trying his best to think of a way to tell her that she could possibly have a father that she knew nothing about.

Chapter 12

      "I really don't know how to feel about everything. I don't want to get my hopes up high for nothing," Gianni said as she talked to Nix over the phone.

      She was awaiting the results of her DNA test and she was nervous about it. It took her a few days to decide if she even wanted to do it or not. Gio was able to convince her once they sat down and talked. He knew so much about Janessa and he had pictures of her from before Gianni was even born. He had her mother's name tattooed on his forearm and he'd had it since before he went to prison. Gianni remembered some of the many conversations that she'd had with her mother and Gio seemed to be the one who got away. He was the man who her mother was in love with and that warmed her heart to know that.

"You don't have to make no decisions right now baby. Wait until the results come back before you do anything."

"I can't believe that Heavy might actually be my uncle. That means that I've been tutoring my cousin all this time. This just feels so weird."

"Yeah, I said the same thing. Nigga was watching you hard as fuck when he was at the club that night. I thought he was on some flirting shit."

"He said that I reminded him a lot of my mama and that's why he was staring. All the questions he kept asking makes sense now."

Gianni leaned her head back and sighed as the nail tech massaged her feet. She had gone to the hair salon earlier and now she was being pampered at the nail salon. She wanted to be cute for the concert at the club the following night. The tips were gonna be something serious. She walked away with over a thousand dollars in one night for the last one. Her savings was sitting pretty and it was only gonna get bigger.

"Call me when you're on your way home so I can order our food from the restaurant," Nix said, interrupting her thoughts.

"I can pick it up if you want me to."

"No, just come straight home so you can relax. They do free delivery."

"Okay, my nails are already done so I shouldn't be much longer," Gianni replied, right as her phone rang. She hung up with Nix and answered for Kori.

"Are you ready for tomorrow night bitch? I can't wait!" Kori yelled.

"Hell yeah I am. I got my hair done this morning and I'm at the nail salon right now."

"Which one?"

"The only one that I go to bitch. You know I don't like switching up on my regulars."

That was all that Kori wanted to hear. She was in her car, so she headed in the direction of her cousin's nail salon. Gianni had been acting brand new for too long and she was ready to get to the bottom of it all. It took her about ten minutes to get to her destination and they talked on the phone the entire time. After a while, Gianni had to go but that was cool with her. She was already parked outside, waiting for her to leave.

It took about another twenty minutes before Gianni exited the shop and got into her car. She had the phone up to her ear, so she probably didn't notice when Kori pulled off and started following her. It was crazy that she had to do so much just to see what her cousin was up to but she felt like it was necessary. Gianni used to tell her everything, but she'd been keeping quiet a lot more than usual.

Kori got on the bridge, making sure to stay at least two cars behind. Gianni was driving in a direction that she wasn't familiar with but she refused to turn around. When she pulled up to a huge two-story house, Kori's mouth opened in shock. She was more curious than ever when the automatic garage door opened and her cousin drove in. Kori parked in front of the house next door, hoping not to be seen. She stared at the house for a while, wondering who it belonged to.

A few minutes later, another car pulled up and Kori got excited. She was anxious to see who was gonna answer the door when the driver got out and knocked. He was carrying bags of what she assumed was food. When the door finally opened, Kori was shocked and confused when Nix appeared.

"The fuck?" she whispered as she continued to stare.

She assumed that her cousin was messing with him but she had no idea that they were living together. That answered a lot of her questions though. She knew for sure that Gianni was no longer living in the shelter but she had no idea that she had upgraded like that. Her cousin went from being homeless to living in a damn palace.

Kori was pulled away from her thoughts when she heard loud laughing. Gianni had come outside to get the food while Nix tipped the driver. She couldn't hear what they were saying, but her chest tightened when she saw him lean down and kiss her. Kori was furious as she watched them disappear into the house before she pulled off. It was fucked up that her own cousin had gone behind her back and started fucking with the one man who she wanted the most. Although the feelings weren't mutual, Nix should have still been off limits.

She was also embarrassed about some of the things that she'd told Gianni about him. She thought it was probably another bottle girl who told on her but it turned out to be her own cousin. Gianni was the reason why he called her into his office to check her. Gianni knew that she was lying, and Kori felt stupid. She was probably laid up with him a few times when Kori claimed that they were together. She couldn't believe that her cousin saved her virginity all those years, only to give it up to a nigga who she barely knew. There was no doubt in her mind that she and Nix were fucking. He didn't seem like the type of man to hang around if they weren't.

Kori had some words for her cousin and she didn't give a damn how she felt once she said them. She planned to give Gianni a piece of her mind when they got to work that night.

When Kori got to the club later that night, she barely had somewhere to park. The concert wasn't until the following day, but there was already a line of people waiting to get inside. She wasn't complaining though. That only meant that the tips would be plentiful. Kori was only fifteen hundred dollars away from getting her surgery. The thought of having a fatter ass excited her beyond words.

"You're late!" Al snapped as soon as she walked into the breakroom. She was actually five minutes early but that was late according to his standards.

"Sorry Al. Am I top or bottom tonight?"

She didn't know why she asked because she never worked the top level anymore. Even the new girls got up there before she did. More than likely, it was Nix who made the call to stop it. That also explained why Gianni was up there permanently. She didn't even come into the breakroom to get her work assignment anymore. She was acting brand new and now Kori knew why.

"I need you to float from top to bottom. They got parties in both areas and I want to make sure there is enough coverage," he replied, exciting her. That was perfect for her since she wanted to be close to Gianni.

After a quick briefing by their boss, everyone filed out of the breakroom and headed to their designated areas. Kori made a beeline for the stairs, hoping to run into her cousin. She didn't see Gianni anywhere but it was cool. A few minutes after she got up there, the doors were opened and the crowd was thick. As soon as Kori started taking orders, Gianni appeared and Nix was right behind her. Kori didn't know how she hadn't figured it out before that day. They didn't seem to be trying to be discreet about anything.

"What's up cousin?" Gianni asked when she and Kori met up at the bar.

"You tell me." Kori turned to face her, ready to go off. Before she could say anything, they were interrupted.

"Damn wifey, you looking good as fuck," Biggie said when he walked up and stood in between them.

"Fuck you, Cortez," Gianni hissed, calling him by his real name.

"Nah, you ain't about that life. Shit, maybe you are. It's been a minute. Maybe somebody else got lucky since I couldn't."

"Not fucking you was the best decision that I've ever made in my life. I didn't even know a dick was supposed to be so big after fucking with that lil shit you packing. No wonder I was able to deep throat it so easily."

Biggie's boys started laughing when she walked off. Biggie only smirked while shaking his head. Gianni's flip mouth was nothing new and he was used to it. That was his first time going to the club that he'd heard so much about but he didn't know that Gianni worked there. His cousin had reserved them a section in VIP, so they all walked up the stairs and headed to their area. A few minutes later, Kori's

232

hoe ass came over to take their orders. He saw her when he first walked in but he ignored her. He couldn't stand her hating ass when he and Gianni were together and nothing had changed. His cousin was flirting with her and she was all smiles.

"Aye Kori, go get Gianni for me!" Biggie yelled over the loud music.

"Do I look like an errand girl to you?" Kori asked as she frowned at him.

"No, you look like a hoe but that's not the point."

Kori wanted to punch his fat ass in the mouth but she walked away instead. She had other people to serve and Biggie wasn't worth her time. She didn't know that Dior was there, but she ended up helping her and her friends.

"How are you paying?" Kori asked once she gave Dior the two bottles that she ordered.

"I'm not," Dior replied while turning her head dismissively.

Kori didn't want to cause a scene, so she walked away in search of Al. She found him on the first floor and walked over to him.

"Look, I gave Dior two bottles and she's refusing to pay. I'm not trying to lose my job over no liquor, so I just left it alone."

"I'll handle it. Get a Hennessey set up for that back table over there," Al replied as he pointed to the customers.

Kori ended up staying on the bottom level for over an hour before she went back upstairs. As good as the tips were, she was ready to call it a night. The club was packed and she knew that it would be even worse for the concert the following day. She would definitely have all the money for her surgery plus a little bit more.

"The tips are bomb as fuck but I'm ready to go home now," Gianni said as soon as she saw her cousin.

"Exactly where is home these days?" Kori asked.

"With my man." Gianni gave her a pointed look like she dared her to challenge what she had just said. Kori was about to go in on her until Biggie interrupted them once again. He was a pain in the ass and she was tired of seeing his face.

"Damn baby. I miss the hell out of you," Biggie said while wrapping his arms around Gianni's waist. He was trying to kiss her neck, but she kept pushing him away.

"Get the fuck off of me!"

"I fucked up baby. You were the best thing that ever happened to me. Give me another chance Gianni. I swear I won't do nothing to make you leave me again."

His hot liquor scented breath made her want to puke. Biggie clearly had too much to drink but he had her fucked up. He pulled Gianni over to his section and sat down with her on his lap. She was trying her best to get away from him, but his hold was too strong.

"Let me go Cortez! One of y'all need to get him!" Gianni yelled while looking over at his friends. They were laughing, but she didn't find shit funny.

When she looked up and saw Nix headed in their direction, she knew that shit was about to get worse before it got better. He was furious and the heated look on his face gave away exactly how he was feeling. Biggie still had his arms around her waist, as Nix walked over and pulled her up. He was livid when he looked on the camera and saw what was going on.

"Do something safe my nigga cause this ain't it," Nix fumed as he pushed Gianni behind him.

"Nigga, mind your muthafucking business," Biggie fumed while getting up and pointing his unsteady finger in Nix's face.

Gianni saw Heavy and Vic rushing up the stairs, but it was too late. Nix delivered a vicious blow to Biggie's face that had him stretched out on the floor soon after. The men who he was with tried to rush Nix, but he was ready. He hit another one and Heavy grabbed two of the others. Vic was already escorting them towards the stairs where another bouncer was waiting.

"Get all these niggas the fuck up out of my club!" Nix yelled before walking off towards his office. Gianni followed him, as Kori looked on in shock.

Gianni walked into the office, but Nix wasn't behind his desk. She went into the adjoined bathroom and saw him standing at the sink. His knuckles were scraped up and bleeding.

"Are you okay baby?" Gianni asked as he hugged him from behind.

"Get the fuck up off of me!" Nix removed her hands from around his waist and walked away.

"What are you mad at me for?"

"The fuck was you smiling up in that nigga's face for? Nigga got you sitting all on his lap and shit." He was in her face yelling, prompting her to take a step back. She had never seem him so upset before, especially with her.

"You act like I wanted to be around his ass. I know you saw me trying to push him away."

235

"No, what I saw was the nigga whispering in your ear and pulling you down to sit on his lap. This is my place of business and I'm out there fighting with niggas because you wanna be a hoe. Get the fuck out. You're fired!" he fumed angrily while sitting behind his desk.

Gianni gasped at his use of language. She and Nix had arguments before but it never got to the point of name calling. Her feelings were hurt but she would never let him see her cry. She had fallen in love with him but she was nobody's fool. She had enough money saved up to get her own place now, even if she had to sleep on an inflatable mattress.

"Fuck you! I don't need you or this job!" Gianni stormed out of his office and slammed the door behind her. Nix regretted his words as soon as he said them, but it was too late.

"Fuck!" he yelled as he jumped up to run behind her.

He didn't know if the niggas who he had fought were still lurking or not and he didn't want anything to happen to her. Most of all, he didn't want her to leave him for good.

"Are you okay boo?" Dior asked, placing her hand on his chest to stop him.

"Move Dior." Nix pushed her out of the way and ran down the stairs.

Gianni had just sped out of the parking lot when he got outside. Nix was in such a hurry that he forgot to grab his keys. He rushed back to his office to get them and forgot to lock the door behind him. Dior watched his every move with a satisfied smirk on her face. She made sure that the coast was clear before she slipped into the office and locked the door behind her.

Dior looked around for a minute before sitting behind Nix's desk. She looked at the computer monitors on his desk that showed every area of the club. She frowned when she saw the monitor that viewed the inside of his house. That surveillance system was the reason why she and Nix were no longer together. Dior remembered how she tried to lie about what she'd done until he presented her with the footage. She was hurt and embarrassed but she was caught red handed.

"Front door," the alarm announced, pulling Dior from her thoughts.

She turned her attention back to the monitor of Nix's home. Her face twisted in confusion when she saw the bottle girl, Gianni, who she sometimes talked to, walking inside. She looked upset as she stormed up the stairs. She disappeared into the master bedroom but there were no cameras in there. When she came back out a few minutes later, she had changed into a fitted t-shirt dress and some furry slippers. She had a duffle bag thrown over her shoulder with a backpack in her hand.

"The fuck?" Dior mumbled as she watched her maneuver around the house like it was hers.

"Front door," the alarm said once again.

Dior sat up in her chair when she spotted Nix walking into the house. Gianni had just grabbed her keys off the counter and was preparing to leave. Her eyes filled with tears when Nix reached out and grabbed her arm to stop her.

"I'm sorry baby. Don't leave me, please," he begged.

Dior felt like she wanted to die. She couldn't believe it. Gianni was the girlfriend who Nix and Nichelle had spoken of. She was the woman who accompanied them to Jamaica and she had to be the woman who he had in the car with him the night Dior showed up at his house. She saw her running down the stairs after the fight and Nix wasn't too far behind her. That went over Dior's head but it all made sense now. Nix was obviously chasing after her.

"Fuck you, Nix. I'm not about to let you and no other nigga talk crazy to me. I didn't even do shit," Gianni said, sounding like she was about to cry.

The tears never fell from her eyes but the same couldn't be said for Dior. She wanted to look away but she just couldn't. Her face was saturated with tears and her heart was shattered.

"I know baby and I apologize. I'll do whatever I have to do to make it up to you. Just please, don't leave," Nix begged as he grabbed the bags from her and sat them on the floor.

"I don't wanna leave."

"I love you, baby."

Hearing him say that to another woman was bad enough. But the look in his eyes made it even worse. Dior knew him well enough to know that he really meant it. Nix was in love with another woman and it felt like a part of her heart was being ripped from her chest.

"I love you, too."

"God, no. This can't be happening to me," Dior said as she dropped her head and cried.

The pain was unbearable and she couldn't take it. The only man that she'd ever loved, loved someone else. Her entire body shook as she sobbed. She never even tried to move on and she wasn't sure that she could. Nix was supposed to be it for her. He was the only man who'd ever seen her naked and the only man who'd she given herself to. He was her first kiss and her date for prom. Nix was a part of every good memory that she'd ever had.

"Don't stop baby," Gianni moaned, prompting Dior to steal another glance at the monitor.

She gasped when she saw what was going on. Gianni was laid out on the counter with her legs spread wide. Nix had his entire face buried between her thighs and Dior had seen enough. The thoughts running through her mind weren't those of an educated woman. She was a woman scorned and she wasn't thinking rationally. Stabbing Gianni in the neck and watching her bleed out was the only thing that she could think of at the moment.

She stole another glance at the camera to see where Al was before she slipped out of the office. He was downstairs, still trying to get order in the club when Dior walked out of Nix's office. Her girls were calling her name but she bypassed them and kept going. Tears blinded her vision as she walked out of the club and got into her car. She ignored her ringing phone and drove home in a daze. Dior always remembered the women in her family talking about women losing themselves in a man. She swore that she would never be one of them but that's exactly what she had become. She loved Nix to the point of obsession and she didn't know if she could ever let him go. Unfortunately for Gianni, she wasn't about to let her have him either.

Chapter 13

"Not tonight bruh. It's gonna be too busy in there. I need all the help I can get," Al said as he sat on the sofa at Nix's house and talked to him.

The club was pure chaos the night before and the fight that Nix had was one of three. He knew that the crowd was gonna be even thicker later on that night before, during and after the concert. They were grateful for the name that the club had made for itself but it was a headache sometimes. Al had already hired more bottle girls, bartenders, and bouncers but it still seemed like it wasn't enough.

"Man, I already know that you need her for the crowd that's coming through tonight, but it's a wrap after that. I can't be up in there fighting every nigga that touch or look at Gianni. After tonight, she's officially a retired bottle girl. She'll be working up in the office with me. She's going to school for accounting, so she can handle the books. Did you use the company card to get everything that she'll need to start?"

"Yeah, I did. I'm not trying to offend you or nothing fam, but I have to ask. Do you really think that's a good idea?"

"What?" Nix asked in confusion.

"Having Gianni work up in the office and shit."

"The fuck are you trying to say?" Nix was highly offended but that wasn't Al's goal.

"No disrespect fam but you know what happened when you let Dior handle the books."

"She's not Dior though. I trusted her snake ass right up until she gave me a reason not to. The same rules apply to Gianni. She's innocent until she shows me otherwise. It don't make no sense for me to be with her if I don't trust her."

"Yeah, that's true. I don't see her being on no foul shit like that though. At least I hope not."

"I've learned not to put nothing past nobody. But, again, I trust her until she proves me wrong. Fuck what a person says. I go by what they show me."

"Who was that nigga that you put to sleep last night?" Al questioned.

"That was her ex nigga. His bitch ass had me fucked up. Pulling her on his lap and shit. Nigga had me going off on my baby and I was dead ass wrong. I had to rewind the cameras when I calmed down to see shit for what it really was."

Once he apologized to Gianni for most of the night, Nix pulled up the surveillance cameras on his phone to see exactly what happened. He wasn't thinking straight the night before and his mind had him seeing only a small part of what really happened. When he looked again, he saw how hard Gianni tried to fight her ex nigga off. The nigga was persistent though and that's what pissed him off the most.

According to Gianni, she hadn't seen Biggie in almost a year. She had seen him in passing and she didn't have nothing to say to him back then either. He had life fucked up if he thought he was gonna come into her man's club and try to get her back. It didn't matter if he knew about Nix or not. He fucked up when he had her and whatever they had was over.

"I hope that nigga don't become a problem for the club. He might feel played about how he got handled."

"I'm ready for whatever. That's exactly why I told you to hire some more security for outside and in. That's one of our moneymakers and nobody ain't stopping our bag."

"You got that shit right. Danny did his thing with upping the prices for the concert and VIP sections. We're about to make a month of profit just from tonight alone."

"What's up with you and that nigga?" Nix questioned.

"Same shit as always. He's trying to look at houses for us to buy and he's not taking no for an answer. That nigga got his daddy ready to write a muthafucking check. He said I got one month to get my mind right or he's done

243

for good. Can you believe that nigga gave me an ultimatum?" Al chuckled nervously.

"Yeah, I can. You know I love you like a brother but I don't blame that man. I'm not being with nobody who refuses to acknowledge that we're together. That's the same shit that I told Gianni. Nigga too grown to be somebody's secret. Fuck that."

"You know that's not even the same situation. You can't compare me and Danny to you and Gianni."

"Why? Because y'all are two niggas?" Nix questioned.

"That's exactly why." Al nodded.

"Well, maybe you need to be by yourself then."

"Dam bruh. Is that how you really feel?" Al was kind of offended, but he knew that Nix had a reason for whatever he said and did.

"You can't expect that man to live the rest of his life in the shadows just because you're scared of who you really are. And let's keep it real. Your mama ain't always been a Christian her damn self. Shit, she used to smoke and drink right in the same club that she complains about you managing."

Al's mother used to be a regular at Club Nixon when they were younger. His grandparents used to fuss at her the same way that she now fussed at Al. She didn't want to hear what they had to say back then and she stayed away so that she didn't have to. When she decided to change her life, it was a decision that she made. Now, she expected Al to just drop everything and sit in the pulpit with her, but that's not where his heart was at.

"Let her tell it, she let the devil use her long enough and she don't want him to use me too." Al laughed but there

244

was nothing funny about it. His mother was a hypocrite in Nix's eyes, but it wasn't his place to voice that out loud.

"Man, fuck that. That's exactly why I live my life for me. I don't, never did and never will give a fuck about what nobody have to say about me. Only you know when you're ready to make a change. And if that time never comes, then it's your life. You're not being fair to yourself either. I just want you to be happy bruh. You're a good dude and you deserve that."

"I know man and I appreciate that. This shit has been keeping me up at night, so I know I have to make a decision soon."

Al sighed in frustration but he knew that his boy was right. He needed to man the fuck up and be honest with himself and everyone else around him. Besides being shunned and disowned by his mother and some of his other overly religious family members, he had nothing else to lose.

"Hey Al." Gianni smiled when she walked into the room.

"What's up girl? I heard that you're quitting on me, huh?"

"I didn't quit. I was fired," she replied while cutting her eyes at Nix.

"No, you were promoted," he corrected.

"I'm still gonna help out tonight though. I know the crowd is gonna be thick."

Although her shift got cut short with Biggie and his drama, Gianni made a killing in tips. She would have probably made more but she hoped to make up for it with the crowd that the concert was bringing in. After that, she was hanging up her bottle girl uniform to work in the office with her man. She was excited to put her accounting knowledge to use and she wanted to do a good job. She would miss her tips, but it was worth it.

"Yeah, I need to bring my ass home and get some sleep. I need to be well rested and alert for tonight," Al said as he stood up and stretched.

Nix walked him out, and Gianni stretched out on the sofa. She needed to take a nap too because she was sure that nobody would be able to take a break. Gianni was lying down watching tv when Nix walked back into the house.

"Look what came in the mail," he said while holding up the envelope from the DNA testing center.

"I'm too nervous to even open it," Gianni said as her heart rate accelerated.

"I know you're dying to find out what the results are."

"I am, but I'm scared too. I don't want to open it right now."

Just then, Gianni regretted even taking the test. She knew that she was being childish, but she wasn't ready to know the truth. She had gone all that time without a father but, secretly, she wanted Gio to be him. Just knowing how much he and her mother loved each other made her wish that she was their love child.

"Ole boy probably opened his already but you don't have to if you're not ready. Come upstairs and let me put you to sleep right quick," Nix said as he picked her up and carried her to their bedroom.

After a few rounds of bomb ass sex, they took a shower and went to sleep soon after. They rode to the club together once they got up and got together. They went in a little earlier than usual because Nix wanted to make enough room in his office for her. He had Al to purchase a brand new MacBook and some software that she would be using. She had transferred all the clubs financial records on it as soon as she powered it on and she was ready to get to work. That was her first official job in her field and she was excited to put her knowledge to good use.

Once that business was taken care of, Gianni got dressed and the doors to the club were opened soon after. She felt like VIP when she got to take pictures with Big Freedia and his crew before the show started. Once they got on stage, the bouncers had to work overtime to keep the crowd in check. Thankfully, everybody behaved and there were no fights or disruptions.

"Bitch, that concert was everything. I almost twerked my lace front off," Nichelle said when she sat down and drank the water that Gianni had just handed her.

"Well, your makeup is dripping everywhere," Gianni laughed while handing her some napkins.

As predicted, the concert was lit and did better numbers than before. They doubled the price on liquor, but nobody seemed to care. A few people left once it was over, but they were quickly replaced by some newcomers. Gianni had made over a thousand dollars and she was looking forward to making a little more. Even Nix had been busy throughout the night. He wasn't able to chill in his section, so Nichelle, her sister and some of her friends had it occupied.

"Tell your man that his bartenders are watering these drinks down a little too much," Nicole, Nix's auntie, fussed.

"My baby is smart. Water that shit down to keep them coming back. Ain't nobody complaining but your alcoholic ass," Nichelle snapped.

When they started arguing, Gianni walked away and laughed. Nichelle and her sister were close as hell but they argued like two old ass ladies. She was stopped twice before she made it downstairs but that was nothing new. She had been on her feet all night and she was happy that it was her last shift as a bottle girl. She knew that her working in the office with Nix was gonna start a lot of gossiping but she didn't give a damn. She had no problem letting everybody know that he was her man and that included Kori.

"Girl, they broke my new ass in this week," Amya, the newest bartender, said when Gianni walked up.

"Yes honey but the tips are well worth it."

"You got that shit right. I've already emptied my tip jar twice."

"That's what's up." Gianni smiled when Nix walked over and stood behind her.

"Let's take a break," he whispered in her ear.

"No sir. It's too damn busy in here for that to even happen."

Gianni blushed and bit her lip as she looked back at him. Their encounter from earlier that day replayed in her mind like an HD pornographic film.

"You better stop looking at me like that before I drag you to my office." She had the most exotic eyes that he had ever seen and he was mesmerized.

"Our office," Gianni corrected.

"Damn, that shit sounds good as fuck, don't it?"

"Move around Jacobi. You gon' get your dick all hard for nothing because I'm not taking a break."

248

"Please baby. Just give me ten minutes," Nix begged as he kissed the back of her neck. He didn't care that a bunch of people were standing around and neither did she. They were gonna find out eventually and there was no better time than the present.

"Okay," Gianni agreed after a while.

"Stop playing Gianni."

"I'm serious. Just let me service these last two tables and I'm coming up."

"Bet," Nix said excitedly as he rushed up the stairs towards the office.

"You and boss man seem mighty close lately," Kori said when she walked up and stood next to her cousin at the bar.

"Where you been at all night? This is my first time seeing you."

"Well, everybody ain't able to be in the same section every night. Unlike you, I have to work the bottom level sometimes too."

"Do you have something to say Kori? If so, be a woman and say that shit."

"As a matter of fact I do. I find it mighty funny how-"

Kori's rant was interrupted when Gianni was hit from behind. She spun around and was shocked when Dior hit her again. Kori jumped back because Gianni went into full savage mode. Dior had obviously come for a fight because she was dressed down in leggings and Nikes. Her hair was pulled back into a ponytail that Gianni used to slam her to the floor.

"You got the right one bitch!" Gianni jumped on top of her and started putting in work to her face.

River and Crystal sprang into action and jumped in to help their girl. Kori hid behind the bar, hoping that nobody saw her. She wasn't scary but, to her, Gianni was getting what she deserved for going behind her back fucking with Nix. For the second night in a row, the club was the center of a boxing match.

"Y'all hoes got life fucked up," Nichelle fumed as she and her sister pulled the two women off Gianni.

Crystal tried to swing, but Nichelle boxed her up real quick and got her mind right. River wasn't stupid, so she chilled out when they pulled her away. By then, Dior was back on her feet and she and Gianni were going at it again. Heavy and two of the new bouncers were making their way through the crowd, trying to get to the brawl. Gianni was doing Dior dirty, but Nichelle and her sister had River in Crystal in check. They couldn't jump in to help, so Dior was all on her own.

"Come on G. Chill out fam. I think she got the point," Al said when he walked over and intervened. He saw Nix trying to make his way from up the stairs but too many people were in his path. Even the bouncers were having a hard time getting through the crowd.

"Stupid ass bitch got me heated. And I got something for y'all scary hoes too since y'all wanna jump in."

Gianni's lip was stinging and so was her face. She knew that she had some scratches and probably a busted lip too.

"Bitch! This ain't over hoe!" Dior yelled as she tried to get to Gianni again. Al was standing in between them trying to keep them from fighting again.

"Why you mad though? The nigga was all yours until you decided to steal from him. You basically stole your own damn money. Kleptomaniac bitch."

Dior didn't have to say why she came at her sideways because she already knew. She'd obviously found out that Gianni and Nix were together and was in her feelings about it. She had the entire game fucked up coming at her sideways though.

"Who stole what from who?" Nichelle asked as she took in the guilty expression on Dior's face.

"Don't get quiet now hoe. Tell everybody how you stole from Nix and he cut your thieving ass off."

Gianni had her back turned to Dior talking to Nichelle, and that was a huge mistake. Dior grabbed a champagne bottle from the bar and smashed her across the back of the head. Gianni went down to the floor, right as Nix made it over to them. He grabbed Dior by the throat and lifted her off her feet as the club, once again, got chaotic. Gianni was out cold, as Nichelle and her sister kneeled down next to her.

"Let me go. I can't breathe," Dior choked out as Nix cut off her oxygen supply.

"Bitch, get the fuck up out of my club. If I see you walk through those doors again, I'm gonna make sure that you meet your mama for the first time," he gritted before pushing her away.

Dior was crushed more by his words than his physical actions. He knew that the subject of her mother was a touchy one but he obviously didn't care. If she didn't know it before, Dior knew for sure that Nix didn't give a fuck about her now.

The bouncers escorted her and her girls out before Nix went to see about his girl. Someone handed Nichelle some napkins and ice that she used to wipe Gianni's face and neck. After another minute or two, she started to stir. Gianni jumped up from the floor like she hadn't been knocked out just a minute ago.

"That hoe wanna play with bottles, huh?" Her adrenaline was pumping and she was ready to go another round with Dior. She staggered a little when she tried to walk, but Nix was right there to catch her.

"Relax baby. You're bleeding," he said while wrapping his arms around her tightly.

"What! Where?" Gianni asked as she looked down at her body. Her head was banging but she didn't see any blood.

"I got you, love. Come on. We need to get you to the hospital," Nix said as he picked her up and carried her out back to his truck.

Al assured him that they could handle everything in his absence but he didn't care if they couldn't. Nichelle rushed out behind them to her car, preparing to follow them. Gianni gasped when she touched the back of her head and came up with two fingers full of blood.

"I'm gonna kill that bitch! I'm bleeding," Gianni cried.

"I know baby but I got you. Just relax. Everything is gonna be okay."

Nix grabbed her hand and kissed it as he drove her to the hospital. He was furious but he had to remain calm for Gianni's sake. She was angry enough and he didn't want to make it worse.

"I don't even have my insurance card. My purse is locked up in the office." Gianni started crying again when they pulled up to the hospital's entrance.

"Don't worry about that baby. They can pull all that up with your social security number."

"Does she need a wheelchair?" Nichelle asked when she walked up. Nix didn't even know that she was following him but he appreciated her being there.

"No, I can walk," Gianni sniffled.

They were happy that the waiting room wasn't crowded when they walked in. Gianni's primary doctor worked at the same hospital, so they already had all of her insurance information in the computer. She only waited for about twenty minutes before she was called to go to the back. She was furious when they had to cut a small patch of her hair to see her injuries but she was grateful that it was in the back. Nix was livid when they told her that she needed a few stitches. He and Nichelle had to go back to the waiting room until they were done with her.

"What did Dior steal from you and when?" Nichelle asked while looking at her son.

"Who told you that?"

"That's not important. Why didn't you tell me? Ain't no way in hell I would have still been around her snake ass if I knew that she did you dirty."

"I wasn't trying to turn nobody against her but fuck Dior." Nix took a few minutes and ran the entire story down to his mother.

Nichelle was furious that she remained cool with Dior after their breakup. Since he never made a big deal out of it, she just assumed that they split on mutual terms. They didn't seem like they were at odds with each other like most couples did. Nix just handled things differently. You could definitely tell that he wasn't raised by her and his father because Dior would have been put on blast a long time ago.

"That hoe better stay the fuck out of my face. And that Crystal bitch is lucky that I didn't really do her as dirty as I wanted to."

"Fake ass hoe. She was the first one to hop on my dick the same night me and Dior broke up. Now she wanna help her fight and shit."

"I know you lying!"

"Bitch told me some shit that I didn't even know. I was thinking about giving Dior another chance until I talked to her."

According to Crystal, Dior had been on some foul shit for a while. She used to check his emails and delete the ones that she didn't want him to see. She used to screen his calls too and he was probably missing out on money because of her insecure ass. Nix had to change all of his passwords on everything after they broke up. She was doing too much shit that he wasn't even aware of.

"Family of Gianni Porter!" a doctor yelled after they had waited for close to an hour.

"Yeah, that's me," Nix said when he and Nichelle walked over to him.

"Well, everything went fine. Ms. Porter received seven stiches and she'll probably have a terrible headache for the next few days. She has a slight concussion, so we want to keep her overnight just to monitor her progress. Visiting hours are over but you can come back and see her for a few minutes."

He led the way, as Nix and Nichelle followed him to Gianni's room. She was sitting up in the bed with a bandage wrapped around her head. She had already changed into a hospital gown since she wasn't going anywhere.

"How you feeling baby?" Nix asked before planting a soft kiss on her lips.

"My head is pounding but I'm good. They just gave me some pain meds but they haven't kicked in yet. I can't go home tonight."

"I know. The doctor just told us. I'm staying here with you."

"I can swing by the house and get some clothes and stuff if y'all want me to," Nichelle offered.

Since Gianni moved in, she didn't go to her son's house unannounced anymore. Gianni did all the cooking and cleaning, so she had no reason to. She never even used her key because she wanted to respect their privacy.

"Nah, we should be good. Hopefully, they'll let her go in the morning. I'll call you if something changes."

"Alright. I'm happy that you're okay boo. Call me if y'all need anything." Nichelle hugged Gianni and her son before she left to go home.

Whatever they gave Gianni must have kicked in because she dozed off not long after Nichelle left. Al checked in with Nix to let him know that they had the club under control. Once Nix made sure that his mother got home safely, he got comfortable in the recliner next to Gianni's bed and tried to get some sleep.

Chapter 14

Gianni opened her eyes and squinted at the extra bright lights. Her head felt like someone was beating a drum inside and her mouth felt like cotton. She tried to sit up but she gave up after the first try. It felt like the room was spinning, so she closed her eyes and laid back. She heard Nix talking on the phone but she refused to open her eyes to see where he was.

"Nix. Can you turn off the light?"

"Let me call you back Al. She just got up."

"Why is it so bright in here?"

"I don't know baby but the light is not on. The nurse came in earlier and opened the curtains though. Let me close them," he said as he got up and tried to make the room darker.

"What time is it?" Gianni asked as she finally opened her eyes and looked around. Nix wasn't wearing the same clothes that he had on the night before.

"It's almost two o'clock."

"In the afternoon!" she screeched.

"Yep. Whatever they gave you had you out for a while. Nichelle came up here while I went home to take a shower. I got you some stuff for you to freshen up whenever you're ready."

"What time am I going home?"

"Hopefully soon. They took your vitals while you were asleep and said they were good. How do you feel?"

"I have a headache but I'm good."

"Yeah, you're probably gonna have that for a while. What are you doing?" Gianni was trying to get out of bed but he didn't know why.

"I need to brush my teeth and take a shower. I have dried up on blood on my neck."

Nix helped her get out of the bed right when the nurse came in to give her some more pain meds. She said that the doctor would be around in a few more hours and she would be discharged then. Gianni felt so much better once she took her shower and got dressed. The medicine helped with the pain and she was able to enjoy the food that Nichelle had just dropped off for them. She and Nix sat up in her bed and watched tv until someone knocked on the door a few minutes later.

"Come in," Gianni called out. When the door slowly opened and Kori walked in, Nix's face twisted up into a frown before he jumped up from the bed.

"Get the fuck out!" he snapped in anger.

"Jacobi!" Gianni screeched.

"Nah, baby, fuck that. Where the fuck was she at when all this shit went down? You broke your neck to help her when she was getting her ass tagged."

"I tried to help but it was too crowded for me to get to her," Kori replied in her own defense.

"Yeah right. You must have been serving up drinks because your ass hid right behind the bar."

Kori's face flushed in embarrassment when Nix called her out. He'd already talked to Rachelle and she told him exactly where Kori was. He didn't want to believe that she would do Gianni so dirty, so he pulled the cameras from his phone to see for himself. Sure enough, Kori's shady ass ran behind the bar and stayed there until everything was over with. He already didn't like her ass and her actions only made it worse.

"Give me a minute to talk to her baby, please," Gianni begged as she looked at Nix with pleading eyes. He wanted to decline but he decided to let her have that.

"Five minutes Gianni. I want her ass gone after that." He gave her a kiss before he walked away, mean mugging Kori the entire time.

"What the fuck is his problem? He's acting like I'm the reason that you're here. He can blame his ex-fiancée for that."

"He's pissed and he has every reason to be."

259

"Yeah but he's pissed with the wrong person."

"Is he?" Gianni questioned while giving her a skeptical look.

"What are you trying to say?"

"You were right there when everything happened Kori. You didn't have to get through a crowd to get to me. We were talking when it all went down or did you forget?"

Kori turned her head and looked away. She was guilty but she was hoping that Gianni didn't call her out on her bullshit.

"Wow. Nix comes into the picture and all of a sudden I'm the bad guy."

"First off, Nix has been in the picture for months. Even when you were lying and saying that y'all were fucking. I almost missed out on a good man because of your deceitful ways. You've been moving funny for a while now, but I tried to ignore all the warning signs. Even when Nix showed me exactly who you were, I still tried to see the good in you. I never thought that my own cousin would be my biggest hater. Especially since I never really had much for you to hate on."

"And you still don't," Kori spat bitterly. "You let that nigga get in your head and turn you against your own family. Where they do that at?"

"That nigga, as you called him, has been more of my family than you ever were. An entire year of me sleeping in homeless shelters, hotel rooms, hell, even my car. Not once did you ever invite me into your home. I probably would have turned you down but the thought would have counted for something. Nix didn't owe me nothing but a paycheck for the hours that I worked. Yet, he opened up his home to me and made sure that I was straight. He barely even knew me but he cared more than you or your mama ever did. And

260

it's fucked up because I have genuine love for you. I had your back even when you weren't around."

Gianni remembered getting into it with Nix when she helped Kori fight Ryan's girlfriend. He asked her if she thought that her cousin would do the same for her and she didn't hesitate before she said yes. Kori had made a liar out of her and she was good on her. Gianni overlooked a lot of things that she did. She even accepted her half ass apologies but she was over it now. She was done wasting time and energy on people who didn't give a fuck about her. Before Kori had a chance to reply to her cousin's rant, Nix walked back into the room.

"Times up. Get the fuck out," he barked angrily. He didn't care that he was being rude or disrespectful. He was sick of Kori and he wanted her gone indefinitely.

Kori looked at Gianni, expecting her to say something but she never did. She looked straight ahead like she didn't want her there either.

"Wow. Despite what you think, I have genuine love for you too." With those parting words, Kori walked out of the room.

"I love you, baby, and I know that your family is small but it's time for you to sever ties with her ass. That bitch ain't right." From her telling everyone that Gianni was homeless to her not helping her fight, Kori was toxic in every way.

"That's already done. Blood doesn't always define family. I just hate that it took me so long to see it."

"Don't let me change your mind if you feel otherwise. I just want you to see shit for what it really is."

"I already do. I'm done with her and that will never change."

"Are you sure about that?"

"I've never been more sure of anything in my life."

"Good," Nix said as he pulled out his phone and dialed a number.

"Who are you calling?" Nix didn't reply but her question was answered when he started talking.

"Aye bruh, hire two new bottle girls instead of one. Last night was Kori's final shift. Fire her ass as soon as she gets there and escort her out," Nix said as he talked on the phone with Al.

Usually, Gianni would be begging him not to do it but she didn't open her mouth. She was tired of being the bigger person and she vowed to no longer have anyone's back who never had hers. She was about to lie down and relax until someone else knocked on the door. Nix thought it was Kori again. He walked over and snatched the door open and found Heavy and his brother standing there with flowers and gifts.

"Hey. I hope y'all don't mind us passing through. Al gave me the info on where you were. How do you feel?" Heavy asked while looking at Gianni. They sat everything that they had for her down on the bedside table when they walked into the room.

"I feel fine. Thanks for the gifts." Gianni smiled.

"I tried calling you a few times last night and this morning," Gio spoke up while walking closer to the bed.

"Yeah, my phone is in my locker at the club."

"I take it you didn't look at the results."

"No, my purse is in my locker too. I got them. I was just too nervous to open it."

"I was too but I gave in eventually. Heavy wouldn't let me hold on to them for too long," he chuckled nervously.

"And?" Gianni was curious as to what the results were. His expression was blank, not giving her any indications one way or the other.

"It looks like you and I are stuck with each other."

He smiled brightly and so did Heavy. Gianni's eyes filled with tears but she was shocked. After all those years of never knowing who her father was, fate had a way of intervening. Once Janessa died, she thought that was the end as far as parents were concerned. She felt blessed that she was given a second chance. Knowing that she was conceived out of love just made it that much more special. She held her arms out for a hug and Gio wasted no time embracing her. Nix and Heavy left out of the room to give them a few minutes of alone time.

Al walked around the club making sure that everything was straight. He had a few new employees, so he made sure to stay close by in case they needed some help. Since he fired Kori and Gianni would be working in the office, he hired a few new bottle girls and had them training with the regulars. It had only been a week but they were working out good so far.

Gianni had been working from home but she was already proving to be an asset to them with their records. She was precise and it felt good for them to see exactly how much revenue they were bringing in daily, instead of weekly how they used to do it. She was feeling better, but Nix wasn't quite ready for her to return.

Besides that, she had been spending a lot of time with Gio. Al was shocked to learn that he was her father but the story made sense once it was told to him. The club had been calm since the last fight and he was praying that it stayed that way.

"Aye Al!" Vic yelled over the walkie talkie. Al had just decided to take a break but he knew that it was too good to be true.

"What's good Vic?"

"Boss man's ex is out here and I can tell that she's about to cause a scene. He gave strict orders not to let her in anymore, but she's asking for you. What do you want me to tell her?"

Dior had to be a special kind of stupid to even show up to Nix's place of business after what she did. Although she had Al by the balls, his hands were tied. He was just the manager, but Nix was the owner. At the end of the day, he made the final decisions. He was in his office and Al didn't want him to go out there and try to kill Dior again.

"Tell her that I'm not here," Al said after a long pause.

"Bet," Vic replied.

Al sighed in frustration because he knew that Dior wasn't gonna go away that easily. He knew that he was right when his phone started ringing. He started not to answer but he knew that he couldn't hide from her forever. Dior wasn't gonna have that kind of power over him. He refused to let her. She didn't even give him a chance to say anything when he answered the phone. She just started going off.

"You must think I'm stupid Al. You don't have no off days. You be at that club more than Nix do. Are you gonna tell them to let me in or what?" Dior asked in a demanding tone.

"Why would you even think it was okay for you to come here after what happened? You must want Nix to kill you."

"Fuck Nix and his bitch. I just wanna relax and have a few drinks with my girls."

"Okay, well you can do that at home. Nix made it clear that he doesn't want you in here no more."

"Well, make him change his mind. You can talk him into doing anything else."

"Nix is a grown ass man. I can't talk him into doing shit. And trust me, you're the last person who he wants to see. Staying away is for your protection more than anything."

"Are you sure that this is how you wanna play it?"

"Just give me some time Dior. The shit just happened last week. It's still too fresh in his mind."

"You have one week. After that, I might not feel like keeping your secret any longer," Dior threatened before she hung up.

"Fuck!" Al yelled while punching the air. It was crazy because he actually liked Dior at one time. He hated everything about her no good ass now.

"What's wrong?" Danny asked when he walked up on him.

"Everything is wrong but we'll talk about it later."

Danny could see that something was bothering him but he didn't press him about it. Al seemed to be in a daze the entire night and he was happy when the club finally closed. He and Danny stayed up talking for hours and he told him everything that happened between him and Dior. Al was always the calm one, but Danny was pissed. He wanted to confront her but Al told him to let it go. He thought that Nix deserved to know, so Al woke up the next afternoon and decided to pay his best friend a visit.

When he pulled up to Nix's house, he sat in his car for a while, deep in thought. He didn't sleep too well the night before but it was worth it. He had some decisions to make and he was ready to make some changes in his life. After getting his thoughts together, Al got out of the car and rang the doorbell.

"Hey Al." Gianni smiled when she opened the door to let him in. She was dressed like she was about to go somewhere. Al was hoping that he didn't catch them at a bad time because he really needed to talk.

"What's up girl? How you feeling?"

"Much better but I still wanna fuck Dior up. Bitch got me missing a patch of hair."

Gianni frowned at the thought. Thankfully, it was in the back and her hair was thick. As long as she kept it down, no one would notice. Her stiches had dissolved and the doctor was confident that it would grow back.

"Don't even let that get to you, G. It'll grown back and it's not even noticeable. Where your man at?"

"He's in the shower."

"Are y'all about to go somewhere?"

"No, I'm about to take a ride with Gio but he's staying here."

Gianni had been spending a lot of time with her father and meeting all of her family on his side. She was excited to know that she had another grandmother and more cousins than she could count. Heavy had four daughters and one of them was the same age as Gianni. Gio had another son but he was killed while he was locked up. She was surprised that most of his family had met her mother and knew her very well. They welcomed her into their circle and they stayed in contact with her. The feeling was foreign but she welcomed it.

"That's what's up," Al said, pulling her away from her thoughts.

"I made some stuffed bell peppers, chicken and macaroni. Do you want me to fix you a plate?"

"Thanks but I'm good." He dropped his head and sighed. Al didn't even have an appetite. He wasn't his normal talkative self and Gianni could tell that something was wrong. She took a seat on the sofa across from him so that they could talk.

"Are you okay?"

"I will be. Just know that you're not the only one who hates Dior's hoe ass."

"That bitch. What did she do to you?"

"Hoe is trying to blackmail me."

"Blackmail you? How?"

"She's threatening to tell people something that I wasn't ready to disclose?"

"Like what? I'll understand if it's something that you don't feel comfortable discussing."

Al hesitated for a while, debating if he wanted to tell Gianni any of his business. It didn't make sense for him to keep it hidden any longer. Pretty soon, everyone was gonna know.

"I'm gay and Danny is my boyfriend," he blurted out.

He stared at Gianni trying to see her reaction. Her face never gave away how she felt or what she was thinking. She looked at him like she was waiting for him to say more.

"And?" she questioned after a long pause.

"What do you mean and? That's enough, don't you think?"

"I mean, I kind of suspected that Danny was gay but I would have never known that y'all were a couple. But, trust me, as fucked up as my life was and is, I have no room to judge. As long as y'all are happy is all that matters."

"What's up nigga?" Nix asked when he walked into the room.

Gianni fixed him something to eat right before she left. Nix sat on the sofa across from Al and ate his food.

"I just told G about me and Danny and she didn't even seem surprised," Al noted.

"So what. The shit ain't even as deep as you're trying to make it seem."

"Or maybe she already knew. Did you tell her?"

"Do I ever tell anybody about y'all? I was with Dior for years and she didn't even know until you slipped up. Don't come at me like that bruh. I'm loyal if nothing else."

"Yeah, you're right. My bad bruh. Shit is just all fucked up right now. I need to rap with you about a few things."

"What's good?" Nix asked.

He sat and listened as Al ran everything down to him. Dior had become a problem for too many people. She was acting like someone who Nix didn't even know. He knew that their breakup didn't bring out the treacherous side of her. It had to have been there all along. Maybe she didn't have a reason to show it when they were together.

"She's trying to be another problem that I really don't need right now."

"Man, I don't want no parts of Dior around me or my club. But I would never let her do you dirty like that. I don't know what the fuck she's so pressed about coming to the club for. But, if it'll buy you some more time until you decide what you wanna do, I'm all for it. Just keep her on the bottom level and away from me and Gianni. Bitch even look at my girl wrong and it's over for her. G still wants to tag that ass and I might be tempted to let her."

Seeing his ex in his club again was the last thing that Nix wanted and he knew that Gianni wouldn't approve. She still wanted to beat Dior's ass and he didn't blame her. But Al was like his brother and he would do anything in his power to help him.

"I appreciate you for even offering but it's not necessary. I wouldn't even put you in that kind of position. Maybe this is just the push that I needed to get my mind right. I talked to Danny about it and it's time for me to be honest with myself and everybody else too. Fuck what people say or think."

"Shit, I've been telling you that for years."

"Yeah man, I know. We found the perfect house and Danny got his pops ready to write the check. I'm not gonna pass up on my happiness just to please other people. This shit is stressful and miserable."

"It's only stressful for you because everybody else is happy and living their lives."

"I already know. I'm too grown for this shit. I already called and told my mama that I was coming to rap with her one day next week when she's free. She's going out of town this week, so I have to wait. I guess I'll talk to Kinsley afterwards."

"She gon' cry," Nix said, making him laugh.

"I already know but fix me a plate nigga. G asked if I wanted her to do it and I said no. That shit smells good as fuck."

"Nigga, you better wash your hands and handle that. It's good as hell too," Nix replied as he finished off the last of his food.

He got up and got some more after Al fixed himself a plate. They sat down and talked and Al felt better about the decision that he'd made. He wasn't dumb enough to think that it would be easy but he was ready for whatever.

Chapter 15

"Hey, my love. How have you been?" Al's mother, Amelia, said when she opened the door and ushered him inside.

He saw Nix's grandparents on their porch, so he went and spoke to them before he made his way next door to the house that still belonged to his grandparents. Unlike him, Al's mother never did have a house of her own. She always lived with her parents unless she found a man to lay up with for a few days. Amelia used to run the streets so much that his grandparents had him more than she did. Since they lived under the same roof, they never complained. Besides, he spent most of his free time next door with Nix anyway. They were both the only children for their parents, but Nix always had Jake to play with.

"Hey Ma. I'm good. How you been?"

"Blessed and highly favored."

"Where's grandma?"

"She's out shopping with your auntie. This is a pleasant surprise since I barely get to see you anymore."

"I know. I be busy with work and stuff."

"You call that den of sin work?" Amelia asked as she ushered him into the dining room where she had been sitting. She had her bible open and appeared to be taking some notes.

"It pays the bills and provides well for my daughter."

"How is my grandbaby? I haven't seen her in a few weeks."

"I'm picking her up when I leave. I talked to her and her mama right before I got here." He would have loved to get his daughter before he got there, but she didn't need to witness the conversation that he planned to have with his mother. He was almost sure that it wouldn't go too well.

"Why don't you make an honest woman out of Kinsley? Y'all already had a baby out of wedlock. God honors the institute of marriage. Alexa deserves to have both her parents under the same roof."

"Whatever Kinsley and I had is over. Besides, I'm already in a committed relationship with the person that I plan to marry," Al revealed, deciding to just get the conversation over with.

You're The Best Part

"Oh baby! I'm so happy for you. My God answers prayers and He never fails. I can't wait to meet her. Or is it somebody that I already know?" Amelia had a huge smile on her face, but he was sure that it wouldn't stay there once he told her who it was.

"Yeah, it's somebody that you know."

"Who baby? Who is it?"

"Danny," Al responded, wiping the smile from her face just like he knew he would.

"I hope that's short for Danielle."

"No, it's short for Daniel."

"As in your good friend Daniel? Is this a joke Aldrin? If so, I don't find anything funny."

"It's not a joke Ma. I've been having these feelings since I was a little boy but I tried my best to suppress them. Danny and I started dating in high school but it was off and on. I tried to lie to myself and hide who I was and that's how Alexa came along. I don't regret my daughter but I'm tired of being ashamed of myself just to please other people."

"Well, you should be ashamed of yourself because I'm mortified. Homosexuality is an abomination and the pits of hell surely await you if you don't repent and give your life to God."

"I've already given my life to God but you don't have a heaven or hell to put me in. Let's not forget about the sins of your past that you try so hard to forget."

"My God has already forgiven me and cast my past transgressions into the sea of forgetfulness. Genesis chapter nineteen versus one through thirteen states that-"

273

"I already know what it says, just like I know what all the other scriptures say. Can you just stop being a pastor for one minute and be my mother?"

"I'll always be both but, no matter what I am, I'll never be okay with the devil using my only child. This is an attack of the enemy but my God will never leave me nor forsake me," Amelia said as she placed her hands on Al's forehead and started to pray for him. She was speaking in tongues and trying to cast out demons that weren't there. She prayed for a good fifteen minutes, and Al sat there and let her.

"Amen," Al mumbled out of respect once his mother was done.

"Thank you, Lord. We have the victory," Amelia said triumphantly.

"I appreciate the prayers mama, I always do. But that doesn't change anything. I'm gay and that's something that you can't pray away."

"Get out! And don't you dare think about setting foot in my house again until you're ready to repent."

Al wanted to say more but his mother rushed to the door and held it open for him. It was crazy how judgmental she was because his grandfather was the pastor before her and he was nothing like that. For years, their choir director was an openly gay man, but Amelia ran him off when she took over. She acted as if she was without sin because she didn't mind casting the first stone.

"I love you, Ma, and that will never change. I just hope that we can one day move on from this," Al said, right before she slammed the door in his face.

Although he was prepared for her reaction, it still hurt. His heart was heavy as he walked to his car and drove away. Spending time with his daughter always lifted his spirits, no matter how down he was. He called Kinsley to let her know that he was on his way, but she didn't answer. She already knew that he was coming, so he just headed over there. It took him about fifteen minutes and he was happy to see that her car was parked in her assigned spot. Alexa had been begging to go to Build-A-Bear so that's where he planned to take her.

Al got out of his car and rang the doorbell of Kinsley's townhouse. Alexa opened the curtain on the huge front window and smiled when she saw him. She always got excited when she saw him and that did him all the good in the world. After a few minutes, the door was yanked open and Kinsley stood there with her arms folded across her chest.

"What do you want?" she asked angrily.

"The fuck you mean. I told you that I was coming to get her today."

"Well, she's not going. I don't want my baby around a bunch of fags," Kinsley snapped, breaking his heart with her harsh words. Calling a gay man a fag was equivalent to being called a nigger by a white person. In his eyes, it was a racial slur.

"Man, my personal life has nothing to do with my daughter."

"Now I see why you never wanted us to get back together. You were too busy sucking and fucking your best friend. If Dior wouldn't have told me, I would probably still be in the dark. I feel sick to my stomach just thinking about it."

Just like Nix had predicted, Kinsley was crying. Al knew that she was in love with him but the feelings weren't mutual. He never led her on to make her think otherwise.

"Who I choose to be with has nothing to do with my daughter. She's well taken care of and always will be."

"Like I just said, she's not going. She's too young to be exposed to that nasty shit. She already got a mama. She doesn't need two."

"Bitch, I'm all man!" Al yelled in his own defense.

"Am I coming with you, daddy?" Alexa asked when she walked up to the door.

"No, you're not. I'll bring you wherever you want to go."

"But I wanna go with daddy." Alexa started crying and that broke Al's heart. His daughter was innocent and she didn't deserve to be used as her mother's pawn.

"Don't do this Kinsley. You're letting your personal feelings get in the way and this has nothing to do with our daughter."

"I don't care. Get away from my house before I have you arrested for trespassing."

For the second time in less than an hour, another door was slammed in Al's face. The second time hurt worse than the first because he knew that he would be lost without his daughter. Al felt defeated as he drove home. He knew that being honest would cause some backlash, but he really wasn't prepared for it. He was happy to see Danny's car still parked in his driveway because he would have usually been gone to his own house by now.

"Hey. How did everything go?" Danny asked as soon as he walked into the house. He was sitting on the sofa watching tv and Al sat right next to him.

"All bad," Al replied as he buried his face in Danny's lap and cried.

You're The Best Part

"Oh baby. What happened and where is Alexa?" He was usually the crybaby and that was out of the ordinary for Al.

"That bitch Dior obviously got to Kinsley before I could. She wouldn't even let me take my baby."

Danny listened, as Al told him everything that happened with his mother and Kinsley. He hated to see him look so lost and broken. Al was always the strong one out of the two of them. Danny would fold under the slightest bit of pressure, but Al was tough. Danny didn't give as many passes as Al did though. If somebody did him wrong, he didn't wait to retaliate.

"Now, I can't make your mama come around. That's something that she's gonna have to do on her own. But Kinsley got the game fucked up. You take very good care of Alexa. She has your last name and you're listed on her birth certificate. In the eyes of the law, you're eligible for joint custody. Hell, you take care of her mammy too. That bitch could never afford to live in those upscale townhomes if it weren't for you paying the rent. It ain't like she got a job. Being a part-time kitchen beautician ain't gon' cut it. I'm about to call my daddy to get on that shit right now," Danny said while grabbing his phone from the coffee table.

"I don't want to put my baby through all that court bullshit. She don't even deserve that."

"And you don't deserve her being kept away from you. I'm sorry Aldrin but I'm not gonna sit around and let nobody walk all over you. We're gonna be homeowners soon and we chose our house with Alexa in mind. The house will belong to her too."

Al only nodded his head and smiled. He loved the fact that Danny was always including his daughter in everything that they did. Danny made sure that all the houses they looked at had a big enough yard for a pool and

277

swing set for his daughter. He also made sure that they would have enough rooms for her to have her own bedroom and play room. Al hated to do it, but Danny was right. He had no choice but to get the courts involved. Kinsley was stubborn and he was sure that she wasn't gonna change her mind.

"Go ahead and make the call."

"Say less. And I got something for that bitch Dior too. She fucked with the wrong niggas," Danny fussed while dialing his father's number.

"Girl, fuck her. I don't give a damn if she is Nix's mama," Crystal fussed as she talked on the phone with River and Dior.

"Exactly. And I don't know why you're going over there trying to kiss her ass. She made her choice. She jumped in the fight to help his new girlfriend and she hasn't answered the phone for you since then," River chimed in.

"First off bitch, I don't kiss nobody's ass. No matter what happened between me and Nix, Nichelle has always been there for me. I just feel like I owe her an apology."

"Like I said, fuck her. Did you see how the fuck my eye looked after all that shit happened?"

Crystal had a broken blood vessel in her eye and a black ring underneath it. She was pissed that Dior felt like she owed Nichelle an apology for anything. She showed them exactly what it was when she jumped in the fight to help her son's new bitch. Now, Dior was banned from the club and so were they. She had been calling Nichelle since everything happened but she didn't even bother answering for her.

"I'll call y'all back later. I just pulled up," Dior said before he hung up.

She got out of the car and knocked on Nichelle's door. Her car was out front, but Quick's wasn't. She was hoping that she was home and not riding with her husband. When she heard the locks being undone, Dior was happy that she hadn't made a blank trip.

"What's good Dior?" Nichelle had her arms folded across her chest and her tone was far from being friendly. She stood in the door and her entire mood seemed angry and aggressive.

"That's what I'm trying to see. I've been trying to call you."

"And I didn't answer for a reason."

"Damn. It's like that Nichelle?"

"How did you expect it to be? You were dead ass wrong for going to my baby's club with all that bullshit. He moved on and you should have let that shit go. I didn't tell you who his new girlfriend was for a reason. I already knew what was gon' happen."

"You didn't have to tell me because I saw the shit with my own eyes. He's not the only one who can watch the

279

cameras." Dior had talked all over herself and she regretted it as soon as the words left her mouth.

"What the hell is that supposed to mean?"

"Nothing. I just came here to apologize."

"No need to apologize to me about nothing. Had I known why you and Nix had broken up when it first happened, I would have cut ties with you altogether. As much as he gave you, stealing was something that you didn't even have to do. I don't respect you for that shit at all. I play about a lot of things but my baby ain't one of them."

Dior only went there to apologize, but Nichelle had her fucked up. True, she had been there for her during some of her toughest times but that didn't give her the right to be disrespectful. She was done being nice and the gloves were off.

"Stop acting like you give a fuck about Nix so much now. You didn't even raise him." When Nichelle walked all the way out of the house and got in her face, Dior knew that she had fucked up.

"No bitch, I didn't, but I damn near raised you. Let's not forget who was there when you graduated high school. You know, when your throwed off ass daddy faked a heart attack so he didn't have to come. He made sure that your sisters didn't come either since they had to rush him to the hospital. I'm the same bitch that decorated your college dorm room and made sure that you had everything that you needed when you moved in. I'm the same one that wiped your tears when your daddy didn't bother showing up for that graduation either. He didn't even give a fuck enough to lie that time. I might have done some shit that I'm not proud of but I was more of a parent to you than the nigga who nutted in your mama to make you. Don't play with me, lil girl."

"I never denied anything that you did for me so no need to bring it up."

"I had to remind you since you felt like talking crazy."

"Look, I just came to apologize. I wasn't trying to implicate you in my drama and I didn't know that my friends were gonna jump in."

"Girl, Dior, miss me with that bullshit. Them hoes came there to fight just like you did. Y'all were dressed for the bullshit. Besides Nix choosing to be with her, Gianni ain't never did shit to you. And be careful of who you call a friend and tell your secrets to. That bitch Crystal was getting the dick even when you couldn't," Nichelle replied, right before she walked into the house and left her standing there.

Dior was stuck for a moment, shocked by what Nichelle had just said. Crystal had been her friend since before Nix became her man. She and River both lived on the same block as her and their houses was where she often ran to seek shelter from her father's verbal abuse. She didn't want to believe that one of her best friends would do her dirty like that but she knew that it was true.

It all made sense to her now. She always found it odd how Nix went out of his way to speak to Crystal. She knew that it couldn't be because it was her friend because he never said a word to River. Hell, he never said a word to her either. Dior was fuming as she jumped into her car and sped off. She was swerving in and out of traffic as she tried to get to her destination as soon as possible. Once she pulled up to the complex, Dior double parked before she got out and banged on the front door.

"Hey girl. You didn't tell me that you were coming over." Crystal smiled when she opened the door. Although she was annoyed with her friend, she was always happy to see her. Instead of replying to her greeting, Dior grabbed her hair and pulled her outside.

"Dirty bitch. I knew that something was up with your hoe ass. You fucked Nix."

Dior was screaming and hitting her with every word that she spoke. Crystal was swinging back but neither woman could be considered much of a fighter. They were doing a lot of hair pulling and slapping until Crystal kicked Dior, making her fall to the ground.

"Fuck you, Dior. That nigga couldn't have loved you that much. He damn sure didn't turn me down."

Crystal was breathing hard and so was Dior. They had never gotten into it that bad before and they had been friends for years. They argued all the time but it was never anything that lasted more than a day. It was fucked up that their friendship ended over a man who didn't want either one of them. Crystal was hoping to take her secret to the grave but she was alive and well and it was out in the open.

"You always were a jealous ass bitch. Nix tried to tell me, but I was too dumb to see it. I had my eyes on them other hoes when the real snakes were right there in my circle. Bitch, on my mama, you better stay far the fuck away from me. Your people gon' be picking out your casket if you don't," Dior warned as she walked back to her car.

Dior wasn't the violent type but her threat had Crystal shook. Everyone knew how much she loved Nix, so she believed her when she threatened to end her life. Granted, Crystal felt bad as hell for what she did but it was too late for regrets. She had been attracted to Nix since she first laid eyes on him but she suppressed those feelings for the sake of her friendship with Dior. River used to joke about fucking him too, but Crystal took it a step further. She played on Nix's emotions when he and Dior first broke up.

He was hurt and vulnerable and she used that to her advantage.

Dior pulled away from Crystal's house right before she walked back inside. Her first mind told her to just leave but she was too angry to listen. She turned back around and pulled up right next to her ex-best friend's car. Dior grabbed the tire iron from her trunk and went to work on Crystal's car. The alarm went off right when she broke the first window. She hurriedly broke two more before Crystal came running back outside.

"You crazy bitch! What the fuck are you doing? I'm calling the police!" Crystal yelled as she pulled her phone out.

"Shady ass bitch. I can't believe that I ever trusted your ass."

Dior was ranting while kicking her car and putting dents in it with the tool that she was holding. She looked deranged and Crystal had never seen that side of her before. She ran inside and grabbed her can of mace, preparing to temporarily blind the woman that she once considered her sister. Dior saw the small can in her hand when she came back out and she was prepared. As soon as Crystal lifted the spray and aimed it at her, she threw the tire iron with all her strength and hit Crystal in the head, knocking her out cold. As soon as her body hit the concrete, Dior ran back to her car and sped away.

Tears fell from her eyes as she drove. Her emotions were all over the place and she didn't know where to run. She felt like she was all alone and the one person who she would usually call didn't want anything to do with her. Nichelle was like the mother that she never had and losing her felt like losing Nix all over again. Talking to her sisters was pointless because they were too judgmental. They would have scolded her for fighting, especially with Crystal.

With a heavy heart, Dior went home and grabbed her bottle of Hennessy. She cried and drank until the bottle was empty before she fell asleep.

"Damn man, I feel like this shit is all my fault. I wasn't even paying attention," Al sighed.

"You didn't do nothing wrong bruh. That entire night was chaotic and we were all preoccupied. I usually don't forget to lock my office door but shit was crazy," Nix replied.

He and Al had just pulled up and looked over the camera footage from the last time Dior was in the club. Nichelle told him about their conversation two days before. Nix was curious about something that she said about the cameras.

He knew that Dior didn't have access to his home or phone, so his office was the only other place where he had monitors. He and Al watched as she snuck into his office and sat behind his desk. She'd obviously seen the footage of him and Gianni having sex and that explained why she behaved the way she did. Dior cried but she never turned away from the monitor. Nix had looked at the footage from that day already but he stopped it after he saw the exchange between Biggie and Gianni. He never thought that he'd have a reason to go view it again.

"The fuck is wrong with that broad. That's definitely not the same Dior that we knew for all those years. I know it sounds fucked up but I'm happy that you didn't marry her ass. It's like she's an entirely different person now."

"I said the same thing but people don't make those kind of drastic changes overnight. That's always been who she is. Maybe we just didn't know her as well as we thought we did."

"I'm so embarrassed," Gianni said when she walked into the office.

"What's wrong baby?" Nix asked.

"Look at this bullshit."

She handed Nix her phone and showed him exactly what she was talking about. He frowned when he saw the video of her and Dior fighting. He got mad all over again as he thought back to all the events of that night.

"Who sent this to you?"

"One of the girls in my study group. She said she got it from her cousin. Ain't no telling who else saw it. Shit got me heated all over again."

"Don't worry about it G. You spanked that ass good. That's why her scary ass had to grab that bottle," Al said, right as there was a knock on the door.

Nix looked at the cameras and saw Danny standing there. Gianni opened the door and he rushed in holding up a magazine.

"This bitch must really be feeling herself! Look at this shit!" Danny yelled.

He loved to read a magazine called *Ready To Rumble* that always put local stories and happenings inside. He flipped to a page in the back and threw it on the desk for all of them to see.

"Man, the fuck is this girl really on. Is this a mug shot?" Al laughed when they saw Dior's picture inside.

"It sure is. Destruction of property through vandalism and battery with a deadly weapon. That bitch went to jail two weeks ago. I wonder who her scary ass used a weapon on this time? Hoe can't fight for shit," Gianni frowned.

"I don't know but I'm about to call my daddy and find out," Danny replied while pulling out his phone.

They listened as Danny gave his father Dior's information. He had to ask Nix for her date of birth but his father was in his law office looking it up.

"I wonder if she's out now," Gianni said.

"Knowing her sisters, she got out the same day," Al replied.

"Are you sure daddy? Did you put in the correct info. Okay, thanks, I'll call you later. Love you," Danny said before he got off the phone with his father.

"What did he say?" Al knew that it had to be bad because Danny looked puzzled.

"That crazy bitch attacked her friend Crystal with a tire iron after destroying her car. Dior is really losing her mind. I thought that was her best friend."

Al looked at Nix and started laughing. Nix had a smirk on his face, but Danny and Gianni were clueless. They knew why Dior attacked her girl and Nix didn't feel no kind of way about it. He was happy that Dior knew the kind of snakes that she surrounded herself with. He tried to tell her but she never listened.

"What are we missing here? What's funny?" Gianni asked.

"It's nothing but I'll tell you about it later," Nix replied. Danny didn't push the issue because he knew that Al would tell him once they got home.

"Well, I'm the star of my own show." Gianni showed Danny the video that was sent to her. He wasn't around when the fight took place, so he was seeing it all for the first time.

"Send that to me, Gianni," Danny requested.

"Let that shit go Danny." Al knew how petty he could be at times. Danny didn't know how to let shit go and he wasn't with the added stress and drama.

"I'll let it go when I give that bitch a dose of karma. Since she likes to ruin lives, let's see how the school will feel knowing that they got an aggressive convict teaching their students. She fucked with the wrong niggas."

"Do it Danny. Fuck her." Gianni frowned.

"Stop being messy Gianni," Nix laughed, right as a loud voice interrupted their conversation.

"Aye boss man. We got a lil problem out here," Vic said over the walkie talkie.

"What kind of problem could we possibly have when the club ain't even open yet?" Nix countered as they looked at the monitor.

"Man fuck!" Al bellowed when he saw Kinsley out front arguing with the bouncers.

"Don't trip bro. I'll come out there with you. Stay in here for a minute Danny. You already know that she's gonna lose it if she sees you." Nix got up and followed his best friend out of his office and down the stairs.

As soon as they walked out of the building, Kinsley walked over to them and threw some papers at Al's feet. She was trying to swing on him, but Nix was holding her back.

"You dirty muthafucker! You're trying to take my baby away from me! How could you even put her through this shit? She's a child Al!" Kinsley yelled and cried.

"Learn how to read dummy. I asked for joint custody. I'm not gonna let you keep my daughter away from me every time you get angry. I haven't seen her in two weeks and that's unacceptable. Don't let the calm demeanor fool you. Behind my daughter, I'll show you another side of me."

"You mean the side of you that would rather fuck another nigga."

"Bitch!" Al was the one who had to be held back that time. Heavy lifted him off his feet before he had a chance to get to Kinsley.

"The truth hurts, don't it? And then you got my baby around all that bullshit. Uncle Danny my ass. Step daddy Danny is more like it."

289

Al was over being embarrassed about his sexual preferences. He and Danny weren't hiding their relationship anymore and he didn't care who knew. He regretted not taking Nix's advice a long time ago. He was tired of giving a fuck about what people said and he was over it. Just like his friend predicted, he was much happier now.

"This ain't got shit to do with Danny and you know it. Keep it real Kinsley. I could have been fucking another bitch and you would have still felt the exact same way. You're mad because I don't want your ass. I've always kept shit real with you from day one. I told you that I didn't want a relationship with you and I never led you on. It ain't my fault that you fell in love and wasted so many years of your life hoping for something that was never gonna happen. I'm a damn good father. You and nobody else can take that from me. Get you a good lawyer sweetheart. I'm going to the end of the earth to fight for mine."

Al pulled away from Heavy and walked back into the club. Kinsley fell to her knees and cried, as Nix tried his best to console her. Al was right and she didn't even have a rebuttal. He never made her think that he wanted her but she always hoped that he would change his mind. She was the mother of his only child and that had to count for something. Sadly, it never did. He took great care of their daughter and he helped her out if she ever needed anything. Al paid her rent and the insurance on the new car that he put the down payment on. He was a good man but she wanted him to be her man. She could compete with other women but there was no way that she could compete with another man.

"I can't believe that he's doing this to me. Can you talk to him for me, Nix, please? I can't afford a lawyer and he knows that."

"Well, stop denying that man a chance to see his daughter, Kinsley. Come on nah fam. You know that Al handles his business with Alexa. Hell, he handles his business with you too. I get that you feel some type of way but what you're doing is fucked up. Y'all daughter don't deserve to be put in the middle of that bullshit. You know how crazy she is about Al. You can't tell me that she hasn't been asking about him."

"Yeah, she has but I don't want my daughter around Danny."

"Why not? She's been around him all her life. She loves him just as much as she loves me. You never had a problem with it before you found out that they were together."

"How could he do this to me? What did I do so wrong to make him turn to another man?" she sniffled.

"This don't have shit to do with you, Kinsley. It's not my story to tell but you and Al need to calm down first, then sit down and have an adult conversation. Y'all are both good parents. Y'all don't have to be together to raise Alexa the right way. Don't let your personal feelings get in the way of what you know is right. That man is hurt about not seeing his daughter and that's fucked up. That ain't even you to do some shit like that."

Kinsley had calmed down and was listening to everything that Nix was saying. He was always the voice of reason and he was right. She was in her feelings and her innocent daughter was suffering because of it. Although she didn't have a man, she enjoyed the free time that she had when her daughter was with Al. She had to get her shit together for the sake of Alexa more than anything.

"How can I drop this court case?" Kinsley asked calmly.

"You can't because you didn't file it."

"I won't fight him anymore. Tell him that he can drop it and I'll have Alexa ready for him to pick her up this weekend."

"How about I tell him to call you later and y'all can discuss it?" Nix offered.

"Thanks Nix. I appreciate you." Kinsley smiled weakly before she walked away and got into her car.

"Shit, I need something to smoke," Nix said as he walked into the club.

He kept going until he exited through the back where the employees parked. He fired up his blunt and rested his back against the building as he smoked it. Nix had a million thoughts running through his head. He was hoping that things worked out for Al. His boy was finally happy and he hadn't seen him that way in a long time.

"Just the person that I wanted to see. I should have known that you were back here getting lifted. Some things never change."

Nix looked up, startled that he was caught off guard since he didn't see anyone coming. He glanced Alicia's way before he turned his head and continued to smoke.

"The fuck you looking for me for?"

"I'm actually looking for your ex bitch. That hoe played with the right one."

"She's my ex for a reason. I don't keep up with my past."

"That bitch was the one who told my husband about us. Stalking ass hoe."

"How the fuck does Dior even know your husband?"

"She doesn't. We talked a few times, so she knew the basics. Shit that I told her in general conversation, she used against me. Bitch went to my husband's job and everything."

Alicia and her husband had decided to go to marriage counseling after she got caught cheating with Nix. Mikell ended up coming clean with her about how he found out and she was livid. Dior was doing too much over a nigga who she wasn't even with anymore.

Alicia's marriage wasn't perfect but Dior had made the shit worse. When she came clean to her husband about everything, he was hurt. He was having a hard time getting over it. They couldn't go a day without him bringing it up until he just got tired of talking altogether. Alicia came home from shopping one day, and Mikell and all of his belongings were gone. She got served with divorce papers the next week and she hadn't seen him since then. She couldn't help but to think back to what Nix had told her. She had way more to lose than he did and he was right. In the end, she lost the love of her life and it wasn't worth it.

"Well, you gotta fault yourself for that. Next time, keep your cards close so people don't know what's in your hand." Nix shrugged, pulling her away from her thoughts.

"It's all good, but what's up with me coming back to work. Are y'all hiring?"

"Nah, your position and every other spot has been filled."

"That's cool. What's up with you?" Alicia walked up on him and put her hand on his chest.

"Not a muthafucking thing."

"You don't have to worry about Mikell no more. We're about to be divorced."

"I was never worried about your punk ass husband. I got a girl and I was good on you even if I didn't."

"Boy bye. When did you get a girlfriend?" Alicia looked at him skeptically, waiting for him to answer her question. When the back door opened, both of them looked to see who was coming outside.

"Don't make me fuck you up out here Jacobi!" Gianni yelled angrily while walking up on him.

"I didn't even do shit," he laughed.

Gianni looked all sweet and innocent but she was ignorant as fuck. Her mouth was reckless and she popped off whenever she felt like it was necessary. She must have been looking at the cameras because she knew exactly where to find him.

"I don't find a muthafucking thing funny! You've been out here talking just a little bit too long. Make sure you keep that same energy when a nigga smile up in my face."

Gianni was pissed as she turned to walk away. Nix had told her all about his little fling with Alicia, but she didn't give a damn. She didn't have nothing to say to her. It was her man who she had the problem with. Nix grabbed her arm to stop her from leaving.

"Don't play with me, girl. You doing all that trippin' for nothing."

"Why is she still standing here then?"

Alicia was just standing there listening to them going back and forth. She was stunned into silence. Nix did say that he had a girl but she would have never guessed that it was one of his employees. And a bottle girl at that. Gianni was always cool but she never really said much. She didn't chill at the bar and talk like some of the others. She asked for what she wanted and was on her way once she got it.

"I don't know and I don't care," Nix replied as he walked off with Gianni and left Alicia standing there. She felt played but it was all good. He didn't have to tell her twice. Nix was good in the bedroom but not good enough for her to make a fool of herself.

"I should have come out there and started swinging." Gianni was serious, but Nix thought it was funny. They went into the office but Al and Danny were preparing to open the club.

"You be watching the damn cameras more than I do." He sat behind his desk and pulled Gianni onto his lap.

"I was waiting for you to dismiss that hoe. You took too long, so I had to come speed up the process."

"Man, fuck her. Let's get married," Nix said out of the blue.

"Shut up," Gianni laughed.

"Nah, I'm dead ass serious. We already live together. What, you plan on leaving a nigga or something?"

"No, but we haven't even been together that long. We're still getting to know each other."

"I told you everything from birth until now. What else do you want to know?"

"That's not what I meant. We're learning each other as we go along."

"So, your answer is no?" he asked while looking at her.

"I didn't say no. I just think we should wait."

"Exactly what are we waiting for Gianni?"

"Honestly, Nix, I'm still learning shit about myself. For years I grieved and suffered in silence. I felt like I was in this world alone after my grandmother died, even though I had other family members. I was depressed, but I had to keep pushing and do what I had to do. I used to pray that I wake up and things were back to the way they used to be when I was a little girl. Have you ever felt like that? Do you ever wish that you can start your life over and do things differently?"

"Nope. Things happened just the way they're supposed to and I don't question it. You gotta think of life like a puzzle. You need all the small pieces to see the big picture. You're a small piece of my puzzle but you're the best part," he replied, making her blush. Nix reached into his desk drawer and pulled out a ring box. Gianni gasped when she saw the beautiful piece of jewelry that he pulled out of it. The emerald cut engagement ring looked expensive and, with his taste, she was sure that it was. He grabbed her hand, but she was reluctant to give it.

"Nix, I told you-"

"I know what you told me, baby, and I'm all for waiting if that's what you wanna do. I still want you to wear my ring. I'm gonna make sure that you wake up every morning and never regret putting it on your finger." She smiled as Nix slipped the ring onto her finger. He knew everything about her, so she wasn't surprised that it was a perfect fit.

"How did I end up getting engaged anyway?"

"Because I don't play that shit with you. Niggas like me don't take no for an answer."

"I'm serious Nix. It's too soon."

"I'm just fucking with you, baby. We can wait as long as you want to. I'm not going nowhere."

"I know because I'm not letting you," Gianni replied as she gave him a peck on the lips.

She had work to do, so she got up and sat in her own chair. When the club opened, Nix went to his section and chilled with Al for a while. He had the same talk with him that he had with Kinsley earlier. Al seemed to feel better about his situation, especially since Kinsley didn't want to take it to court. He still wanted to have something in writing just in case she started acting crazy again. Nix loved to see his friend happy and that was the goal that he had been trying to obtain for years.

Chapter 17

“What's been going on over there girl?” Kori asked as she sipped her spiked ghetto punch.

She and Amya were at a hole in the wall wing spot grabbing something to eat. They hadn't seen each other since Kori got fired, so they were playing catch up.

Kori was shocked when Al stopped her from clocking in to work the night that she went to see Gianni in the hospital. She shouldn't have been though because she had a feeling that it was coming. Nix looked like he hated her and she knew that he was the one who made the call.

Admittedly, she missed Gianni and she even tried calling her a few times. Her cousin never answered and she was sure that Nix was the reason. She was still having a hard time knowing that the two of them were even together. He appeared to really be feeling her cousin and the feelings seemed to be mutual.

"Girl, you don't have enough liquor in your system yet for me to tell you all that's been happening around there," Amya replied, snapping Kori out of her thoughts.

She still didn't really know everybody yet but she was learning. Some of the bottle girls talked a lot and she was always listening. Her uncle Vic told her a lot of what was happening too and most of it was unbelievable, if she had to say so herself.

"What do you mean. What's been happening like that?"

"You must not talk to Vic too much anymore. That nigga knows everything."

"Girl, fuck Vic. He pulled a few strings to help me get on at his friend's bar but I haven't seen or heard from him since then. I guess he's trying to be a good husband now."

Kori hated her new job and everything about it. The bar was small and shabby but it was better than nothing. The tips were trash compared to Club Nixon. The best part of it all was the older men who frequented the place. They loved young girls and she was making a killing finessing them out of their hard earned money.

"You scared that nigga when you got pregnant. All of his kids are grown and his wife would have left his ass. I guess he decided to fall back once you got rid of it."

"Fuck him. What's been going on?" Kori took a sip of her drink while giving Amya her undivided attention.

"Well, for one, Al and Danny are in a relationship."

She regretted saying anything while Kori was drinking because she spit out a mouth full of liquor. Some of it landed on Amya's arms and she frowned in disgust.

"Girl, I'm sorry but I wasn't expecting you to say that. When you say a relationship, what exactly do you mean?"

"A relationship bitch. They're a couple, as in boyfriends."

"Nah, I can't see that. I had my suspicions about Danny but Al ain't gay. The hoes used to be on him like crazy."

"Maybe so but he probably wasn't on them. Did you ever see him with anyone or has anyone ever claimed to be with him?"

"Now that I think about it, no, I haven't."

Kori thought back to the few bottles girls and customers who used to try to get at Al. He never seemed interested, but she didn't think anything of it. He was all about work and she assumed that he didn't want to mix business with pleasure. Al was a very private person, so she just figured that he might have had a girl at home. She never thought that it was because he was gay.

"It was the talk of the club for a few days but nobody cares anymore. That's their life and it's not even that deep. They're both cool so I wish them all the best."

"What about my cousin? What has she been up to?"

"I don't see her as much since she works in the office with her man now."

"She's not a bottle girl anymore?" Kori asked in shock.

"Nope, she does the books now. I guess Nix didn't want her being a bottle girl anymore after that fight. She be in the office or chillin' in Nix's section with her daddy."

"Gianni doesn't have a daddy."

"Bitch, everybody got a daddy," Amya replied while looking at her like she was crazy.

"Yeah but she doesn't know who hers is.

"Apparently she does because he's always coming to the club for her and his brother."

"Who is his brother?"

"Heavy," Amya revealed, shocking Kori once again.

"Girl, this is just too much. So Heavy is her uncle now. That don't even sound right."

"That's your cousin. I would have thought you knew before anybody else."

Kori hadn't told her about what happened between her and Gianni, and she didn't plan to. She felt bad about how she handled things with her cousin. She let her jealously cause her to make some stupid decisions that she was regretting.

"What's up cousin?" someone asked, making Kori lift her head to see who it was.

She smiled when she saw Greg standing there but the gesture wasn't for him. The man who was standing there with him was cute as fuck. His neatly twisted dreads hung to the middle of his back. He was tall just like she liked her men and his body was lean. He was a shade lighter and he wasn't as buff but he almost reminded her of Nix. There was a bar next door to where they were and Greg had been known to hang there. Kori hadn't been around that way in a while, so she didn't know if he still did.

"Hey cousin. What's been up with you?"

"Ain't shit. Stop being rude and introduce me to your friend."

"You didn't introduce me to yours but this is my girl, Amya. Amya, this is my cousin, Greg."

"What's good, beautiful?" Greg grabbed Amya's hand and kissed it.

"Hi, it's nice to meet you." Amya smiled politely but she got a bad vibe from him almost instantly. His eyes looked sneaky and his friend just looked as grimy.

"And you are?" Kori asked flirtatiously while looking at the other man who her cousin was with.

"I'm Jaron but you can call me Ronnie." He licked his lips as his eyes locked in on her breasts that were spilling out from the tank top that she had on.

"Are y'all in a hurry or would y'all like to join us?"

Amya looked at Kori and frowned when she said that. She got a bad feeling from both men but she didn't know them well enough to judge. She cringed when Greg took a seat next to her and struck up a conversation.

"What are you drinking beautiful?" Ronnie asked Kori.

"Have we met before? You look so familiar." Kori was trying hard to figure out where she knew him from but she was coming up empty.

"I don't think so. I would have remembered if we did. We can change all that though."

"Ole boy who owns the club where you work is his people," Greg said.

"Nix?" Kori knew that she wasn't crazy and she could definitely see the family resemblance.

"Yeah, that's my brother, even though they all try to deny it."

Ronnie sounded salty and the frown on his face gave away exactly how he felt. Unlike Nix, he had it hard growing up. His mother got addicted to crack and his grandparents didn't give a fuck. They gave him a place to stay and fed him but he was on his own after that. They always told him that Quick was his father and Ronnie tried reaching out to him when he became a teenager. Quick dismissed him, calling his family liars, even though he looked just like the men in the Nixon family. He said that he only had one son and he wasn't claiming nor taking care of another one. Ronnie was hurt but that was the story of his life. He never made that mistake again. As far as he was concerned, he didn't even have a father or brother.

"I didn't know that his mama had any other kids."

"She doesn't. We have the same daddy. The nigga never claimed me or did shit for me, so fuck him."

"What do you know about that nigga who owns the club?" Greg asked his cousin.

"Besides him being your brother-in-law, not much."

"Gianni fuck with that nigga." As far as Greg knew, his sister was still fucking with Biggie. Then again, he hadn't seen or talked to her in years. Everything that he knew about his baby sister came from Kori.

"Yep, she lives with him and everything."

"Where does she live?" Greg questioned.

304

When Kori opened her mouth to answer, Amya looked at her like she was crazy. Giving out Nix's personal info was going too far. Obviously, Gianni and her brother didn't have the best relationship if he didn't know anything about her.

"I don't know," Kori said as she watched Amya visibly relax.

"You still work over at the club?" Greg was fishing for info, but Kori's girl seemed to be blocking him from getting it.

"No, I don't work there anymore."

"Are you ready to go Kori?" Amya asked, hoping that she said yes.

"You drove so I guess so." Kori rode with her so she really didn't have a choice.

"I can bring you home if you're not ready to go," Ronnie offered. Kori wanted to play shy but she was too grown for that.

"You can go ahead Amya. I'll call you later," Kori said to her friend.

She didn't have to tell Amya twice. She grabbed her stuff and stood to her feet. Amya was big on good and bad vibes and she wasn't feeling their present company.

"What's good Amya? Can I get your number?" Greg asked.

"I'm sorry but I have a boyfriend."

"Good for you but I don't give a fuck about the next nigga."

"Maybe not but I do."

"Well, fuck you then. Ain't no need for me to be a gentleman and walk you to your car." Amya shook her head as she hurriedly walked away.

"Why you do my girl like that?" Kori laughed.

"Man, fuck her. What's good cousin? Is that job paying you right? If not, I might have a business proposition for you." Greg had a sly smile on his face as he spoke.

"What kind of business proposition?"

"One that will benefit the both of us. Let's go and I'll tell you all about it."

Just like his mother, Kori was out there being a hoe for free. Greg never understood women like that. They had a certified moneymaker between their legs and he was trying to get paid. Kori was young and attractive. With his help, she could possibly bring in more money than Janessa did.

"Man, I'm starving. I could have told Nichelle to cook something if I would have known that you weren't," Nix fussed as he looked in the refrigerator.

"Why do you keep opening the refrigerator? It's InstaView. You can see what's inside without opening it every ten minutes. Your ass is too grown to still be depending on people to cook for you."

"I'm not depending on people. I'm depending on my fiancée."

Gianni always smiled and blushed when he said that. She wore his ring proudly, but they hadn't discussed marriage again since he asked her the first time. She wasn't in a hurry and neither was he. They were learning more about each other every day and that was the fun part.

"I told you that my school work comes first. I had a lot of homework to do. I'll go grab us something from somewhere once I'm done."

It would have been easier for her to pull up to a drive-thru to feed him but he was a difficult nigga. She had to order from a restaurant and go inside to get it. Gianni's workload had picked up because she was near the end. Nothing came before that and Nix knew better.

"I guess I can wait."

"Or you can go get it yourself. As a matter of fact, that's what you need to do. I'm busy," Gianni replied, right as the doorbell rang.

Nix looked on the camera and saw Quick standing there. He grabbed his wallet and keys before he opened the door to greet him.

"What's up boy?" Quick asked as he gave him a fist pound.

"Ain't shit but you're right on time. Come run me to Outback to get something to eat."

"Let's roll," Quick said before they both walked to his car.

307

"I know you didn't just pop up on me for nothing. Nichelle does it all the time but you usually come for a reason. What's good?"

"How much do you know about this new girlfriend of yours?"

"Gianni?" Nix questioned. Quick had never questioned him about a woman before and he was confused as to why he was doing it now.

"Shit, that's the only woman that I know you're with. Am I missing something?"

"Nah but I'm curious as to why you wanna know anything about her."

"I just wanna know how much you really know about her. You put a ring on her finger kind of soon."

"I know all that I need to know about her and that's all that matters."

"I just think you're moving too fast with her."

"Nigga, I was conceived from a one night stand. The fuck you mean."

"Yeah but me and your mama got to know each other over time."

"That's the same shit that Gianni and I are doing now. What's the difference?"

"I'm just saying bruh. You knew Dior since y'all were kids and look at what she did."

Nix didn't know why he was surprised that his father knew. Nichelle always did talk too damn much.

"I appreciate your concern but I'm good."

You're The Best Part

"I'm just saying bruh, you're letting her in too soon. Ain't no way in hell she should be doing your books and shit. Now she knows how much money you make and she's probably sitting there plotting. I bet her ass gon' pop up pregnant soon. Just watch and see what I tell you."

"When have you ever known me to make a decision without thinking about it first? It's a little too late for you to assume the role as my father. I'm a grown ass man now. And if she does get pregnant, I'm gonna take care of my baby like I'm supposed to. That's more than I can say for you."

"Fuck what you talking about. I am and I always will be your father. I don't give a damn who raised you. I don't want you to let pussy cloud your judgement and stop you from using common sense."

"Nigga, pussy is everywhere. That shit never moved me and it never will. You seem to be the only person who have a problem with my relationship with Gianni."

"I don't have a problem with your relationship. I just want you to be smart about the shit."

"This coming from a nigga who went on a crime spree with his pregnant girlfriend and made another baby that he don't claim while she was locked up. I'm good on advice from you."

If it were anybody else, Quick probably would have shot him for talking reckless. He didn't raise his son but he loved Nix and Nichelle more than he loved himself. He did a lot of things when he was younger that he couldn't take back. He regretted not getting his life together when Nix was younger to be a better role model for him. Now, he and his son were more like friends and Nix looked at Quick's parents as his own.

Even when he was in the position to raise his son, Quick was too busy chasing hoes. By the time he and Nichelle stopped running the streets and settled down, Nix was a teenager. They tried to get him to come live with them but he wasn't having it. He had always been strong willed and outspoken. They never had to wonder what he was thinking because he always told them.

"Alright nigga. Don't say that I didn't try to warn you if shit go left."

"Like I said a minute ago, I'm good," Nix replied, signaling the end of their conversation.

Quick nodded his head in understanding but he left it alone. Nix would die if he knew that his father had been asking around about Gianni. His wife and parents seemed to love her. Granted, Gianni was cool, but he just felt like she dropped out of thin air. She had never been to jail and she was about to graduate from college. Other than that, there wasn't much more that could be said about her.

"I'll see you later bruh. I might pass by the club later on," Quick said once he dropped Nix off at home.

Nix nodded, not bothering to tell his father that he wasn't gonna be there. Quick pissed him off trying to give out unsolicited advice. As fucked up as he was, Nix would be a fool to listen.

He walked into the house, but Gianni was no longer in the living room studying. All of her papers were still there, so he was sure that she didn't go too far. When he walked into their bedroom, Nix paused when he saw about ten of her purses thrown on the bed. Gianni was in the walk-in closet looking through another one.

"What's up baby? What are you looking for?"

"I lose everything. I need to stop switching purses so much."

310

"Do you need some help?" Nix asked with an amused smirk.

"No, I'm good. I'll look in the other purses later."

"You got too damn many. Come eat before your food gets cold."

Gianni looked annoyed but she shrugged it off and followed Nix downstairs. They talked as they ate. Once they were done, Gianni finished her homework and they chilled and watched movies for the rest of the night.

Chapter 18

Dior was fuming inside as she looked at her sister, Grace, talking on the phone. Grace tried hard not to show any emotion on her face but Dior saw her as she kept sneaking peeks at her. Their father was loud as hell and she heard every word that he said. Even when Grace tried to turn her volume down, he could still be heard clearly.

"It's not as bad as it seems daddy. We're family and we'll get her through this," Grace said.

"Who the hell is we? I'm not giving a dime of my hard earned money to pay nobody else's bills. The damn job barely paid anything to begin with and she went and got herself fired. How stupid could she be?" Walter fumed.

He was always talking down on her job when he only had a middle school education. He had been a construction worker all his life but he made teaching seem like it was the bottom of the barrel. She didn't make as much as her sisters did but her job paid the bills. Well, it used to before things went left.

Dior was excited when she got called into the principal's office at her school two weeks before. She had put in for a master teacher's position and she stood a good chance of getting it. When she saw the vice principal and one of the supervisor's from the district office, she just assumed that that's what they were there for. She was shocked into silence when they played the video of the fight she'd had in Nix's club. She was even more surprised when they pulled up a picture of her mugshot.

She still couldn't believe that Crystal's hoe ass actually had her arrested. Dior was sure that she was the one responsible for her losing her job too. She didn't plan to tell her family what was going on but their father found out anyway. One of Walter's fishing buddies had a granddaughter that taught at the same school. Word spread fast once Dior was let go and her father was livid.

"Calm down daddy. You know you haven't been feeling well. Don't get yourself all worked up for nothing," Grace coddled.

"Crystal ain't been nothing but a good friend to her. Why would she attack that poor girl? I told y'all a long time ago that something wasn't right with her. She don't act nothing like you and your sisters. Y'all took after your mama. I can't believe that my wife lost her life to bring that one into the world."

"That's enough daddy. I keep telling you that words hurt and you need to be mindful of what you say."

"I ain't tell not one lie. You see that boy came to his senses and called off that wedding."

"Okay daddy. Go lay down and I'll be over there later to bring you something to eat."

"Alright baby. I love you and I'll see you later."

Hearing him tell her sister he loved her ignited a fire within Dior. He had never uttered those three little words to her and, sometimes, she needed to hear them.

"Fuck him!" Dior spat as soon as her sister got off the phone.

"Dior!" Grace gasped.

"Yeah, I said it and I meant it."

"That's still your father."

"Well, when the fuck is he gonna start acting like it!"

Dior jumped up from her sofa and started pacing her living room floor. She was experiencing a mixture of emotions and she felt like she was going crazy. She was stressing and nobody gave a fuck about her. Nichelle was too busy kissing Gianni's ass. Her friendship with Crystal was over and River refused to takes sides in the matter. Dior felt all alone and she had nobody to talk to.

"Calm down Dior."

"Why did you come here Grace? Huh? You don't give a fuck about me and you never did."

"That is not true and you know it. I love you and I'm here to help. Why didn't you call me, Dior?"

315

"Call you for what? I have some money saved up, so I'm good. I don't need y'all looking down on me for nothing else."

"I've never looked down on you and I'm not about to start. I just came here to make sure that you were okay since you never answered the phone when we tried to call you."

"Fuck you, too. I'm good on all y'all."

"I get that you're upset but I'm not the enemy."

"Yes, you are! You were just as bad as daddy was. You saw the way that he treated me, Grace. You were there to witness the way he talked to me. Yeah, you tried to take up for me but that wasn't enough. Why did you leave me there in that toxic ass situation? You're the oldest and you were supposed to protect me."

Dior cried as she said some of the things that she'd always wanted to say. Thanks to their mother's six figure insurance policy, all three of her sisters were homeowners at a young age. They used to get her to spend some nights with them but nobody got her permanently, and she always hoped that they would.

"You're right Dior and I'm sorry. I had a lot going on back then. I was married and trying to have kids in between furthering my career. You were probably too young to notice, but I had some issues of my own. I suffered with depression when I couldn't give my husband the kids that he kept asking for. I love my babies but using a surrogate was not something that I wanted to do. It wasn't my intentions to neglect you but I couldn't help you when I needed help too. I had so many regrets and not being there for you more is one of them. I love you and I don't ever want you to doubt that," Grace cried as she opened her arms for a hug.

She loved her little sister and the guilt for how their father treated her ate at Grace. Dior was innocent and she didn't deserve that. She even tried talking to their father but he was old and stubborn. Dior was what they called a change of life baby and their mother had complications from day one. Her doctor even recommended terminating the pregnancy because of all that he knew could go wrong. Walter was all for getting rid of the child but his wife refused. She had Dior and ended up having a massive heart attack in the delivery room. Since then, Dior was looked at as a curse to her father and that's exactly how he treated her.

"I love you, too," Dior replied as she walked into her sister's embrace. She needed that more than anything and she felt better than she'd felt in a while.

"I know that you have some money saved up but you don't need to touch that. We'll take care of all of your expenses until you can find another job. We need to see about getting those charges expunged too. That won't help with your job search."

"Thanks Grace. I appreciate you."

"We're family and that's what we're supposed to do. You need to come with us to Disney World next month since you're not working anymore. I wish you would have booked with us when we first did it."

"I thought your daddy was coming. That's why I declined."

"You know he's not flying anywhere but you should come. I got you if you decide to join us."

"Thanks but I'm good."

Her sisters, their husband and kids had rented a huge house and were staying in Disney World for two weeks. Dior and Nix had gone with them a few times before and they always had a good time. She would have loved to go again but she didn't want to intrude. She didn't have a man or kids, so it didn't make sense.

"I gotta go but I'll have a cashier's check for you next week," Grace said before she grabbed her purse and left.

Dior knew that her sister was only helping her out of guilt but she didn't care. She had a little over twenty thousand dollars in her savings and she planned to hold on to it as long as she could. If Grace wanted to pay her bills, she was gonna sit back and enjoy her paid time off.

"It's looks like you're enjoying your newfound unemployment status," River joked as she looked at Dior.

"What's not to like? My bills are paid and I can shop and do whatever I want to without a care in the world."

It had been almost two months since she got fired and Dior hadn't started job hunting yet. Grace was true to her word and she had a cashier's check for Dior when she said she would. Her other two sisters deposited money into her account every other week and she appreciated them. Dior had been working since she was seventeen and she was enjoying her time off. When River called and asked her if she wanted to go shopping, she jumped at the chance. They were now having lunch at one of their favorite Chinese restaurants. Her sisters were on their way back from Disney World and they invited her out to dinner the following day.

"But seriously, Dior, how have you been?" River asked sincerely.

"As good as I can be. Sometimes I just sit back and think about how so many things have changed over the past year. I really thought that Nix and I would be married with kids by now. You and Crystal were supposed to be my bridesmaids and life was supposed to be good. I just can't believe she did me like that."

"Yeah, she was wrong and I told her so. But you were wrong too. I understand that you were upset but beating her ass should have been sufficient. You didn't have to destroy her car and knock her out with a tire iron."

"Fuck her. That bitch better be happy that she's still alive."

"You might need to talk to somebody about your anger issues. It seems to be getting worse the older you get."

"I just don't have time for the bullshit. My anger isn't getting worse. My patience are getting shorter," Dior corrected, right as her phone rang to Grace's ringtone. The waitress came over with their bill but River grabbed it before her friend could.

"I got it," River said, right as Dior answered her phone. She knew that her friend wasn't working, so she didn't mind paying for their food.

"Hey sis. Are y'all back?" Dior asked.

"We just landed but we're still on the plane. I need a huge favor Dior. You know I wouldn't ask you if it wasn't important."

"Okay. What's up?"

"Daddy had a doctor's appointment today and found out that he has an upper respiratory infection. His doctor just called and told me that he called in a prescription for him. Can you pick it up and drop it off to him?"

Grace had just turned her phone off of airplane mode and her notifications were going crazy. When she got a message from her father's doctor, she got scared until she listened to what it said. Walter had been under the weather lately and she felt bad about leaving him to go out of town. He assured her that he was okay and she talked to him several times a day.

"No," Dior said without an ounce of hesitation.

"Dior, please. The pharmacy closes in an hour and I don't think I'll make it in time."

"How did he get to the hospital? Why can't he get his prescription the same way? I told you after his birthday that I wasn't stepping foot in the house again and I meant that."

"The hospital transportation van picked him up but they only bring them to and from their appointments. Please Dior. I'm asking as a favor to me."

"Fine. What pharmacy do I need to go to?" Dior conceded.

"Thanks so much Dior. I'll text you all the info now. His insurance will cover the cost, so you don't have to pay anything."

"Okay," Dior replied before she hung up.

"What's wrong?" River asked once she got off the phone. Dior was frowning like she'd gotten some bad news.

"Nothing. I have to run an errand for Grace."

"Oh okay. Well, it was nice spending the day with you, bestie. We have to do this again soon." River gave her friend a hug before they went their separate ways.

Dior was annoyed as she went to the pharmacy and got her father's prescription. She was only doing it as a favor to Grace. Her sister had been good to her and she didn't want to seem ungrateful.

When she pulled up to the house, Dior was praying that Walter was asleep. She planned to leave the medicine on the living room table and be on her way until Grace instructed her otherwise. Her sister wanted her to put the medicine in his hands so that he could start taking it right away. The house was quiet when Dior used her key to enter.

"Is that you Grace?" Walter called out from his bedroom.

"No muthafucker," Dior mumbled as she made her way down the hall towards his annoying ass voice. Walter was laid back in his recliner when she opened the door and walked into his bedroom.

"Oh, it's you. Where is Grace? She was supposed to be coming to bring me my medicine."

"Well, Grace ain't here. She asked me to go get it." Dior handed him the bag and he snatched it from her hands.

"Why couldn't she come bring it to me?"

"Does it matter? You got it and that's all that counts. Complaining ass."

"You better watch how the hell you talk to me," Walter hissed, right before he went into a violent coughing spell.

"Fuck you!" Dior spat angrily. She was fed up and respecting him wasn't happening anymore. She tried that in the past and it didn't work. She looked at him in disgust when he coughed up something into one of the Kleenex that he was holding.

"Get your disrespectful ass up outta my house and leave my key on the dresser. I don't know who the hell gave you one anyway. I never question God but I wanna know why. A beautiful soul lost just to give birth to a demon. Why did He take my wife and leave me stuck here in hell with you?"

"I've been wondering the same thing. Why couldn't it have been you instead of my mama? I'm sure I would have been better off without you."

"I regret the day I brought you home from the hospital. I wish I would have buried you instead of my wife."

That last comment did it for Dior. Although he may have always felt that way, it was a different story for him to voice it. He didn't care about how the things that he said or did made her feel. Tears fell from Dior's eyes as he continued to ramble about how much of a burden it was to keep her. She was in a daze as she walked over to his bed and grabbed a pillow. He didn't even see Dior coming since she approached him from behind. Walter gasped in shock when she put the pillow over his face and applied pressure.

"Evil bastard." Dior frowned as she used all the strength she had to end his miserable life.

"Help!" Walter's voice was muffled as his arms flailed weakly.

Dior cried as she thought back to every hateful thing that he'd ever said to her. She remembered every birthday that he never celebrated and every big event that he'd never attended. When things didn't work out between her and Nix, her father actually laughed. Dior was heartbroken and crying, and he found humor in her pain. According to him, Nix saved himself years of bad luck by marrying her. It was then that Dior realized just how much she hated her own father. She knew without a doubt that she disliked him but it was deeper than that now. She hated his very existence and she didn't want him to exist anymore.

Dior was in another world and she didn't realize how long she had been holding the pillow over her father's face. He had stopped fighting a long time ago, but she had zoned out. When she removed the pillow, Walter's eyes were open and so was his mouth. Dior closed them both before she put her impromptu murder weapon back in the bed.

"You look much better with your mouth closed," she sneered as she looked at Walter's lifeless body.

She took his pulse just to make sure the deed was done. She smiled when she didn't feel anything. Walter always said that she was a murderer and now, she really was. Dior jumped when her father's phone started ringing. When she saw that it was Grace calling, she started to panic. She had to find a way to get in front of the situation. Walter was seventy-five years old and something was always wrong with him. Him dying wasn't hard to believe but not by murder.

After pacing for a while, Dior grabbed her phone. As bad as she wanted to call Grace, she couldn't at the moment. She watched enough tv to know that she should call for help first before calling anyone else. That's how a lot of killers got caught. They called their accomplices or someone else before calling the police or an ambulance. Dior got into her acting mode and dialed those three familiar numbers.

"Police, fire and medical," the lady said when she answered the phone.

"I need help! Please hurry! My father is not breathing!" Dior yelled into the phone. She called out her father's address and begged them to hurry.

"Okay ma'am. Help is on the way. I need you to calm down for me and listen."

Dior was crying and mumbling as the woman gave her instructions on how to do chest compressions and mouth to mouth. She stood there looking at her father with hate-filled eyes, assuring the woman that she was doing everything that she told her to do. Dior had no plans on touching him, especially if it meant bringing him back to life. She was hoping that the pits of hell were opening up to receive him.

The wailing of the sirens pulled her away from her thoughts. Dior rushed to the door to let them in right before she called her sister.

"We're in the car headed home now," Grace said when she answered the phone.

"Grace! You need to get to daddy's house now!"

"Why? What's wrong Dior?" Grace asked as she instructed her husband to head to her father's house. She put the call on speaker and texted her other sisters. Dior sounded frantic and she knew that something had to be wrong.

"I just came to bring him his medicine and found him in his recliner unresponsive."

"Oh, my God! Call for help Dior!"

"I already did. They just got here."

"Okay, I'm on my way now," Grace replied before she hung up.

"Damn, I'm good." Dior smiled, giving herself an imaginary pat on the back. She seemed to have missed her calling. Maybe she should have been an actress instead of a school teacher. The performance that she'd just given was Oscar worthy if she had to say so herself.

It took about fifteen more minutes before Dior's sisters pulled up to the house. She didn't know how but she miraculously squeezed out some more tears.

"What's going on? Did they say anything?" Grace asked as she walked over to her.

"No, they're still in there working on him."

"That's not a good sign," their sister, Elise, said as her husband pulled her in for a hug.

"God, please don't let him die," Daria, the second oldest of the bunch, prayed.

Grace grabbed her sisters' hands as they all bowed their heads in prayer. Dior knew that it was in vain but she went along with it anyway. As soon as they were done, one of the paramedics came out to deliver the bad news.

"I'm so sorry. We tried everything that we could but he didn't make it," the man stated solemnly.

"No! Please no! I shouldn't have left. I knew that I should have stayed here with him," Grace sobbed as her husband tried his best to comfort her.

Dior looked at her sisters with their men and children surrounding them and she longed for that kind of companionship. Although she wasn't grieving, it would have been nice to have someone there to comfort her anyway.

"Are you okay auntie?" Grace's oldest daughter, Lexus, walked over and asked. She was a teenager and almost taller than Dior. She gave her auntie a hug and Dior appreciated that.

"Yeah, I'm okay." Dior hated that she was the cause of everyone's pain but she'd been hurting for years. It felt good to end the life of the person who caused it.

"Did he say anything when you got here Dior?" Grace questioned after a while.

"No. I walked into the room to give him his medicine and I immediately knew that something was wrong. He looked like he was struggling to breathe, so I called for help."

"He's been feeling bad for the past few weeks but he sounded fine when I talked to him earlier. He even told me that he was feeling better."

Grace was beating herself up for leaving when she knew that her father wasn't feeling his best. Everyone assured her that it wasn't her fault but she was having a hard time receiving it. When they carried her father out, she really lost it. She cried so much that she started throwing up. That was the only thing that Dior felt bad for. As for the man who they'd just loaded into the coroner's van, she felt nothing but relief.

"His old evil ass probably got a section reserved in hell," Nichelle said as she walked around the mall with Gianni.

She hadn't talked to Dior since she showed up at her house a while ago attempting to apologize. She was shocked when she saw her father's obituary in the newspaper the day before stating that his funeral was the following morning. Had things not gone left, she would have been there to support her. Nichelle was sure that Dior wasn't grieving since he treated her like shit since the day she was born.

Dior was like a daughter to her at one time but she turned into someone that she no longer knew. The things that Nichelle had been hearing about her lately was not the same girl who her son had fallen in love with. Dior had worked so hard to become an elementary school teacher and she didn't even have that anymore. Danny was serious about making sure she got fired and he succeeded.

"I never heard of no shit like that before in my life. How is it her fault because her mother died giving birth to her?" Gianni questioned as she looked at some dresses.

She was doing a countdown and she had less than a month before she graduated. She was excited and ready to get the degree that she'd work so hard for. Gianni didn't want to get caught slippin' at the last minute. She was trying to find her graduation outfit now.

"Girl, his old ass had issues. He used to treat that girl like a dog. If you didn't know it, no one would even be able to tell that he was her father."

"That's fucked up," Gianni said while shaking her head.

She and Nichelle continued to browse a few stores until she found two dresses that she liked. The shoes that she purchased matched both. Since she couldn't decide which one she like best, Nichelle convinced her to get both of them.

"You should buy two more casual outfits and do a photoshoot," Nichelle suggested.

"I thought about that but I might be too late."

"You're not too late. I follow this chick on Instagram and she's a beast at that shit. She got a studio with props and all that. I think you should do it."

"See if she has anything available within the next few weeks. I don't want to buy more clothes for nothing."

Nichelle got right to work messaging the photographer. She and Gianni took a seat on a bench in the middle of the mall, hoping that she replied quickly.

"Yes! She said that she just had a cancellation for next week. You have to pay a deposit like right now if you want it."

"Book it and tell her to send me the invoice."

Gianni got even more excited when she saw some of the photographer's work. She was even better than Nichelle said and she couldn't wait to work with her. She and Nichelle started walking through the mall again looking for the perfect outfits. Once they were done, they decided to go to Victoria's Secret to get some lingerie and fragrances.

"Come on man. You can pick up all that expensive shit if you want to. It's coming right out of your cut," a man barked as soon as they entered the store.

Gianni would recognize that voice from anywhere and it always made her cringe. She had a frown on her face when she locked eyes with her brother, Greg.

"What's up beautiful? How you been?" Greg asked with his signature sneaky grin. He touched the chain on her neck and she slapped his hand away.

Seeing him was bad enough but seeing Kori and another woman standing there had her shaking her head in pity. The man who Nix said was his father's unclaimed son was a few feet away. It didn't take a genius to figure out what was going on. Kori, just like Janessa, was letting Greg use her body for profit. As pissed off as Gianni was with her cousin before, she would have never wanted to see her go out the same way.

"Fuck off," Gianni snapped.

"Hey cousin," Kori spoke. Instead of speaking back, Gianni grabbed her by the arm and pulled her away. Nichelle stood there and mean mugged her husband's illegitimate child and waited for her daughter-in-law to return.

"What the hell are you doing here with Greg?" Gianni asked in a harsh whisper.

"He's my cousin and your brother. I didn't know that there was anything wrong with us hanging out. I've been calling you for weeks and you never answered. Is that all that you have to say to me?"

"I really didn't have shit to say to you until I peeped out what was going on."

"Wow. Nix got your head that gone. It's bad enough that you let the nigga fire me. Now he got you not fucking with me at all. I admit that I was wrong about some things but it's not that deep."

"This don't have shit to do with Nix. That ain't my club to make no decisions one way or the other. Had I known that Greg had you out here selling pussy, I would have begged him to let you come back."

"You got me fucked up. I ain't selling shit," Kori denied with a guilty look on her face.

"You don't have to lie to me because I already know what it is. You never knew this but he had the same arrangement with my mama. Greg is grimy as fuck and that's what he does. Now, I can't stop you from doing what you do but at least be smart about it. Protect yourself Kori. Don't go out like my mama did," Gianni replied with a look so serious, Kori got chills.

She watched as her cousin walked away with Nix's mother and started looking around the store. Kori was stuck for a minute until she was pulled away from her thoughts.

"Lil bitch always did think she was better than me. I guess that's because my mama always made her feel that way," Greg spat as his eyes followed his little sister.

He looked at Gianni in disgust. She reminded him so much of their mother and he hated her just the same. He was a grown ass man but he couldn't seem to let go of the hurt from his past.

"The fuck is that nigga looking at. Who is that?" Nichelle asked when she saw the way that Greg was looking at them.

"That's my sad ass brother but he's nobody to worry about," Gianni replied.

"I'm not too sure about that boo. The look he's giving you is anything but friendly."

"Fuck him. I got bullets for his bitch ass too."

Gianni and Nichelle continued to shop long after Kori and her crew left. She was hoping that her cousin took heed to her warning, but that was on her if she didn't. Once they were done, they headed outside to the parking lot. Gianni huffed in annoyance when she saw Biggie and his boys getting out of a truck that was parked right next to her.

"Tell your bitch ass boyfriend that he's a dead man walking. All them bouncers and security cameras can't follow him everywhere," Biggie threatened as his flunkies nodded in agreement.

"Nigga, my son ain't never scared. The fuck is you to think you put fear in somebody!" Nichelle barked angrily.

"Bitch, you can eat some bullets right along with your hoe ass son." Biggie looked like he was trying to walk up on them but he had Gianni fucked up.

"Nigga, I dare you. Fuck with it if you think it's a game." Gianni pulled her gun from her purse and cocked it.

Biggie looked at her and frowned but he was no fool. He was the one who taught Gianni how to load and shoot a gun, so he knew that she wasn't bluffing. She carried her piece faithfully, just like he'd taught her to. He was in his feelings that she decided to pull it out on him though. He had done a lot for Gianni after her mother and grandmother passed. It was fucked up that she was taking another nigga's side over his.

"I guess they can mark your headstone right next to his," Biggie warned before he walked away.

"Stupid muthafucka should know better than to threaten somebody and walk away!" Gianni yelled after him. She waited until they were out of sight before she and Nichelle put their bags in the car and drove away. Nichelle's car was parked in Nix's driveway, so Gianni headed straight home.

"Oh, my man is here. I can't wait to tell him about that fat fucker. Nigga got me heated." Nichelle frowned.

Quick's car was parked in the driveway when they pulled up. He and Nix were walking outside as soon as they got out of the car. Nichelle was cool, but her husband gave off a weird vibe. He had never done anything wrong, but Gianni hated the way he stared at her. It wasn't anything inappropriate but it made her feel weird. She was happy when he and Nichelle got into their separate cars and left because he creeped her out.

"Damn baby, I thought you were just getting a graduation dress," Nix said when he started grabbing all of the bags from the trunk.

"I was but Nichelle booked me a photoshoot. Is everything okay?" Gianni asked while playing with the initial on her chain. He knew that she only did that whenever she was nervous.

"Yeah, everything is good. Why do you ask?"

"I don't know. Your daddy just be looking at me sideways sometimes. It's just weird."

"What do you mean weird? I'll get at that nigga if he makes you feel some kind of way."

"No, it's okay. I might be reading more into it than it is."

Nix knew that his father wasn't a big supporter of their relationship but he never paid attention to the way he looked at her. Quick had life fucked up if he thought that he was gonna intimidate her or have her afraid of him. Nix made a mental note to have a talk with him whenever he saw him again.

"Tell me about this photoshoot," Nix requested while changing the subject.

Gianni ran everything down to him as he helped her put her stuff away. She was starving and she was happy that she cooked before she left. She was drained so, once she ate, she and Nix took a shower and went to sleep.

Kori gripped the sheets tight as her fifth and last customer of the night stroked her from behind. Her mind was a million miles away and she wasn't paying attention to what was going on. She was usually into what she was doing, but she couldn't seem to focus since she ran into Gianni a few days ago. Her cousin put something on her mind and she just couldn't shake it.

"Man, fuck this. I can stay at home and get pussy from my wife if this is all I get," her customer said as he got up and started getting dressed. Kori wasn't feeling what they were doing, so she really didn't care how he felt. He walked out of the room and slammed the door right before Greg rushed in.

"The fuck is you doing Kori! Nigga losing more money than I'm making!" Greg yelled angrily.

Kori started out strong in the beginning but she had been slacking lately. He and Ronnie hadn't hit a lick in a while but he would probably have to mask up soon if she kept fucking up like she was doing. Ronnie sold weed too, so he was good even when Greg wasn't.

"I'm sorry cousin but I'm not feeling this no more. The money is good but I'm not trying to die behind it."

"What are you talking about? You know I got you fam. I'm right outside the door if one of them niggas get rowdy," Greg replied as he lifted his shirt and showed her his gun.

"That's not what I'm talking about. I'm not trying to go out like auntie Janessa did."

"What my mama got to do with this?"

"I didn't know that she died doing the same thing that I'm doing now. I can use the money but it's not worth it."

"Man, that shit ain't true. I know you ain't out here listening to all that bullshit that Gianni be spittin'."

"How do you know that Gianni told me anything?"

Greg had a look of guilt on his face when she asked him that. Gianni never liked to discuss her mother's life leading up to her death. The fact that she warned Kori and the two of them weren't even on speaking terms spoke volumes. Kori had never known Janessa to sleep around, so she believed her. The entire family was shocked when they learned that she had AIDS, but Kori wasn't trying to go out like that. She didn't always use protection but she made it a point to start. She'd already made an appointment at the free clinic to get checked for diseases. Gianni had her scared and she wasn't ashamed to admit it.

"Because she's been saying the same shit since our mama died. I used to tell Janessa just like I told you. Stop giving the shit away for free. If you gon' spread your legs, at least get paid for the shit. You started fucking that nigga Ronnie and he didn't even offer you a dollar. Help me understand the logic in that."

"I fuck niggas because I want to. I don't know shit about these muthafuckers that you bring through here," Kori said as she got up and started getting dressed. She didn't care that her cousin was standing right there and Greg never even tried to look away.

"Are you serious right now? All this money we're getting and you're trying to let it go."

"I'm just scared Greg. This shit ain't even me anyway. I don't know what the fuck I was thinking. I'd rather struggle to make ends meet."

"You sound dumb as fuck. You've made close to two thousand dollars in less than a week. What job is gonna pay you that kind of money?" Greg questioned, making Kori stop to think.

He was right, but she was still hesitant. Kori now had enough money to get her surgery and she was ready to book her flight. Still, she would be on bed rest for a while so she could use some extra cash. Her man was working again, but she liked to have her own stash.

"Just let me think about it Greg. I'll hit you up," Kori replied as she grabbed her purse and rushed out of the room.

"Fuck!" Greg punched the wall and he was happy that he didn't do any damage.

He didn't need them to keep the deposit that he paid on the room. Kori was on some bullshit and he needed to come up with a game plan quick. Ronnie had something in mind, but it was kind of risky. Going through with his plan was a guaranteed payday if they made it out alive. It would also mean putting Gianni in harm's way but that was a risk that Greg was willing to take. If his sister had to die for him to get his money up, then that was fine by him.

"Are we going by grandma and nana daddy?" Alexa yelled from the backseat when they pulled up to Nix's grandmother's house.

You're The Best Part

Danny looked over at him and gave him a comforting smile. Nix's grandmother, Mrs. Flo, had invited them to dinner and they happily accepted. Nix and Gianni were already there waiting for their arrival.

"No baby, not today," Al replied.

He hadn't spoken to his mother since he told her about his relationship with Danny. His grandmother tried calling him several times but he never answered for her. Al was closer with her than he was with his mother. Having her turn her back on him would hurt worse and he wasn't prepared for it. His nana was there for him when his mother was too busy running the streets.

Al had been in a good mood lately and he wasn't gonna let anything ruin it. He and Danny were in the process of closing on their dream home and he was spending time with his daughter again. Al was grateful to Nix for talking some sense into Kinsley but he didn't let her off the hook that easily. He had Danny's father draw up some paperwork to guarantee that she never pulled some bullshit like that again. Al wasn't on child support and he had no need to be. He took care of his daughter and he loved doing it. Alexa told him that her mama had been going out on dates and he was happy to hear it. Kinsley wasn't a bad person and she deserved to be happy.

"That food smells good and we haven't even gone inside yet," Danny said when they rang the doorbell. His stomach rumbled when the aroma of the home cooked food hit his nostrils.

"Mrs. Flo don't be playing. That's why I told you not to eat anything," Al replied.

"Hey my loves. Y'all come on in and fill up on some of this food," Mrs. Flo said when she opened the door. She gave them all a hug and ushered them inside.

337

Al led the way to the dining room. He paused when he walked in and saw his grandmother sitting at the table.

"Nana!" Alexa yelled while running up to her.

"Hey, my sweet baby. You look so pretty." The older woman smiled.

"Hey nana," Al spoke as he walked over and kissed her cheek.

"Come with me into the other room Aldrin. You and I need to have a talk. Since I can't get you on the phone, I figured this was the next best thing."

It seemed as if everyone in the room got quiet, waiting to see what was going to happen next. Al paused for a minute but he followed her out of the dining room and into the kitchen.

"I already know what you're gonna say grandma."

"Do you? Because I haven't even figured that part out."

"I'm sure you're disappointed in me too."

"No, I'm proud of you. I know that it wasn't easy telling your mother the truth, but I commend you. I'm ashamed of the way she handled things but just know that she doesn't speak for me. You already know my beliefs, so I don't need to reiterate them to you. It's not my place nor my job to judge you and I never will."

"Thank you, grandma. That means a lot to me." Al smiled as he hugged her.

"And that is my house," she said while pointing next door. "Amelia doesn't get to say who can and can't come in there. You are always welcome."

You're The Best Part

"I'd rather you come to visit us instead. We'll be closing on our house soon."

"Congrats baby. You know I don't do no driving with these bad eyes. I'll be ready whenever you wanna pick me up though."

"How's my mama?" Al asked her.

"She's fine but she better go to her prayer closet and have a talk with God. The bible says judge not lest ye be judged but she must have skipped over that part. My poor husband is probably rolling over in his grave. Our membership has gone from over two hundred to barely eighty. She's running our church into the ground."

She shook her head as she and Al rejoined everyone in the dining area. Danny smiled when he saw that Al was in a good mood. He didn't know what he and his grandmother talked about but he was happy that it had him in good spirits. A few minutes into their meal, Quick and Nichelle walked in. They joined in on the conversation and they all were having a good time.

"What's wrong baby?" Nix asked Gianni. She was fidgeting in her seat and she wasn't doing that before.

"Nothing, I'm good," she replied with a forced smile.

She didn't want to cause a scene and tell him how she really felt. Quick was making her uncomfortable with the way he kept staring at her. He would look at something on his phone and then look up at her. He did that a few times before he looked at her and scowled. Gianni was ready to go after that but she didn't want to rush. She was happy when Quick went outside to smoke. She helped Mrs. Flo and Nichelle clean up before she and Nix left and went home.

Chapter 20

“ “I'll probably be home before you. I'm about to leave from by Gio and stop to get gas,” Gianni said as she talked to Nix on the phone.

“Nah, go straight home. I don't like you stopping at the gas station when it's dark outside. I'll fill it up tomorrow. I shouldn't be too much longer. We ran out of just about everything we had, so this was a big delivery.”

Nix, Al, and Danny were at the club restocking the bar. He had to triple his order but he wasn't complaining. Gianni had been doing a great job with the bookkeeping and he was making a killing. Danny was just the promoter, but

Nix decided to offer him an assistant manager's job that he happily accepted. He was in the process of hiring two more supervisors to help out, especially on the weekends. Al barely took any time off and he never complained. Since he would be having his daughter a lot more, Nix wanted him to enjoy his time with her in their new home.

Gianni had spent the day out with Heavy's wife and daughters. They went to the spa for a day of pampering before grabbing a bite to eat. Afterwards, she went to Gio's apartment to chill with him but she was about to be heading home.

"Okay. Did you eat yet? I can stop at a restaurant and grab something for you if you didn't."

"I'm good baby. Nichelle dropped something off to us not too long ago."

"Cool. Well, I'll see you in a little while," Gianni said before she hung up.

"Everything all good?" Gio asked as he looked over at her.

"Yeah, he's still at the club."

"Tell him to be careful. I don't trust that Biggie nigga. I asked around about him. He's a low level dope boy but I don't trust these lil niggas out here. Shit is altogether different than when I was coming up. I would hate to body another nigga but, for you, I will."

"Please don't. We just found each other. I'm not trying to lose you again. Biggie ain't nobody to be worried about. He was always nothing but mouth."

"Underestimating a nigga is the worst thing you can do sweetheart. Niggas be out here trying to make a point, especially when they feel played."

342

"Yeah, that's true. I told Nix about it so we're being extra careful." Gianni yawned.

"I'm sorry my baby. I know you're tired from hanging with your cousins all day. I just wanted to see you before you went home." Gio stood to his feet and pulled her up from the sofa.

"Yeah, I've been up since about five this morning."

"I already got my outfit picked out for your graduation. Thanks for giving me an invitation."

"I know that this is new to both of us but you're my father. Why wouldn't I invite you?"

"Are you sure that you don't need anything? You know I got you if you do."

"No, but I appreciate you. I still have all the money that you gave me a few weeks ago."

Gio had more money than he probably knew what to do with. Heavy was as real as they came and he held on to every penny that his brother left him with. In return, Gio paid off his younger brother's house and blessed him and his wife with new cars. He gave Gianni a cashier's check for twenty-five grand and he was always offering her more. He was living in an apartment because he was too scared to purchase a home. He swore that the Feds were watching him since he got released and he wasn't taking any chances. He was scared to buy a car too but he really needed one. He hated having to call around for rides all the time. Heavy offered to put everything in his name and Gio was thinking about taking him up on his offer. They could always have the titles transferred after a while. He didn't trust many people but Gio trusted his brother with his life.

"I'm so proud of you, baby, and I know that your mama would be too. She always wanted a little girl. That's all she used to talk about. She loved to shop, so I know that's why."

"Yes and we did a lot of it," Gianni said, smiling at the fond memories.

Gio walked her out to her car and she hugged him before she left. Although Nix hated fast food, Gianni still indulged. She had eaten when she was out a little while ago but she was hungry again. She had b0een dying for a whopper, so she stopped at Burger King and got one. The burger was gone before she made it home but she was nice and full when she pulled up. All she wanted now was a shower and a bed. She didn't feel like pulling into the garage, so she parked in the driveway and got out of the car. Nix had spoiled her and he always moved her car whenever he came home.

Gianni had her head down when she walked up to the door, trying to locate her house key. She felt a presence behind her as soon as she opened the door, but it was too late for her to react. She was forcefully shoved into the house and fell on the tile floors. Her first thought was that Gio was right. She had underestimated Biggie and he'd obviously caught up with her. Gianni was usually more observant when she drove but she had gotten comfortable. She looked up, expecting to lock eyes with her ex-boyfriend. Unfortunately, she was staring into the scowling face of Quick instead.

"What the fuck are you doing?" Gianni yelled angrily.

"Shut the fuck up! You might have my son and the rest of my family fooled, but I saw right through your scandalous ass from day one."

"What the hell are you talking about?"

"Where did you get that chain from? The first time you try to lie to me, my son is gonna come home to a dead bitch," Quick threatened. He snatched the chain from her neck to make sure he wasn't trippin'. Once he saw what he needed to see, he became even more enraged.

"That was my mother's chain. I kept it after she died."

"Where did your mama get it from?"

"How the fuck should I know?" Gianni screeched.

She had a feeling about who gave Janessa the gift but she would really seem guilty if she revealed it. Besides, it was just a theory and she didn't know if what she believed was even true. With all the men that her mother dealt with, it would be almost impossible for her to figure that out. Janessa used to get gifts all the time but it wasn't Gianni's place to ask her where they came from.

"Lying ass bitch!" Quick fumed as he lifted his fist and hit her in the mouth.

Gianni screamed out in agony but that didn't stop him from hitting her again. Her bottom lip split open thanks to the ring on his finger and she had never felt that kind of pain before in her life.

"Ahhh!" she yelled as blood poured from her mouth and onto the floor.

"This chain belonged to my dead brother. I gave it to him as a birthday gift the month before he was killed. I had it specially engraved just for him. I am my brother's keeper," he said, reading the fine print.

Quick turned the chain around and showed Gianni the engraving that she never even knew was there. She had worn that chain more times than she could count and she never even paid attention. To her, it was sentimental because it belonged to her mother.

When he saw it on her neck at his mother's house, Quick couldn't stop staring at it. He kept looking at the picture of Jake in his phone with the chain on his neck to compare it to the one that she was wearing and they were identical. Whoever gave her mother the chain was probably the same person responsible for killing his brother and trying to kill his son. In his mind, Gianni was there to finish the job.

"I don't know where it came from, I swear."

"My brother got killed the night that this chain was taken from him. My son almost lost his life too. It ain't no coincidence that you were wearing this chain and living up in the house with him. Who sent you at Nix?"

"Nobody sent me at him. I met him when I started working at his club."

"You got one more time to lie to me and it's over for you."

Quick pulled a gun from his waistband and pointed it at her head. Gianni's entire body was shaking as her young life flashed before her eyes. She couldn't believe what was happening and she was confused by it all. Nix was the only man that she could honestly say that she loved. She was reluctant to give him a chance but she was thankful every day that she did. Had she known that his father was going to be the one responsible for ending her life, she would have never even gave it a second thought.

"I'm gone bruh. Are you sure that y'all can handle the rest without me?" Nix asked while looking at Al and Danny.

"Yeah, we got it. We're almost done," Al assured him.

Nix nodded as he went to his office to grab his keys and wallet. He locked up everything before he headed to the back parking lot where his car was parked. He didn't know why but he got a funny feeling all of a sudden. Everything was good as far as he knew, so he didn't know why he started feeling weird. Nix tried to shake the feeling as he drove towards the bridge that led to his house. A car almost cut him off before he got on the ramp and almost made him hit the guard rail. He was about to blow his horn until the window was lowered and shots were fired. Biggie had a sinister grin on his face as he tried to end the life of the man who had embarrassed him in a club full of people.

"Fuck!" Nix hissed as he pressed on the gas.

His back window shattered as bullets continued to be fired in his direction. Biggie must have followed him from the club but there was no way in hell he was gonna lead him to his house. Gianni told him about their little run-in at the mall but he brushed it off like it was nothing. That was a stupid mistake that he was currently paying the price for.

Cars swerved and tried to drive away from the gunfire as Nix dropped down on the first exit. He maneuvered in between cars, hoping that no innocent drivers got hit with a bullet that was meant for him. His gun was underneath his seat but he couldn't get to it. He would probably crash and leave himself wide open for an ambush if he did.

"Damn man," Nix said when he looked behind him and saw the old school Cutlass keeping up with him.

He was coming up on another bridge but he didn't want to get on it. He got in the lane like he was getting up on the ramp and the car followed him. They had stopped shooting but they were still gunning for him. Nix waited until they were right behind him before he jumped the curb instead of getting on the bridge. The car wasn't fast enough when they tried to follow him. They ended up hitting the guard rail and smashed the front of their car. Nix slowed down and watched as Biggie and the driver jumped out of the smoking car and ran. His first mind told him to turn around and handle them niggas but that wasn't a smart move. There were too many people around. Instead, he took the long way home just to make sure nobody else was behind him.

Nix was a little shaken but at least he was alive. He was able to breathe a little easier until he pulled up to his house and saw Quick's car parked in his driveway behind Gianni's. His father knew that he was at the club and he didn't tell him that he was coming over. Quick made Gianni nervous for some reason and Nix wasn't feeling him being there with her all alone. Nix grabbed his gun from under his seat and looked around as he got out of his car. His front door was slightly ajar, making him cock his gun and pause before entering.

"You got one more time to lie to me and it's over for you!" Nix heard his father yell.

348

He heard Gianni whimpering, making him rush inside to see what was up. His pressure rose to dangerous levels when he walked in and saw his father holding a gun up to his girl's head. Gianni's mouth was leaking blood, making a puddle on the floor beneath her.

"The fuck is you doing!" Nix fumed as he kicked the gun from his father's hand and made it fly underneath the sofa. Quick grunted when his son kicked him in the stomach because he wasn't expecting him to do that. He doubled over in pain as Nix picked Gianni up from the floor and ran to the hallway bathroom. Her mouth was bleeding badly and he was nervous.

"I told you that this bitch wasn't right. Look at this shit," Quick said as he rushed into the bathroom holding the chain that he snatched from Gianni's neck. He was still in pain from being kicked but it was nothing that he couldn't handle.

"What the fuck does her chain have to do with anything?" Nix bellowed.

"That's just it though. This ain't her chain. This belonged to Jake. What the fuck is she doing wearing a chain that was taken from my brother the night he got killed?"

"I don't know and I don't give a fuck. Come on baby. I need to get you to the hospital." Jewelry was Jake's thing and he had lots of it. Nix never paid attention to everything that his uncle wore because it was never that deep to him.

"Are you serious right now? This bitch was probably sent here to do you in. She's probably the one responsible for you getting shot in the first place. Put her the fuck out and let her get help the best way she can," Quick fumed as he stood in the doorway like he didn't want Nix to pass.

Chenell Parker

"Get the fuck out of my house and don't even think about coming back."

Nix pointed his gun at his father with a look of pure hatred in his eyes. Quick had done a lot of foul shit in his life but that had to be the worst. It was unforgivable in Nix's eyes and he was done with him. If Quick wasn't his father, he would have put him out of his misery and hid his body.

"Damn, so it's like that." Quick looked hurt that his only son had pointed a gun at him. If it was anybody else, he would have pulled his spare gun from his ankle strap and put a bullet in their head. Since he loved Nix more than life, he would have never even dreamed of doing anything to hurt him.

"Just like that nigga. Get the fuck out!" Nix repeated angrily.

Quick nodded his head and turned to walk away. He grabbed his gun from under the sofa and left, slamming the front door behind him. Nix picked Gianni up and carried her out to the car. She was crying softly and his heart broke with every tear she shed. He didn't know what Quick was talking about and he didn't care.

When they got to the hospital, Gianni assured him that she felt good enough to walk. As soon as they signed in, she saw the triage nurse before she was sent to the back for a doctor to check her out. Nix was on fire when he learned that she had to get stitches. He called his grandparents and they were just as angry as he was. They wanted to come to the hospital but he told them not to.

He should have known that they were gonna call his father to tell him off and Nichelle was calling his phone soon after. When Nix didn't answer, she started up with the text messages. Quick told her some of what happened but she called Nix to get the rest of the story. His father also saw the bullet holes in his truck and they were both panicking.

Nix wasn't even thinking because he drove the bullet ridden truck to the hospital instead of taking Gianni's car.

"Maybe I shouldn't have called Gio," Gianni mumbled as she looked over at Nix. He was sitting in the room with her, waiting for them to come in and do what they needed to do. Gianni's mouth was no longer bleeding but she was still holding a towel over it.

"Why? What's wrong?" Nix grabbed her hand and kissed it. He kept apologizing to her about what happened but it wasn't his fault. Gianni wasn't mad with him but she hated everything about his father.

"He said that he's on his way up here and he's pissed. I told him not to come though."

"Nobody is more pissed than I am. The fuck was that nigga thinking," Nix fumed.

"I have something to tell you," Gianni said, right as the doctor walked into the room.

"Okay, so we have some good news and some not so good news," the doctor said.

"Is something wrong?" Gianni asked in concern. She felt like she was about to start hyperventilating. The thought of her possibly having a disease had her on the verge of a panic attack. Just then, she felt stupid for trusting Nix and not making him use protection. He had never given her a reason not to trust him though. He took a test just to ease her fears.

"The urine sample that we collected determined that you're expecting."

"Expecting what?" Gianni's heart dropped when she said that.

"A baby," the doctor chuckled.

351

"Are you sure?" Gianni questioned.

"Very. The bad news is that we can't give you the pain shot that we usually give for this kind of procedure. We'll have to use numbing cream on the area instead. Tylenol is not the best pain reliver but that's really all that you can take in your condition. A cold compress will also help to alleviate the swelling. The nurse will be in to administer the numbing cream and I'll be back to stitch you up and discharge you."

"Pregnant," Gianni mumbled once they were alone again.

"Now I'm really pissed the fuck off!" Nix was livid as he stood up and paced the floor. Not only did Quick manhandle his girl, but he put his unborn child in jeopardy too.

"Relax Jacobi. I'm sure that everything is fine. I can't be that far along."

"I'm so sorry baby. I'm gonna fix this shit, I swear." He had tears in his eyes as he pulled Gianni into a tight hug and kissed the top of her head. That was her second time being in the hospital because of him and he vowed that it would be her last. It was his job to protect her and he felt like he was failing her.

"Stop apologizing Nix. You didn't do anything wrong. I'm okay but you got some explaining to do."

"What do I need to explain?"

"You can start out by telling me where you hid my birth control pills. I know I didn't lose them twice," Gianni said, calling him out.

She remembered searching every purse that she had for her pills and Nix even offered to help. She never did find them but she went to her doctor to get some more. Not even

352

a week into getting them, she somehow misplaced those too. She got so consumed with school and finals that she never did get any more.

"Nah, I didn't hide your pills."

"Stop lying Nix."

"Real shit baby. I didn't hide your pills. I threw them away," he smirked.

"Are you serious?" Gianni asked incredulously.

"Stop always playing with me, Gianni. You go against everything that I say. Nigga gotta go to the extreme just to lock your ass down. You already turned down my marriage proposal. The least you can do is give me some babies."

"I didn't turn down your proposal but this is not the best time for us to be trying to start a family. I'm about to graduate and I planned to go right to work afterwards."

"And you still can. I'll never stop you from doing that. This ain't the time for regrets love. This is my first baby and I'm excited. Nobody, including you, is gonna make me feel bad about it. I don't care that I went to the extreme to get it."

"I don't have any regrets. I would have preferred to wait but it's too late for all of that now."

"Exactly. I got us baby and that's all that you need to worry about. I'm ready to sell that house and get us another one."

"What! Why do you wanna sell your house?"

"It's too accessible G. I'm sick of Dior popping up when the fuck she wants to and I hate that people can just

353

walk up to the door whenever they feel like it. I'm trying to move to a gated community with some security and shit."

Although Dior hadn't shown up over there in a while, he still didn't feel like his house was secure enough. He was too easily accessible to too many people. He already had an enemy out there that he had to handle.

"I love your house," Gianni pouted.

"See, and that's another thing. You keep saying my house because you moved in with me. I want the next house to be ours. I just got too many fucked up memories in that one. I won't even feel comfortable with you being in there by yourself after what happened today."

"I understand."

"This is just a few more pieces to add to our puzzle. The big picture at the end is what counts," he winked.

Gianni was about to say something else until the nurse walked into the room. She numbed the entire area around her mouth right before the doctor came in. Nix frowned the entire time as she was given stitches for the second time since they'd been together. Her lip was swollen but she wasn't in any pain. He was hurting more than she was and he was tired of people coming at her sideways.

"Okay, my dear, you are good to go. Be sure to follow up with an OBGYN to get your prenatal care started. If the pain or swelling gets worse, don't hesitate to come back to the emergency room or go see your primary healthcare provider. I'll write up your discharge paper and have the nurse bring them in," the doctor said before she left.

"How do you feel baby?" Nix asked her.

"I'm good. I don't even feel anything." Gianni kept the towel over her mouth because she knew that it looked a mess.

When the door opened again, they were expecting it to be the nurse. When Nichelle walked in, Nix jumped up from his chair but Gianni pulled him back. He had no reason to be mad with her because she didn't do anything.

"I'm so sorry about all of this Gianni. We're gonna get to the bottom of everything, I promise," Nichelle said as she walked over and tried to hug her. Nix stood in front of Gianni, blocking her from doing so.

"Nah, don't come in here with that fake ass love. We're good on you and your husband," Nix fumed.

"Nix, stop. She didn't do anything wrong."

"Fuck that Gianni. You don't know her like I do. Quick don't do shit without telling her about it first."

"Baby, I swear, I didn't know what was going on and I still don't. I would have never let your father do something so stupid. All he said was that it had something to do with his dead brother. He was upset. You know how hard he took it when you and Jake got shot. He wasn't himself."

"That nigga had a muthafucking gun up to my girl's head threatening to kill her! She just had to get six fucking stitches in her lip because his bitch ass hit her while she's pregnant. If he felt some type of way about anything, all he had to do was come talk to me like a man. Gianni ain't have shit to do with what happened to me and Jake. Fuck Quick and, if you wanna take his side, then fuck you too!" Nix fumed.

"Pregnant!" Nichelle yelled in shock right as the nurse walked back into the room. She was cautious about entering, especially since she heard all the yelling on the other side of the door. She quickly handed Gianni her discharge papers and gave her the green light to leave.

"Let's go baby. I'm done talking."

Nix grabbed Gianni's hand and led her out of the room. Nichelle was still walking behind them trying to plead her husband's case, but Nix wasn't trying to hear it. All three of them walked into the parking lot together but they went their separate ways. Nix got into his truck and pulled off, right as Quick walked over to talk to his wife. Nichelle looked sad and he wanted to know why.

"What happened?" Quick asked.

Before she had a chance to answer, a truck came speeding into the parking lot. Gio jumped out of the passenger seat and was about to walk into the emergency entrance until Nichelle stopped him.

"Gianni already left!" she yelled.

Gio walked over to her with a scowl on his face. Gianni told him not to worry about coming to the hospital and he listened for a while. The thought of another nigga putting his hands on her had Gio ready to catch a case. He called his cousin to pick him up to go see about her. Seeing Quick standing there had him enraged. Gio hauled off and punched him in the face, knocking him to the ground. Quick tried to get up but a kick to the stomach stopped him.

"Bitch ass nigga!" Gio huffed, as Quick slowly stood to his feet. He was reaching for his gun when Nichelle intervened.

"Stop it! What the fuck is wrong with y'all?" she yelled while pushing her husband back to his car. Quick spit out a wad of blood as he looked over at Gio walking back to the truck that he'd just pulled up in.

"That muthafucker is dead," Quick swore as he got into his car and started it up. That was the second time that day a nigga put their hands on him. Nix got a pass since he was his son but Gio had the entire game fucked up.

"It's over Quick. You've done enough damage for the day."

"You must be crazy. That nigga sucker punched me and you think I'm about to let that shit go. You already know what type of nigga I am. Walking away ain't even in my blood."

"He did the same thing to you that you did to his daughter. You're always overreacting and making shit worse. I'm tired and I can't take this shit no more. Thanks to you, my fucking son just basically washed his hands with me and I didn't even do shit," Nichelle cried. She was hurt by what Nix said to her but she understood why he said it. She wasn't trying to defend her husband but that's exactly how it sounded to him.

"That nigga is in his feelings right now but you know he don't mean that shit."

"I'm so over all this bullshit Quick. We've been doing the same shit since we were kids and I'm tired. I got a fucking grandchild on the way that I probably won't even have a relationship with, thanks to you."

"How was I supposed to know that she was pregnant? I was only trying to find out how she got my dead brother's chain but nobody seems to care about that."

"Fuck that chain! Put some of that same muthafucking energy into finding out who shot up my fucking baby's car. Your priorities are all fucked up."

Nichelle was crying and he felt bad for how everything happened. She was right and he did overreact a

357

lot. He could have easily had a mature conversation with his son about his feelings but he took things to the extreme, just like he was known to do. As much as he wanted to fuck over Gio, he had to respect his mind. He shouldn't have put his hands on his daughter and he owed Gianni an apology. He wasn't sure that she would accept it but he was gonna try. He also needed to apologize to his son. Nix could be stubborn just like him, so he had to be careful with how he went at him. Quick still had a lot of questions but he had to move differently. If not, he could run the risk of losing his wife, son, and his unborn grandchild.

Chapter 21

"Where the fuck are you, Quick? You better not fuck this up for me. It took Flo long enough to even get Nix to agree to come over there," Nichelle argued.

"I got you, baby. I'm not gonna be late. This is important to me too," Quick replied.

"One hour, Quick, and don't be late."

She hung up the phone and she was just in time. Biggie had just walked out of the barbershop and got into his car. Quick had two guns on his lap that he had cocked and ready. Ryan drove off after a few minutes and followed their target.

It didn't take Quick long to find out who had taken a shot at his son. Biggie had signed his own death certificate and didn't even know it. The streets were talking now but Quick wanted to know where all the snitches were at when his brother got killed. Nobody seemed to know anything and that was years ago. Jake and Nix had never fucked with anybody. They sold their lil weed and chilled out. It was fucked up that somebody did them dirty like they did. It was even more fucked up that they robbed his brother after he was already dead. That shit hurt more than anything.

"Don't lose that nigga. I need to get this shit done before my wife have a fucking stroke," Quick barked angrily.

"That nigga ain't getting away from us," Ryan assured him.

It had been a minute since he went on a mission with his uncle. He really didn't want to go but Quick wasn't the kind of nigga that you said no to. He looked out for Ryan all the time and that was the least he could do. His uncle and his father were already at odds with each other and he didn't want to be on Quick's bad side either.

Although Nix was more than capable of handling himself, Quick always had his son's back. Nix and Jessie had been having some minor disagreements about the construction business and Quick confronted his brother about it. Jessie was no fool. He didn't want problems with his crazy younger brother, so he backed down. He was the manager but, at the end of the day, Nix was the boss. Jessie never got over the fact that his father handed everything over to Nix but that was his own problem. It was a done deal and nothing was gonna change.

"Did you get any info from that bitch that you be fucking with?" Quick asked while looking over at his nephew.

"I'm trying Unc. I don't want to seem too obvious and shit. I don't want to keep bringing it up every day. She might get suspicious."

"I don't give a fuck how you do it, as long as it gets done. Let me hurry up and handle this nigga so I can get home to my wife."

It had been two weeks since Nichelle talked to their son and she was going crazy. Nix wasn't fucking with them at all and she blamed Quick for everything. Gianni had graduated and she couldn't even go like she planned to. She drove around the house two days before and saw a *for sale* sign out front. She came home and cried herself to sleep that night.

Quick didn't know how to fix the mess that he'd created. His wife was stressing and he felt bad to have been the cause of it all. Gianni snuck and called Nichelle a few times and told her what was going on. She gave them a lot of insight into some things that they didn't know. Quick felt even worse about what he'd done to her when he learned of some of the details.

Nichelle was losing it, especially since finding out that Gianni was pregnant. Just the thought of not being in her first grandchild's life had her stressing something serious. Quick didn't want to get his parents involved but his wife insisted. If no one else could get to their son, she knew that his grandparents could. Nix had too much respect for them to ever disobey their orders.

At first, Nix kept declining their dinner invitation, claiming that he had something to do. When Flo called and told him that she wasn't taking no for an answer, he finally decided to take them up on their offer. He wasn't trying to

361

repair his nonexistent relationship with his parents. Quick felt bad for his wife because she hadn't done anything wrong. He called from Nichelle's phone to apologize to Gianni but she hung up in his face.

"Got that fat muthafucker," Ryan said when Biggie turned onto a dead end street.

His car slowed down right before he pulled into the driveway of a house at the end of the block. Quick instructed Ryan to hit his lights as he crept up the street. He pulled his hoodie over his head right before he jumped out of the car and stayed low. As soon as Biggie opened his car door to get out, Quick upped both of his guns and started shooting. Biggie didn't even see it coming. He had a gun underneath his seat that he didn't even have time to reach for. His body jerked with every bullet that hit him until he stopped moving altogether. Quick still wasn't satisfied. He went right up to him and fired two shots into his head right before he ran back to Ryan's car.

"Another problem eliminated. Take me home, so I can take a shower. I'm not trying to hear Nichelle's mouth no more," Quick said, as Ryan backed up off the dead end street and sped away.

"Damn man. That nigga didn't even see it coming."

Ryan shook his head as he headed towards his uncle's house. Quick was one of the most unstable niggas that he knew. He was fearless and he didn't have a remorseful bone in his body. Well, that's what Ryan used to think. He didn't know what happened between Nix and his father but it seemed to be bothering Quick. Nix was the only person who got away with talking crazy to Quick. He had a soft spot for his son and he was trying to make shit right between them.

"Handle that business nigga. I don't need to hear no more excuses. You already know how important this shit is

362

to me." Quick looked at his nephew to let him know just how serious he was.

"I got you, Unc. I'm about to head that way now. I'll hit you up tomorrow," Ryan swore, right as he stopped in front of Quick's house.

Quick got out of the car and jogged up the stairs. He had made a lot of enemies, so he looked around before he opened the door and went inside.

"I was just about to call your ass again," Nichelle said as she held up her phone to show him.

"Chill out girl. I told you that I would be here."

"What happened?"

"You already know what happened. That nigga is plant food now."

"Good. Fuck him and his life. Nigga tried to kill my baby. He had life fucked up. Go take your shower. I already got your clothes laid out."

"Relax Nichelle. Everything is gonna work out." She was worried and she drove him crazy when she was like that.

"I don't know Quick. You know how stubborn Nix can be. I just feel like I'm losing my baby all over again," she sniffled.

"Come on baby, don't start all that crying again. I fucked up but I'll do anything to make this shit right. They got every right to be mad at me but you ain't do shit. I just gotta take my lick."

"Hurry up and get ready. My nerves are bad and I'm anxious."

Nichelle paced the floor as her husband walked away to take his shower. She didn't have the best relationship with God but she was sending up a few silent prayers. She had fucked up for most of her life but she just wanted a chance to get it right. At forty years old, Nichelle was tired of doing the same thing. The club scene was starting to get old. She had been partying since she was twelve years old and it was time out for all the bullshit. Thankfully, she didn't look like all that she had been through and she was grateful. She was ready to change for her grandchild more than anything.

Nix held Gianni's hand as they sat at his grandmother's dining room table and listened to her talk. He wasn't in the mood for a lecture on what the bible said about honoring his parents. He honored the people who raised him and he always had. Nichelle and Quick got exactly what they deserved from him and that wasn't much. Gianni hated everything about his father but she loved Nichelle to death. She still wanted her around, but Nix wasn't feeling it. He didn't appreciate how his mother defended Quick and he was good on her at the moment.

"You owe your parents an apology Jacobi," Flo said, pulling Nix back into the present.

"For what? I wasn't the one who started the mess that we're in."

"No, but you shouldn't have talked to them the way that you did. And you definitely better repent for kicking your father. You know better than that. JB and I raised you but they're still your parents. We're family and this is not how we're supposed to behave."

"Family ain't supposed to split your lip and put a gun to your head either, but it happened," Nix snapped.

"I messed up bruh. I'm man enough to admit that. You're right. I should have been a man and talked to you about how I was feeling. From the bottom of my heart, I apologize to you, Gianni. I was wrong and I accept full responsibility for that," Quick replied.

Humbling himself to anyone was never his thing. But, for his son, he would go to the ends of the earth. Quick admitted that he had Gianni all wrong. He didn't know that his parents had known her all her life. He knew her grandmother very well since she was his mother's good friend. He felt like shit when he learned all that she had been through. He was only trying to solve the mystery of his brother's murder. It wasn't his intention to bring her even more grief.

"You have to learn to forgive Nix. I know we raised you better than that. Now, I'm not saying that your father was right but y'all have to find a way to get past this. If not for yourselves, do it for the life that Gianni has growing inside of her," Flo pleaded.

Gianni was only nine weeks into her pregnancy, but Nix was looking forward to becoming a father. JB was a great example for him to follow and he wanted to get it right. Unlike his own father, Nix swore that his child was gonna come first. He hired the same realtor that Al and Danny used to sell his old house and help them get a new one. Nix only wanted to look at secure gated communities or private streets with armed security. He was serious about the safety of Gianni and his baby, even if it meant protecting them from his own family.

"I already forgave them. That don't mean that I have to be in their presence. You always tell me to protect my peace and that's exactly what I'm doing."

"I get that you're upset with Quick but what did I do?" Nichelle asked.

"You mean besides coming to the hospital defending and making excuses for him?" Nix countered.

"I apologize if that's how you took it but that's not what I was trying to do. I'm not perfect Nix and I never have been. I was a baby who had a baby and I didn't know what to do. I'm thankful for your grandparents raising you to be the man that you are. Quick and I weren't right and there's no telling how you would have turned out if you came to live with us. No matter what happened in the past, you're still my baby and I love you."

Nichelle got up and gave Nix a hug. He just sat there at first until Gianni kicked him underneath the table. She had been quiet the entire time and let him do all the talking but he was too damn stubborn. His mother burst into tears when he hugged her back. Admittedly, Nix felt kind of bad for giving her the silent treatment but she should have chosen her words carefully before she said anything. She was the Bonnie to Quick's Clyde and her husband did no wrong in her eyes. She might not have meant any harm by what she said but emotions were high that day.

"I love you, too," Nix replied.

"Thank God," Flo said as she raised her hands in the air.

Nichelle rushed over and pulled Gianni into a hug. She felt like she could finally breathe again and she was thankful that her prayers were answered. She was ready to plan a baby shower and shop for her grandchild. She wanted to ask them about the house being for sale but she didn't want to press her luck.

"Tell me everything that I missed. I want to know about the graduation and your first doctor's appointment. I hope you're taking prenatal vitamins. And don't be lazy Gianni. You don't want to have a hard labor." Nichelle was rambling but she was excited. She felt like a huge weight had been lifted from her shoulders.

Quick smiled, happy that his wife was back in their good graces. He knew that he had a long way to go before he was forgiven if they ever forgave him at all. Just like his wife, he wanted to have a relationship with his first grandchild too.

"Let me rap to you outside for a minute Nix," Quick said as he got up and walked to the front door.

Nix was hesitant but he eventually got up and followed him. For some reason, he felt like he was betraying Gianni by even talking to him. When he looked back at her, she gave him a reassuring smile. The swelling in her lip had gone down in two days and the stitches dissolved in five. Her smile was just as beautiful as ever but the emotional pain would always remain.

"What's good?" Nix asked when he stepped out onto the front porch.

"I just wanted you to know that you can breathe easy now. I eliminated that little problem that you had."

"Preciate it," Nix nodded.

"I got Ryan trying to get some info from ole girl so I can take care of that other issue. Man, I know that saying I'm sorry is not enough but-"

"You're right, it's not. I get why you felt some kind of way because I would have too. Jake was like my brother and it fucked me up when he got killed. It was even worse for me because I didn't get a chance to say goodbye. I just don't respect how you handled the situation. All you had to do was tell me what was up and let me talk to my girl myself. Shit ain't sweet with us right now and I doubt if it ever will be again. She don't feel comfortable around you and I can't blame her for that."

Nix hated that he couldn't identify his uncle's killers but he was too busy fighting to stay alive himself. He couldn't remember anything about the assailants and that haunted him every day of his life.

"I understand. I can't do nothing but respect her mind," Quick replied, right before his son walked back inside.

"Baby, look at this," Gianni rushed up to him and said. She had her phone in her hand with her Instagram page pulled up. She rarely did the social media thing and she was a silent follower whenever she did.

"Damn," Nix said when he saw the pictures of Biggie that everyone was putting up.

They had rest in peace up under all of them, as well as other messages of sorrow. Word definitely traveled fast because the news hadn't even named the victim yet. Gianni and Biggie had a lot of mutual friends and they were all commenting. Apparently, Biggie had just pulled up to his baby mama's house and was shot multiple times before he even got out of the car.

"Social media gets the story before the new stations do," Gianni said.

"Always. That's how most muthafuckers get caught up too."

"It's fucked up but I'm not about to sit here and pretend that I'm sad about it. That nigga tried to end your life and ended up losing his. That's how karma works though."

"Fuck that nigga. How you feel baby? You good?"

"Yeah, I'm okay. You?" she countered.

"I'm good as long as you are."

Quick stayed outside while Gianni and Nix talked to Nichelle for a while. They told her about their plans to move and she was on board to help out any way she could. Gianni had applied to work for an online accounting firm as an independent rep and she was hoping to hear something soon. She still planned to help out at the club and Nichelle offered to babysit whenever they needed her to. She was prepared to give up the streets and everything else for her first and only grandchild.

Chapter 22

"I can't believe that you let your baby be around all that bullshit. I would never," Dior said as she talked on the phone with Kinsley.

"Girl, I don't even care anymore. Alexa loves their new house and that's all that matters to me. She doesn't think anything of it. She just said that her uncle Danny lives with her daddy at his new house. They respect her and that's all that I care about," Kinsley replied.

"Where did this new attitude come from? You wouldn't even let him see her at first. I can't believe that you're okay with it now."

"I'll never be okay with it but there's nothing that I can do. You know how much I loved Al but it was time for me to move on. I met somebody and things have been going good so far. Nix had to make me see the bigger picture and he was right. Al and I decided to get along and coparent for the sake of Alexa."

"Fuck Nix. How can you take the advice of a nigga who don't even have kids?"

"The same can be said about you. Besides, he has a baby on the way," Kinsley revealed, making Dior's heart drop.

"That bitch is pregnant!" Dior said it louder than she meant to but she was shocked.

"And engaged from what I heard."

"Nix hasn't even known her that long. That bum bitch is probably just using him for his money."

"And? You did the same thing."

"Lies bitch. I was with him long before the money. We had each other's backs. Now, I can admit that I fucked up but I righted my wrongs. Nix and I would have gotten back together a long time ago if it wasn't for the snake that I considered a friend."

Dior hated Crystal with every fiber of her being. She regretted telling her so much of her relationship business. She was sure that she was the reason why Nix never took her back. Dior wanted to beat her ass again every time she thought about it. The restraining order that Crystal had on her was the only thing that stopped her.

"Girl, forget her. That's some jealous hearted, hating shit right there. But anyway, how are your sisters doing?" Kinsley asked.

You're The Best Part

She knew about Dior's strained relationship with her father, so she never bothered asking her how she was doing. Kinsley went to the funeral and Dior didn't even shed a tear. Her sisters were falling out but she didn't even look sad.

"They're fine I guess. Grace was his favorite, so she's still taking it kind of hard. We can barely finish packing up the house without her breaking down."

It was no surprise to know that Walter left everything to his oldest daughter. Grace was fair though. She hadn't gotten the check from his life insurance policy yet but she was splitting it all with her sisters.

Dior was the only one who wasn't a homeowner and Grace offered to let her keep the house. She didn't even think twice before she declined. That house held too many painful memories for her. Not only that but it was the same house where their father died at her hands. She wouldn't have even felt right sleeping in there. She hated that house just as much as she hated him.

Grace decided to donate the furniture and all of Walter's clothes to charity. They had a lot of sentimental things that she boxed up and took to her own house. The home was in near perfect condition, so she planned to sell it and split that money with her sisters too.

Once it was all said and done, Dior was gonna be at least fifty thousand dollars richer. She wasn't even thinking about looking for a job. She was content staying at home letting her sisters pay all of her bills.

"Well, let me go girl. Alexa is with her father and I have a date. I'll talk to you later," Kinsley said, right before they got off the phone.

Hearing her say that had Dior a little down. She was so hung up on Nix that she never even tried to move on. Besides River, she didn't really have any other friends.

Kinsley was cool but they only got tight because they used to date two best friends. Dior swore that she was about to start living her life to the fullest. She was ready to start dating again too and finally get over her first and only relationship.

Dior pulled up to her father's house and sighed. She was hoping that they could have everything finished so that she didn't have to come back. She hated being there more than anything. She saw her sisters' cars parked out front, along with another one that she didn't recognize. Grace told her that she had a few realtors coming over so maybe that was one of them.

She sighed when she got out of the car and walked up the stairs. When she opened the door, Grace's face was full of tears but that was nothing new. She was always overcome with emotion whenever they went to the house. When she walked over to her, Dior opened her arms, ready to give a big sister a comforting hug. She was shocked when Grace lifted her hand and slapped her hard across her face.

"You killed him! How could you do that to your own father?" Grace screamed as she wrapped her hands around Dior's neck.

"Grace, no. Let her go," Elise said as she pulled her oldest sister away.

Daria looked at her in disgust as Elise consoled Grace. She was sobbing uncontrollably as she fell to her knees. Dior was shocked that they knew and she wondered how they even found out what she had done. She never even noticed the two white men in suits who were standing there looking at her.

"Dior Harris, you're under arrest for the murder of Walter Harris," one of the men, who she now knew as detectives, said while cuffing her. She tuned him out as he read her rights. It was her second time hearing them and she really didn't care. Her sisters looked on with pain filled eyes but she felt no remorse.

"I just wanna know why Dior," Grace sniffled as she looked over at her.

In her heart, she knew that something wasn't right. She had talked to her father not too long before she asked Dior to drop off his medicine. Walter told her that he was feeling better and he sounded like he was. She attributed his death to him suddenly taking a turn for the worse but not everyone agreed with her.

Grace's husband was the one who mentioned something about getting an autopsy. When Grace asked the coroner's office about it, they agreed to do one but they told her that it would be months before the results came back. They were backed up and an elderly man who died in his home wasn't considered high priority.

When the results came back, Grace was crushed. Her intuition was right and her father's cause of death was ruled a homicide by asphyxiation. The detectives called her the following day and asked her to come down to the station to answer a few questions. When Grace told them everything that happened, Dior was at the top of their list of suspects. She was the only one who had seen him that day and Walter's neighbors confirmed that. No one else had entered or exited the house besides her.

"Are you seriously asking me something so stupid?" Dior questioned, pulling Grace back to the present.

"We know that things weren't always great between y'all but-"

"But what, Grace? Huh? But fucking what? Y'all will never, ever know how it feels to walk even one day in my shoes. You will never know how it feels to have the one man who is supposed to love you unconditionally, hate your very existence. How it feels to be blamed for something that you had no knowledge or control of. I knew that he hated me and he never tried to deny it. And the fucked up part about it all is that y'all knew it too."

Dior was crying but not over her father's death. She was hurt and nobody, not even her sisters, could understand her pain. She had no regrets and she wasn't remorseful. If anything, she was pissed that she hadn't done it sooner.

"I can't say that I understand how you felt Dior because I don't. I tried to be there for you as much as I could to take some of the sting away."

"Yeah, well, it didn't work and I'm done talking." Dior turned her head away, dismissing her sisters and the entire conversation.

"I'm sorry Dior. I'm so sorry," Grace said as she stepped up and hugged her.

Elise and Daria hugged her too, even though she was handcuffed and couldn't hug them back. They were all emotional for so many reasons. They hated what their baby sister had done to their father but they also felt guilty about it.

Dior had it hard and she always did. They were so consumed with their own lives that they never really took into consideration how she truly felt. They thought that by showing her extra love and attention, the pain that their father inflicted on her wouldn't be so bad. They were obviously wrong and her actions proved that. They could have done more and they would have to live with the guilt of knowing that.

"We have to get her out of here. She'll most likely be arraigned in the morning to see if she'll get a bond or not," one of the detectives said as they led Dior out of the house.

"I'll call a lawyer and be there tomorrow!" Grace yelled after her.

"We'll all be there," Daria said, as Elise nodded in agreement.

They were sure that a lot of people wouldn't understand why but they were gonna be by their sister's side every step of the way. It was time for someone to really have Dior's back and, for once, her sisters were going to be the ones.

"Fuck," Nix grunted, as Gianni's warm mouth glided up and down his dick.

He was sleep, but she knew exactly how to wake him up. Her mouth was like a suction cup as she used her small hand to massage his balls. Nix had a death grip on her hair as his toes curled underneath the blanket. Gianni had his dick shoved down her throat and she didn't gag once. He felt his nut building but she wasn't done with him. She got up and turned her back to him before she slid down on him in the reverse cowgirl position. Gianni gyrated her hips like she was dancing and had Nix moaning and gripping the sheets. He was thrusting his hips upwards and he was ready to tap out. Gianni always talked shit when he came before her, so he had to take control of the situation.

Nix sat up in the bed and quickly switched their position. He had Gianni face down with her round ass up in the air. He gave her cheeks a hard smack before he filled her up once again.

"Shit baby," Gianni moaned when Nix started giving her long, deep strokes.

She hissed when he pulled her hair and started fucking her harder. She threw her ass back at him just like he always wanted her to. Nix loved that he was her first and only sex partner. He taught Gianni how to please him and he was always satisfied. She did everything just the way he liked. Nix pulled her back into him for a kiss before he picked up the pace and had her coming all over him and the sheets. He felt his release building up and it wasn't long before he unloaded into her and collapsed in the bed.

"Damn G. You got me out of breath and shit," Nix huffed.

"Nah nigga, the weed got you out of breath," she laughed.

Gianni was an early riser, so she got out of bed and went into the bathroom. She took a quick shower and got a warm towel to clean her man up. Nix went outside on the patio to smoke right before he went back to sleep. Gianni had already taken out what she wanted to cook, so she got her dinner started early. She talked on the phone with Gio while she cooked her cabbage, baked chicken, and cornbread.

Her father hated Quick just as much as she did. Gianni thought it was funny when she learned that Gio knocked him on his ass outside of the hospital. Nichelle told her about it too and even she felt like her husband deserved it.

"Don't forget to save me a plate," Gio said.

It was almost two that afternoon and her food had been done since noon. Nix must have really been tired because he was still sleeping. Gianni was pregnant but he slept more than she did.

"I always save you a plate. It's not like you have a woman to cook for you," Gianni laughed.

"Nah, I'm good on that for right now. They be trying to sneak their asses in here but I'm straight. You make sure I get fed and that's good enough." As soon as he said that, Nix walked down the stairs and into the kitchen.

"Are you ready to eat?" Gianni asked him.

"Yeah but you can relax baby. I'm about to smoke something right quick. I'll fix it myself when I'm done," Nix replied before he went to his smoke room. He stayed in there for about thirty minutes before he walked back into the kitchen. He was in there for a while and Gianni didn't know what he was doing. She wrapped up her call with her father before she went into the kitchen to join him.

"What the hell is this?" Gianni pointed to her pan of cornbread that was covered in some kind of pink paste.

"The cake you baked. You forget to put frosting on it so I did it for you. All we had was strawberry though."

"That is cornbread, not cake. Oh, my God. You need to stop smoking so much."

"My fault baby. It was sweet so I thought it was a cake. That shit taste good as fuck too." He shrugged.

"I'll fix your food next time. I knew your ass was in here too long."

Gianni laughed as she took a picture. She was rarely on social media but she felt like that was something worth posting. Her cousins were gonna fall out laughing when they saw it. When her phone rang, she though that one of them was calling her. She smiled when she saw Nichelle's number pop up instead.

"Hey boo. Are you busy? I wanted to come over there and show y'all something," Nichelle said when Gianni answered for her.

"No, I'm not busy. You can come over."

"Good, open the door. I just turned on y'all street."

"Who was that?" Nix asked when she hung up the phone.

"Nichelle," she replied while going to open the door.

"I hate to see how she act when you have the baby. Damn. We got six more months to go and she already be here every day. That shit bout to stop when we move though."

He and Gianni had looked at two houses already and she loved them both. Nix was trying to live like the boss he was, so he wasn't satisfied. He already had two offers for the house they were in now, but they had to wait until they found them something else.

He wanted them to get married before they moved, but Gianni was still on that waiting bullshit. She was already pregnant so he didn't know why.

"Hey y'all," Nichelle said when she walked inside.

"What's good?" Nix spoke back while Gianni waved.

"Baby, wait until y'all see this shit. I could have sent it over the phone but I just had to see y'all faces," Nichelle said as he pulled her phone from her purse. She scrolled for a few minutes until she found what she was looking for. She turned her phone around for them to see and the look on their faces was just like she expected it to be.

"The fuck did she do this time?" Nix shook his head when he saw the news article that had Dior's picture up top. He didn't even bother reading the story, but Gianni was all in it.

"She killed her daddy!" Gianni's face was a mixture of shock and confusion.

"Man, I know that girl ain't kill that old ass man," Nix replied.

"She sure did. It was classified as a homicide by asphyxiation. Now, I'm not saying that she was right but you were around for years Nix. You know how dirty her daddy used to do her. Truthfully, I'm surprised she didn't do it sooner," Nichelle said.

"Yeah, he used to fuck over her a lot but damn." Nix remembered having to stop Dior from going to her father's house for a while when they were together. She used to always cry and be so depressed whenever she came back home. He got tired of having to comfort her because of something that her father had said or done. To protect her peace, he told her to stay away.

"I can't stand the bitch no more but I feel kind of bad for her. His old ass was just too mean. I know her sisters are probably taking it hard," Nichelle assumed.

She sat around and talked to Nix and Gianni for a while. Since she didn't feel like going home to cook, she ate while she was there. She wouldn't dare ask to fix Quick a plate, so she planned to grab him something before going inside.

Nix and Gianni still weren't fucking with her husband and she didn't try to push the issue. She was happy that she was back on their good side and she couldn't worry about nobody else.

"I'll call you tomorrow and let you know how the appointment went," Gianni said when she walked Nichelle out to her car.

"Okay and don't forget to ask him when you'll be able to find out what you're having. We need to do a registry and start thinking of baby shower themes."

"I will," Gianni promised before she drove away.

She went back inside and found Nix stretched out on the sofa. He reached out and pulled her to lie down on top of him.

"That stomach ain't flat no more." He smiled.

It was funny to him how Gianni was the first woman to ever get pregnant by him. He and Dior tried, but it never happened. He even had a pregnancy scare with the woman that he dealt with after her but it was a false alarm.

"I know. It's starting to fill out a little." Gianni had just noticed it herself when she looked in the full-length mirror earlier. It wasn't noticeable to anyone else but they both knew her body and they saw the minor changes.

"Baby Nixon is loading. Everybody in the family will have the same last name except for you."

"I can if that's what you really want."

382

"What do you mean if that's what I want? I wanted it since the first day I asked you. I know we moved fast as hell G but this was obviously meant to be. The life that's growing inside of you is proof of that."

"Yeah, you're right. Okay, let's do it."

"Stop playing with me, girl."

"I'm serious. You already trapped me with a baby. We might as well make it official," she laughed.

"How do you wanna do it?" Nix asked excitedly.

"Something small and intimate. We got too much going on right now to do anything big."

"That's true but I got a big ass family baby."

"Shit, I do too now," Gianni laughed. "Maybe we can do a courthouse ceremony and a nice reception afterwards. You know Nichelle will be happy to handle that."

"Shit, that sounds good to me."

Nix was excited. Not only was he getting his baby, he was getting a wife too. A family of his own was all that he ever wanted to be content. It didn't happen when he wanted it to or with the person who he thought it would be with. He wasn't complaining though because he felt blessed that it was happening at all.

Chapter 23

"Chill out with all that shit Nichelle, damn," Nix frowned.

It took a little over a month before he and Gianni made things official and became husband and wife. They went to the courthouse earlier the day before and they were now at their reception. As usual, Nichelle was doing the most with all those crocodile tears that she was shedding. Even his grandmother was calm and she was usually the one who did all the crying.

"Leave me alone boy. My only baby got married today. I have a right to cry," Nichelle sniffled. She did the same thing at the courthouse and Nix was over it.

Thanks to his grandmother, Quick was there too. Flo got to Gianni and begged her to let him come. Nix was furious, but she assured him that she was okay with it. Quick was no fool though. He was there but he made sure to stay his distance. He gave them a ten thousand dollar cashier's check as a wedding gift but he got Nichelle to give it to them. Gianni had to beg Gio to relax because he wanted to tag his ass again. She wasn't about to let anyone ruin her special day.

She was overcome with emotion too when Nix told the DJ to play a song that he dedicated to her. *Best Part* by Daniel Caesar and H.E.R. said everything that he needed her to hear. Gianni really was the best part of him. She was the missing piece that completed his puzzle. Their unborn child was all the proof that he needed to let him know that they were meant to be. His new bride was happy and that was all that he cared about.

Gianni was on the dance floor with some of her cousins having fun. She hadn't really had any fun since their vacation to Jamaica. She couldn't drink but she was still having a good time. She had on a white, off shoulder maternity dress that she lifted up so she could dance. Nix was sitting at the table with Al and Danny having a few drinks. For the first time ever, he closed his club and gave everybody the day off to attend his wedding reception.

"This is what we should do. I'm not trying to spend a bunch of money on a wedding. We can go to the courthouse and have a nice reception afterwards," Danny said while looking at Al.

"Nigga, you know you're too extra to have something so small," Nix laughed.

"Nah fam. We ain't spending all that money for other people to enjoy. Y'all did the right thing. Shit, y'all are about to have a baby and move into a bigger house," Al noted.

He and Gianni had finally found the perfect house. It was on a private street with armed security out front. They closed on it the week before and had already started moving some of their furniture in. Nix had the same surveillance system set up inside and out. His old house hadn't sold yet but three different people were interested in buying it. He was happy because he was getting way more than what he paid for it. Since she was pregnant, they decided not to do too much for their honeymoon. They were going to Cancun for a week but they weren't leaving until the following weekend. Gianni's doctor said that it was okay for her to fly since they had a connecting flight and it wasn't that long.

"How is everything with Kinsley? Is she still behaving?" Nix asked.

"Yeah, she is. She even lets Danny pick Alexa up now. She got a new man and I like the nigga already. Alexa said he's nice so that's all I care about."

Al had met Kinsley's boyfriend and he seemed cool. He was a social worker at a high school and his daughter seemed to really like him. He didn't live with Kinsley but he was there a lot. Kinsley had calmed down a lot and she was even cool with Danny again. Al gave all the credit to her new man since he seemed to be the one to get her mind right. Maybe he was counseling her too and it was definitely working.

"I still can't believe that crazy bitch Dior killed her own daddy," Danny commented.

"Shit, I can. You weren't around all the time to see all the shit that she went through. He did that girl dirty and the reason why was fucked up. I'm happy that her sisters didn't leave her to go through all that shit by herself," Al replied.

"Yeah, me and Gianni saw her sister, Grace, twice when we went to the clinic. She's a pediatric nurse at the clinic where Gianni's doctor's office is located. They got her a good ass lawyer who's trying to get her charges reduced. Even though I been stopped fucking with her, I hope she can get a lesser charge. I saw firsthand how dude did her. She used to be trying to do everything to make him happy but that nigga was just mean. He wasn't like that with the other ones though."

Nix didn't feel bad for her when she lost her job and went to jail for what she did to Crystal. That was shit that she did on her own free will. But, when it came to her father, his heart really went out to her.

"You might wanna sit your wife down for a few minutes. She looks worn out," Danny laughed.

"Go grab me a bottle of water Danny. Gianni outchea trippin'," Nix fussed as he got up and went to go get her.

"What's wrong?" Gianni asked when Nix pulled her off the dance floor and made her sit down.

"You're doing too much love. Look at how you're sweating." He grabbed a napkin from their table and wiped her face. Her makeup was a mess and the eyeliner had her with racoon eyes. When Danny came back with the water, Gianni drank the entire bottle in one long gulp. He got her another one and she drank half of that one too.

"I'm so tired," she panted while fanning her face.

"I know you are. Relax baby. You've been on the dance floor since the reception started."

Nix rubbed her tiny baby bump as they sat down and talked. After a while, it was time for them to cut the cake. They didn't have any gifts to take home because everything was gift cards or monetary. Once the reception ended, everyone went their sperate ways. Gianni was so happy when they got home. She took a long, hot bath before she and Nix climbed into bed.

"Kori called me today," Gianni said after they were silent for a while.

"For what?" Nix asked.

"I don't know. I didn't answer." She sighed and he could tell that she had something more to say.

"What's good baby? What's on your mind?"

"I don't know. Am I stupid for missing her?"

"Nah, ain't nothing stupid about you. That's your people and y'all used to be close. If you feel like that, call her."

"A part of me wants to and another part of me feels like we need to leave everything just like it is. I am kind of worried about her though. I know she's out there fucking with Greg on the same shit that my mama was on."

"Like I said, call and see what's good with her if you want to. As far as what she's doing with your brother, there's nothing that you can do about that. You tried to warn her and the rest is up to her. Ain't nobody about to stress you out though."

"You got that right. Maybe I just need to think about it some more," Gianni replied.

She hadn't seen or spoken to her cousin in months and she missed her. She knew that things would never go back to the way they were before and she didn't want them to. Nix didn't even want Kori to know where they lived and he had good reason. Gianni would always respect her husband's wishes, even if it meant not ever having a relationship with her toxic cousin again.

"Bitch, my grandson is about to be fly as fuck. I'm going broke behind mine," Nichelle said as she walked around the Canal Place mall with Gianni.

Gianni was now five months pregnant with her and Nix's first son. He was too excited to be having a boy and she was happy that they didn't have to think of a name. It was no secret that he wanted his first born to be named after him. Nichelle was already buying stuff for him and going overboard as usual. Nix was no better. He had stuff delivered to the house just about every day. They were all moved into their new house and the old one was almost sold. The paperwork was still being done, so it wasn't all the way official just yet.

"I might not even need a baby shower if you and Nix keep buying everything."

"Bitch, please. You're definitely having a baby shower and that shit is about to be epic. These hoes be waiting on me to half step but that will never happen."

"What hoes?" Gianni asked while looking at some maternity dresses. She and Nix were doing a maternity photoshoot with the same chick who did her graduation pictures. She sent Gianni a few outfits that she wanted her to purchase for them before then.

You're The Best Part

"All the hoes that Quick used to fuck with before we got married. And, trust me, it was a lot of them. You're lucky that Nix was raised by JB. He got to see how a man is supposed to love and treasure his woman at a young age. Quick was too busy running the streets to catch that life lesson. He got it now though."

"I love your son but he's the lucky one. I never did mind being single. I'll cut a nigga off in a minute if shit ain't right. I was by myself for over a year before I met Nix."

"I know that's right but you got a good one. And I'm not saying that just because he's my son. Hell, I can't take none of the credit for the way he was raised," Nichelle admitted.

She and Gianni continued to shop until they got hungry. The food court didn't have much to choose from, so they decided to grab a smoothie until they could get something better. They stood in the line of the café and talked until it was time to order.

"Can I help you?" the lady behind the register asked. Gianni's head snapped up when she recognized the familiar voice. Kori wasn't even paying attention to who she was helping. When the customer took too long to answer, she looked up into her cousin's face.

"What's up?" Gianni spoke right before placing her order. Kori's eyes bulged in shock when they traveled down to her pregnant belly. Gianni was talking but she didn't even hear what she was saying.

"My bad cousin. What did you want?"

"What's the best one? I just need something to hold me over until I leave."

Kori told her some of their bestsellers, right before she and Nichelle placed their orders. They were about to walk away once they got their smoothies until Kori spoke up and stopped them.

"Can I talk to you for a minute Gianni?" she called out after her cousin.

When Gianni nodded her head, Kori told her boss that she was taking a break. She walked from behind the counter and found a table for them to sit at. Nichelle excused herself and walked away to give them some privacy.

"What's up?" Gianni asked once they were alone.

"Not much but I see that a lot is up with you. Congrats on the baby. What are you having?"

"Thanks. It's a boy."

"I tried calling you a few weeks ago."

"I know. I was at my wedding reception when you did."

"You got married!" Kori didn't mean to get so loud but she wasn't expecting to hear that.

"Yep," Gianni replied as she held up her ring finger.

"Wow. Congrats again."

"Thanks Kori, but what's good? I know you didn't ask to talk just to congratulate me."

"No, I didn't. Honestly, I wanted to apologize to you. There is no excuse that I can give and I'm not even gonna try. I was in my feelings about you dealing with Nix because I had a crush on him. We never messed around or slept together. I'm sure you already knew that but you deserved to hear it from me."

"It's no love lost Kori. Now, I can't sit here and tell you that shit will go back to the way it was because that would be a lie. My husband is all about protecting our peace and he ain't feeling you. We're family, so I do want us to stay in contact. Although I have other cousins that I recently discovered, I can't just forget about you."

"What other cousins?"

Kori listened, as Gianni ran everything down to her about how she met her father. It sounded unbelievable but that was her cousin's life.

"Yeah, he's uncle Heavy now, even though I don't call his ass that," Gianni laughed.

"That's so sweet. Amya told me something about your father being in the club but I didn't know what to make of it."

"Yeah, it's nice to know that I have some other family out there."

"And speaking of family, you were right about Greg. I made a stupid mistake that I ended up regretting."

Greg had been on Kori's back about continuing with their little arrangement. The money was good and she was tempted to do it a little longer. That all changed when her man came home and hit her with some horrific news. Larry had contracted chlamydia and he was furious with her. She was the only woman that he'd been with in years and he knew that he got it from her.

Kori was mortified when she went to the clinic and was given the same diagnosis. She was still fucking with Ryan but he was good since they always used condoms. Since she got pregnant that first time, he wasn't taking any more chances. Kori knew that she got it from one of the men who Greg solicited for sex. Gianni's warning replayed in her head and she was thankful that she got out when she did.

She hated that she contracted a disease at all but she was thankful that it was something curable.

Larry left her and she couldn't even blame him. Kori still worked at the bar but she got a part-time job in the mall to help with expenses. Ryan threw her a lil change every once in a while but she still had to work for what she wanted.

"Girl, Greg don't give a fuck about nobody but himself. I didn't fuck with him for a reason. I know we're family but he's the kind that you have to love from a distance," Gianni said, interrupting her thoughts.

"I heard about what happened to Biggie too. People were saying that he was messing with a married woman and her husband followed him home and killed him. His girlfriend was pregnant with his third child too. That's fucked up."

"It is but that's life. I hate to hear about what happened to him though."

Gianni wouldn't dare tell Kori about her run-in with Biggie or about him shooting at Nix. Her cousin talked entirely too much for that.

She sat there and talked to Kori until her break was over. Admittedly, it felt good to say some of the things that she'd always wanted to say to her cousin. Gianni battled with herself on if she should return her cousin's call. She decided against it but it was obviously meant for them to talk. She still loved her cousin and she always would. Unfortunately, she was gonna have to love her from a distance too.

Chapter 24

“ “A re you sure that bitch gave you the right info?” Quick asked as he and Ryan sat in the truck watching everyone who entered and exited the building.

“Yeah, she said this is the spot. Be patient nigga,” Ryan answered as he took a pull from his cigarette.

“Nigga, I am being patient. We've been coming here for weeks and ain't seen shit yet. That bitch probably played you.”

“What would be her reason to play me? It ain't like I told her why I was asking about the nigga. Just chill out.

You know how this shit can go Unc. We got at that Biggie nigga fast but it don't always work like that."

"I don't need you to preach to me, nigga. I don't give a fuck how long it takes. Getting at this nigga is as important to me as breathing. This shit has been a long time coming. That bitch better not be on no bullshit. She can get it too."

"Well, I guess she's safe. Look at who just rolled up," Ryan replied while pointing at their target.

He was talking on the phone as he walked up to the bar that he was known to frequent. He stood on the side of the building smoking a blunt, but that was the wrong move for him to make. Ryan hit the lights on the truck and drove around the side of the building. Quick was out of the truck before it even stopped with his gun at his side. He wasn't trying to kill him though. He needed some answers before he put him out of his misery.

Quick was ducked down in between two cars and Ryan acted as the lookout. When his nephew gave him the thumbs up, he quickly walked over to his target and hit him in the back of the head with his gun. He didn't even see him coming and that's exactly how he wanted it. Quick caught his limp body before it hit the ground. He pulled him over to the awaiting truck and threw him in.

"Burn out nigga," Quick said when he got into the truck and closed the door.

He didn't have to tell Ryan twice. He sped off in the direction of the abandoned grocery store that was now home to tons of drugs addicts. They congregated on one side of the building drinking and getting high. Ryan pulled up to the other side and killed his lights once again. The moon illuminated the sky just enough for them to be able to see the face of their enemy.

You're The Best Part

"Damn Unc. How hard did you hit this nigga?" Ryan asked when they pulled him out of the truck.

Quick didn't bother with an answer. He grabbed the bottle of water that he'd been drinking and poured it over the unconscious man's face. He started to stir as both men looked down at him in disgust.

"The fuck!" Greg yelled as he looked up at the two unfamiliar men.

"Stay your bitch ass on the ground like all the rest of the snakes," Quick sneered when he tried to stand up.

"What's this all about? Do I even know you?" Greg asked. He was directing his comments to Quick since he seemed to be the ring leader of the two man show.

"Nah nigga and you don't want to know me."

Quick took the chain that he got from Gianni and pulled it from his pocket. Gianni didn't want to seem guilty, so she told Quick that she didn't know where the chain came from. She ended up telling Nichelle the truth about where she believed it came from.

According to Gianni, Greg asked her for the chain at their grandmother's funeral. He told her that he gave it to their mother as a gift and he wanted it back. Gianni thought that he was lying just to get the chain from her. Greg would do anything for a dollar, so she brushed it off. Besides, he was in jail at the time so there was nothing that he could have done with it. She brushed it off and forgot all about it until Quick said something about it belonging to his dead brother.

Quick knew that Gianni didn't get along with her brother, but Nichelle told him that her cousin was in the mall with him once before. Since Ryan still fucked with her sometimes, he got his nephew to get some info from Kori.

"What's that?" Greg asked when Quick showed him the chain. He knew exactly what it was but he was hoping that he sounded convincing when he played dumb.

"I'm the wrong nigga for you to play games with. My brother got killed and this chain was taken from his neck while he bled out in the middle of the street."

"Man, I didn't have shit to do with that. I was locked up. I just got released this morning."

"That explains why we couldn't find you for a few weeks."

"Exactly. You got the wrong dude."

"Nah, cause see, this didn't just happen. I got the right nigga but how this ends all depends on you. Tell me something good."

"Like what? I don't know shit."

"You know your sister is married to my son. You're Gianni's brother, right?"

"Yeah, that's my little sister," Greg replied excitedly. He had a hopeful glimmer in his eyes but he was wasting his time. Quick laughed at how Greg's mood changed.

"The fuck is you getting so happy for? Shit, she hates me just as much as she hates you. Saying her name won't save you. As a matter of fact, she's the one who was in possession of the chain. According to her, you gave it to your mama."

"That's a damn lie. I've never seen that chain before in my life. She's the one who you need to be questioning. It was probably her and her ex nigga who did that shit. You need to be going after her ass, not me."

You're The Best Part

"Bitch ass nigga, she's pregnant with my grandson!"

Quick frowned as he kicked Greg hard in his stomach. He was sure that his steel toe boots probably left a print but he didn't give a fuck. He was even more of a hoe than he thought he was. Greg was trying to throw his own sister under the bus just to save himself.

"Ahhh! Fuck!"

"See, we're like family. I didn't want to have to do you dirty but you forced my hand. All I wanted was some answers but you feel like playing games." Quick pulled out his gun and aimed it at Greg's head.

"Alright! Okay! I'll tell you what I know. Just promise me that you won't kill me."

Quick nodded his head and gave Greg his undivided attention. His emotions went from angry to sad to hurt, as he listened to everything that the other man had to say. He didn't like to show his feelings, so he kept his game face on the entire time. Once Greg was done, Quick didn't even feel the need to waste time. He raised his gun and let off three shots, all to his head. Ryan wanted to say something but he could tell that his uncle was in his feelings, Instead, he remained quiet and drove Quick home.

"Same time tomorrow. I'm ready to end this shit once and for all," Quick said before he got out of the truck. Ryan only nodded his head in response. He drove away once his uncle went inside. He had to work in the morning but, afterwards, he planned to take a nap before he had to bring his uncle to commit another murder.

"Damn Unc. Where are we going?" Ryan asked as he drove to the undisclosed location that Quick was directing him to.

They had victim number two in the back of the truck, just like they'd done the night before. He wasn't as easy to get to as Greg was. He watched his surroundings a little bit better and he gave them a little chase. Ryan had to drive as Quick got out of the car and went after him. A shot to the leg disabled him before they caught up with him and threw him in the back of the truck.

"The fuck y'all want with me man!" Ronnie yelled as a burning pain shot through his entire leg.

"Damn bruh, I'm offended. You said that you wanted us to bond like father and son. What happened? Did you change your mind?" Quick taunted.

"Nigga, fuck you!"

"Nah lil bitch, fuck you."

Quick hit him with a closed fist and split his bottom lip. He was joking but there really was nothing funny about the situation. He instructed Ryan to turn off into the wooded area that was coming up before he told him to stop. Quick didn't utter a word before he got out of the truck and pulled Ronnie out with him.

"Do what you gotta do nigga. I'll never beg another man for nothing, not even my life."

"Good because you're gonna die no matter what you say," Quick assured him.

Unlike his boy, Greg begged and pleaded for his life. After he told Quick everything that he needed to know, he cried and asked him to spare his life. Apparently, he didn't even know Jake or Nix and the entire idea was Ronnie's. Greg was only trying to make some quick cash, but it was Ronnie who pulled the trigger that ended his brother's life and wounded his son. It was fucked up because it wasn't even about Jake or Nix. He did all of that just to hurt Quick.

It was crazy to him how it all went down. Gianni having possession of the chain was just a weird coincidence. She had no knowledge of where it came from or how it was obtained. That fact alone make Quick feel even worse for what he'd done.

"Do what you gotta do but it still won't bring your brother back," Ronnie smirked, pulling Quick away from his thoughts.

He looked up at the man who shared some of his same facial features, a man who he once idolized from afar. The same man who looked him in the eyes and told him that he would never acknowledge or accept him as his son. He was a young boy at the time but the pain of his words stayed with him for years.

For as long as Ronnie could remember, his family told him that Quick was his father. He never knew why he didn't come around and he never asked anyone. His mother was a crackhead, so he assumed that had something to do with his decision to stay away.

Ronnie used to see Quick and Nix around all the time and he always wanted to go approach them. Nix used to be with Jake all the time and he didn't look too friendly. Quick didn't look friendly either but he took a chance and stepped to him anyway. Ronnie's feelings were hurt after their first and only encounter but he held his head high as he walked away.

Ronnie was never the same after that day. He walked around with a lot of hate in his heart and he started unleashing it on other people. He hated his mother for putting him in that position and she was often at the receiving end of his wrath. After beating her unconscious once before, he got locked up and met Greg.

When he confided in him about his personal life, Greg had his own sob story. He hated his mother too but for an entirely different reason. The two of them stayed in contact once they were released and Greg was the getaway driver when Ronnie got at Nix and Jake. He was pissed because the wrong man died that night. He wanted Nix's blood on his hands instead of Jake's. Ronnie wanted to take the one thing from Quick that he seemed to love the most.

He wanted to get at Nix again but the opportunity never presented itself. Ronnie and Greg both stayed in and out of jail and he hadn't seen Nix for years until he went to his club that night. He went back a few nights later to peep shit out but it was a waste. They had too many cameras around the building and security was tight. He would have never imagined that Greg's sister would be fucking with the nigga. Greg didn't care though. He was talking about robbing Nix and killing his sister too if it came down to that. Ronnie was down for whatever but they never got the chance to put a plan in motion. Just like before, one of them was always getting locked up.

"I must say, you got more balls than your bitch ass friend. That nigga didn't even try to go out with dignity. After he snitched on you, he cried and begged for his life like the hoe he is."

"That's all on him but ain't no hoe in my blood. The one thing that my bitch ass daddy ever gave me was heart. I guess I'll see your brother in hell. I only wish your bitch ass son was joining me," Ronnie replied, right before Quick emptied his clip into his body and watched as the life drained out of him.

Technically, he had just killed his own son. Emotionally, he didn't feel an ounce of remorse.

"You good Unc?" Ryan asked him. He stood there quietly the entire time as Ronnie and his uncle went back and forth. He saw the emotional changes on Quick's face but he didn't speak on them.

"Take me home," Quick mumbled.

Ryan nodded his head as they both walked back to his truck, leaving Ronnie's body there for the city workers to find. They were doing work in the area, so he probably wouldn't be there too long. They rode to Quick's house in silence, both lost in their own thoughts. When Ryan pulled up to the house, Quick got out without a word or a backwards glance.

The house was cold, dark, and quiet when he walked inside. It was almost two in the morning but Nichelle was still up waiting for him.

"Are you okay baby?" Nichelle asked him as she swung her legs onto the side of the bed.

She already knew what was up but she wanted him to give her details. Instead of answering her, Quick dropped down to his knees and buried his face in her lap. Her husband hadn't cried since he lost his baby brother but he was sobbing like a baby. Quick was always such a strong man, so that had her worried. She didn't pressure him to talk; she just rubbed his back and let him release his liquid pain.

"All that shit was my fault man. My fucking brother lost his life because a nigga was trying to get back at me. I almost lost my only son," Quick wept.

"I know that you're hurting baby but that is not your fault."

Nichelle tried hard to hold in her tears but it was almost impossible. She felt like she was to blame for some of what happened too. She was the reason why Quick never acknowledged his son. She was no fool and she didn't need a paternity test to tell her what she already knew. Ronnie and Nix were brothers, but she refused to accept it. Now, her husband had the weight of the world on his shoulders and she didn't know how to take the pain away.

She rocked him for a while until he seemed to feel better. Quick went to take a shower while she fixed him something strong to drink. He seemed to be feeling better after a while but he was still too quiet.

"I need to do something tomorrow or maybe the day after," Quick said after sitting there deep in thought.

"Okay baby. Whatever you want." Nichelle didn't even ask him what he wanted to do. Just like always, she would have her husband's back and be there when he needed her.

Chapter 25

Gianni groaned as she reached around the bed for her ringing phone. Nix was knocked out and she knew that he was tired. They had another concert at the club and he had to help out. Although he hired a lot of new people, Nix wanted to make sure that everything ran smoothly. He got inside after four that morning and Gianni got up to make him breakfast. Once they ate, they both went back to sleep.

"Yeah," Gianni mumbled groggily when she picked up the phone. She was too tired to even see who it was calling her.

"Gianni?" Kori sniffled.

"What's up Kori?" She sat up and looked at the clock and saw that it was after one in the afternoon.

"I'm sorry to have to call and tell you this cousin, but Greg got killed." Her voice was cracking and she sounded like she was crying.

"Who told you that?"

"Somebody called my mama. They found him two days ago in an abandoned parking lot. He had his license on him and he still had grandma as his emergency contact. I guess that's how they found my mama. They need somebody to come down there to identify him."

"For what? It ain't like nobody gon' bury his ass. Do you or your mama have insurance on him because I damn sure don't?"

"We don't either but we can't just leave him there like that."

"I don't see why not. Truthfully, he's already been identified if he had his license on him."

"Yeah, that's true but that's not it."

"What else happened?"

"They found his friend Ronnie's body last night. This shit is so unbelievable."

"Not really. I can't speak for the other dude but Greg was grimy as fuck. Ain't no telling what he was out there doing."

"That's true but I feel so bad."

"I don't know why."

Gianni frowned at the phone as if Kori could see her. She was doing too much and she wasn't even that close to Greg. He was her brother and she wasn't about to shed any tears over him. She had an idea about what happened but she would go to her grave before she ever spoke on it.

"I don't know if you knew this or not, but I still be talking to Nix's cousin, Ryan. For some reason, he asked me about Greg a few times and I don't know why. It just seems strange now that he's dead. Do you think he could have had something to do with it?"

"I'm gonna pretend that I didn't hear what you just said. And if you had any common sense, you wouldn't repeat that to anyone," Gianni warned.

"I would never. I'm only saying it to you. But, what about Greg?"

"What about him? After thirty days, the state will throw him in a pine box and dig a hole. That's as good as it's gonna get."

"My poor cousin. Maybe we can do a Go Fund Me or something."

"Bye Kori. I'll call you back later." Gianni was hoping that she didn't regret talking to her cousin again. She wasn't in the mood for all the extras.

"The fuck did she want?" Nix muttered in his sleep-filled raspy voice.

"Calling to tell me that Greg and your fake ass half-brother got killed," Gianni replied.

"When?" Nix sat up and wiped the sleep from his eyes.

"She said they found Greg two days ago and the other one last night. She's talking about going to identify Greg and setting up a fundraiser to bury him."

"She must be out of her muthafucking mind. You ain't doing shit!"

"I already made that clear."

"Let her do it if she's so concerned."

Nix laid there and stared up at the ceiling. He didn't even have to wonder about what happened because he already knew. Gianni shed light on something that would have probably remained a mystery to them. When she told him that she believed her brother gave her mother that chain, Quick started piecing it all together.

Nix hated himself for not being able to identify his uncle's killer but he was clinging onto life himself. He couldn't remember the car that they drove up in or their height and build. Besides all the pain that he was in, everything else about that night was a blur. The ringing of the security phone pulled Nix away from his thoughts of the past. Someone had to be at the gate because that was the only time that the phone rang. Nobody said that they were coming over, so Nix didn't know who it could be.

"This can't be real. I just want to sleep," Gianni whined, making Nix laugh.

"I got it," Nix replied as he got up from the bed.

"No baby, I'll do it. I know you're tired. I'm just being lazy."

"You're not being lazy. My son needs his rest. Just relax."

"You don't have to tell me twice." Gianni turned over on her side and got comfortable.

Nix answered the phone and was told that Nichelle was at the front gate. She usually called first but it was cool. Nix gave them the okay to let her in, right before he threw on some sweats and a t-shirt. More than likely, she was coming for Gianni but Nix was about to send her on her way. His wife was tired and Nichelle didn't know when to leave.

Nix jogged the stairs right as his mother rang the doorbell. He opened the door and resisted the urge not to slam it in her face when he saw Quick standing there with her. His father had never been to their new house and that's how he wanted it to stay. His wife didn't feel comfortable around him and he wasn't about to force her to interact with him. His apologies meant nothing because the damage was already done.

"Y'all can't be serious right now." Nix frowned.

"Just hear me out bruh. I'll be on my way as soon as I say what I have to say," Quick pleaded.

"I'm not trying to hear nothing else from you right now."

"Good because you're not who I want to talk to. Where's Gianni?"

"Now you got me fucked up!" Nix yelled angrily.

"Clam down Nix. You know damn well that we would never show up to your house on no bullshit. She's pregnant with our grandson. Upsetting her or stressing her out is something that we would never do."

"Nah, she's good on whatever y'all have to say."

"Nix please," his mother begged. Her husband asked her to bring him over there and he had a good reason.

"Gianni is sleep anyway, so y'all gotta go."

"I'm up," Gianni noted as she walked up and stood behind her husband.

"Go back upstairs and lay down baby. They were just leaving," Nix assured her.

"It's okay Jacobi. Let him say whatever he has to say."

Nix wrapped his arm around his wife's waist, never even bothering to invite his parents in. He glared at them with a frown, letting him know that he wasn't going anywhere.

"I know that things aren't good between us Gianni and they probably never will be. I just want you to know that I regret what I did and that shit will haunt me for the rest of my life," Quick said.

"Is that all?" Nix asked impatiently.

His father ignored him and continued saying what he had to say. Quick pulled the chain from his front pocket and extended it towards her.

"This chain means a lot to me. It was the last birthday gift that I got for my little brother before he died. The sentimental value is worth more than any amount of money that I can ever obtain. I also know that it means a lot to you too. You lost someone you loved and it became a sentimental part of your life as well. I've found peace with my brother's death and I hope this chain brings you the same amount of comfort. It's yours," Quick said as he put it in her hand and walked away. Nichelle followed behind him as they got into her car and drove away.

Nix was speechless. He had never heard his father speak so passionately before. Gianni had tears falling from her eyes, as he pulled her in to a comforting hug. Although it was obtained in a horrible way, that chain meant a lot to her. He appreciated Quick for thinking of her in that way. He couldn't say that things between his father and Gianni would ever be good, and he wasn't gonna rush her.

"I know that this is not what you all were expecting but it's the best that we can do under the circumstances. Getting off with probation was almost impossible," Dior's attorney said as she talked to her and her sisters outside of the courthouse. Her brother-in-law was there too but he didn't seem to be on her side.

Dior stayed locked up for an entire month before the lawyer that her sisters hired was able to get her bond reduced. Grace used some of the money from their father's insurance policy to get her out and she had to wear a house arrest monitor. Her sister's husband didn't agree with her getting Dior out, but she did it anyway. He wasn't always around, so she didn't expect him to understand. Grace didn't even want him to be there, but he insisted on accompanying her.

"What do you want to do Dior? Personally, I think you should take the plea deal. Going to trial might not be the best option," Grace said while looking over at her sister.

Dior's charge was reduced to manslaughter and it helped that she had never really gotten into trouble before. Besides the incident that happened with Crystal, she had never gone to jail before. The lawyer also got her sisters to write letters to the presiding judge on her behalf. They painted a clear picture of the verbal and emotional abuse that Dior had suffered over the years. They weren't trying to tarnish their late father's name but they had to tell the truth.

When they were done, even the prosecutor sympathized with Dior. She had a childhood that sounded almost identical to hers but her abuse from her mother was physical. As much as she would have loved to let her walk away, she still had a job to do. She reduced the charges to manslaughter and offered a deal of three to five years. It was a slap on the wrist but, if Dior lost at trial, she was facing up to ten.

"I agree with your sister. The plea deal is probably your best bet. You could probably be out in two providing you don't get into any trouble. Even if you did have to do the entire five, it's better than ten. I'll give y'all a few moments to discuss it. I'll be inside whenever y'all are ready," the attorney said before she walked away.

"There's really not much to discuss. I would be a fool to go to trial knowing that I'm guilty. I'm gonna lose," Dior spoke up.

"I hate that this is even happening. I can't even stand the thought of having to visit you in jail," Grace said.

"Why not? You have to visit the grave yard to see your father," her husband spat angrily.

"Why are you even here? It's clear that you don't give a fuck about me or what's going on." Dior frowned.

"You're damn right I don't. You killed your own father and you're standing here expecting sympathy. If you ask me, ten years behind bars was too lenient for what you did."

"Well, it's a good thing nobody is asking you. You're just mad because Grace used some of the life

412

insurance money to get me out. I'm sure you already had plans on what you were gonna spend it on."

"Okay, that's enough. This is not the time for us to be bickering. We all just want what's best for Dior," Grace said as she raised her hand to stop them from arguing.

"Who is we? Give me the keys baby. I'll be waiting for you in the car," her husband said, right before she handed him the keys to their car.

"Bye! Bitch ass nigga!" Dior yelled after him.

"That's enough Dior! This is not easy for any of us but arguing and name calling is not gonna get us anywhere. Let's go in here and tell this lawyer what you've decided to do," Grace said as she walked away with her three younger sisters following behind her.

As usual, she was the mouthpiece for everyone. Dior was sure that her other two sisters probably wouldn't have even supported her if Grace hadn't. She had always been the one to call the shots but she never led them wrong. She had a good heart, so it was easy for them to follow her lead. Although Dior still harbored some resentment towards her for what happened in her past, she appreciated her for not turning her back on her like some other siblings probably would have.

About an hour later, they were walking out of court. Dior accepted the plea deal and was ordered to turn herself in the following morning. The judge was ready to lock her up right then and there, but her lawyer fought for an extra day. Dior had already given up her apartment and she was staying in a furnished Airbnb. She didn't feel comfortable staying with any of her sisters, especially Grace. She'd sold her car too and her sister promised to send her all the money in increments while she was locked up.

As bad as Dior wanted kids, she was happy that she didn't have any. She was sure that going to prison would have been much harder if she had to leave her children behind. Truthfully, she probably wouldn't have done what she did at all if she had any.

Nix got everything that he wanted but it wasn't with her. He married Gianni and they were expecting their first son. River stayed in contact with her and she always had all the latest gossip. Dior wasn't about to say that she was happy for him because that would be a lie. At one time, she loved Nix more than she loved herself and she didn't want to see him happy with anyone else. Unfortunately, that was happening anyway.

Even that bitch Crystal was out there winning. She was engaged to her man and they were expecting their first child. Dior still hated everything about her and she regretted wasting so many years on that fake ass friendship.

"Let's do a ladies' night tonight, just the four of us," Grace suggested, shaking Dior from her thoughts.

"Where?" Dior asked.

"We can do it at your Airbnb. Let's pig out on food and liquor and just act a damn fool."

"Sounds good to me."

Dior was smiling on the outside but she knew that it was only temporary. She planned to enjoy a night of fun with her sisters before she had to turn herself in for the next three to five years.

Chapter 26

"Come on baby, you got this. One more big push," Nix coached as he held his wife's hand.

The time seemed to fly by, and Gianni was in the delivery room giving birth to their son. They were ready for his arrival and he had more than enough of everything that he needed. Nichelle did way too much for the baby shower and he probably wouldn't even get to use everything that he had. Nix planned to have a few more, so he told Gianni that they were saving everything.

"Smile Gianni. This is being recorded," Nichelle said as she held her phone.

"Chill out Nichelle. She's pushing. How the hell you want her to smile?" Nix fussed.

"Okay Mrs. Nixon, on the count of three," the doctor coached.

Gianni gripped Nix's hand tight as she pushed with all her might. She felt instant relief as soon as her son slid out of her and that had to be one of the best feelings in the world. She was nervous when her water broke early that morning. The pain that she felt afterwards was indescribable but it was all worth it when she heard her son crying.

"Yeah, he's definitely a Nixon with that big ole head," Nichelle said as she followed her son over to the incubator to the cut the baby's umbilical cord.

"Please don't make me put you out. It's only because of Gianni that you're even in here." Nix frowned.

He was supposed to be the only one present for the birth of his son, but Nichelle begged to see her first grandchild enter the world. He said no, but Gianni and her soft ass heart overruled him. She always fell for Nichelle's sob stories, but he knew better.

"Stop being so sensitive boy. Let me snap a few pictures of him, so I can go show everybody."

Gio and a few of Gianni's other family members were there, along with Quick and his parents. Everybody was excited about the new addition to the family but none more than the new father.

"You did good baby. How you feeling?" Nix asked when he walked back over to Gianni.

They had just laid the baby on her chest to allow her some bonding time. Aside from his head full of hair that he obviously got from her; it was too soon to make out who he really looked like.

"I'm happy that it's over." She smiled weakly.

"I wonder how long we have to wait before we try for another one. I'm about to ask the doctor."

"I dare you. He's not even an hour old yet. Are you serious?"

"Dead ass. I told you that I want a house full."

"And I told you that I don't. I'm not trying to push out a damn baby every year. I'm working remotely right now but I told you what my plans are."

Within the next year, Gianni planned to open her own business. She wanted to do financial consulting, credit repair, taxes, and a lot of other things related to financial services. She would still be able to do the books for the club but she had her own dreams that she wanted to fulfill.

"I got you, baby. You can still do everything that you want to do and more. See, you'll be working in the daytime while I'm home with the kids and then you'll have them at night while I run the club."

"And when do you plan to sleep?"

"I don't care about all that. We can do this," Nix assured her.

"I'm not trying to talk about that right now Jacobi. I just had a baby and you're already talking about more. Let's figure it out with this one first."

It took a little while before Gianni was cleaned up and taken to her room. She slept for most of the day while people came in and out to see the baby. Nix entertained them because she was drained. When she finally woke up that night, her room was full of balloons, flowers, and gifts.

"Look at her, Cobi; she finally woke up," Nix said as he sat in the chair next to her bed and cradled their son.

"Boy, I was tired and I still am. Did they ever say how much he weighs?" Gianni yawned. She was out of it, so she didn't even hear when they came back and told her all of that info.

"He's seven pounds even. Al's grandma sent you some gumbo but I asked the nurse to put in in the refrigerator. I can get her to warm it for you if you're ready to eat."

"No, I'll eat it tomorrow. I'm good for right now."

"Nah, you haven't eaten anything since you've been here. You're about to eat right now."

Nix pushed the call button for her nurse. When she came into the room, he asked her to warm Gianni's food and she happily complied. He put their son down for a minute while he helped her sit up in bed to eat. Gianni didn't realize how hungry she really was. She ate the entire container and the piece of cake that Al's grandmother sent for dessert.

"That was so good."

"I knew your ass was hungry," Nix laughed.

"Did Gio see the baby?"

"Yeah, he did. Everybody has been up here. I let Quick come in and hold him since you were asleep."

"I know that shit ain't sweet between me and your daddy, but I don't want it to always be tension whenever we're in the same room."

"It's whatever you want love. I'm good as long as you are."

418

"I just want our son to know his entire family on both sides. I can't say that I'll ever break bread with the nigga but we can be cordial. Gio ain't fucking with him at all so that's a whole other story."

"Can you blame him? I barely wanna fuck with his ass."

He and Gianni talked for a little while longer before she drifted off to sleep again. When she got up the next morning, Nix helped her take a shower before he left to go get them some breakfast. The baby was sleep while she scrolled through her social media pages. When someone knocked on the door, Gianni yelled and granted them entrance. She was shocked when the door opened and Kori and her aunt Karen walked in. Gianni hadn't seen her aunt since she asked her to leave her house because her new man was moving in. She requested money from her a few times via Cash App but that was about it.

"Congratulation niece. Let me come see my great nephew," Karen said as she walked over to look at the baby.

"Thanks. Sanitize your hands before you hold him," Gianni requested.

"He's so cute, cousin, but he doesn't look like Nix," Kori said.

"Bitch, if you came here to throw shade, there's the door," Gianni pointed.

"I wasn't being shady. I was just making an observation."

"He doesn't look like anybody yet. He's only a day old."

"He'll get his features in a few days. He's a cutie though." Karen smiled right as the door opened.

Nix paused when he opened the door and saw Kori and another woman standing there. The unfamiliar woman was holding his son and he wanted to know who she was. Gianni saw the puzzled look on his face, so she hurriedly spoke up to answer his unasked questions.

"Baby, this is Karen, my auntie. Karen, this is my husband, Jacobi." Gianni saw the frown that graced her husband's face, but it went away almost as quickly as it came.

"He's handsome. It's nice to finally meet you, nephew."

"Are you ready to eat baby?" Nix asked, not even bothering to return her aunt's greeting.

"Yeah," Gianni replied, right before he helped her sit up in the bed.

He didn't give a fuck that he was being rude. They didn't give a damn about his wife and he felt the exact same way about them. He and Gianni had been together for over a year and that was his first time ever seeing her auntie. She called a few times when Greg got killed but that was only because she thought that Gianni had him in insurance. Karen and Kori tried to organize a fundraiser but they gave up once they realized that Gianni wasn't on board. Nix was happy that his wife was no fool though. She probably wouldn't have seen a dime of the money that they collected anyway.

At the end of the day, Greg was thrown in a pine box and buried in an unmarked grave by the state just like Gianni predicted. Some girl who Ronnie was dealing with gave him a viewing and cremation. It wasn't the ideal service, but he faired out better than his boy.

"How have you been niece?" Karen asked.

"Better than ever," Gianni replied with a genuine smile as she looked at Nix.

"You came up in the world I see. Kori showed me some pictures of your house on Instagram."

Nix was about to snap but she grabbed his hand to calm him down. Kori looked embarrassed and she could have killed her mother. The last thing she wanted her cousin to know was that she was stalking her life behind the scenes on social media. They had just got back on track a few months ago after not speaking for a while.

Gianni had hit the jackpot with Nix. She was living the life that Kori and some other women had only dreams of. She remembered clowning her cousin about staying a virgin for so long, but it obviously paid off. Gianni had her reevaluating her own life. Kori had been thinking about going back to school to better her own life. Looking at her cousin made her realize that being the underdog wasn't always a bad thing. She didn't want to end up like her mother and always depend on a man to make her happy. For the first time ever, Kori was single and lived alone. She still had men friends but it felt good not to be attached to anyone. She didn't deal with Ryan anymore since her cousin was killed because the entire situation felt weird to her.

"Not bad for a girl who once lived in a homeless shelter, huh?" Gianni replied after a while. She could see that her comment made her auntie uncomfortable and that was her goal.

"Well, we just wanted to come by and see our newest family member. We got a few runs to make, so we'll see you later," Karen said. Nix stood up and took his son from her before she and Kori left.

"You see what I'm saying G. That bitch is still a hater. She wasn't expecting her mama to tell on her shady ass."

"Fuck them. Let them keep watching on Instagram. That's the only way they're gonna see it."

When the door opened a few minutes later, Alexa came running into the room with a gift bag followed by Danny and Al.

"Hey Uncle Nix. I got a present for my baby cousin. Can I hold him?" she asked excitedly.

"Yeah, sit in the chair so you can hold him." Nix smiled. Danny took a few pictures of her holding the baby and she was all smiles.

"Congrats you guys. Sorry that we couldn't be there to witness everything." Gianni smiled while holding out her arms to hug them both.

Al and Danny had gone to the courthouse that morning and got married. Danny's parents were the only ones in attendance and that was fine with them. They were going to Disney World for their honeymoon so that they could take Alexa with them.

Al's mother still didn't want to have anything to do with him. His feelings were hurt but he was learning to live with it. His grandmother kept her word and he picked her up on some Saturdays to come spend the day with him.

Kinsley had her own life now and she had just recently found out that she was pregnant again. She had come around a lot since she found out about the two of them being together. They didn't have any problems out of her and that made life for Al much easier.

"It's okay. Y'all had a good reason. He's absolutely adorable. I can't wait to spoil him," Danny smiled as he took the baby from Alexa.

You're The Best Part

"Yeah because this is as close as we'll get to having any. Alexa is more than enough?" Al laughed, as Danny nodded in agreement.

"I know Dior is probably in prison banging her head again the bars," Danny said, making everybody laugh.

There was a small write-up in the paper about her case a few months ago. Dior got off easily in a lot of people's opinions. Not many people knew about her history with her father, but Nix had witnessed it firsthand on more than one occasion. He didn't fuck with her like that at all but he was happy that she got a slap on the wrist. Hopefully, she would use that time to think about some of the decisions that she had made lately.

Their friends stayed there a little while longer before they were left alone again. Gianni's doctor told her that all was well and she and the baby would be going home the following day. Nix was serious about asking the doctor when they could start trying for another baby. He told him that they should wait at least a year but he wasn't trying to hear that.

"Nah see, that nigga is trying to mess up my plans," Nix said once the doctor left.

"What plans?" Gianni questioned.

Gianni laughed as he sat there and mapped out when they were going to start trying again. He wanted their kids to be a year apart, so he wasn't trying to wait for an entire year before she got pregnant again. She didn't have any objections to whatever he wanted to do.

Although Gianni wasn't an only child, she always felt like one. Greg wasn't shit and he was the worst big brother ever. Gianni definitely wanted more than one child and she wanted them to be close. She wanted her babies to have a bond and always have each other's backs. She didn't have that growing up but she found it when she met and married Nix.

3 years later...

"I'm so nervous. Please God, I need some good news. I can't take no more boys," Gianni said as she crossed her fingers.

The ultrasound tech laughed, but she was dead ass serious. Nix was serious about having his kids close together. He and Gianni now had three boys ages three, two and one. She was six months pregnant with baby number four and they were both praying for a girl. They were doing a three dimensional test to make sure that the results were accurate.

Being in a house full of males was not fun. Her two oldest boys were potty trained but they peed everywhere but the toilet. Gianni lost count of how many times a day she had to clean their bathroom. All three of them were active, thanks to Nix. They loved football and they ran through the house all day. He was a great hands-on father. He didn't put anything before his boys like his parents had done with him. His wife and kids were his top priority and always would be. Gianni was thankful for all the help that they had though. Besides Nichelle and Quick, Gio, Heavy and his family always had the boys to give them a break.

Al and Danny helped out a lot too. Kinsley had another baby girl that she let them christen. That came as a shock to everybody, but they loved her daughter just as much as they loved Alexa. She was married now and seeing her happy was all that Al ever wanted.

"Man, this better be my damn girl. If not, we're trying again next year," Nix spoke up.

"Boy, you got me fucked up. I'm getting my tubes tied no matter what it is. I don't even know how it feels not to be pregnant."

"You're married love. You can't do nothing without my consent and I'm not signing shit!"

"That is so old Jacobi. Women don't need their husbands' consent to do nothing to their bodies anymore."

"Okay, here we go. Are y'all ready?" the tech asked them.

"Hell yeah," Nix replied. He held Gianni's hand as they watched her administer the test. They waited with baited breaths until she finally told them something.

"It's a girl!" she yelled excitedly.

"Yes! Finally!" Gianni cheered. They had Jacobi Jr,. Jacori and Jabari. Now, she was getting her princess Jade.

"Damn man, it's about time." Nix smiled.

"How do you think I feel being in a house surrounded by men?"

Gianni was all smiles as she got dressed and ready to leave. She called Nichelle and Nix heard her screaming through the phone. She had been dying to get a granddaughter and he knew that his baby was gonna be spoiled. The boys were with her and Quick now, and he was sure that his daughter would be there just as much.

"Are you hungry baby?" Nix asked Gianni.

"Yep." She nodded.

They weren't too far away from one of their favorite restaurants, so he headed in that directions. When he and Gianni got out of the car, he was about to open the door for her to go inside. When the door opened, he was shocked to see Dior and another man walking out. She looked embarrassed to be seen in her work uniform but she held her head high and kept walking. He didn't even know that she was out and he damn sure didn't know that she worked at one of their favorite spots.

"Well, I guess we won't be eating here too much anymore," Gianni commented as they waited to be seated.

"We don't have to come to this location. They have two more to choose from," he reminded her, right as the waitress came over to bring them to their seats.

"Order my drink and appetizers for me, baby. I'm going to the bathroom."

Gianni walked away as Nix looked at the menu. They had been there too many times to count, so he didn't know why he even bothered. When the waitress came, he put in their drink and appetizer orders right as Gianni was walking back to the table.

"Are you serious about getting your tubes tied?" Nix looked at his wife and awaited an answer.

"Yes, I am. We're getting our girl like we both wanted."

"But I want more than one girl though."

"We don't have the best track record with kids Nix. It took us having three boys just to get her. I'm tired of always being pregnant."

"Now see, you're going back on your word."

"No, I'm not."

"Yes, you are. I kept my end of the bargain. You told me that you would give me as many kids as I wanted as long as you didn't have to give up your career to do it. You got your own building with five employees working for you. I did my part and you need to do yours."

"Nigga, I've been doing my part for the past three years. My pussy needs a break," Gianni snapped, making her husband and the waitress who had just returned laughed.

She apologized to the woman for her use of language but she meant every word she said. Nix got to do the fun part but she had to carry the extra weight around for nine months and push it out. She loved her babies and she wouldn't trade them for anything in the world but she needed some down time.

"We have to compromise love."

"What's there to compromise Nix? Four kids is more than enough."

"Let's make a deal. We'll have one more after Jade. If it's a girl, you can get your tubes tied. If not, we have to try one more time before you do it."

"Are you even listening to yourself? You're sitting here talking about having six kids like it ain't nothing."

"Might be five if you have another girl."

"There are no guarantees on that Nix. God. What the hell did I get myself into?"

"Something that only death can get your ass out of. Children are a blessing baby."

"Yes, they are but we've been blessed enough."

"You can never have enough blessings. It ain't like we can't afford it."

"That's not the point," Gianni replied, right as her phone rang.

They both looked at it, but Nix frowned when he saw Kori's name pop up. She and Gianni still talked occasionally if she felt like answering for her. Kori had graduated from college in medical coding and she worked at one of their local hospitals. She married some old looking man and had a son who looked just as elderly. She was always calling Gianni for their kids to have play dates that would probably never happen. She was still a shady bitch and some things would never change.

"Ignore that hoe and let's finish our discussion."

"There is nothing to discuss," Gianni said while declining her cousin's call.

"Come on now love. Don't make me be extra again like I did when you got pregnant with Cobi. Just make this easy on both of us."

"Okay, let's compromise."

"I'm listening." Nix ate his appetizers that were just placed in front of him while giving his wife his undivided attention.

"We can do it just how you said but I need a two-year window."

"Nah baby, that's gonna mess up my plan."

"Boy, fuck your plan. I need a break Nix. I seriously don't remember how I look without a belly. People are probably tired of seeing me pregnant."

"Fuck what people have to say or think. Nobody have to provide for you and my kids but me. Just think of it as another small piece of our puzzle."

"Oh God. Here he go with this puzzle bullshit again."

"That's some real shit baby. I told you a long time ago that life is like a puzzle. You need all the small pieces to see the big picture. You're a small piece of my puzzle, but you're the best part," Nix said as he made his wife blush and smile just like always.